A WEDDING FOR THE SINGLE DAD

MEREDITH WEBBER

REUNITED WITH HER DAREDEVIL DOC

SUSAN CARLISLE

MILLS & BOON

First Published in Great Britain 2021
by Mills & Boon, an imprint of HarperCollins*Publishers*
1 London Bridge Street, London, SE1 9GF

A Wedding for the Single Dad © 2021 by Meredith Webber

Reunited with Her Daredevil Doc © 2021 by Susan Carlisle

ISBN: 978-0-263-29756-0

MIX
Paper from
responsible sources
FSC® C007454

A WEDDING FOR THE SINGLE DAD

MEREDITH WEBBER

MILLS & BOON

CHAPTER ONE

'WHO THE HELL are you?'

'Says the man lying in a creek bed and lucky to be alive! Shoulder bad? Possibly dislocated, from the look of things,' Lauren said, hoping she sounded cooler and more in command than she felt. There'd been something about the very English male voice that had made the demand sound more abrupt than it might otherwise have.

Something about it, too, that had skittered down her spine.

She'd come expecting injury, but not an enormous man—at least six foot two or three—with night-dark tousled hair and a chippy attitude.

She smiled at him to cover her own uncertainty—she just didn't do skittery spines.

'I'm your friendly neighbourhood rescuer, Lauren Henderson, although what you were doing flitting around up there in Henry's home-made flying machine I can't imagine.'

She'd drawn closer to the man by now, and he didn't look any smaller. From his snapped retort—'It's an ultra-light!'—it was clear he also wasn't any happier.

'Which doesn't answer the question, but I guess I'd better have a look at you. There's a team trudging up the path somewhere behind me, but even on a stretcher you'll be more comfortable if I get your shoulder back into place before they carry you down.'

A grumbling noise suggested that he might argue about being carried down the gully, but really he had no choice.

She approached him fairly tentatively, and not only partly because of the rocky terrain—the dangers of wounded wild beasts were featuring in the forefront of her imagination...

There was no sign of blood, which didn't rule out the possibility that he wasn't lying in a puddle of it, and his eyes—an unusual dark blue—were alert.

Too alert?

'Apart from your shoulder, are you in pain?' she asked, easing her backpack off her shoulders and setting it to one side as she knelt beside him.

'I fell out of the sky! Of course, I'm in pain. Ouch!'

Lauren had been feeling around his head as he muttered at her, and touching the slight lump on the back of his skull had caused the 'ouch'.

'Can you move your legs and your good arm?' she asked, and although he groaned as he did it the three limbs moved fairly normally.

'Well, let's get your shoulder sorted,' she said, 'before the others get here.'

'What do you mean—get it sorted?'

The man was in pain, so she bit back a smart retort.

'Pop it back into place. You'll still need to be carried out and have it X-rayed when you get to civilisation, because there will be damage to the cartilage and tendons.'

She'd removed 'the magic green whistle', as football players called the handy device, while she was speaking, and now passed it to him. 'Take about six breaths,' she said.

Dark blue eyes narrowed suspiciously. 'What's in it?' he asked.

'Methoxyfluorane,' she said calmly, getting herself into position beside his left shoulder, prepared to lift his arm whether it hurt him or not. But the man was in a lot of pain—she had to grant him a little leeway...

Also, he was very intriguing *and* very attractive. And quite possibly—probably—her new neighbour. Henry's nephew or great-nephew, she seemed to remember...

She watched him breathe in the pain-relief drug and hid a smile as it obviously started to work, relaxing the tension in his body.

'Now, I'm just going to bend your arm at the elbow and move it like this, and with a bit of pressure I should be able to slip it back into place.'

'Are you a qualified paramedic? Should you be doing this?'

Okay, so methoxyfluorane hadn't improved his mood. But he *had* crashed down from the sky, and he was probably feeling extremely foolish for having attempted to fly the ultralight, as well as being in a great deal of pain.

So she smiled sweetly at him.

'No and yes,' she said, and before he could voice further objections she lifted his folded arm and moved it upward and outward until she felt the joint slip back into its socket.

'Better?' she said, although she knew it would still be painful—just not agonisingly so.

He muttered something she was charitably willing to accept as assent, and she began to examine the rest of him. Bloody graze on his left hand—he'd probably put it out to break his fall—and his left ankle looked a little swollen.

'Sore?' she asked, moving it slightly.

More muttered complaints followed as she unlaced his light canvas shoes.

'I'm going to take off your shoe and sock so I can bandage it,' she told him. 'If we leave them on and your ankle swells, your shoe will have to be cut off—which would be a pity with such good-quality footwear.'

More mutterings. This time she gathered something about what a woman would know about men's footwear. She ignored the words and went ahead, removing his shoe, and then his sock, revealing a long, pale foot, with blue veins visible beneath milky skin.

The bare foot made him seem vulnerable, and for all his tetchy remarks she suddenly felt sorry for him.

Which, she decided, was distinctly better than the physical reaction she'd had earlier...

She'd just finished binding the ankle when voices told her the SES team had arrived.

'He okay?' the lead man asked.

Lauren nodded. 'I've just reset a dislocated left shoulder—it'll need to be X-rayed—and checked him over for other injuries. His left arm will need to be put into a special sling for a while, and his left ankle...'

But the team were no longer listening.

'Geez,' one of them said, peering up at the tangle of fine wood and plastic in the midst of the dead black trees that bordered the gully. 'Is that old Henry's flying machine up there? Boy, he'll be cranky up in heaven!'

'Or down in hell,' another suggested, and all four laughed before slowly returning their attention to their patient.

'You did that?' they more or less chorused, all shaking their heads in disbelief.

'Okay,' Lauren said, calling them to order as they started to suggest the punishments old Henry would have meted out to someone crashing his most favourite toy. 'You've actually got a patient here, and if you want to get him down the track in daylight I'd suggest you get him strapped onto whatever you're carrying and start moving.'

'I don't need to be carried.'

Not muttered, but definitely not happy.

'You might have other injuries, and possibly concussion,' she told him, adding firmly, 'So you *will* be carried.'

Recalled to their job, the team set to work, and as they slid the pieces of stretcher under the injured man Lauren could practically read their minds.

Although in case she'd been in any doubt Joe, their leader, muttered, 'Cor, he's a big bugger!'

'I'll take the head end and you can go two each side,' she said. 'The ambulance will be down on the road. You can radio for their two guys to start up the track to help.'

They worked well, the team, getting the bits of board under the patient and snapped together, strapping him firmly onto it.

'Just use the magic whistle if you need to,' Lauren reminded the man, as they all got into position to lift him.

He gave her a look of such disbelief she had to smile.

'They *have* done it before,' she said, and he shut his eyes, as if better to pretend this wasn't happening.

He'd been rescued by—he couldn't think off-hand of a bunch of comedians to compare this lot to—vaudeville slapstick clowns, perhaps?

Campbell Grahame shook his head—big mistake, as it brought the sore lump on it into contact with the board to which he'd been strapped. He clutched the device his rescuer had called 'the magic whistle' to his chest, wondering if he should take a few more puffs as the lurching downhill journey was anything but comfortable.

His rescuer!

Maybe he'd think about *her* instead of the pain.

She'd seemed to appear from nowhere, startling him as he'd tried to work out just how seriously he was injured. *And* told himself how stupid he'd been! He'd been angry with himself, as well, for flying so far in an old machine he didn't know at all. Apart from anything else, it had been totally irresponsible.

He turned his attention back to his rescuer.

Totally unsympathetic, she'd been, whoever she was. But perhaps brisk efficiency was what was needed in rescue situations.

Still, a rescuer with long, tanned legs, clad in short red shorts and a singlet that clung to a curvy upper body like a second skin...? The men at least were in uniform—with the words State Emergency Service embroidered on their shirts.

The peaked black cap she was wearing, pulled down tightly on her forehead, meant he hadn't been able to see the hair tucked under it, but dark eyes and eyebrows suggested it would be brown or black.

He raised his eyes to take another look at her face, hoping she was concentrating on where she was putting her feet rather than on him.

But it was a surreptitious glance, just to check that her face was as lovely as he remembered it.

It was.

It was well put together, with a straight nose and wide, shapely lips, a small, determined chin—yes, she was something of a beauty...although he did wonder if other people would think so.

Perhaps it was just a face like any other, and he'd imbued it with beauty because she'd rescued him?

Whatever. The fact remained he'd been damnably rude to her.

He sighed, and the beauty—he was pretty sure she *was* a beauty—said, 'Don't be afraid to use the whistle. This isn't exactly the smoothest ride you'll ever have, and there could be other things wrong with you.'

But he knew there weren't. The team had carried out the basic tests—blood pressure, heart-rate, breathing—and although he felt pain as they trekked down the rough track, he knew it wasn't anything serious.

So he could think about the woman again—tall, as well as good looking...

'What's your name?'

His question came out without much forethought, and she frowned down at him, as if she wasn't certain of the answer.

Had she already told him?

He couldn't remember...

'Lauren Henderson,' she said eventually, before adding, 'And yours?'

Cam frowned. He *had* introduced himself earlier—but had that been just to the team?

Surely she'd heard?

'Campbell Grahame—I'm usually called Cam.'

One of the two men who held the stretcher at Cam's shoulder level turned briefly towards them, but a slight slip on a rock had him turning back, concentrating on where he was going, almost immediately.

'How do you do, Cam?' Lauren said, in the slightly husky voice that somehow suited her. 'I won't shake hands because I'd probably drop you.' Silent for a moment, she then said, 'And what *were* you up to—flying over the forest in old Henry's ancient machine?'

All four of the heads he could see in front of him turned at this question, and he wondered if perhaps they should leave conversation until they were well away from the rough track by the creek bed.

But she *had* asked...

'I thought it might be useful to spot any injured wild-life returning to their burnt-out homes.'

'You've never heard of drones?' It was a question edged with sarcasm, but perhaps—

'Is that why I crashed? You had a drone up and it hit me?'

She gave a huff of laughter and shook her head. 'You crashed because you were flying so low your left wing-tip hit a tree, and you were lucky I did have a drone up—because otherwise it would have taken a full-scale search, and almost certainly plenty of man hours, to find you. The forest might be burnt out, but there's thick re-generation in the undergrowth, and with the deep gul-lies even a helicopter search would have been difficult, if not impossible.'

'Well, that's telling me,' he muttered to himself, feel-ing put out that he wasn't being treated more kindly, considering he was injured. Not that he'd earned any kindness, the way he'd been earlier—though his bad tem-per was more to do with his own foolishness than these innocent rescuers.

They continued down the path in silence, and as the journey went on he realised just how far this group had walked to rescue him—idiot that he was to have even got into the damn microlight.

'Do you do this often?' he asked.

'Rescue blokes from crashed flying machines?' one of

the men responded. 'Not so much. But I reckon a couple of dozen times a summer we get call-outs to search for someone who hasn't come back when they should...a fisherman stranded on rocks in the lake as the tide rises, lost bush-walkers, kids—we keep busy.'

Intrigued now, Cam wanted to know more. 'Only in summer?'

Another of the men shook his head. 'Nah! Winter's actually worse—cooler for people who want to walk some of the trails though the bush, who then get off the trail and end up lost.'

'Not that there'll be much bush to walk in this year,' another said, gloom shrouding his words.

And then the talk turned to the bushfires that had so recently ravaged the area. Most of South Eastern Australia had suffered to some degree, and Cam, who'd arrived in the country six days ago, in the aftermath of the fires, had discovered that as well as inheriting a veterinary practice from a great-uncle he'd only met once, many years earlier, he'd inherited a small hospital for injured wildlife—complete with, and run by, mostly volunteer helpers.

And an ultralight!

He bit back a groan, more of anguish than agony. Flying the wretched machine had seemed like a challenge. And it had brought back such vivid memories!

The only time he'd met his great-uncle, Henry had helped him build his very own ultralight, and taught him how to fly it. So, seeing what must have been Henry's old machine in the shed, it had been hard to resist—particularly as his daughter had been so excited that Daddy could fly such a thing.

Showing off to Maddie. How pathetic had that been? Idiotic too.

Maddie!

Hell!

He looked up at rescuer number one. 'Can someone radio the vet surgery and let my mother know I'm okay? She'll be worried.'

'I'll do it,' one of the men at the foot of the stretcher said, keeping hold of his burden with one hand, while the other tapped away at a radio Velcroed to his chest.

No need to tell them his mother was the last person who'd be worried. She was probably trailing along the lake's edge with her fishing line, with Maddie following in her wake like a small shadow, her own fishing line tangled around the small rod, because to her shells had far more appeal than fish.

But at least his mother would know to listen to messages on the surgery line as well as the home phone when she returned from her excursion.

New voices and laughter preceded the arrival of the ambulance crew, who greeted everyone cheerfully, assured him he'd soon be more comfortable in their care, and then joined the effort of carrying him down to the road.

He was about to lose Lauren Henderson from her place at the head of the stretcher.

As she moved away he reached out with his good hand and caught her fingers. 'I'm sorry for being such a bear,' he said. 'I was just so annoyed with myself for bringing Henry's machine down. It was a stupid and totally irresponsible thing to do.'

She smiled at him. 'It was,' she agreed, but the smile had taken any sting out of her words.

Then she was gone, striding on ahead of the team carrying him down the track.

He wanted to ask about her—who she was, and what

she did. She hadn't been sympathy personified, but she'd reset his shoulder—besides which, she was damned attractive.

Knowing someone's name really told you nothing, he was thinking when the paramedic who'd taken her place said, 'The doc reported a dislocated shoulder—looks like she got it back in place. Left one, was it?'

He nodded his reply—mainly because, back in place or not, his shoulder was hurting like the devil, and he really didn't want to be taking any more of the drug.

And why is that? a small voice in his head asked.

He closed his eyes, as if he might shut out the question, but he had a suspicion it might be pride—not wanting these tough men carting his considerable weight down the mountain to think him a weakling.

Stupid pride, at that!

He lifted the little 'whistle' to his lips and took a deep breath.

'Take a few,' said the man at his head. 'Moving you to the ambulance will hurt a bit.'

Cam took a few more puffs. Given the Australian talent for understatement he'd already encountered in his short time here, it was likely going to hurt like hell!

Lauren didn't wait to see her patient loaded into the ambulance. She turned and went back up the path. Telling herself her plan was stupid and futile failed to stop her forward momentum.

As a child, she'd helped Henry—or mainly watched— as he'd built his little ultralight, and it deserved a better end than to be stuck in the burnt-out scrub at the head of the gully. And rescuing the bits would distract her from the reaction she'd felt when the stranger had grabbed her hand and pressed it gently as he'd apologised.

For some reason, that slight touch had left her fingers tingling.

Think about the wreckage!

Even if she couldn't rescue all of it, if she could just recover the frame and the little leather seat Henry had fashioned out of an old saddle...

She thought back to those days when she'd been Henry's little shadow—far closer to him than she'd been to her own father when she was small. Probably because her father's practice hadn't involved animals large and small.

Henry hadn't talked much about his family, although hadn't he once visited a sister or a niece back in England?

Mary?

Marion?

Madge?

It had been Madge—a niece. Maybe she'd inherited the old house and the veterinary practice?

And if he lived with his mother—the tall man with the blue, blue eyes who'd made her spine skitter and her fingers tingle—then that was probably Madge, because the house certainly hadn't been on the market. The lakeside gossip net would have known if it had been.

But living with his mother? Unusual in this day and age... Although she'd lived with her father for years— for ever, almost...

Was he a vet, that tall man with the very blue eyes?

Silly question. Henry had talked occasionally about his great-nephew with a veterinary practice in London— spoken of him with pride. And if she'd ever thought about it, she should have guessed he'd inherit Henry's place and his practice.

But who'd leave London to come to a practice in the bush?

And why should it matter to her, anyway?

Just because he was good-looking?

Because he'd sparked something in her although he'd been abrupt and cranky?

And made her fingers tingle when he'd caught her hand.

And he was going to be living next door.

This last realisation made her feel…not exactly queasy, but unsettled inside.

Puzzling over it kept her feet moving, so she was soon past where she'd met the man, and the wreckage of the ultralight was much more visible—and not as badly shattered as she'd pictured it.

Carefully avoiding any chance of slipping and injuring herself, she gathered up the pieces—one almost complete wing, the bones of the shattered one, and the cockpit, as Henry had grandly called the seat and control panel—and some other bits and pieces not immediately recognisable.

Wishing she'd stopped long enough to get some big bin bags, she untied her light jacket from her waist and tied it around the awkward bundle. She hitched it on to her shoulder and set off, yet again, down the rough track.

By the time she reached her house, drenched in sweat, she was regretting what now seemed like a totally irrational decision.

Just what was she intending to do with the wreckage?

Rebuild the thing?

She dropped the bundle just inside her back gate, unwrapped her jacket and used it to mop the sweat from her face.

'Are you going to put it together again?' asked a quiet, precise voice, and she turned to see a small child with dark tousled hair standing at the fence, dark blue eyes fixed intently on her.

'I'm not sure I'm clever enough,' she answered honestly, seeing the wreckage more clearly now.

'My father could help you,' the little girl told her. 'He knows how.'

Lauren smiled, because the words held such certainty. This was a child who firmly believed her father could do *anything*—although, if the father was who Lauren guessed he was, putting the ultralight back together again was probably the last thing he'd want to do.

Time to change the subject.

'Does your mother know where you are?' she asked.

The small child climbed onto the gate and began to swing back and forth on it. 'I don't have a mother,' she said. 'Daddy said she left to find herself. But I think you *are* yourself, and that's where you are.'

It was slightly convoluted, but Lauren could see where she was coming from, and was amazed yet again at the wisdom of children.

'Do you have a name?' she asked—although she should be asking exactly who was in charge of her, and what she was doing at her back gate.

'I'm Maddie,' she said. 'It's really Madge, after my grandmother, but Daddy says that's a name for an old person not a...' she paused, as if trying out the next word in her head, and finally came up with '...youngser like me.'

'Well, Maddie, perhaps your grandmother is looking for you and you should go home. Do you know the way?'

The girl rolled her eyes. 'It's just next door,' she said, and Lauren thought she heard the echo of an unspoken *Stupid!* lingering at the end of the statement. 'Although it's not as next door as the next door was when we lived in London.'

From London to Paradise Lake. From a bustling, cosmopolitan city to a virtual backwater with a string of houses around a tidal lake. What a huge shift in their lives.

A huge shift in work, too, for the man she'd rescued. From city vet to a country one—and a different country at that.

Had he realised that when he'd come out here?

Did he intend to stay, or merely check out the place and put it on the market?

'I could walk you home,' she offered, concerned about the child, because she'd been quite right. 'Next door' here was about three hundred metres away, and once the sinking sun disappeared it would be gloomy in the sparse bushland between the two houses.

'If you like,' Maddie told her, climbing off the gate. 'We have heaps of baby animals at our place—more than ten, anyway. People come in to help, because some of them are hurt, and some are too little to live in the... Well, we'd say *woods* in England, but here it's called the bush—even if there isn't any bush to live in.'

She waved a hand towards the blackened hills behind them, while Lauren realised that it must be another after-effect of the fires that she'd heard nothing of these new people in Henry's house—not a hint of the gossip which was usually the life-blood of Lakesiders' conversations.

There'd been a locum, of course, and she'd met him one time. And she'd known that volunteers were working all hours to keep the wildlife hospital and sanctuary going. She had done a couple of night shifts there herself, but because she entered and left through the gate in the animal cage, she hadn't met or even considered the new owners.

She took Maddie's hand, and was just leading her to the track she always took between the two places when a tall, dishevelled and totally distracted figure appeared, his left arm held tight to his chest by a sling, his left ankle tightly bandaged.

Campbell Grahame stopped and leaned on the stick he held in his right hand.

'You shouldn't be out walking after that fall,' she said.

But he ignored her, calling out to his daughter and grabbing her as she raced towards him and flung herself at his legs.

'What have I told you about wandering off into the bush?' he demanded, though he didn't sound as cross as she imagined he must be feeling after finding her missing.

'But I only went next door. And this nice lady is going to build the flying machine again after she's walked me home.'

'You must be out of your mind,' he said, and then must have realised he'd already been far too rude to her today. 'Sorry. That was rude. I've been worried about Maddie.'

'I said you'd help her,' Maddie offered hopefully.

The man just shook his head and awkwardly scooped her up with his right arm, his stick now waving uselessly in his hand.

'You should let Maddie walk,' Lauren said, changing the subject before it became even more complicated. 'You shouldn't be bearing your own weight on that ankle, let alone hers.'

He frowned at her, but did let Maddie slide back to the ground.

Okay, the man was in pain, and he must have been worried sick about his daughter's disappearance—but, really, one 'sorry' didn't cover his rudeness.

She looked him directly in the eyes as she responded, daring him to make another prod at her. 'Are you always this aggressive, or has the accident dented your masculine pride? Or is it because you were rescued by a woman?' she asked, aware that it had happened before in the macho world out here in the lakes.

Without waiting for an answer—or an excuse—she turned on the spot and marched back towards her house.

Maddie's, 'Now look what you've done!' came clearly to her through the still, early-evening air. 'And she's a *very* nice lady!'

Beautiful, too, Cam thought as he took Maddie's hand and turned back towards Uncle Henry's house—their house now, he supposed. Not that they *had* to stay here. A few weeks seeing to some necessary repairs, a bit of paint to brighten the place up, and then Cam and his mother could sell it and go back to the UK.

The locum the lawyers had arranged was still running the business and he could stay on—he might even like to buy it. If not, the solicitors could find another buyer.

The thought made him feel even more depressed than the pain in his shoulder. She'd been right, that woman— now soot-stained, probably from rescuing the ultralight— he shouldn't be walking around. But he hadn't wanted his mother to go looking for his daughter—that could have ended up with both of them being lost in the bush...

The bush.

Could he really go back to the UK after seeing the beauty of this lake and experiencing the sense of community around it? Meeting a few of the locals...learning that he owned, apparently, a wildlife hospital and sanctuary, not to mention some of that burnt-out bush behind the house... Henry and some friends of his had planted trees there—a variety of the special trees whose leaves koalas ate—to encourage the local koala population to stay in the area.

For so long he'd dreamt about Australia—this strange land at the bottom of the globe.

Sell out?

He didn't think so.

They were in sight of the house now. The stately old stone building looked so incongruous among the holiday shacks and the new modern houses that straggled along the shores of the lake. He'd learned that it had been built by the owner of a local coal mine, back when the area had first been settled, and the owner had obviously believed strongly in his own importance.

Even with the old servants' quarters at the back now annexed by the wildlife hospital and sanctuary, and his veterinary rooms set up on the ground floor at the front, it was still a lot of house for three people. Spacious and elegant, if somewhat shabby.

'I've forgotten her name…the lady who lives next door…but her house looks even bigger than ours. And there's a sign outside with pictures of cakes. Do you think she's a cake-maker?'

He thought of the tall, slim woman who'd not only popped his shoulder back into its socket but had then also helped carry him down the hill.

'If she is a cake-maker, I don't think she eats many of them,' he said to Maddie.

She grinned with delight. 'Because she's not roly-poly, like Madge says I'll get if I eat too much cake?'

He smiled down at this small human who held his heart in her currently rather grubby hands. 'Exactly,' he said.

And they were both smiling as they entered the house through a French door on one side of it, directly into a rather dim but potentially pleasant sitting room.

* * *

Having shifted the pieces of the ultralight to her back shed, Lauren went upstairs to shower and change. She studied her soot-stained self in the bathroom mirror and shook her head. Pity to have made such a terrible first impression on her new neighbour!

Really? a voice in her head replied. *Why should it bother you what impression you made?*

She didn't answer the voice, not wanting to admit that she'd found him attractive—*very* attractive. And definitely not wanting to admit that seeing him had caused nerves in some parts of her body to jangle, and tighten, and heat—nerves that hadn't felt much for years.

Certainly not warmth.

As for heat…?

Good grief!

What was she thinking?

She sighed. It was because she had no life—that was all it was. Years of medical training, the horrors of internship, and then eight years caring for a wonderful but increasingly difficult father had limited her social life to zilch. No wonder someone—a *male* someone—taking her hand and giving it a gentle squeeze had made her skin tingle.

Had that *ever* happened before out here in the very beautiful but isolated Paradise Lake community? No. The residents were mostly retired, or newlyweds building their first house in the place where they'd come for holidays as children.

Single men were scarcer than hen's teeth, and as for married men…

Disaster!

But she loved the lake, and she had taken over her father's practice as well as his care when his forgetfulness had finally had to be acknowledged as dementia rather than just old age.

Don't brood.

She'd shower, wash her hair, pull on some jeans and a top and—

And then what?

Take herself to dinner at the new restaurant that had opened further along the shore?

She shook her head, her wet hair flapping about her face. Pulled out a dry towel and rubbed at it roughly, remembering times when she'd have spent half an hour drying it carefully, persuading it into gentle waves that looked as natural as she could make them.

Looking good for David.

As she dragged a comb through her still-damp hair, she wondered where that had come from.

It had been years since she'd given David even a passing thought.

And, more to the point, why was the man she'd rescued today intruding into her brain?

Surely not just because he was an attractive man?

An attractive man who'd made her spine skitter and her skin tingle...

He was a new neighbour, nothing more, and obviously married as he had a child.

Although hadn't the child—Maddie—said something...?

The thought of her encounter with the man at the head of the gully reminded her that she hadn't downloaded her drone's latest pictures. She'd sent the drone home, grabbed her backpack, and then raced off to find whoever it was she'd seen crash.

Glad to have something to do, she went to her office

and detached the SIM card from the small machine's belly, pushed it into her computer, and sat down to study what it had picked up.

Nothing much, she decided, when she reached the point where her neighbour had crashed. But as the drone had obeyed her instructions and flown back home before she'd headed out on her rescue mission, it had crossed a new area.

And what was that she could see?

A lump in a burnt-out tree—exactly what she'd been looking for. The lumpy shape of a koala.

She checked the co-ordinates but really didn't need them, for she could see the back fence of the wildlife sanctuary.

She zoomed in.

Could it have come from the sanctuary?

She shook her head.

She'd been there yesterday evening, and knew none of the recovering koalas had been released for over a week. Even those that had been released had gone into suitable forests far removed from the fire grounds.

No, this little fellow—and he or she *was* little—had somehow escaped the worst of the fires and was trying to find a new home.

In a burnt, and therefore leafless tree...

She grabbed a rope and her spiked climbing shoes and hurried towards the sanctuary, wondering who was on duty tonight, hoping it would be someone who could help her.

'Oh, Beth!' she groaned as she let herself in through the security gate in the outer yard. 'Are you on your own here tonight?'

Petite and seven months pregnant, Beth smiled at her. 'Just me, and I'm shutting up soon. The animals that need night feeds have gone home with Helen. There are only two of them, and she says they're pretty good, so she can feed them both at once. The new vet came in to look around early this afternoon, though.'

The new vet with a dislocated shoulder…although his shoulder wouldn't have been dislocated then…

Henry's great-nephew, with a voice that sent a shiver down her spine.

But was he here to take over the practice, or sell it and move on?

Enough.

She needed to concentrate on the animal in danger. Night was falling fast, and to try a rescue in the dark would be foolhardy, to say the least.

But on the other hand…

She headed for the inner door—the one that led into the veterinary surgery.

His shoulder had been X-rayed and expertly strapped to his chest, and he'd been walking—albeit with a stick…

She knocked on the connecting door, loudly, because it was more likely he was in the house itself and wouldn't hear a gentle tap.

The door opened immediately!

'Yes?' he said, sounding abrupt.

But when she saw the glass beaker in one hand and the pipette in the other, she realised she'd interrupted something he'd been doing.

Following her gaze, he said, 'Sorry. I've just been testing some of the old supplies at the back of the cupboard. I'll be right back.'

She'd have liked to tell him again that he shouldn't be moving about on his ankle, but as she was about to ask his help in an operation more complicated than beakers and pipettes, she kept her lips firmly closed.

And shut her mind firmly to the man himself who—as a man, for heaven's sake—was causing her more problems than her concern for his welfare.

Internal problems.

Physical problems.

Things she hadn't felt in years.

The shivery spine and tingling fingers had only been the start...

Get with the program!

'There's a small koala, not far from here. My drone picked it up,' she said, as she confronted her grumpy neighbour for the second time—no, third—today. 'The problem is, he's up a burnt tree, and will have realised there's no food, so as soon as it's fully dark he'll climb down and head further into the burnt area and we might not find him again.'

She paused, hoping the look on her new neighbour's face was incomprehension, not disbelief.

She tried again. 'I can climb up and get him. I just need someone to hold the rope and the bag and take him from me so I can climb down.'

He frowned at her, a quick glance taking in her coiled rope and spiked boots, and the bag she'd grabbed as she'd walked through the sanctuary to his door.

'I know you're not one hundred percent, but I can't ask Beth to help me, and it would take too long to get one of the other volunteers here, so do you think you could? Please?'

The silence seemed to echo through the room, and then he smiled in a way that made her wonder if this was a good idea. Plenty of men smiled at her—but none of those smiles sent warmth bubbling through her veins.

Really, this was getting out of hand!

How could she possibly be attracted to a total stranger?

She was tired—exhausted, in fact—after two treks up the gully today, so it was probably just her imagination anyway.

'I suppose one good turn deserves another,' he said, and smiled again. 'I'll get my walking stick and you can lead the way.'

She threw him her grateful thanks and moved back into the sanctuary, where small wombats poked their noses from old hollow tree trunks and sleepy koalas barely noticed her.

She breathed deeply, smelling the so-familiar scent of eucalyptus leaves, and told herself he probably smiled at everyone that way.

Breathing certainly calmed her nerves, so when he reappeared she was able to say, 'It's just out here—not far,' and lead him out through the side gate of the sanctuary.

She pointed into the second row of the burnt-out plantation. 'Don't look at the tree. Look for the lump in it.'

'Got it,' he said. 'But how do we go about this?'

He lifted the coiled rope off her shoulder, his fingers brushing the bare skin on her upper arm.

'This one's easy,' she said, resolutely ignoring the accidental touch, for all it had shaken her. 'See that branch just below the animal? We throw the rope over that, then I swing on it to make sure the branch will take my weight, rope myself up, and climb. You just have to play out the rope. You're really here just in case I slip, so you can stop me crashing to the ground.'

She took the weighted end of the rope from him and swung it around before flinging it into the tree.

'Okay, the branch looks strong enough. Just let out

the rope so the end falls back to the ground, then we'll detach the weight and attach me.'

He played out the rope, but his silence was a little unnerving.

'Sometimes you have to climb up to attach the rope,' she said—nervous chatter, she knew, but it was better than silence. 'Or attach it in stages as you climb, so if you do fall, you don't fall far.'

She tied the rope around her waist, grabbed the bag, and handed it to him.

'Make sure you hold him by the scruff of his neck when I pass him to you, and the sooner you get him into the bag the better. They're fighters, and their claws are sharp and can really rip into you.'

She headed for the tree.

'And keep one foot on the rope!' she reminded him as she began to clamber up the trunk.

Struck dumb by the rapid sequence of events, Cam could only shake his head. *Keep one foot on the rope*—he understood that part. She didn't want him struggling to put a panicked animal into a bag and forget he was also the brake on her rope.

Stars were beginning to appear in the sky, and his neighbour was already halfway up the tree.

Did she do this often?

He wanted to ask, but also didn't want to distract her—particularly now, as she was persuading the recalcitrant and possible wounded koala to let go of his perch.

Then she started back down, with the animal making grunting noises—protesting strongly at this treatment.

Cam wound in the rope, secured the coil beneath his feet, and lifted the bag so she could slip the captive into it.

'There!' she said. There was satisfaction in the word,

but keeping the animal in the bag—one-handed—was easier said than done.

'You can lift your foot and let me jump down now,' said his neighbour—Lauren—and he realised she was still several feet above the ground.

He lifted his foot and held out his spare hand to steady her as she landed lightly beside him.

'Thanks,' she said, with a smile that made him wonder if this had all been a dream: the beautiful smiling woman, sooty again from the tree, the animal still complaining in the bag, the fading sunset behind the burnt-out forest where they stood and the glimmer of a silvery lake in front of them.

She was not at all the kind of woman who usually sent his body into a perfectly natural male response. Not that this could be compared with anything usual!

The timing couldn't be worse—just settling into a new life, Maddie to think of, a practice to learn and run, a divorce to be settled—yet still she turned him on.

It had to be an enchantment of some kind.

He checked her out again—a quick, sidelong glance—wondering...

'Come on,' she said. 'We have to check him out.'

CHAPTER TWO

'Why do you do this?' he asked, as they walked the short distance back to his house and the wildlife sanctuary.

She turned towards him and even in the near darkness he saw the flash of white teeth as she smiled.

'I suppose because I can,' she answered, adding, 'And I'm good at it.'

He wished he could see her more clearly, read her expression—not that he'd learn much, he guessed.

So he asked. 'How come?'

'I grew up doing it,' she said. 'I don't know how much you know about koalas, but about twenty-five years ago koala numbers were being decimated by the chlamydia pecorum infection. In an attempt to wipe it out large numbers of animals were caught, treated—cured, really—tagged, and rehomed back in the bush. My father and Henry were at the forefront of the effort in this district around the lake.'

'I heard about it and assumed that was possibly why Henry started the wildlife hospital and sanctuary at the back of his house.'

'Your house now, isn't it?'

They were approaching the house, and he looked at it and nodded his head. 'Such as it is,' he said.

She chuckled—such a soft, musical sound he had to smile.

'Mine's worse,' she told him, pausing to drop her climbing shoes and the rope at the edge of the path where it divided to go east and west. They were going west.

'I get builders in,' she said, 'to fix one thing, and they discover a dozen worse problems.'

'You might give me some names,' he said, 'but first— is it too much to ask that you give me a hand with our friend here? I *am* a vet, and I have treated the odd un-usual animal back home, but although I've read up on them I've no practical knowledge of koalas.'

He held up the bag, in which a very disgruntled koala was still complaining loudly.

Lauren felt a moment's hesitation, even though she'd fully intended to get the koala sorted before she left.

So, was the hesitation because talking to this man was so easy?

Or because it was so long since she'd had a man to talk to—just talk…?

Stupid!

For a start, he was probably still married—there was the child, Maddie, even if her mother was off 'finding herself…'

And secondly… Well, she'd prefer not to think about the secondly—which was, to put it bluntly, her physical reaction to this man. It had to be the result of prolonged celibacy that had her blood warming when he spoke and her skin tingling if they accidentally brushed against each other.

But she could hardly walk away and leave him with an injured animal and no idea where to begin his treat-ment of it.

He brushed her cheek with a finger. "I've missed you. Do you think we could extend our temporary arrangement a little while longer?"

"I don't know if that's a good idea."

He took her hand. "In truth, I'm not sure either. But I know I want to see more of you."

Her arms came around his waist. She raised her mouth to his. "I want to see you too."

Travis's mouth met hers. He'd found nirvana once again. He forced himself to keep the kiss light, not gobbling her up as he wanted to.

With a soft sigh, Dana returned his kiss. Her hands traveled over his chest to circle his neck.

He pulled away to nibble behind her ear. She moaned and leaned her head to the side giving him better access. He gladly took it. "You promised me a tour. Do you mind if we start in your bedroom?"

She grinned and took his hand before leading him down the hall. At the stairs, they climbed.

His heart picked up its pace as his manhood grew. "You know what I thought about for the last three days?"

"What's that?" she whispered.

"You, and a nice soft bed."

Dana's heart fluttered. She'd had similar thoughts, as well. It had taken her a day to figure out why Travis hadn't called. He didn't have her number or know where she lived. That put her in a quandary.

Did he want her to call? They agreed on the here and now. Did he want more? Had what they'd shared in the forest just been heated moments and that was it? Should she make up a reason to call him? That, she didn't feel good about. Games weren't her thing. So she'd done nothing.

By the time she'd gotten the message he'd called the

station, she'd already started second-guessing what had been between them. At first his voice had sounded terse on the phone, so she'd waited to see where he was headed with the conversation before she became too agreeable. He met her halfway so she'd decided to do her part by inviting him to her house. She had been dying to see him, to touch him, to kiss him.

After stepping just inside her bedroom, she paused. She didn't make a habit of inviting a man to her house. It had been years since she'd done so.

Travis came up behind her, wrapped his arms around her waist and pulled her back against him. His manhood stood tall and ready between them. A shiver went through her, sending blood to her center. She didn't want to give up a moment like this anytime soon. If she could help it.

"Now this I didn't expect. You're such an amazing bunch of contradictions."

By the movement of his head against hers, she could tell he looked around. Dana wasn't sure if that was a good thing or bad. She viewed the room as if seeing it through his eyes. It had ruffled curtains surrounding the two large windows. A brass bed sat catty-corner on one side of the room, covered in a handmade quilt with a floral pattern. Against the headboard were a number of pillows of different sizes. Wall lamps hung on each side of the bed. An overstuffed paisley-covered chair had a home in another corner. Nearby was a large antique chifforobe and a French provincial desk in front of the back window. Bright-colored paintings of different areas within the national forest hung on the walls.

"It's all feminine-looking and yet you act so tough on the outside."

She turned in his arms so she could see his expression. "Is that a bad thing?"

"Hell, no. That's like having the perfect piece of candy, hard on the outside and very gooey and perfect on the inside."

"You called me candy before. I think I'll take that as a compliment."

"It was meant that way." He kissed her temple before his lips traveled down to her neck where he stopped to nibble.

She closed her eyes and enjoyed the touch of his lips. As Travis worked his magic, he walked her backward toward the bed. She gave no resistance. Her fears had been groundless. Travis still wanted her.

"Did I mention how much I like your house? I especially like that big porch across the front. But I'm thinking this may be my favorite room."

"I don't get to spend much time here this time of the year. Mostly I live at the station."

"Tonight I hope I can make you wish you were here more often."

The back of her legs touched the mattress. Her gaze met his.

His eyes had turned a smoky blue. They flamed with desire.

She suddenly felt self-assured and sassy. "How do you plan to do that, Dr. Russell? Do you have some kind of magic wand?"

He rubbed his hips against her. "I think you know that I do."

"Is that all talk or is there going to be any action behind it?"

He gave her a wolfish grin. "I think instead of telling you about my powers I'll show you." His lips took hers in a deep, delicious and determined kiss.

She no longer doubted his desire for her. She had

turned into nothing but begging heat. It only became worse when one of his hands cupped her behind while the other one moved over her bare thigh. His finger slipped under the elastic of her panties to brush her curls. Her center throbbed like a drum. His mouth moved to taste the skin above the top of her shirt. "I like these shorts far better than I do your cargo pants. Sexy, very sexy."

She cupped his cheek. "All nice and smooth. I sort of like that rough manly look."

"I'll keep that in mind." He rubbed his face against her palm.

Dana pulled him to her. Her hands running down his back to the hem of his golf shirt. She wanted to touch his skin. Needed to. Her body sizzled with sensation.

Travis stepped back enough she could remove it. With it gone, he pulled her to him. Her nose buried in his chest.

She inhaled. "You smell so good."

"Not like dirt, smoke and sweat I hope."

"No. You smell like Travis. I remember it from years ago. A smell I'll never forget."

Travis kissed her deeply as if she'd said something very important to him. Breaking the contact, he placed his hands on her waist and lifted her, then fell on the bed with a bounce. He gave it an extra bounce, making her do so, as well. "Nice. I might never leave."

She liked the idea too much but that wasn't the type of relationship they agreed on. "You could be alone much of the time this time of the year."

"Then I need to make the most of now. I'd hate for you to have to run off."

She looked at him sweetly. "What about our supper?"

His mouth found one of her breasts and teased it through the material of her shirt and bra. "I've decided to have dessert first."

"I guess the tour will wait too."

"Uh-huh. I'll see the rest of the house later." He looked up and met her gaze with a grin. "Maybe next week."

CHAPTER TEN

FOR DANA, THE next two weeks passed in a blur of Travis. All she wanted to do was stay in bed with him. Her life had turned into what she'd always dreamed it could be. What she'd always wanted it to be. To have a man in her life she could admire, who made it clear he wanted her and who made her feel special. She felt truly blessed.

Yet she knew that one day soon Travis would call an end to it. They didn't talk about the future. They lived in the moment. She wasn't sure how long she could continue to do that no matter how sweet she found their time together. Commitment was important to her, knowing she belonged. A forever place.

She'd been called out to fight a fire once during that time. For the first time she had not been eager to leave. All the times she left with excitement pumping through her veins. While she'd been gone the excitement had been about returning to Travis. The necessity of sleeping on the cool ground had never bothered her before, but now she knew what it was like having Travis hold her in his strong arms and against his solid body.

He stayed at her house most nights. They were slowly growing into what looked like a real couple. They rose early, made love, then Travis prepared breakfast and they took their coffee out on the porch to watch the sunrise. In the evenings, she cooked dinner. He'd yet to say anything about reading something into that. She wondered more than once if he saw it as the sign of her deep feelings.

One night Travis had to go to his office to see a patient after hours. She joined him. He asked her to help him do vitals as he examined the woman having breathing problems. Dana liked that he appreciated her skills and trusted her.

During their first weekend together they slept late. Travis did some paperwork while she tended to her flowers. With that done, they mucked out the barn and saw to the horses. Travis acted eager to help, and just as he had in the forest, took her direction. That evening they went to dinner at a local restaurant. As far as she was concerned they'd been wonderful days.

In the middle of their second weekend Travis said, "I have a medical association dinner to attend next Saturday night. I'd like you to go with me."

Such a fancy meeting wasn't her usual type of event. Growing up with just her grandfather who didn't do much socializing outside of church on Sunday, she didn't know much about being social. Even her prom she'd missed. Not because she wasn't asked but because she knew her grandfather didn't have the money for a dress. "Those really aren't my thing. I don't have anything to wear."

"All you need is something nice. Nothing fancy."

That sounded just like a man.

"As far as I'm concerned you look good in anything." He grinned. "But look your best in nothing."

She gave him an appalled glance and lightly slapped his arm. "I'm sure everyone would appreciate that."

"Please come with me, Dana. It's just dinner." His eyes

pleaded. That look she had a difficult time resisting. "I'd really like you to come with me."

How could she say no? "I'll see if I have a dress or a nice pants outfit I can wear."

"If you decide to buy one or the other let me get it for you." He wore that begging look again.

She liked that Travis wanted to do something nice for her. "You don't have to do that."

"I know, but I'd like to."

The idea of letting him care for her didn't fit her usual independent personality. But this time she would let him have his way. Still it niggled at her that she had no idea where this relationship was going.

The night of the dinner meeting Travis decided to dress at his condo. He said he wanted to make their evening out be like a date.

Dana had bought a new dress. A summer-sky-blue color, it was a simple shift with no sleeves. Nothing fancy. She splurged for a pair of silver sandals and had taken the time to have her hair trimmed. Going through her small jewelry box, she located the necklace and matching bracelet that had been handed down to her by her mother and put them on. The only things she owned that showed they might have cared.

Looking at herself one way and then the other in the full-length mirror, Dana had to admit she looked her best. That gave her confidence for the evening. The fact she'd be with Travis who was such a stunning man helped, as well. She had no doubt he'd take care of her and not leave her to fend for herself.

When she opened the door for Travis, he just stood there staring at her, as if stunned. Growing self-conscious, she touched her hair.

"You look absolutely gorgeous."

"You don't look half bad yourself." Unable to resist touching him, she ran her hands down the lapel of his black suit. He wore a blue shirt that matched his eyes and a tie of the same, striped blue and black. To say he looked dashing would've been an understatement. "I don't think there'll be a better looking man there."

"And I may get in a fight because all the men are looking at you."

She smiled. "That's not likely to happen."

He offered her his arm and helped her down the front steps, opened the car door to his late-model luxury car and saw her settled inside.

As they made the circle in front of the country club, Dana said, "I've never been here before. Heard about it, but not been here." She hated places like this, felt intimidated by them.

A valet attendant saw to the car. Travis escorted her to the door. The moment they stepped inside the building someone called Travis's name. He directed her over to the man. With his hand at her waist, which gave her reassurance, he introduced her. Travis made small talk for a minute and they continued down a large open hallway. Others spoke to him and in each instance he took the time to make sure she met them. For someone who had moved back to town fairly recently and been gone for a number of years, he knew a lot of people.

They kept moving until they entered a large banquet room. People mingled with drinks in their hands and around dining tables set for a meal.

Paying more attention to the women than the men, Dana was relieved to see she had dressed correctly. She didn't have to look hard because most of the women in the room were looking at Travis. He was without a doubt the best-looking person there. She smiled. He was hers. For tonight.

"Why the frown?"

She pushed the thought away and forced a smile. "I didn't know I was."

"Would you like a drink?" Travis asked.

"A white wine would be nice."

Travis left her and went to the bar. She looked around the room filled with well-dressed people. All the women seemed to have manicured fingernails and fashionable haircuts. She knew her hair was more functional than stylish and her nails were cut short with no polish.

This wasn't a group she fit into. Travis needed someone who belonged in his world. How long would it be before he realized that? She looked at him. Her heart would break when he realized it and left her.

A plump woman with short curly brown hair approached. "Hi. I'm Doris. You must be Dana. I'm Travis's nurse."

"Oh. Hello."

"It's nice to meet you. Travis can't say enough about you. You've made him smile. I like that. He came to town far too serious and sad."

Dana wasn't sure what to say. "Thank you."

"He talks about you constantly. He's crazy about you."

Heat went up Dana's neck yet she liked hearing that. She was certainly crazy about Travis. Too much so. She had stepped past her promise to herself not to get too involved with him. She was destined for hurt.

"I fully expected you to be wearing a Wonder Woman outfit." Doris looked her over. "Lovely dress."

"Thank you. It can't be that bad?" What in the world had Travis been saying?

Doris gave her a knowing grin. "Oh, yeah. It's nice to see you're a mere mortal."

"I can assure you that I am." Dana had to get the conversation going in a different direction. "Are you the nurse who took care of his burn?"

"I am." The woman nodded.

Dana leaned toward her like she planned to tell a secret. "Then you know he's a much better doctor than he is a patient."

Doris laughed, one that made her eyes squint.

Travis returned, then handed the wineglass to Dana. She took a sip.

"I see you've met, Doris."

Doris gave him an angelic look. "Yes, we were having a little girl talk about you."

Dana grinned at Travis's stricken look. "Should I be worried? I don't need my nurse and my...uh friend ganging up on me."

Dana's stomached tightened. Travis didn't even know what to call her. What was she to him anyway? A longer-than-usual fling?

A man not much taller than Doris came up beside her. "This is my husband, Sheldon."

"Hello," he said to both Dana and Travis.

The men shook hands.

Her husband put his hand on Doris's shoulder. "I'd like for you to come met someone."

"Okay." She looked at her and Travis, "we'll see you later then."

She and Travis nodded then wandered around the room for the next fifteen minutes speaking to different couples Travis knew. As people started finding their tables, they located theirs, as well. Three other couples joined them.

Travis knew all of the men. They worked at the hospital. They introduced their wives and Travis saw to it she was introduced, as well. As they ate dinner, Dana remained perfectly happy to eat and listen to the conversations around her.

They were being served dessert when the woman sitting next to her asked, "Dana, what's it you do for a living?"

Dana hesitated for a moment then she squared her shoulders. She had a job to be proud of. Just because historically it was a man's profession and dirty didn't mean it was any less important. "I'm a smokejumper."

The woman's eyes widened and she looked at her as if she wasn't sure how to respond. "Like one of those people who jumps out of an airplane into the forest to put out fires?"

"Yes, I'm one of those."

"That's amazing." The woman sounded as if she meant it. She turned to her husband. "Did you hear what Dana does for a living?"

"No."

She told him loud enough it got the entire table's attention.

Travis ended his conversation with the man on the other side of him and turned toward her, putting his arm across the back of the chair.

"I've watched news stories about people who do your type of work," one man said.

Travis squeezed her shoulder. "Dana's the best. She also has an advanced EMT and Wilderness First Responder certificate."

Was Travis trying to make them believe she belonged in their world by selling her qualifications? Thankfully the spotlight was taken off her and turned to focus on a man who had come to the podium in the front of the room.

She looked at Travis unsure of what his reaction had really been to everybody's response to her job. He gave her a smile of reassurance. Over the next hour a number of people spoke, giving reports. She wasn't interested, nor did she even understand, but she listened patiently. She would really have liked to go home.

Under the table, Travis put his hand on her thigh. She squirmed. When he brushed his thumb upward, her center tingled. The man just did something to her.

They were on their way out when a snow-white-haired man stopped Travis. "Can I speak to you alone for a moment?"

Travis looked at her.

She nodded. "I'll wait for you in the lobby."

The two men stepped off to the side. She continued on down the hall to the front of the building. She took a spot beside one of the large windows near the main entrance. She watched as the attendants worked bringing cars to those who waited. Glancing at her watch, she checked the time and looked up when there was a flash of lightning. Her crew was due up next for a jump.

She heard a female voice say, "Can you believe that she's a smokejumper, of all things!"

Dana turned to see who spoke.

A tall, leggy woman with red hair and long fingernails done with French tips had her back to her. She stood with another woman.

The red-haired woman continued, "She looks nothing like what I expected Travis to be interested in. When we dated he gave me the impression he was looking for a woman who wanted a good time, not hearth and home. Maybe he's just playing with her like he played with me."

"I thought she was lovely and certainly more interesting than the usual people that attend this dinner," the other woman said before she walked out the door toward the cars.

Seconds later Travis joined her. "Sorry I took so long." He kissed her temple. "Henry was asking me to consider being an officer in the medical association."

"That sounds important. Do you want to?"

"I told him I needed to think about it." He led her toward the door. "It always looks good on your vita to be an officer in an association. That alone makes it tempting."

They joined the line to wait on the attendant. The same woman who had been talking about her stood in front of them.

She turned with a smile on her face. "Hello, Travis. How have you been?"

"Marlene, it's nice to see you."

Marlene looked at Travis as if he was dessert and she'd missed it. She ignored Dana.

Travis's arm came around Dana's waist and he pulled her close to his side. "Marlene, I'd like for you to meet Dana Warren."

"Hello, Marlene." Dana offered her hand to Marlene but she didn't take it, her eyes never leaving Travis. As hot as the weather was, there was frost in the air.

Travis continued as if he didn't feel the undercurrent. "Marlene and I met when I first moved back to town. She's a pediatrician."

The implication was they had dated. "That's nice."

Travis nodded his head to the right. "Marlene, I believe that's your car."

A sleek red two-seater sports car pulled up.

"There's ours." Travis led Dana away.

"It's good to see you again," Marlene called.

Travis said nothing as if he hadn't heard her.

As they made their way to the car, Dana said, "I'll take it you two have some kind of history."

"A very short and unillustrious one."

"Is that so?" She watched Travis closely.

"She's a barracuda and I'm not interested in a fish."

Dana couldn't help but chuckle. It was an adequate description of the woman.

"I much prefer a different type of woman. She was far too much like my ex-wife, only interested in the status she thought two doctors together could bring her. She liked that idea far better than me. She didn't take me breaking it off with her well."

Dana stomach dipped. Would that be how it ended with them? "Is that so?"

He looked at her. "I told her up front. She'd didn't want to believe me."

Wasn't that what was happening with her? She'd started to believe there could be more. She needed to get out before he decided it was time he did.

Travis let out a self-satisfied sigh. The evening had gone well. Dana had been a perfect partner. He had known she'd had some major reservations about attending. He understood where her self-esteem issues came from, but by now couldn't she see the successful person she had become? A smokejumper, the best of the best in her profession. She ran her own crew. Owned her own ranch. So why the insecurity?

The very idea she worried she wouldn't know how to act in a social situation he found laughable. She'd proven herself tonight. She might have been uncomfortable at first, but her fears had been groundless.

He took her hand and brought it to his thigh. She'd turned quiet. "It wasn't so bad was it?"

"No. It wasn't so bad." Dana sounded like she meant it. "It's not something I want to do every night."

"There's only one thing I wanna do every night." He looked at her and wiggled his brows.

She laughed. That amazing sound he liked so much. The one that made him feel good about life.

Silence settled over them. A few minutes later Dana asked in a soft voice, "Travis, what're we doing?"

A note in her voice made his chest tense but he kept his response lite. "What do you mean? We're on the way to your house."

"No." Her tone sharpened. "You know what I mean. This relationship. We don't make sense."

"Sense? What doesn't make sense?"

"You're a doctor. I'm a smokejumper. We're not even in the same world."

"Lots of people don't work in the same world. I don't see the problem." He was confused about where the conversation was headed.

"Travis, you live in a different world than I do. Like tonight, you have fancy dinners to go to. I eat MREs. I sleep on the ground. You like a luxury mattress. We just don't make sense."

He shook his head. "Those things don't really matter."

"But you hold a position in town. You've been asked to be a member of the medical board. I'm not the right woman for you. I don't do social functions or fancy events."

"That's garbage. You did just great tonight. What's this all about?" Travis navigated the drive grateful they were home where he could see her eyes. When had he started thinking of her house as his home? That sounded too

'Of course I'll help,' she heard herself say, hoping she sounded brisk and efficient, and not as dubious as she felt. 'You need time to learn what you can and can't do with wildlife. Just don't lose your heart to any of them—or, worse, let Maddie get too attached. They all go back into the bush eventually.'

He opened the gate into the mesh cage, and in the low light within she saw the grey pallor of his face.

'You've done too much!' she said, cursing herself for her stupidity. 'I shouldn't have asked you to help. We should have let him go—take his chances.'

He shook his head, but she'd already found a stool for him to sit on, and as she guided him towards it, her arm around his back, she took the bag from him.

'Did the hospital check you for concussion or mention you could have it?'

'They asked if I had anyone at home to keep an eye on me, and I assured them I did.'

Not that his mother wouldn't be perfectly capable of caring for him, but she had Maddie to think of as well, and probably wouldn't want to be up and down all night checking on him.

'Well, you just sit for now, but tell me if you start to feel woozy.'

She checked him out as unobtrusively as she could. His colour had certainly returned, and his eyes seemed bright and focussed.

'I won't fall off the stool, if that's what's worrying you,' he said. 'Now, let's get this animal sorted. I'm following the locum around, and beginning to learn what's where in the vet surgery, but I haven't spent more than a few minutes out here.'

Lauren hesitated. There was something about this man—Cam—that made her feel...not uncomfortable, exactly, but disturbed. As if the normally reliable nerves and tissues inside her were sending messages through her body…messages she couldn't understand—or didn't want to.

Nonsense. Get on with it.

'I've done this often enough,' she said, hoping she sounded more casual than she felt. 'And it will give you a chance to see how to go about things.'

She hesitated again, now more worried about his health than the effect he was having on her.

'Do you need something to drink—or some food? I don't want you fainting. I'd never get you upright again!'

He smiled at her, sending that strange warmth through her veins again.

Bloody hell.

She knew what she must look like—tall, skinny, slightly sooty…well, very sooty, if she was honest…

And obviously he was just smiling because she'd been kind. Right?

'I had soup and toast with Maddie earlier,' he said, 'so no food—though I am glad to get my weight off my ankle.'

Relieved, Lauren turned her attention to the animal.

'You probably know all this just from your general practice, but it'll be quicker and easier if I do it this time.'

He smiled again.

'I'd never met a koala until I came here a week ago,' he said, waving his hand towards the resident population of eight recovering animals. 'While as for wombats— I'm not entirely sure I'd even dreamt of meeting one.'

'Not covered in your general course at uni?'

He shook his head, the smile still hovering.

Get on with the job in hand, Lauren told herself.

At least that should counter the weird reactions she was having to this man.

Be professional. Big breath!

'Okay, I'm going to have to anaesthetise him to check him out, and it will be easier to do that while he's still in the bag. Would you mind holding it a bit longer while I get what I need?'

She handed him the bag and hit the code to get into the locked storeroom, where medication and equipment were kept. There, she grabbed a syringe and an ampoule of the anaesthetic they used, a mask, and a small cylinder of oxygen, just in case.

'Will you inject into an upper limb?' Cam asked, and she saw he had the animal on his knee.

He had managed to uncover its furry face, and one shoulder, while keeping the claws tucked away in the bag.

'Yes, that's easiest,' she said, and slid the injection into the animal.

'I do know all about cleaning the site before injecting, and all those rules,' she explained as she disposed of the sharps and other rubbish, 'but you have to weigh that up with the stress we're putting on him.'

'Or her,' Cam said, smiling again as he lifted the now comatose koala from the sack.

'What next?' he asked.

Her mind went blank. She had to get out more, if a man's smile was turning her into a turnip-head!

'Now we look at him,' she said, adding quickly, 'Or her.'

She settled the little bear on a clean paper towel on the bench in front of them and checked the body. 'Her,' she said, with confidence this time.

'And start fluids, I would think?' he said. 'Do you give them in a drip or intramuscularly?'

'IM,' Lauren said. 'And regularly—until she's well enough to take water from a dish. If she's been wandering through the fire grounds we can expect burns to her feet, and maybe her face—see here?'

She showed him a small patch of reddened, blistered skin near the snout, then lifted each foot, again red and blistered. But the belly fur, although dark with soot and debris, seemed uninjured.

'If the burns are too extensive, surely you'll have to euthanise?' he said.

Lauren nodded, probing at one of the hind pads that seemed to have a deeper burn.

'These look first-degree, I'd say,' Cam said, and again Lauren nodded, amazed at how quickly she'd relaxed now they were both in a more professional mode.

'Except maybe for this left rear. But at least that means they're easier to treat. We need to soak them first,' she said. 'Ten minutes in a weak saline solution so we can debride any burnt skin before we dress the burns.'

'And just how to you do the soaking part?' her helper asked.

Lauren heard the smile in his voice and looked up. Smiled back. 'Give her a bath,' she said, crossing to the sink and filling a basin with warm water. 'She'd hate it if she was awake, but while she's sedated it's quite easy. She needs all the burnt rubbish out of her fur anyway, before we can check for any other injuries.'

'Maybe you should be the vet here,' Cam said, and Lauren grinned.

'I have been for the last few months,' she said, easing the koala into the basin. 'The fires threw everyone out of kilter, and the locum Henry's lawyers had appointed didn't manage to get here until a couple of weeks ago.

But nor did a huge number of our usual holidaymakers, so my practice wasn't as busy either.'

'You're a doctor?'

She lifted the little bear out of the basin and placed her on a towel while she changed the filthy water, returning with a clean dish and pausing to glance at the man who'd asked the question, his head now bent over the bear as he tried to keep all four paws in the water.

'I am—but I didn't tell you that, did I?'

He looked up and grinned, restarting all her physical sensations.

'I think the rescue team and the paramedics all calling you "Doc" was a bit of a giveaway,' he said. 'I owe the whole lot of you thanks for the rescue, but also an apology. I was so furious with myself for doing something so irresponsible as flying the machine, I was positively rude.'

'You were hurting, too,' she reminded him, inordinately pleased by the apology.

He smiled again.

Oh, dear.

'That's no excuse,' he said. 'I knew it was stupid, but Maddie was so excited when I told her I'd flown one before, well...'

A rueful smile this time, but just as effective at jangling her nerves.

If she concentrated on the job at hand she could ignore the smiles, she told herself, and changed the water for the second time.

'There's necrotic tissue turning white on the front paws.' Cam pointed it out to her.

'That's good. We can take her out now, and dry her, and cut off all that dead skin before treating her.'

She dried the small animal carefully, then set her down on a clean towel.

'Can you keep a hand on her while I sort out what I'll need?' she asked.

Cam reached out with his good hand to hold the animal gently, avoiding the damaged areas—learning through touch, Lauren thought, and respected him for it.

Knowing the sanctuary so well, she quickly found what she needed, and gave the little animal her first injection of fluids.

'If I had two hands I could at least do the debriding for you,' he said, but she brushed away his words.

'I've done it often enough that it's almost second nature for me now,' she said as she snipped. 'We use that antibiotic ointment and then a non-adhesive dressing,' she said, as he peered at the different things she'd produced from the cupboard.

'Then you have to bandage them?' he asked, looking up at her.

His head was so close she found it difficult to answer. 'Bandages—of course!' she finally managed, turning away and all but running to the refuge of the supply cupboard. 'We bandage the pads like we'd bandage the palm of a hand, leaving her claws free to hold a grip on her perch.'

The words tumbled out as she began the job, the table between them now.

'And you just leave the nose?' he asked.

Somehow the sensible question settled her nerves, and she was able to glance across at him. 'I think that's your job,' she said. 'What would you do?'

'Leave it and keep applying the cream.'

His voice was beautiful—deep and rich—and the English intonation invested it with something special.

Not rude at all now...

Despite the ache in his shoulder, and a general sense of pain all over his body whenever he moved, Cam found himself enjoying this experience—enjoying being with this woman as well as learning about the treatment of the little bear. Not that they *were* really bears, koalas, but Uncle Henry had sent Maddie a toy one when she was born, so he'd always considered them to be bears.

There was something restful about this woman. Definitely competent, but quietly so, assured—and confident in her own skin. It was how he wanted Maddie to grow up—but how did you achieve that, given things like peer pressure and the widespread influence of the dreaded Internet?

'Is something wrong?' Lauren asked, and he realised he must be frowning.

He shook his head and had to smile. 'I'm letting myself panic about things that might never happen—worrying about how to bring Maddie up to be herself and proud of it. Stupid, I know, when she's only four.'

'A very bright four-year-old, from the little I've seen of her.'

He sighed. 'Yes, she is that! But so was her mother.'

A deeper sigh.

'Was?' Lauren asked. 'Her mother's dead?'

He gave a huff of laughter that sounded perilously close to a snort.

'Not dead,' he said, 'but she might as well be for all the interest she takes in her daughter. She left us two years ago, certain that some god, or fate, or some higher

power, had a purpose for her and she had to find it—to...
Well, I think just to save the world, generally speaking.
No big challenge! Last I heard she was here in Australia, way up north in the rainforest. Trees are one of the
many things she's dedicated to saving.'

He heard the edge of sarcasm in his own voice—weary
sarcasm, for there'd been long battles fought on the subject...fought and lost.

'Maddie barely remembers her—which is sad, as she
was a good mother when she felt like it, thinking up fun
games, telling stories, walking in the park to see the
squirrels.'

Was that an echo of sadness in his voice now?

He hoped not.

He had realised very early on in their marriage that it
probably wouldn't last. The magical, mystical wild child
who had so comprehensively spellbound him was, in reality, careless and unreliable, not to mention emotion-
ally fragile, needy, and totally exhausting to be around
twenty-four hours a day.

Realising his mind had wandered, he tuned back in
to Lauren, who was saying something about the size of
their patient—something to do with feeding.

'I'm sorry, I was miles away,' he said, and she smiled.

'That's okay—it's actually a wonder you're still able to
sit there after the fall you had. I was saying I think she's
probably feeding mainly on leaves now, but I'll give her
some milk because it's easy and should help her settle.
We use a soy-based infant formula.'

She waved the feeding bottle she had in her hand and
wrapped an old woollen cardigan around the wounded
animal, which was just beginning to stir.

'This might make her feel safer—remind her of her
mother's pouch,' she explained. 'There,' she added, as she

tucked the sleepy animal against her chest and looked down into button-bright eyes. 'Would you like some milk?'

She slid the soft rubber teat into the koala's mouth and Cam reached out and touched the soft fur on her head.

'She really is quite beautiful...damaged paws and all,' he said, in a slightly awed voice.

'She is that!' Lauren said, and they both watched as the little animal investigated the teat with her pink tongue before finally taking some milk. 'Good girl,' Lauren said.

And, although exhaustion was telling Cam he should take himself off to bed, he found he couldn't leave, mesmerised by this woman talking quietly to the injured and undoubtedly traumatised animal. It was a picture he'd probably keep in his mind for ever.

As the animal's eyes closed, and the teat fell from her mouth, Lauren stood up, mentally wondering where to leave the little koala.

'I'll just settle her in a box under a tree, so she can climb out if she wants to,' she said.

Looking up at Cam as she spoke, she read the grey pallor of exhaustion in his face.

'Oh, for heaven's sake! I'm so stupid—letting you stay here while I sort her out. You should be in bed. I shouldn't have asked for your help.'

She slid the animal into a cardboard box, and pushed it up against a tree trunk that had some fresh green leaves tied to it about two feet above ground level.

'Come on,' she said, moving towards the man on the stool. 'Let me give you a hand back into the house.'

He reached for his stick with his right hand but she waved it away, sliding her arm under his right shoulder to help ease him to his feet.

'Now, put your free arm around my shoulder and lean on me,' she said as he teetered unsteadily.

'I'm really quite all right,' he protested feebly.

'And I'm a Martian,' Lauren retorted. 'Come on— one step at a time.'

The fact that he *was* leaning on her told Lauren just how exhausted he must be. At least he'd eaten and could go straight to bed.

Bed.

Bed was the last thing she wanted to think about, given the way this man she held so closely—for nothing but support, mind—was making her feel...making her body feel.

Forget all that—she'd think about it later. Right now she had to find somewhere for him to sleep—in a house where the bedrooms were all upstairs.

He'd never make it.

'Let's head for your living room,' she suggested. 'In Henry's day there was a good couch in there. It won't be long enough for you, but we can prop your legs up at one end and your head the other and it will save you the stairs.'

'And who is "we"?' he asked.

She turned to look at him—so close she could see the beard shadow on his chin and the tilt of a smile on his lips. 'Me!' she said, possibly with more force than was necessary as she tried to ignore her reaction to those smiling lips. 'Trust me, I'm a doctor!'

Though a fine doctor you are to have let him sit for so long, she finished in her head, as the weight of the man pressed close to her.

It was disconcerting, to say the least.

No, it was far more than disconcerting. But that was also something she could think about later...

'Nearly there,' she said, far too cheerily, as they crossed the tiled entry and went into the living room, straight towards the couch. 'Now, are you okay to sit?' she asked when they reached it, thinking that if he dropped down onto it too suddenly he might jar his shoulder.

'Very slowly,' he growled, and she knew he understood.

Eventually, with cushions from the armchairs, she had his length settled.

'That's fine,' he said. 'Stop fussing!'

So she did—although she knew the nights got chilly and he would need something to cover him.

She went back into the wildlife hospital area. Locals knitted and donated all manner of things for the animals, and there, in one of the cupboards, she found a couple of bright crocheted blankets.

'They would be pink!' he muttered at her as she spread them over him.

'It suits you,' she said. 'Now—pain relief. Did the hospital give you something?'

'I don't need it,' he said, and she laughed.

'You're doing that man thing of grinning and bearing it,' she teased. 'It's not going to make you look like a wuss if you take a couple of tablets. Where will I find them?'

'Wuss? I'm being a wuss, now?

'*I* think you're being a big baby.'

The small voice made them both turn to see Maddie, in a long nightdress, standing in the doorway, a toy koala tucked under one arm.

'What are you doing out of bed?' her father demanded. 'And where's your grandmother?'

'She's asleep,' Maddie said, coming closer to her father and sidling up until he could put his arm around her small body. 'And I heard voices.'

This probably wasn't the time to tell the child she shouldn't be coming downstairs on her own to investigate voices in the night, so instead Lauren asked, 'Do you know where the tablets your father brought home from the hospital might be?'

Maddie nodded, and handed the toy koala to her father. 'You hold Gummie and I'll show you,' she said, and she headed off out through the door, clearly expecting Lauren to follow.

'I'll get you some water as well,' Lauren said. 'You'll be all right here with Gummie?'

She was smiling as she said it, and although all she received by way of an answer was a baleful glare, she was fairly sure he'd stay where he was. He was in too much pain to do much else, she guessed, as she followed Maddie towards the kitchen.

'I imagine those tablets are up in that cupboard so you can't reach them,' she said, walking into the room to find Maddie dragging a chair towards a high kitchen cupboard.

'Yes, but Daddy needs them,' she said, abandoning the chair and pointing to the cupboard she'd been aiming for.

Lauren retrieved the painkillers, read the label and checked her watch, surprised to find that it was after ten. She'd come for help at about six, so he certainly hadn't had any pain relief in the last four hours.

She washed her hands, then released two tablets from the aluminium strip, filled a glass with water and, herding Maddie in front of her, headed back to the living room.

'Will you stay and look after my daddy in the night?' the child asked, and Lauren looked down and saw the worry in her eyes.

'He really doesn't need looking after now,' she said gently.

Maddie nodded, but Lauren couldn't fail to read the mutiny on her face.

'But I could stay if you'd like me to,' she told the child, who lit up with utter delight.

'I'll stay and help too,' Maddie promised.

And Lauren began to realise it was going to be a very long night.

CHAPTER THREE

'WHAT ON EARTH are you doing here?'

The grouchy question brought Lauren out of her dreams of unburnt forests and back to the real world in a second.

She glanced over at the second armchair, wondering briefly if it was as uncomfortable as hers, but Maddie was still sound asleep. Finally she looked at Cam, who appeared exhausted, dark-jawed, and not very happy.

'There are two painkillers on the table to your right,' she said, 'and some water. You might want them before you try to stand.'

'I haven't time to wait for them to work,' he muttered, squirming as he tried to untangle himself from the crocheted covers.

'Here, let me!' Lauren said, standing carefully as she realised her cramped sleeping position had her own joints complaining.

She crossed the room and disentangled him, then shifted the cushions that had propped up his legs so he could swivel around and stand.

Handing him his stick, she bent her knees and slid her arm under his right shoulder to help ease him to his feet.

'Just take it slowly,' she warned.

He was pushing against the pain, and would probably

have had them both on the floor if a woman hadn't appeared in the doorway.

'He always was stubborn, even as a child,' said the
woman—who must be the missing Madge. 'And far too
proud to accept a bit of help. Makes him cranky, people
helping him. I put it down to losing his father when he
was only young—Maddie's age, really. Felt he had to be
a man from then on, and hated not being able to do everything his father had.'

Somehow they were upright.

'Thanks, Ma,' Cam growled at the woman, before
turning to Lauren. 'Now I'm on my feet, I think I can
manage the bathroom on my own.'

'I need to get home anyway,' Lauren said, backing off
with her arms up, surrendering. 'I'm Lauren Henderson,'
she said, turning to the new arrival. 'I live next door. I
stayed because Maddie was worried about her father.'

Aware she must look a sight—still sooty in parts, and
wearing slept-in clothes—she headed out of the room,
across the entry, and escaped through the front door. It
was only when she got to where the paths merged, and
bent to retrieve her spiked shoes and rope, that she realised she was starving.

She could vaguely remember having a cup of tea when
she'd returned from the gully the second time, and whatever
she'd eaten with that had been her final meal of the day.

She should have raided her neighbour's kitchen last
night, but by the time she'd settled Maddie in one of the
cushionless armchairs, and herself in the other, she'd
been too tired even to think about it.

Cam brought the old motorbike slowly out of the scrub
and looked up at the mellow yellow of the stone building in front of him.

He lowered his legs to the ground to get his balance.

He also tucked his left hand back into its sling, aware he shouldn't have had it out for even such a short time.

He looked at the building again, seeing it as somehow warm and welcoming.

Had she—Lauren, he reminded himself—had the stone cleaned in some way so that it looked so much better than the drab greyness of Henry's—*his!*—home?

'Just nip inside and ask if we can see the doctor for a minute,' he said to Maddie, who'd dismounted to stand beside him.

She didn't hesitate, disappearing through the front door and turning to speak to someone in the entry. He smiled to himself, imagining the small but determined child doing battle with a receptionist—the guardian of the dragon's lair.

Dragon?

Lauren?

He was spending too much time with Maddie, for whom dragons—mostly friendly—lurked in every corner.

He was just beginning to think he'd have to abandon his means of transport and go in himself when his daughter reappeared, helmet swinging from one hand, the other towing Lauren behind her.

'She had to finish with someone else,' Maddie announced as she delivered her prize to her father.

'Are you *mad*?' the prize demanded, in what seemed like an echo of those other words she'd spoken to him. 'Riding around on Henry's old motorbike with only one hand?'

He shrugged, unwilling to say that yesterday's koala adventure had left his ankle far more painful than his shoulder, especially as she was still frowning at him.

'I did cheat and use the other hand—and the shoulder feels fine. You did a good job!'

She brushed away the compliment, no doubt aware he was buttering her up.

'Isn't there a car?' she asked, then answered herself. 'I guess the locum is using the four-wheel drive, but I'm sure there's another car—'

'Then you might remember the size of it,' he said, and won a half-smile.

'Bit hard to get in and out of?' she guessed. 'Painful, too, I'd imagine. Not that you should be driving with only one hand, so that was a silly suggestion anyway.'

'Anyway, Madge has taken the small car into the village. That's why we're here.'

'You've escaped? Made a dash for it?'

He grinned at her and shook his head. 'My mother,' he said in mock-repressive tones, 'has gone shopping for a leg of lamb. Apparently, women living on their own never cook themselves a leg of lamb.' He paused, and then added, 'Men either, I suppose. But, anyway, she wants to thank you for rescuing me yesterday, and would like you to come to dinner tonight.'

'You assume I live alone?' she asked, eyebrows rising, and he sighed.

Bad enough that he lived with two women—well, one and a half—who argued with him all the time, but now this neighbour—his only close neighbour, his quite beautiful neighbour...

'We were together on our koala rescue mission for several hours last evening and you didn't call or text once. Not a single "I might be late" message, or an incoming phone call from a worried husband, friend, relative, partner...whatever. Then you stayed the night—which, I realise, you did for Maddie, not for me, but still...'

He paused, trying to work out how they'd got so side-tracked.

Back to the subject of his visit. 'So, will you come to dinner? Seven?'

'Madge makes great puddings,' Maddie put in as she pulled on her helmet and clicked the straps together.

'Thank you. I'd be happy to join you,' Lauren said, and he felt a surprising flip of pleasure at the thought. 'But you shouldn't really be moving around too much on that ankle—and get that hand back in the sling as soon as you get home.'

'We rode very slowly, and only on the bush track between our houses.'

'Well, go home and rest anyway,' she said severely, shaking her head at his folly, although he thought he glimpsed the sparkle of a smile in her eyes.

'Yes, Doctor,' he said, raising his hand to his forehead in a smart salute, then turning to settle Maddie on the bike behind him, checking her helmet was secure.

'We go very slowly,' Maddie piped up, 'because Daddy really doesn't know how to ride a motorbike! He just likes finding things in Uncle Henry's old shed and trying them out.'

He watched Lauren roll her eyes and shake her head, and had to grin. 'It's been a while since I rode a motorbike,' he said.

A call from inside had her turning away.

'Seven,' he called after her, really pleased that she'd left the scene before he kicked the engine into life and wobbled his way down the path.

Lauren was glad she had patients to take her mind off this latest encounter with her neighbour—although, as she should have realised, he was one of the main topics of their conversation.

'It's nice to have some young people up this end of the lake again, isn't it?' said Mrs Brimblecombe, while Lauren took her blood pressure.

'Aren't you counting me as young?' she teased, smiling at the woman she'd known since she was a child.

'Of course you're young,' her patient said. 'But there's the new vet, and Kelly, who's started that café just along the shore a bit, and Beth and her new baby coming...'

Lauren wrote out the prescription Mrs B had come for while the lady listed all the young people and families who had moved to this end of the lake in the last six months, and although Lauren only half listened, it still seemed a lot.

How had she not noticed it, this influx of youth?

Because you're no longer what most people would consider a youth, she reminded herself.

But as she saw Mrs B out through the door and ushered in another elderly local—Mr Clarke—her mind was back on the new vet.

Now, he *was* young.

She wondered how long a veterinary course might be in the UK—here it was five years, longer if one wanted to specialise, but over there—

'I was asking if you had all the pieces,' Mr Clarke said, quite sharply, alerting Lauren to the fact that she'd missed quite a bit of his conversation.

'Of the ultralight?' she guessed.

'Of course the ultralight,' Mr Clarke said. 'I was saying I might be able to help you put it back together. A few of us thought we could help. As a tribute to Henry, you know.'

Am I that old, she wondered, *that aged pensioners of the area are offering me their help?*

'I'll have to have a good look when I have some time,' she said, aware of the lameness of her answer.

But if she accepted their help she'd be committing to endless mornings or afternoons listening to discussions on their bowel problems, or comparisons of their drug routines. She'd had experience of that on the rare occasions when she'd dropped into the sailing club for a drink.

She'd been thinking the rebuilding of the ultralight would be a break away from work...

She fixed her mind on her patient, listening to his list of symptoms, sloughing off the purely irrelevant items on the list, like the funny noises in his left ear, and deciding, after she'd done the regular checks, that there wasn't anything much wrong with him.

'Although you do have quite a build-up of wax in both ears,' Lauren told him. 'I can easily syringe them out.'

'My mother told me that you should never put anything smaller than your elbow in your ear,' her patient said, then he smiled. 'I suppose that's silly, because you can't get your elbow into your ear, can you.'

He proceeded to try the process with both elbows and both ears, while Lauren quietly prepared what she'd need.

'It's not that I mind that they're all so healthy,' she said, over a delicious dinner of roast lamb. 'It's just that occasionally I'd like—I don't know—perhaps a challenge.'

'Be careful what you wish for,' Madge said to her. 'That one—' she nodded towards her son '—can get into trouble just sitting at his desk. I mean, how many vets do you know who've been bitten by a tiger?'

'It was a very small tiger,' Cam said quickly, but Lauren was shaking her head in disbelief.

'A tiger?' she echoed.

'It was at the zoo,' Cam said, defensive now. But he could see he wasn't going to get away with that. The gleam of mischief in Lauren's dark eyes told him that much, while that same gleam raised far too many disturbing sensations within his body.

Attracted to the girl next door—what a cliché!

'And it was just a cub,' he said, hoping his voice sounded less distracted than his mind was.

Lauren was hanging on Madge's every word, her lips quirked into a teasing smile, loving these tales of him as a foolish young student.

'A cub bite that put you in hospital for a week,' Madge reminded him, relishing his embarrassment.

'It had bad teeth.'

He was even more defensive now, but the smile on Lauren's face told him she was enjoying this as much as Madge.

Not that he minded Lauren smiling and laughing at him.

In fact, his earlier impression that she was beautiful was enhanced by that smile.

'Pardon?' Lauren had spoken. He shouldn't have been thinking about her smile.

He had far too much on his plate, what with learning about the practice while the locum was still here, settling Maddie into school, and just generally getting himself organised. He had to do something about Maddie's mother, too! Get that part of his life organised. She wasn't coming back, so it was time he insisted she sign the divorce papers.

How could he concentrate on all these things if a simple smile from a woman he barely knew threw him into a spin?

'I wondered if it was septicaemia that had you in hospital?' Lauren was asking, the smile still lingering in her eyes despite the fact that septicaemia was a serious issue.

He shrugged, and took a gulp of the red wine he'd found in the cellar. 'They didn't say so, but it had to be something similar.'

'Poor you,' she said, with a slighter smile this time, taking a decorous sip from her wine.

'And then there was the elephant seal,' Madge reminded him.

Cam looked apologetically at Lauren. 'Once she's started thinking of all the most embarrassing moments of my life it's hard to stop her.'

'Oh, but I'd love to hear about the elephant seal,' Lauren said.

He knew she was teasing…quite liked it, in fact. But it was time to bring this to an end.

Right now his life was complicated enough, without introducing a smiling, teasing and, yes, tempting woman into it.

If Kate would only sign those divorce papers…

He pushed the thought away and joined the conversation.

'Next thing we know we'll be back in my childhood, with Madge bringing up my being chased by the Loch Ness monster.'

'*Were* you chased by it?' Lauren asked, with so much merriment dancing in her eyes that he wanted to kiss her.

'He only *thought* it was the monster,' Madge put in—which, Cam knew, would only make Lauren more determined to pursue it.

'Oh, look at the time,' he said. 'Please excuse me for a few minutes. I've got to read Maddie's bedtime story.'

'I want Lauren to read it.'

The determined voice from the top of the stairs suggested she'd been there for some time.

'No—' he began, but Lauren was already pushing back her chair.

'I'd love to—if you'll both excuse me? That lamb was delicious, Madge. I'll be back soon.'

'She's in the small bedroom to the right of the stairs,' Cam said, then took a very deep breath and looked at his mother.

'Really, Ma you didn't have to trot out all those stories.'

'Nonsense, she loved them,' Madge replied, her face alive with delight. 'She's really nice, isn't she? And Poppy, the young woman who was in the sanctuary today, says she's single.'

'Ma!' Cam said, turning quickly to make sure Lauren hadn't escaped from Maddie after only one story.

'Well, it's time you started thinking about marrying again. Maddie needs a mother, and I can't stay with you for ever. I've got my own life to lead.'

'Maddie's already got a mother,' he reminded her. 'She could still return!'

'Do you want her to?'

'I don't know,' he muttered, but the new image in his mind of a laughing woman with warm brown eyes told him that answer wasn't entirely true.

Glory be, he thought. *Who knew Uncle Henry's bequest would lead to such a dilemma?*

The story was about a family going on a bear hunt, and as Lauren read she wondered what it would be like to have a family—to be part of one. A family with children like Maddie, always interested and keen to know things.

Like so many children who'd grown up without a

mother and without siblings, she'd often dreamed of having a family of her own. And then, what seemed like a very long time ago, she'd had...not dreams so much as expectations that all those things would happen.

Engaged to David, expecting life to spread out before her in the seemingly normal way...for her, nearly through her medical degree, 'normal' had seemed like a wedding, children, family holidays here at the lake.

Caring for a beloved parent with Alzheimer's hadn't been in the plan, and it certainly hadn't fitted in to David's plans. But how could she have walked away from the man who'd brought her up—been mother and father to her? And how deep could David's love have been that he'd refused to countenance any compromise?

That had hurt the most.

Would Cam...?

She batted away thoughts of Cam—it was a totally senseless comparison. She might be attracted to him, but surely that was just physical. And even if it wasn't, he was far too young for her—there had to be a ten-year gap between them, and the memory of David—the pain of losing him—still lingered deep in her subconscious... had left a lack of trust...

'You missed a page,' Maddie told her, bringing her back to the present with a jolt.

She turned back, read the page, and eventually finished the story, by which time Maddie was sound asleep. But sitting there, watching the sleeping child, made her wonder if she really wanted to go back downstairs.

She felt at peace—something she was unlikely to feel in the vicinity of Campbell Grahame who, with his eruption into her life, had stirred all kinds of strange sensations within her. Sensations she hadn't felt or even thought about for years, and definitely shouldn't be thinking about now. He was a married man with a child, and presumably his wife could return—having found herself—at any time.

A memory of Maddie's voice telling her that Madge made lovely puddings reminded Lauren that said pudding had probably been made and, as a guest, she would be required to at least sample it.

She headed back downstairs, aware of how familiar the house was to her, and yet now, with its new inhabitants, unfamiliar as well.

'It's a nursery pudding, really,' Madge announced as Lauren came back into the room. 'Just bread and butter pudding. But the family love it, and I know Cam will always sneak a bit when he can't sleep and is wandering the house in the middle of the night, wondering how he came to be sharing his life with so many strange creatures.'

So he had nights like that, too? Only when it was her she was usually wondering about getting the guttering fixed, and whether she could afford to have that done, *and* the chimney swept before winter.

'I don't suppose you can give us the name of a good chimney sweep?'

The question, seeming to come directly from her thoughts, startled her, and she stared at the man, trying to see some sign that he could actually read her mind.

Freaky!

'I thought Maddie would like to have a real fire to sit in front of, make toast and snuggle up, even if it doesn't really get cold enough to justify it.'

'Oh, it gets cold enough,' Lauren assured him, seizing on a bit of the conversation that was easy to answer.

'Then we'll need the chimney checked,' he said. 'Henry might not have used it for years.'

'I do know someone. I need to get him to check mine

anyway, so I'll give him a call and let you or Madge know when he can come.'

Good, rational conversation.

Far better than considering the effect this man was having on her, or debating with herself over David's desertion...

'This pudding is delicious, Madge. And you're right—not only do I never bother to cook roast lamb for myself, but it's years since I made a dessert of any kind.'

'Then you must come every Tuesday,' Madge announced. 'That's always our roast night.'

Did she want to get so involved with these people?

See more of Cam in a domestic setting like this?

Some instinct—self-preservation—suggested not.

She was well over David now, and she had a new and different—not to mention extremely busy—life. But that didn't mean she'd forgotten the pain of his rejection—the pain of loving and losing, the talk in the gossip-starved Lakes area.

'She's not wearing the ring any more...'
'I heard he's taken up with someone else...'

The gossip had reverberated through the community, exacerbating the pain and her feelings of loneliness. To go through that again...

'We'll see,' she said. 'Things are quiet at the moment, but come the school holidays, when all the city people arrive, I'm usually too busy for anything regular.'

To prevent further pressure from Madge, she turned to Cam, who'd been concentrating far too hard on his pudding.

'How's our little koala today?' she asked. 'Have you seen her?'

He looked up and smiled at her, as if well aware of why she'd changed the conversation.

'She's well, and eating leaves,' he said. 'The volunteers who were there today tell me we have to change the dressings on her paws every two days, so I'll do that tomorrow and check the wounds. And we had a baby wombat brought in today. I've read up, over the years, on the animals Henry talked of in his letters, but I had no idea they could be so small...and almost totally hairless. Maddie and I both fell in love with it.'

'They're born about the size of a jelly bean, and then they crawl up into the mother's pouch—which, in wombats, is backward-facing, so it doesn't fill up with stones and dirt as she shuffles along. They attach to a teat there, and it kind of swells in their mouth to keep it attached until it's big enough to occasionally poke its head out.'

'A backwards pouch?' Cam sounded totally incredulous. 'In all the reading I've done I've never picked up on it being a backward-facing pouch.'

He shook his head, smiling at the thought, and she rushed into practical speech to avoid thinking about his smile.

'It makes sense—but what had happened to the mother of your new arrival?' Lauren asked, knowing that very small hairless wombats should still be tucked into their mother's pouch.

'Hit by a car,' Cam told her. 'But thankfully the driver had enough sense to check the pouch.'

Lauren smiled. 'Enough sense and enough knowledge,' she said. 'For many years Henry had a ten-minute slot at the end of the local news once a week, and besides showing some of the animals the sanctuary cares for, he educated people on the animals themselves.'

Cam laughed. 'Judging from the number of animals we have in the sanctuary at the moment, he did a very good job of it. And who'd have thought there was a special formula product developed just for baby wombats?'

'You don't know the half of it. Wait till you have to feed a snake.'

He looked at her in horror. 'No—no way! I draw the line at snakes. In fact, I didn't know people would bring them in.'

Lauren smiled at him. 'They don't. I was teasing. Although there is a family on the other side of the lake that handles snakes. If you ever have one in the house, there should be a phone number for the snake-catcher on that board by the phone.'

Cam was shaking his head. 'Snakes in the house? I'm going back to England! That damn ultralight nearly killed me, Henry's motorbike would never pass a safety test, and now you're telling me snakes might come into the house?'

'Not often,' Lauren said, trying not to smile as she teased him. 'And not if you keep the fly screens on your doors closed—which you really have to do, mainly because of the mosquitos.'

Cam groaned and held his head in his hands.

'Take me home, Ma!' he pleaded.

And now Lauren did laugh. Madge called him a wimp and joined in.

'I must be going,' Lauren said when they'd all settled down again, although Cam was still muttering about the dangers of life in Australia. This was a different Cam—light-hearted and fun to be with. And dangerous, given her reaction to this new version of him.

'You didn't even mention the spiders that can kill a person with one bite,' he grumbled, still complaining. 'I hope I'm not expected to look after them as well!'

'Oh, no,' Lauren told him cheerfully. 'The snake man

does them too. He's an accredited breeder and handler, and he milks them for the development of anti-toxins.'

Cam shuddered, but as Lauren had got to her feet, and was helping Madge clear the table, thanking her for a wonderful meal, it was obvious she was about to leave.

'I'll walk you home,' he said.

She turned to him. 'It's a couple of hundred metres on a path I've known all my life,' she said. 'Besides which, you should still be taking it easy on that ankle.'

'Oh, let him walk you home,' Madge said. 'His ankle's fine and it will keep him out from under my feet in the kitchen. He's got no idea how to stack a dishwasher.'

Madge wasn't lying. Normally he'd go into his office and write up the day's work—such as it had been—while she tidied. The locals were still understandably nervous about bringing their pets to a new vet, even if he was related to Henry, so continued to see the locum.

But Ma pushing him to walk Lauren home?

By a silvery lake that shimmered in the moonlight?

What could possibly go wrong? a sarcastic voice whispered in his head.

'You really don't have to come with me,' Lauren said quietly as they left the house together.

'You want me to sneak back into the house and hide from my mother?' he grumbled.

She smiled, and all the small snapshots of Lauren he'd taken in his head over the last few days were highlighted by that smile. With her well-proportioned features and that fall of golden hair—he'd been fooled that first day by her dark eyes and brows—she really was quite beautiful.

And he was—

What?

Smitten?

Good grief!

That was far too strong a word.

Maybe it was just fascination—she was so unlike any woman he'd ever known.

And beautiful.

Maybe it was just lust. Although he didn't think lust would have him waiting, almost breathless, for her smile. Or wanting to hear her voice, speaking quietly, just to him, no matter the topic. And surely it had to be more than lust when the teasing glint in her eyes could leave him mute.

He knew for sure that this, whatever this was, had never happened to him before. Not with girlfriends, or Maddie's mother—anyone, in fact. Yet here he was, walking one step behind her, wanting to reach out and clasp her hips. Or walk alongside her so he could sling an arm casually around her waist and then, as their pace slowed, turn her to him and kiss her in the night-scented bush.

His heart was hammering in his chest, while his mind was lost in lustful imaginings.

Control—he needed control.

He stepped into her before he realised she'd stopped, and she turned around, a little frown on her face.

'I was just saying the path's wide enough for us to walk together, rather than you trudging behind,' she said. 'Is your ankle bothering you? Should you turn back?'

Given the strength of his imaginings, it was all he could manage just to shake his head and move up beside her. To find his voice.

'Why aren't you married?'

It was unfortunate, finding his voice right then! Of all the things to have come blurting out. She'd think him mad!

But the question was out, hanging in the air between them like words in a balloon in a comic.

Idiot!

She studied him for a moment, then smiled. 'Did you actually mean to ask that?' she said.

Hoping he didn't look as embarrassed as he felt, he shook his head, then rushed into more speech. 'No, and I'm sorry. That was very rude and none of my business. I don't know what I was thinking. Can we just forget I asked?'

She smiled again, and tucked her hand into his arm to get him started on their journey once again.

'That's okay,' she said. 'I get asked often enough that it doesn't offend me. I just haven't had time.'

He waited. There'd be more, he was sure. But she—they—walked on as if everything had been explained.

'You haven't had time?' he said finally.

'That's right,' she said, totally at ease—or seemingly so—while he was floundering like a fish cast ashore by a rogue wave.

'So, you've nothing against it as such—marriage?'

He'd obviously lost his mind, gabbling on like this, especially as they'd come out of the scrubby bush now, and could see the shimmering lake spread out in front of them.

How had marriage got into the conversation?

It was none of his business why this beautiful woman was or wasn't married.

But the question hadn't had her storming off, removing herself from close contact with a madman. She'd slowed down, and was looking out at the lake in all its glory as she answered.

'Not really,' she said. 'Things just got in the way at the time when marriage was happening to everyone around me. And once all your friends are married, you realise that the pool of available men has greatly decreased—especially when you live in a community as widespread but small as the Lakes.'

Her voice was so even, so placid, she might have been discussing a business venture or even a shopping list, yet underneath the words he heard an echo of...sadness?

So when she changed the subject, saying, 'It's really beautiful, the lake, in all its moods, but I love it in the moonlight—it's so serene...' how could he not slip his arm around her waist and draw her closer to him.

Close enough to kiss.

Had she felt it too? That sudden surge of physical attraction that had him turning her towards him, easing her closer to his body, feeling her softness matching his harder planes?

He kissed her neck, nuzzled it for a moment, and felt her shiver from the touch. So when they did kiss, the power was there—the attraction, or the lust, or whatever it was between them—and it stole his breath, leaving him speechless.

When she eased away he let her go, resuming his place by her side, putting his arm around her waist—walking her home in the moonlight.

They wandered more slowly now, his arm still around her waist, and he felt like a schoolboy walking his first girlfriend home.

Lauren was relieved when the roof of her house loomed above the bushes.

Nearly home!

She could feel the tension in the man who walked so close beside her and knew her own matched it. She really needed to get inside—to put some space between them and work out just what was going on.

First his question about marriage.

And then *that kiss*!

It had not only left her breathless, but also lost, somehow.

What did it mean?

And, more puzzling, why on earth had she responded? She had kissed him back—felt his need and her own hunger...

'As if!'

'As if...?' he echoed, and she realised that her final thought had actually come out of her mouth.

'I really don't know,' she said, reaching her front gate and turning towards him. 'Just random thoughts chasing through my head and then—'

'As if?'

He repeated it with a smile and she looked at him, standing there in the moonlight, tall and solid—a good-looking man who'd turned up in her life a bit like a genie out of a bottle and ruffled the waters of her usually calm existence.

And she'd kissed him!

Well, he'd kissed her, but she'd definitely kissed him back, reawakening desires she'd thought forgotten, if not long dead. Making her think impossible things, dream impossible dreams...

She barely knew him, and he had a ton of baggage in his life, yet already he'd not only got under her skin, he'd somehow sneaked deeper, into parts of her that had been locked away for a very long time.

'Thank you for walking me home,' she said, and slipped away before she did something foolish—like give him another quick kiss goodnight!

Inside the house, she turned on the lights, determined not to peek through the window and see if he was still there.

Instead, she leant her back against the door, her legs still trembling slightly, and then slid down to sit on the floor, hugging her knees with her arms and wondering about age and levels of maturity...

CHAPTER FOUR

'THIS IS MADNESS,' Lauren muttered to her receptionist as she showed out the fifth patient of the morning and realised the waiting room was still full.

'They mainly want to gossip about the new vet,' Janet whispered. 'Seems they all know you had dinner there last night!'

Shaking her head at the speed of the Lakes' bush telegraph, Lauren sighed. 'Yes, but their excuse is that they need new prescriptions, which I then have to write out—*after* actually checking to see they're okay.'

She bit back another sigh. It was her own conscience making her a little tetchy. She'd slept badly, thoughts of the man next door crowding in her head, and now she found herself overbooked with patients who really only wanted to gossip. Not that she could blame them; any newcomer was newsworthy around the Lakes.

'I think I'm next—when you finish chatting,' a loud male voice declared.

'And I'll be right with you, Mr Richards,' Lauren answered. 'Just go through to the nurse's room and she'll take your blood pressure.'

'Which will be sky-high with all this waiting,' the man grumbled, but he did move in the direction of the small treatment room presided over by Judy, who had been Lauren's father's nurse before Lauren had even started.

At least Judy wouldn't put up with his complaints!

'His blood pressure *is* high,' Judy said, just minutes later, when she showed Mr Richards into Lauren's room.

Lauren sighed and looked at the figures Judy had entered into the computer.

'Mr Richards,' she said, smiling in what she hoped was a persuasive manner, 'won't you even consider Meals on Wheels? If only for a few weeks? You'd be amazed how much better you'll feel.'

His florid face grew even redder, until he seemed to glow from some inner fire. 'I eat perfectly well,' he told her, in a voice that brooked no argument.

But she had to try!

'You don't really,' Lauren argued, patiently and politely. 'You eat a pie and chips or fish and chips at every meal. The only reason you're not even more overweight is that you have to walk to the fish market for your fish and chips, or to the bakery for your pies.'

'I get the pies frozen at the supermarket now. Chunky steak, frozen in packs of four, and you can get chips there too—in the freezer section.'

Lauren heard the silent *so there* at the end of his sentence, and only just managed to stop another sigh escaping.

'You can also get fruit and vegetables at the supermarket while you're there—you can even get them in the frozen section, so all you have to do is cook the veggies and unfreeze the fruit. There's mango, and berries of all kinds, some melon... If you just add a *little* variety to your diet it would be a help.'

Mr Richards scowled at her. 'I get by,' he said.

'With a blood pressure that's off the charts, and forty

kilos overweight, you won't be getting by for much longer,' she reminded him—they'd had this conversation almost weekly for *so* long.

'Mightn't want to!' her patient retorted.

Lauren was struck dumb.

Was he saying he deliberately abused his body because he would rather be dead? Did he even take the medication she was already prescribing for him?

She thought back to when she'd first seen him as a patient, more than ten years ago. He'd only recently retired then, turning his farm over to his son and coming to the lake so his son could run it as he thought best.

Mr Richards had been fit and healthy—with slightly high blood pressure and still recovering from his wife's death some years before. But he'd had his dog, brought with him from the farm...

'Is it because you miss Bonnie?' she asked quietly, and caught the look of pain in his eyes. 'Why not get another dog?' she asked. 'Then you'd have plenty of exercise and training a pup would keep you busy. Your Bonnie was one of the best-mannered dogs I've ever met. The residents at the nursing home loved having her visit.'

Mr Richards eyed her suspiciously, but she sensed interest in her suggestion.

'And where would I get a dog? Bonnie came with me from the farm,' he said, still querulous, but softening.

'I'll ask around,' she said gently, 'and let you know. Now, buy some fruit and vegetables at the supermarket on your way home. You'll have to get used to eating them, because I know Bonnie always loved a slice of apple— and you once told me she also ate vegetables.'

He looked dubiously at her, taking the prescription she'd written and studying it.

'I mean it,' she said. 'I'll find you a dog if you start to

eat more healthily and get yourself a bit fitter. Get up to the bowls club on Friday afternoons and try the barefoot bowls they play there, with people of all ages. It's fun, and you might decide to take up the game.'

'Hmph,' was all he said.

But she felt she'd possibly jolted him enough to start taking care of himself. And when he actually put out his hand to shake hers before he left—just as he always had years before—she felt she might have won a small victory.

Now all she had to do was find a dog!

Ask a vet, was the immediate answer to that problem, but even thinking about Cam brought heat to her face.

She'd put up a notice at the Community Hall instead.

The patients kept coming, so the usual midday closing of the morning surgery stretched closer to one, and she was rostered on at the wildlife sanctuary from one-thirty.

Ask a vet, her head reminded her, but the more sensible part of her brain told her she could quite easily get into the sanctuary through the side gate and needn't see Cam at all.

Memories of the kiss came flooding back, along with the heat she'd felt earlier.

She shook her head, as if that might clear it—might stop her feeling like a teenager reliving her first kiss!

How on earth had she come to respond as she had?

Attraction, she admitted to herself. It happened between men and women. It just hadn't happened to her for a long time—lying dormant at first, to give her time to heal from the pain of David's loss, and then deadened by her need to concentrate on her father's well-being more than her own.

Why on earth was it affecting her now?

Be sensible. Look at it without emotion.

That was her sensible self talking.

So, yes, he was intelligent, and good company...when he wasn't in pain and grumpy about it. And attractive. *Very* attractive.

Taller than she was—a huge plus for a tall woman— *and* about ten years younger than her. They hadn't discussed age, but she had learned he'd married while still at university.

And, apart from that fairly significant—to her—issue, did she really want another man in her life?

Want to go through the highs and lows of...what?

Falling in love?

That was what teenagers did!

Surely she was too old for such a thing.

Although, would it be such a bad thing?

Falling in love?

She sighed; it was a default setting with her now, the sighing.

If she was honest, it was cowardice holding her back— she was afraid. Not of love itself, but of the power it gave someone else over her, and anyway the whole idea was ridiculous.

'As if!' she muttered to herself.

She made herself a sandwich and a cup of tea, concentrating on thinking about the patients she'd seen to avoid any further thoughts of the vet.

Although... Patients!

All of them had heard about her rescue of Cam and, while most of them wanted to find out all they could about the new arrivals in their small community, a few of them had been focussed on their own problems.

She had given those patients her full attention, aware

that it was often in what was left unsaid that she could pick up on what was truly bothering them.

Beth was getting painful Braxton-Hicks contractions, and worrying that they might mean she'd have a premature baby.

Lauren had assured her that they could start any time from the third month, and told her that, yes, they could be painful. But she wasn't certain she'd allayed Beth's fears. She'd examined her carefully, assured her that the pregnancy was proceeding exactly as it should, and reminded her that she—Lauren—was only ever a phone call away should Beth have any concerns.

And Muriel Carter, a spry eighty-year-old, was getting more frequent occurrences of atrial fibrillation. They didn't worry her unduly, although the disturbance made her feel tired, but her daughter, who was a doctor, had wondered if she should have a surgical ablation—a procedure in which tissue in the atria was scarred by extreme heat or cold to stop the electrical impulses that caused the fibrillation.

Lauren had gently pointed out that the operation, involving a wire entering the heart through a blood vessel in the groin, didn't guarantee success. In fact, only about sixty-five per cent were successful. But she'd written a referral for Muriel to take to a heart specialist in Riverview, the nearest big city, and suggested she discuss it with him.

Finishing her sandwich, Lauren rinsed her cup and plate and left them to dry on the sink.

She considered changing out of her 'professional' outfit of trousers and a neat shirt, then told herself not to be stupid and headed for the sanctuary, which was—blessedly—Cam-free.

Helen, who ran the place, greeted her with the news

that their latest 'baby' was doing well, and that Cam had been in to replace the dressings on the little koala's paws.

'He seems a really nice man,' Helen said, before taking Lauren around all the animals currently in their care, pausing at one of the young swamp wallabies. 'I think this one might be ready to be released,' she said, 'but you remember how young he was when he came in? He'd never been out of his mother's pouch. And although we've all been taking him outside onto grass in different places, he's really just a big sook, and he always comes back to whoever's taken him out.'

'And you're wondering if he'll manage on his own?' Lauren asked.

'Will you know if he doesn't?' a deep voice asked, and they both turned to see Cam standing behind them.

'Not really,' Helen admitted, and the dejection in her voice told Lauren that she really didn't want to let the little fellow go.

'What about Amanda, who often does the night feeds for us? Lauren suggested. 'She lives up at the swampy end of the lake, where these fellows belong. She might take him to her place for a few days, then leave her back gate open for a while so he can come and go until he gets used to it.'

'Brilliant!' Helen smiled with delight. 'I don't know why I didn't think of it. I'll phone and see if she's home, and if she is I'll take him up right now.'

Helen bustled into the office, leaving Cam and Lauren alone and, as far as Lauren was concerned, acutely embarrassed.

Because they'd shared a kiss?

Or because she'd responded to his kiss?

It was definitely her response making her feel embarrassed right now—it had been as if his lips on hers had released some spark of passion she hadn't known was there! And now the memory of the damn kiss was stuck in the forefront of her mind, the heat it had generated gathering again in her body.

For heaven's sake, she was a mature woman—she needed to get over it!

'Do you fret this much about all the animals you care for?' Cam asked.

Delighted to have a normal conversation, Lauren said, 'The wallabies more than the others. Koalas aren't particularly sociable, and we just release them into a patch of forest that has the type of eucalyptus leaves they eat, and a small colony of koalas within it, and they seem to find their own way back into normal life. And kangaroos don't seem to notice an extra one joining their mob. But these little fellows...'

She slid her hand under the small animal's chin and tilted up his head.

'Look at that face! These are also called Pretty Face Wallabies, and they tend to worm their way into your heart.' She paused, then admitted, 'Well, Helen's heart! I'm more a wombat-lover myself. There's something so self-sufficient about them.'

He cocked an eyebrow, as if to say *just like you*, but she ignored it and began to check the whiteboard, which showed what would need to be done on her shift. It appeared to be mainly cleaning and checking stock.

'Did you want something?' she said, turning back to Cam, who was still standing just inside the door.

'Well, yes,' he said. 'But just information, really.'

He paused, and Lauren wondered what kind of information *she* could give him.

'I was wondering,' he said, eventually, 'where one

could take someone out for dinner in this area. Are there any good restaurants anywhere close?'

Maybe he means Madge, Lauren told herself, even as a niggle of something she didn't want to think about unsettled her equilibrium.

'Well, it depends,' she began. 'You know the village…?'

'The cluster of shops and houses at the near end of the pier?' he asked.

She nodded and smiled, and said, 'We call it the jetty. I don't think it's grand enough to be a pier.'

He returned her smile, and what little equilibrium she'd managed to find all but fled.

Deep breath!

'Yes, that's the village, and towards the end of it—'

'I thought *we* must be the end of it—there are no houses that I've seen beyond mine.'

'We're the western end,' she said, desperate to keep the conversation on something safe, like eating places, so she didn't have to think about last night. 'But on the other side of the jetty, right on the lake, there's a café-type restaurant. It hasn't been open long, but it seems to be gaining a faithful following and a reputation for good food.'

'Eastern end of the village…right,' he said, as if he was mentally writing it down.

'And if you want something a bit more posh then there's the dining room at the golf club. Do you know where that is?'

'It's behind the school. I saw it when I took Maddie up there the other day. Apparently, she's old enough to start there in the kindergarten class, but she doesn't think she should be relegated to that when back home she's going to a real school.'

Lauren had to smile. She could just see Maddie making her point about such a demotion to what she might consider 'little kids' school'.

'Is she still going to start there?' she asked, and Cam nodded.

'Of course,' he said, with great dignity. 'I do still have s*ome* control over a four-and-a-half-year-old.' Lauren was still smiling when he added, 'Though for how much longer, I don't know. I swear she's four going on forty!'

'She's a great kid,' she said. 'And now I really must do some work. I have patients again from four till six, and if I don't finish my chores here Helen will get cross.'

'Rubbish!' Helen said, emerging from the office. 'You and the other older volunteers are the only ones I trust to do their jobs right. I swear some of the young ones come just so their boyfriends or girlfriends can meet up with them here—probably without their parents knowing.'

Smarting slightly over the 'older volunteer' status she'd been given—heaven knew, some of the other volunteers were in their sixties and seventies—Lauren nevertheless began her cleaning, picking up the straw that had been strewn on the ground in the early morning and bundling it into bags.

Cam's voice startled her. She'd thought he'd left but, no, he was right there beside her, bundling straw into a bag.

'So, if you work till six, would seven be all right? I've discovered the four-wheel drive car the locum has been driving is actually Uncle Henry's—so mine, in fact. I'll call for you at seven?'

Lauren straightened up, clutching none-too-clean straw in one hand, a bin bag in the other.

'Call for me? Whatever for?' she said, glad Helen had already left to deliver the wallaby to his new home.

'To take you out to dinner,' he said, as if it was the most obvious thing in the world.

'Out to dinner? Me?'

He shrugged awkwardly, given the sling still holding his shoulder in place. 'On a date?' he offered, managing in spite of his height and solid build to look sheepish.

'On a date?' Lauren echoed, but weakly, because even as she said it she knew there was nothing she'd like more than to go out to dinner with Cam.

As a friend, of course.

But a *date*…

The very idea caused a sizzle up her backbone—which, surely, should be a warning not to go? Not to get too involved.

He's married, she reminded herself.

'I'd love to have dinner with you,' she said, 'but a date…?'

She studied his face for a moment, saw the teasing gleam in his blue eyes, and knew she had to make her point and make it quickly, before she got herself lost in some kind of relationship that couldn't go anywhere.

'I'm probably ten years older than you—you do re-alise that?' she said. 'So I don't think our dating is at all appropriate.'

He smiled at her—which she wished he wouldn't do.

'Is there someone else in your life? Or do you worry over what people might think?'

'No and no!' she said. 'I just don't think it's a good idea. And, while there's no one else in *my* life, aren't you forgetting you're still married? You definitely shouldn't be dating!'

'Okay, then,' he said, with a smile and another half-shrug. 'No date, but just dinner together. Do you recommend the café you mentioned?'

It was her turn to shrug. 'Like I said, it's not been open long, and I've been meaning to go, but I haven't got around to it. I *do* hear good things about it.'

He beamed at her, causing so much consternation in her usually reliable body that she scowled at him and said, 'And you can stop smiling like the cat that got the canary, because it is *not* a date!'

'Whatever you say, ma'am,' he said, snapping a half-salute, and leaving the room.

Feeling enormously pleased with himself, Cam retreated to his part of the building, arriving there to find a message from the locum, reminding him that today would be his final day.

Good, he thought, *I'm ready to make this place my own.*

He'd talk to Lauren tonight about tradespeople. The surgery was looking tired, and he wanted to paint the waiting room, bring in some new furniture, and do a complete overhaul of the operating theatre and treatment room.

It was a half-day at the surgery, with the afternoon kept free for farm visits, so with the receptionist and locum both gone he answered the phone when it rang.

An agitated female voice garbled at him, so he caught only a few words, like 'fever', or maybe 'stevia', and something that sounded like 'backpackers'.

She couldn't possibly be calling about feverish backpackers, and his mind spun as he tried to find a possible animal.

'Did you say "alpacas"?' he asked finally.

The woman said, 'Of *course* alpacas—what else would I mean? Stevie's down! Can you come now?'

Stevie? Not fever?

He shook his head, but assured her he could, and she gave him directions to her place further around the lake.

He grabbed the four-wheel drive's keys off the board, and was about to head out when he thought of something.

He dashed through into the sanctuary, where he found Lauren in a store cupboard.

'I don't suppose you know anything about alpacas?' he asked.

She frowned at him, then shook her head. 'Related to camels, aren't they?'

'I *do* know that much!' he said.

'Rye grass,' she said, remembering a long-ago trip to a farm with Henry. 'They can get something called rye grass toxicity.'

'And…?'

'I think they fall over—but whoever owns them will know all that. Just ask the owners. They love to tell vets things. It's like patients and doctors, when the patient has looked up all his symptoms online and discovered he has multi-organism, acute blue spyridium disease.'

Cam laughed. 'Does such a thing exist?' he asked.

Lauren shook her head. 'Not that I know of—but they do find the weirdest things on the Internet, so maybe it does.'

'Okay, I'll ask the owner,' he said. 'See you at seven.'

'You'll be lucky to make it,' she said. 'If the owner is who I think she is, she knows more about alpacas than anyone in the district—if not the world—and loves to educate.'

Cam walked away with a smile on his face. This was the beginning of a new life for him—and in more ways than one. Alpacas, for a start, were not something he'd run across as a London vet.

And Lauren…

He knew his grin had grown wider—but what the hell? Just knowing he'd be seeing her again in a few hours made him...

Made him what?

Want to bounce around a little with excitement?

But that was downright juvenile, so he contented himself with feeling happy.

Very happy.

Extraordinarily happy.

But somewhere below all this delight questions were niggling. It wasn't as if this was his first date since Kate had left him—he'd been quite serious about one young woman he'd taken out—but he hadn't felt like this before.

It was as if Lauren had lit something inside him—brought a dying ember back to life—so the attraction he felt towards her was different in some way. A whole-body kind of experience...which was simply ridiculous even to think about!

He'd be content with happiness...

But then the sane voice inside his brain warned against getting too far ahead of himself, and he picked up the alpacas' address and set out to meet them.

When Lauren had finished her chores, the stock cupboard looked neater than it had in months. Concentrating on the task had helped her to stop herself thinking of the evening ahead.

Thinking *too much* about it, at least.

Pathetic.

She walked swiftly home, aware she needed to shower and change before beginning her afternoon session. Having to hurry helped her not to think about Cam.

Almost not think about Cam...

Although thinking about what decent 'going out'

clothes she had in her wardrobe wasn't exactly *not* thinking about Cam.

She smiled to herself—of course it was thinking about Cam. It was about wanting to look good for him...wanting him to think she looked good.

She shook her head—better than sighing—and reminded herself that she had patients to see...patients who required one hundred per cent of her concentration.

She'd think about Cam later...

Edward Forrest was her first patient—a friend of Henry and her father's, although he'd been a bit younger than them. 'The three old codgers' they'd called themselves, and since Henry had died Edward had become increasingly isolated.

From the moment he rolled into the surgery on his electric buggy and didn't smile at her, she was aware that his gout must be playing up.

She moved forward to greet him and took both his hands in hers. 'Not so good?' she said gently, and he shook his head. 'I'd better have a look,' she said, and knelt to unwrap his heavily bandaged left foot. 'Are you trying to drink more water?' she asked, as she finally revealed his angrily swollen big toe.

Edward huffed and puffed a bit, and finally admitted that he'd tried to keep drinking water, adding, 'Not that anyone can actually drink two litres of the stuff a day, like that diet sheet you gave me said. There's not enough time in a day, and even with just a few glasses I'm spending half my time peeing.'

Lauren smiled up at him. 'Just keep up with drinking what you can. Forget two litres and try to get into a habit of a glass when you get up, one with your morning cuppa, one at lunch, one in the afternoon and one at dinner time.'

She'd checked his file before he'd come in, and found a note that he'd been growing tomatoes the last time he'd had a flare-up. Growing them and eating them off the bush whenever he was in the garden…

'What have you been eating lately—surely the tomatoes are finished?' she said.

'Prawns,' he announced, in such a tragic voice Lauren had to smile. 'Young Josh came in with a great catch and brought some around, so…well, I had to *eat* them, didn't I?'

'Presumably with a few beers to wash them down?'

'I did not,' he said, sounding most offended. 'You said to cut down on the beer, and prawns go a treat with red wine.'

Lauren closed her eyes. 'Red wine is alcohol too, you know,' she said as she fetched clean dressings. 'You really do have to cut down on *all* alcohol, Edward, if you want to prevent these flare-ups. And the more water you drink to wash the uric acid that builds up in your toe out of your system, the less pain you'll have.'

He muttered something that could have been, 'You've told me that a hundred times,' but Lauren ignored him and wrote him a prescription for the corticosteroid she knew he'd used before.

'Now, remember—take two for three days, then one for three days—'

'Then a half for three days. I know all that,' he told her, as he examined the wrappings she'd placed around his foot. 'That's not too bad,' he said of her work. 'If I keep it wrapped people don't bump into me.'

'Just start taking better care of yourself,' Lauren told him, as she saw him out.

Her next patient was only wanting a new prescription—and, it seemed, a chat about the new vet and the drama up the gully the previous weekend.

'I'd love to be able to chat,' Lauren said, 'but there seem to be more people than usual waiting today, so I'd better crack on.'

The patient departed, and another arrived, and it was life as usual—checking the tonsils of a small child, the ear of a teenager who'd tried a bit of self-piercing and ended up with an infection, and two more older locals mainly wanting info on the new vet.

'Bless their hearts,' Janet said as they locked up, 'It's the biggest excitement in their lives since Henry's death!'

With Janet gone, and nothing to worry about for any of the patients she'd seen, Lauren could no longer *not* think about this evening's outing.

She went up the stairs and through her room to the bathroom.

Shower, wash hair, then think about it!

Towelling her damp hair, she stood in front of her big old wardrobe, peering in at her collection of what she called 'going out' clothes. Not that going out to anywhere in the village required much more than basic decency.

Although, now she thought about it, in summer, when the area had an influx of holidaymakers, some of the teenagers in brief bikini tops and low-slung short shorts barely reached that level.

She returned the towel to the bathroom and combed her hair—still damp, so a darker gold than usual—then went back to the wardrobe. Which was when the absolute stupidity of her behaviour struck her. She'd regressed to her teenage years, when wearing just the right thing had been vitally important.

She should just wear jeans and a top, as the nights were cool.

Except, for the first time in for ever, she had a reason to dress up.

Lauren had to smile, imagining the reaction of the locals if she appeared in one of the lovely outfits she termed her 'wedding' dresses—beautiful clothes she'd bought for special occasions, like friends' weddings. She might look good, but she'd embarrass both herself and Cam, as the village really wasn't a 'dressing up' kind of place.

So, back to jeans and a top. She had a new pair of skinny jeans she'd bought in Riverview recently, and a caramel-coloured knit that she'd bought at the sales up there at the end of last winter. Lightweight, and V-necked, it would be perfect over the black jeans—casually saying *I'm not dressed up*, and yet making her feel good because the jeans were sexy and the top was new.

And, if she was honest, she knew the outfit would definitely suit her!

Unable to remember the last time he'd worried over what to wear made Cam feel jittery.

Jeans and a shirt—nothing easier.

Except he had a small fashionista sitting on his bed.

'You're not going to wear *that*, are you?' Maddie demanded, as he dragged a rugby shirt from the cupboard.

'Why not?' he asked, but he was already putting it back where it had come from.

'You want to make a good 'pression,' Maddie told him.

'I think Lauren's first impression of me, lying on my back in the gully, is probably stamped in her head for ever, so I don't really think she'll notice what I'm wearing.'

'Go for that blue shirt hanging at the end,' she said,

pointing to a fairly well-worn corduroy button-down. 'And roll the sleeves up a bit. And don't tuck it in.'

'And just how did you become an expert on mens-wear?' he asked, surprised by her decided views.

'Uncle Matt always looks good, and that's the sort of stuff he wears.'

With a slow shake of his head Cam realised she was right. In fact, Matt—his oldest friend—had given him the blue shirt years ago, trying to spruce up his suddenly single friend...

Lauren opened the door when she heard the vehicle pull up outside. Too late now to change her top, which she'd decided might be too dressy.

There was so much tension in her body she worried she might shatter at the slightest misstep.

Stupid, really, when all she was doing was going to dinner with a friend.

She breathed deeply, forcing her body to relax, trying to remember what 'normal' felt like.

'You brought the car,' she said, stating the obvious as she pointed to the four-wheel drive. 'It's only half a k, and it's a lovely night; I thought we could walk. If your ankle's all right, that is?'

He bowed and said, 'Then walk we shall! My ankle's fine. I'll leave the car here and take it back later.'

His arm was free of its sling, and with a blue shirt making his eyes seem impossibly bluer, he really was devastatingly good-looking.

And he was studying the front of her house with a slight frown.

'Maddie mentioned the cakes,' he said.

Lauren smiled at him, relaxing. 'Our old house-keeper—Dad's and mine—was the area's champion cake-maker. She made them for weddings, engagements, baptisms—anything and everything. Even made them when there was nothing special on. Mrs Blair is long gone, but I haven't the heart to take down the cake signs—not when in between making cakes she helped make *me*.'

He turned to her and smiled. 'That is such a nice thing to do,' he said, and the words sent warmth spiralling through her.

Dusk had fallen, but the path around the lake was clear of scrub. He held out his right arm as she joined him, and she tucked her hand into his elbow.

That was only politeness, she told herself, but it brought her body closer to his, and her misgivings about this expedition returned. Given the attraction she felt towards the man, should she really be taking the opportunity to be closer to him?

Yet it felt comfortable...right...

'So, how were the alpacas?' she asked, and he turned to catch the smile that followed her words.

'You *knew* what that woman Celia was like, and did nothing to warn me,' he said, accusation clear in his voice.

'She's a lovely person, you must admit,' Lauren said, still smiling.

'She is—but she's also totally daft about her animals,' Cam responded. 'They're more like children to her—they've all got names, and they *answer* to their names, and they run to her like children do. And can she *talk*! She knew one thousand times more than me about alpacas. But I had a date—yes, I know what you think, but it's easier to just call it a date—and I needed to get away.' He paused, then added, 'It *was* rye grass toxicity—but only one animal. Her beloved Stevie had it, and he'd gone down, and she said he wouldn't get up although he was kicking feebly. She wanted me there to kill him humanely.'

'Oh, dear…poor you,' Lauren said, well aware of how emotional the scene would have been.

'She sat on the ground and held his head while I injected him,' Cam said.

And he sounded so astonished by this behaviour, Lauren had to ask, 'But don't pet owners often hold their pets while they die?'

Cam sighed and stopped walking, turning to look out over the lake for a few minutes.

'Sometimes, yes…but they don't wail in the most broken-hearted manner. I nearly cried myself,' he said. 'For an alpaca I didn't even know!'

Lauren turned to him. 'I'd be more worried about the rye grass than Celia's behaviour. And why only one animal was affected. Did you check the others?'

It was his turn to smile as he turned back towards her. 'If you call "checking" chasing the herd up and down the field to see if any of them fell down, then, yes. Apparently, that's what happens—and who was I to argue.'

'And Stevie?'

'We should walk on or we'll never get there,' Cam said, steering her back along the path. 'Well, it turned out,' he said after a moment, 'that Celia had bought a bale of feed from a different distributor, but hadn't yet cut the strings. It was in the back of her utility, parked by the fence of Stevie's pen, and he'd been putting his head over and munching on it. Celia's certain she has no rye grass in any of her fields, so thinks it must be in the new feed.'

'She'll soon sort it out,' Lauren said, walking more slowly as they approached the village.

Perhaps they should have driven, she thought. And kind of sneaked in…?

She felt embarrassed that she'd even thought of it.

Not that it would have made the slightest difference, whatever they'd done. They'd be seen at dinner and it would be all over the local community within hours. Memories of the talk there'd been way back when David had disappeared from her life surfaced briefly, and she had to remind herself that she'd ignored it then and could do so again.

Not that one dinner out would start much gossip… would it?

She glanced at her companion, but he was looking out over the lake again, taking in the picturesque beauty of the trawlers moored at the end of the jetty, the moon just rising behind them.

'It *is* a beautiful place,' he said quietly, and she felt a rush of pleasure at this compliment to her home.

They continued in silence. Cam was pleased just to take in the beauty of the place, especially with Lauren by his side. He sensed a tension in her, and guessed that, at the moment, it was more to do with local gossip than their age difference.

He'd already heard from many of the people he'd met through work how wonderful she was—not only as a doctor, but with her volunteer work—and he knew that the gossip wouldn't harm her. Embarrass her, maybe, but she was held in such high esteem in the town it couldn't damage her.

Should he tell her that?

Would it ease her tension? Relax her back into the laughing, teasing, wonderful woman he was beginning to know?

Or *was* her tension to do with the age thing…silly though that seemed to him?

Unable to reach any conclusion, he looked around and realised they'd reached their destination.

CHAPTER FIVE

PARADISE EATERY the sign proclaimed. There were tiny fairy lights strung along the building's guttering and threaded through the potted trees on either side of the front door.

Lauren was already being greeted by the woman at the front counter, and Cam followed the two women to a table.

'Cam is my new neighbour, in Henry's place,' Lauren said. 'Campbell Grahame, meet Nell Wright—owner of this establishment.'

Nell shook his hand, welcoming him, and added, 'You're the new vet, aren't you?'

'I am—and I've taken over completely now the locum's gone. He seems to think I've learned all I need to know, but I rather doubt that.'

'Well, I've only got a tortoise, so I probably won't be calling on you professionally,' Nell said. 'I'll get you both a menu.'

She returned with menus and an offer of drinks.

'What would you like?' he asked Lauren.

'A light beer, please, Nell,' she said, and Cam followed suit, rather pleased he wasn't going to have to consult a list of wines. He didn't know if the Australian wines he'd consumed back home went by the same names in their home country.

Nell departed and he turned towards Lauren, seeing in the room's soft light how the sweater she was wearing set off her golden-coloured hair and emphasised her dark brown eyes.

She was beautiful—but he knew she wouldn't thank him for saying so.

Work conversations would probably be easier. Which reminded him...

'I don't suppose you know anything about pregnancy testing alpacas, do you?'

She laughed with delight, shaking her head at the same time.

'Inappropriate dinner table conversation?' he suggested, and she clearly took pity on him and reached out to pat his hand where it lay on the table.

'No, it just surprised me,' she said. 'But sadly I don't—I can't be any help at all!' She frowned for a moment, then added, 'Wouldn't it be much the same as testing cows? Or maybe sheep?'

His turn to laugh. 'Lauren, I'm a city vet—straight from London to this totally alien environment, where I have to treat burnt koalas, dying alpacas, and heaven only knows what next. Yes, we did cover large animals at vet school—even elephants—but I probably didn't take a lot of notice as I knew I wanted to be a city vet.'

'Oh!' she said, suddenly grave. 'So did you *want* to move here, or just feel obliged to because of Henry leaving the place to you? Couldn't you have sold it?'

She sounded concerned for him, and he'd have liked to pat *her* hand in return, but both of them had disappeared beneath the table.

'We were delighted to move here—Maddie especially,

and for me it was a tremendous gift. My very own practice. In the place I'd heard so much about from Uncle Henry's letters. I couldn't have been happier. But I assumed it would still be mainly domestic pets—which, from the study I've done of Henry's books, it seems to be.'

'Just the odd alpaca thrown in?' Lauren teased.

He grinned at her, unsure if the delight he was feeling was purely to do with Lauren, or simply because he was out with an attractive woman for the first time in what seemed like ages.

Looking at the smiling woman across the table, he knew it was Lauren making him feel so good. In fact, he doubted any other woman would have made him feel the same.

He was considering telling her how great she looked, when she glanced up from the menu she was studying and said, 'I remember going around with Henry when I was a teenager to preg-test sheep. He used a portable ultrasound, I think at about forty days after they'd been run with the rams, but I could be wrong about the timing.'

'I'll have to ultrasound an alpaca? A small herd of alpacas?' he asked, thinking of the rather weird, long-legged and long-necked animals.

'You do have a portable one, I imagine?'

'Of course,' he said, taking a gulp of his beer in an effort to stabilise his whirling thoughts.

How had they gone from him telling her how good she looked—even if only in his thoughts—to ultra-sounding herd animals?

It was probably a good thing, he decided, given this outing wasn't a date. But it *had* told him one thing—he had to get on to Kate and insist she sign the divorce papers she'd been sitting on for months. Well, maybe not insist—because he lived with the fear that if he pushed too hard she'd take the matter to court and put his custody of Maddie in jeopardy.

He focussed his attention back on Lauren and realised she was still talking about alpacas.

'Celia will handle it all,' she assured him, and then turned to the waiter. 'I'll have the prawn pasta, please, and a small salad on the side.'

Totally discombobulated, he shook his head and looked at his own menu. 'Eye fillet, medium rare,' he said, 'and a side of vegetables, please.'

The waiter bustled away, and Lauren smiled at him across the table.

'I bet "vegetables" here mean a half a plate of chips and some sprouts and carrot and broccoli in a little bowl because they don't fit on the plate.'

'And *what* is wrong with steak and chips?' he demanded.

She grinned at him. 'Not a thing to a long, slim beanpole like you. You can carry a bit of extra weight. But me... Although I'm tall, any weight I put on goes straight to my belly or my butt, leaving my arms and legs as thin as twigs.'

He smiled at her. 'Fishing for compliments? I can't see your legs or arms, but you look just stunning—and I imagine your life is far too busy for you to be putting on weight.'

She smiled and drank a little more beer—embarrassed, he thought, but pleased as well.

What on earth was she doing, going out with this man? Date or not, it felt so comfortable, so enjoyable, she'd be hard pushed to say no should he ask her again.

But he was married, and there was the difference in their ages...

And yet...

'You know,' she said, because he deserved honesty, 'I can't remember when I last had a normal conversation with another adult. I mean, I see adult patients every day, and the people at the sanctuary as well—even the other SES workers at training days and meetings—but, honestly, it's not the same. It's just chat.'

She studied his face, which told her nothing, then pushed on.

'It's wonderful,' she said, 'and I'm glad you asked me.'

His smile lit up his face to such a degree that she wondered if she'd said the wrong thing...given him the impression that she was enjoying their—dreaded word—date!

But of course she *was*.

'So, we'll have to do it again,' he said, right on cue. 'Maybe try the golf club? Or go up to the city to somewhere fancy.'

It's not a date, she wanted to remind him. But then she thought, *Why the hell not?* Why shouldn't she get out and have a bit of fun? It had been so long she'd almost forgotten the pleasure of pleasant, undemanding company.

Their meals had arrived while she was considering these astounding revelations, and without a second thought she reached out and pinched a chip from his plate.

He lifted the plate and brought it closer to her, obviously intending to push some chips onto her side plate.

'Have some more,' he said, but she waved the offer away.

'That was me reverting to childhood,' she explained. 'Whenever I went out to dinner with Edward, Henry and my father, I'd pinch chips from their plates.'

'What about your mother?' he asked.

She smiled and took a quick breath. 'I never knew her. She was diagnosed with breast cancer while she was pregnant with me and she refused to have an abortion, or any treatment, in case it interfered with the pregnancy. She died soon after I was born.'

He shook his head, such disbelief on his face that she knew he was thinking about the sacrifice her mother had made—it was the same thought that had kept her on track all through her life.

'How on earth did your father manage?' he asked.

Lauren smiled. 'Same way you did with Maddie after your wife left. People just do the best they can. Dad had Henry and Edward too. Henry was a bit older, and had never married, but he was the prop that kept my father going. Between the three of them, and my mother's mother, who came for a few days whenever she could, I think they did a pretty good job.'

Cam looked up from the steak he was cutting and smiled at her. 'I think they did an excellent job.'

'Ah, but you didn't think that the day I rescued you,' she reminded him, and he laughed.

'I was so cranky with myself for flying that darned machine I couldn't think straight,' he said, and smiled at her. 'I do apologise—again. You were wonderful. *Are* wonderful.'

Embarrassed by his praise, Lauren picked the prawns out of her pasta—which was delicious. Suddenly she was not very hungry. But she needed something fiddly to do to stop her thinking about Cam's praise.

Was he just a flirt, or was he fancying himself in love with her?

Surely not the latter. They barely knew each other!

But something in his eyes when he'd told her she was wonderful had had the glow of—what?

The same attraction she was feeling towards him?

The same feeling that there was some kind of electric current flashing between them…?

They finished the meal with a soft, gooey apple and rhubarb crumble and ice-cream, after which Lauren declared she was very glad they'd walked as they could walk off some of it on the way home.

Then they argued about the bill. Cam insisted he'd asked her out, and intended to pay; Lauren countering that with her 'not a date' stance.

'I'll pay next time,' she told him, after he'd insisted, and after it had become clear that arguing further would cause a disturbance in the busy restaurant.

'So, there'll be a next time?' he teased as he tucked her hand into the crook of his elbow again and eased her closer to his body.

'How can I say no,' she grumbled, 'when it was the best time I've had in ages?'

'How many ages?' he asked.

And she knew he really wanted to know.

She sighed.

Knew she should explain…

'I studied in Sydney, and did my GP training placements down there, then came home for a holiday with Dad. I hadn't seen him for a while, although we'd talked on the phone, and I suppose I must have been a little worried about him, because I told David, my fiancé, that I might have to stay a while.'

'And "a while" turned into for ever?' Cam asked, and slid his arm around her shoulder in a comforting way.

She nodded. 'It was soon evident that my dad wasn't

managing—he was forgetting things, losing words, and his mind was wandering when he should have been working. Henry was aware of it, and he was the one who told me Dad had been losing more than words—he'd been losing patients to other doctors. I knew I'd have to take over completely. I brought in a young man to take care of Dad when I was working—to take him for walks in the bush, which he loved, or out on Henry's boat…did you know you have a boat? And I took over the practice, getting in help when I needed, and became Dad's primary carer.'

'And David?'

Lauren stopped walking and turned to Cam. 'David couldn't handle it—couldn't understand that I wouldn't walk away from the man who'd made me what I was. You're bringing up a daughter—you must know the limits it places on your own life. Dad had done that for me.' She was silent for a moment before adding, 'But David's life was in Sydney, working his way through an orthopaedic specialty—he had no time for a long-distance romance.'

She paused, turned to walk again.

'I think I was more upset about my poor choice of life partner than the actual break-up. I threw my engagement ring in the lake—which upset him far more than his desertion upset me. He seemed to think I should have given it back for his next fiancée.'

'Getting even?' Cam said, and Lauren smiled at him.

'More getting rid of the past.'

They walked on again, and Lauren was suddenly conscious of the fact she'd just told Cam more than she'd ever told anyone. For years she'd guarded her heart against the hurt David's rejection had caused. She'd kept it tucked away, pretending to understand and not be unduly bothered—mainly to protect her father from feeling guilty that she'd given up so much for him, back in the early days when he'd have understood.

But now…?

To talk about it…and to Cam of all people…

For whatever reason, she'd opened herself up in a way that made her feel vulnerable, so when their pace slowed, and Cam turned her towards him, she didn't resist, but nestled in his arms and raised her head for the kiss she knew was coming.

You're just seeking comfort, her head told her, but her response to his kiss was more than just comfort.

It was hunger—as raw and needy as she had ever felt.

But this was Cam—her neighbour—someone she was likely to see nearly every day. And even as his response sent her heart into overdrive, and long-forgotten sensations stirred her body, the warnings in her head grew more strident.

How would she feel in the morning, when all the doubts she had about a relationship with Cam would come surging back? His age, his marital status, her fear of being hurt again… And the unspoken one—the fear of what might lie ahead of her…the shadow of her father's illness.

She eased away, dropped her head so his lips kissed her forehead. 'It's too much of a muddle,' she whispered. 'Too hard for me to think about—to think clearly at all.'

He drew her close again and nuzzled her neck. 'Were you always this sensible? Have you always analysed every move you make?'

She couldn't think with that nuzzling going on, making desire burn hotter.

She eased away again. 'I think I probably have,' she said, and this time she stepped away and turned resolutely towards her house. 'It wasn't that Dad and Henry ever set rules for me. But I was always conscious of not wanting them to—well, to be disappointed in me, I suppose. I was conscious, as I grew older, that they'd probably given up a lot of their own pursuits to bring me up.'

Cam gave her a one-armed hug. 'So,' he said, with amusement in his voice, 'Great-Uncle Henry not only left me a house, a veterinary practice, an animal sanctuary and a flying machine, but also a woman of principle! Is that it?'

She smiled at him. 'Kind of...' she said. 'I just don't know...' She sighed. 'I don't *get* muddled,' she added, a little later. But it sounded feeble even in her own mind. 'This is just totally beyond anything I've ever imagined, and I don't know how to *begin* to think about it.'

She studied his face.

'Let's walk,' she said, and took his hand to lead him on along the path to their homes.

Cam didn't know how to think about it, either. This woman was unlike anyone he'd ever known.

Was it that she was so principled?

Yes, but he'd known plenty of other principled people—his own parents, for a start—and he rather hoped it was a trait he had himself.

So it was something else that made Lauren different—and even more attractive than just the physical pull she had on him.

She'd stopped walking, pausing to look out at the lake, and he studied her, so beautiful in the moonlight, with the silvered lake behind her, the silence of the bush around them.

'I think you might just have bewitched me,' he said. 'Because all I can think about is how soon we can do this again.' He drew her closer and kissed her chastely on the lips. 'Friends?' he asked as he drew away.

She smiled at him. 'Friends!' she whispered, and then turned to take the track to her house, leaving him to go on to his vehicle, shaking his head at the way a simple dinner out had grown into such a muddle.

It really was the only word.

His fault, of course. Wanting to rush headlong into things the way he had with the ultralight.

He gave a huff of laughter.

Comparing Lauren to an ultralight?

No way!

Lauren went into the house, closed the door and leaned against it. She stayed upright this time—behaving like the adult she was. But the contact with Cam had shaken her—and not only physically. It had affected her perception of who she was.

She had always seen herself as a strong, independent woman. And in recent years her life balance of work, volunteering, exercise and get-togethers with friends had been all she'd needed or wanted. She *liked* the solitariness of her life—the need to please only herself in choosing what to do, what to eat, what holidays to plan.

She knew it came from being a solitary child, happy making up her own games in the bush around the house, too far from the village and the school for other children to be around. At boarding school for her senior years she'd become friends with others like her—young people from distant places who went back home when each term was finished.

Then at university, right there in the same college as her, had been David, and the two of them had become a couple—bringing a new type of isolation with her friend and lover...being a couple in the midst of singles.

So why change the habits of a lifetime and get involved with the man next door? The *young* man next door...

Although, apart from the ultralight adventure, he didn't come across as young. Probably being left to bring up a small daughter alone had matured him beyond his years.

With a sigh—it was becoming a habit, this sighing—she slid into her normal routine, checking the downstairs doors were all locked before climbing up to her room, where she walked to the open window and leant on the sill to stare out at the night.

Was Cam looking out at the lake too?

Silly thought. She really had to stop thinking about it—about him.

The melody of the mobile phone in her pocket startled her. Not because she never had night call-outs, but because she'd been so lost in her own thoughts.

'I hoped you were still up.' Cam's voice was urgent. 'It's a dog—left on my front step, wrapped in a blanket. He's badly injured and I need help if I'm going to save him. Could you come?'

'Of course.' It was the only answer. Aware that his veterinary nurse lived close to Riverview, she realised why he'd rung her.

She quickly pulled off her good sweater and pulled on a T-shirt. She'd grab a jacket from the rack near the front door—and shoes. Her ankle-height wellies were by the front door, too. She'd wear those.

Within minutes she was at Cam's place, and saw the lights were on in his veterinary rooms. She made her way there, going in through the open door, closing it behind her.

'Cam?' she called.

'In here—the surgery. You know it?'

Indeed, she did. She'd loved watching Henry with the animals.

Cam's 'going out' clothes were covered with a green gown, and as she walked in he pulled down the cloth mask that covered his mouth and nose.

'I've put a gown out on the bench for you, and a mask and gloves with it,' he said, then returned his mask to its place and his attention to his patient.

He glanced up when Lauren joined him at the table, his blue eyes angry and intent. 'I think he's been injured in illegal dog-fighting,' he said, barely taking his eyes off the animal as he probed the gashes and tears in the poor dog's skin and muscle.

'I thought that had been snuffed out—illegal dog fighting,' she said. 'I haven't heard of any in the area—although I suppose I don't go to places where I might hear.'

He glanced up at her again. 'I think it just goes further underground when the authorities try to stop it,' he said, and she could hear the bitter anger in his voice. 'This is a fairly isolated area—I imagine that out beyond the lake and the village there are plenty of sheds the organisers can use...and possibly some own a shed or two as well as dogs.'

'What can I do to help?' Lauren asked, and he looked up from his examination of the injured dog as if surprised to see that she was there.

'I've mixed some disinfectant in that bowl over there. If you could take a cloth from that pile and try to clean him up a bit... Later we'll need antibacterial solution to clean out the wounds, but for now I just need to see the extent of the damage.'

Cam was swabbing wounds on the animal's head, so

she began at the other end, wiping off mud and blood and who knew what from the animal's skin.

'He's got old scars and some bruising,' Lauren said, cleaning his belly and seeing a clear boot mark.

'The owners treat them badly—starve them, beat them…anything to make them angry enough to fight.' His voice was hard with a fury that seemed to burn in him.

'Oh, Cam…' she whispered, as the thought of what this animal had been through hit her. 'There are some quite deep bite marks here on the side of his shoulder,' she said, as she worked her way from the tail up. 'And from the look of that tear on his face that you're swabbing, he's been badly mauled.' She paused, then asked quietly, 'Have you thought of euthanising?'

'No way.'

The words were ground out from between gritted teeth.

'I am going to get this guy back on his feet and then talk to the police about the bastards who did this to him. They must have some inkling that this is happening, and they're the ones who need to stop it. This is illegal, and the penalties are harsh, but they're so secret, these fights, that the venues change—perhaps even week to week. And that means the law doesn't have the time or the manpower to pursue them—at least, not in the UK.'

'And you do?' she murmured, feeling rather fearful that he was angry enough to put himself in danger. She knew enough about dog fighting to know that a lot of people made money out of it.

'I'll make a fuss,' he growled. 'That's the least I can do. Now, if you'll help me turn him, we'll clean up the other side and get started on repairs.'

But as they turned the dog they saw the pool of blood, and the torn blood vessel that had leaked it.

'Damn—I thought I'd checked that!' Cam muttered. 'I'll clean it up and suture the leaking blood vessel before we do any more.'

He was holding the seeping vessel with his fingers, peering around helplessly.

'Look,' Lauren said, 'you know where to put your hands on everything you need. I'll hold that while you set up.'

He glanced at her with a grateful smile and stepped aside so she could take his place. Her fingers slid over his to grasp the blood vessel, and his closeness as they swapped brought a flash of the warmth she'd felt earlier.

Idiot, she told herself. *We have a life to save here, so get with the programme.*

Working with Cam was special, in a challenging kind of way. She just hoped his very real anger at the practice of dog fighting wouldn't lead him into trouble.

Trouble?

She barely knew this man, but she instinctively felt that 'trouble' might be his middle name.

His Great-Uncle Henry had had a streak of bravado a mile wide—he'd always been willing to have a go at anything, no matter how impossible!

Fifteen minutes later, with the bleeder sutured and the dog relatively clean, they could see the extent of the damage.

'Okay,' Cam said, 'now for some surgery. You ever been a surgery nurse?'

She smiled at him. 'Not as such. But I did do a surgical rotation during training, and a couple more in my intern years, so if you keep the orders simple I should be able to manage.'

Cam insisted they both gowned up in fresh gear—and even allowed her to help him on with his gloves after he'd washed his hands with the particular care of a surgeon. She followed him at the basin, washing her hands and pulling on new gloves and mask.

He checked their patient's heart-rate and pulse, shaking his head at the fact that an animal so badly injured should still be not only hanging in, but hanging in strongly.

'Nothing like the will to live, is there?' he said to Lauren, the blue eyes above his mask shining with admiration for the plucky animal.

And, even in this fairly critical conversation, Lauren felt her knees go wobbly at the gleam in his eyes.

Concentrate, she told herself.

Cam paid attention to the facial injuries first, leaving the deep bite marks behind the dog's ear untended.

'That's where the worst infection is likely to be,' he said. 'I've flushed them out as much as possible, and I'll leave them open so I can keep an eye on them.'

He moved a portable X-ray screen and positioned it above the left front leg, which was badly mutilated, but the X-ray, when they both peered at it on the little office screen, showed no breaks to the bones, although the shoulder tendons were badly torn.

It was two hours before Cam was finally satisfied that he'd done all he could for the dog at the moment, and the animal was swathed in bandages.

'How will you keep him quiet enough to allow the wounds to heal?' Lauren asked, scratching at a small patch of unbandaged skin on the dog's back.

'With so much damage, I'll sedate him for twelve

hours,' Cam said. 'I just hope that when it wears off he feels bad enough not to want to move. I don't want to keep him in a crate, which would be the obvious answer. He was probably kept in one most of this life, and he'll be terrified. The poor chap is traumatised...'

He hesitated, his eyes on the dog, his hand absently fondling the animal's head.

'I'll put him in a kennel out in one of the runs,' he decided finally. 'They're all empty at the moment, apart from one very pregnant cat. I'll keep them well apart and I'll just close off the open run so he can't get out into the rather patchy grass.'

But Lauren was barely listening. 'You think he's been kept in a crate?' she whispered, her heart aching at the thought of this dog's life. On impulse, she added, 'Can I have him when he's better? I have a patient who really needs a dog, and I've told him I'll find one. This fellow can come and convalesce with me, and I'll introduce him to Mr Richards as soon as he's up and about again—the dog, not Mr Richards. And if he doesn't want him, I'll keep him. My last dog died two years ago, and I haven't felt up to replacing him before now.'

'We'll have to see,' Cam said, sounding so exhausted that Lauren suddenly realised how late it was—close to three in the morning.

'I should go,' she said. 'And, no, you definitely don't need to walk me home.' She put her hands on his shoulders and looked deep into his tired eyes. 'I'll be fine,' she said, and won an exhausted smile. 'You go to bed.'

'All alone?' he managed.

She gave him a little shake. 'As if you're fit for anything else...'

She kissed his cheek and stepped away from him, but he caught her hand.

'I want to come with you.'

She squeezed his fingers, then disentangled them. 'Look,' she said, touching his shoulder, 'if you're really worried I'll take Henry's old bike and be home in no time.'

His smile was a weak effort.

She kissed him again, quickly on the lips, then turned him towards the stairs, and said, 'Go to bed! Now!'

Only after he'd settled the dog in a bed in one of the kennels, and cleaned up most of the mess, did he follow her orders.

She didn't take the bike, preferring a quiet walk home along the path she knew so well. The peacefulness of it helped the tension of the operation—of Cam—to slowly subside.

When she did get home, she showered, fell into bed, and was still asleep when Janet arrived for work, calling up the stairs to her that there were patients waiting!

Cam was awoken by a small hand tugging at his arm.

'Daddy, there's a dog in one of the kennels all over bandages! He looks sad and I think he's hungry.'

Cam opened his eyes and peered blearily at his daughter. 'What were you doing out at the kennels?' he asked.

Maddie smiled at him. 'I went to visit the cat. Madge came with me, with the food. No kittens yet, but she's so big they must be coming soon!'

He closed his eyes, aware that he needed to get up, showered, dressed and fed, and to be ready for any patient that might come in.

'Be a love and slip downstairs and ask Madge if she'll make me some coffee. Tell her to use Henry's old filter machine—I'll need more than one cup.'

'But what about the dog?' Maddie asked, edging backwards towards the door.

'Later,' he said. 'Now, go!'

With his first coffee in hand, he walked out to the kennels, where the dog lay quietly, stiff with tension in spite of the sedation.

Cam squatted beside him. 'Hello, old boy,' he said gently. 'You'll be feeling a bit rough, but we'll soon get you well.'

He moved the bowl of clean water closer, talking all the while, hoping his tone would tell the dog that he was safe.

'I'll be back later,' he said, and hurried back to his rooms, where a parrot who needed his toenails clipped was waiting for him, and Madge was sitting at the reception desk where his nurse usually sat.

'She went off with the locum,' Madge murmured to him as he carried his patient into the treatment room. 'She left a note, and an address for you to send on any mail and wages, if they're due.'

Oh, great, he thought. But his attention was on the bird, who was eyeing him closely, as if deciding where best to nip him.

'He's really gentle, and very old, so he won't bite,' his owner said.

Wrong.

One look at the clippers and the bird let out an indignant squawk and nipped him sharply on the thumb.

But the job was soon done, the thumb bandaged, and his next patient—a constipated poodle—had arrived.

Somehow he got through the morning, and he had finally closed the door, aware that he should be writing up all the notes his nurse would normally do, but craving a small nap instead, when Lauren arrived.

'I thought I'd sit with the dog for a while…just talking to him.'

'Forget the dog—you're an answer to a prayer.' He paused then added, 'No, don't forget the dog. I have to look at him anyway, and if you've the time to talk quietly to him that would be excellent, but first of all do you know anyone who'd like a kitten, or a job as a veterinary nurse?'

It said a lot for Lauren's equanimity that, although she smiled, she honed in on the immediate problem.

'Don't vet nurses need special training?' she asked.

'Usually,' he said, 'but if I can't get a qualified one straight away, even just someone to sit at the desk would do…'

He looked so uptight—this usually ultra-casual man— that she immediately crossed to his desk and lifted the phone.

'The agency who supplies temps when my nurse or receptionist go on leave might know someone,' she explained as she waited on hold. 'Some don't last long because we're an hour's drive down from Riverview, and they don't like the commute, and if they rent down here they miss the city's social life.'

The phone was finally answered at the agency and Lauren asked about trained veterinary nurses. The woman she spoke to was someone she knew, who assured her there was a young woman living on the lake somewhere who was fully trained.

'She'll get back to me,' Lauren reported to Cam, when the conversation had finished, and explained to him that one might be available locally. 'Actually, she'll probably phone you, as I rang from your number.'

He just stared at her, as if stunned that she'd made it sound so easy.

'So, the dog…?' Lauren said, bringing him back to the reason for her visit. 'How is he? May I go and talk to him?'

'What about the kittens?' he said.

Lauren shook her head at his persistence. 'Are they even born yet?' she asked, and he shook his head in turn. 'Then wait until they are, then wait again until they're about a week old and totally furry and adorable, tumbling over each other. Then take some pictures and put them up in the shops in the village—they'll be gone in no time.' She hesitated before adding, 'You might have to promise to spay them when it's time, but that shouldn't be a bother.'

He grinned at her. 'Thanks a bunch,' he said.

But she'd stopped listening, her thoughts back on the dog. 'So, can I sit with the dog?'

Cam frowned, obviously weighing up some objections. 'You'll need to be careful,' he said. 'He's probably been abused all his life, and he'll see all people as abusers, so he might try to get in first with a snap or a bite.'

Lauren smiled at him. 'He's so trussed up, I doubt he can do me much harm,' she said.

But Cam still looked worried. 'There's another thing…' he said, and she waited.

And waited!

'You might get too close to him,' he finally admitted, 'and that might not be good for you *or* him.'

'Why ever not?' Lauren demanded. 'I've already told you I know someone who'll take him when he's better.'

'That's as may be,' Cam said, clearly still worried. 'But he could turn out to be too aggressive, even dangerous, and he might have to be put down anyway.'

'No way!' Lauren told him. 'Don't even *think* about that until we see what a little kindness and friendship might do for him.'

She could see Cam was unconvinced, and she knew that he was operating, as she was, on not enough sleep.

'Just let me spend some time with him,' she added. 'I'll be very careful.'

She could tell he was about to agree, but would insist on accompanying her.

'I'll be fine, and I think he'll be better with one person rather than two,' she said, touching him on the arm. 'Just tell me the code for the gate and then go have a sleep.'

He did so reluctantly, and as soon as she'd repeated the numbers she left his rooms and headed for the kennels.

She was pleased, when she considered it, to be out of Cam's presence. Away from the unsettling feelings he caused her...from the urge to move close to him, to—

Don't even go there, she told herself.

What with one thing and another, there'd been far too much togetherness between them lately—and for all the strange sensations it was causing in her body it was feeling far too comfortable.

Almost normal...

CHAPTER SIX

HER AFTERNOON PATIENTS WERE, again, mainly people needing new prescriptions and wanting to know just what was going on with their long-term single doctor.

Like in any small country town—or village, really—anyone new was newsworthy, and for a male newcomer to be seen out and about with the local spinster... Well, she'd known it would start the tongues wagging...

'They say he's a nice man, the new vet,' one woman said. 'Did his wife die?' she asked.

Which brought up something Lauren really didn't want to think about.

She avoided answering the question with a blood pressure check, and went on to ask about her patient's grandchildren—always a welcome topic.

But his marital status was questioned again by her last patient, a schoolteacher pretending interest in Maddie but really after gossip.

Lauren avoided that too, by asking about the woman's eldest, who was up in Riverview at university. Doing well, apparently.

'It's all they're talking about,' Janet said to her when she'd shown the final patient out. 'It's because you went out to dinner with him—now everyone knows.'

'Knows what?' Lauren demanded, far too abruptly,

because she knew that Janet would always be thinking of Lauren's interests.

'You know what people are like,' Janet said. 'And anyone new gets talked about. So you'll have to accept a little gossip about yourself and the new vet, even if it was only a very casual dinner.'

'It *was*!' Lauren snorted, then realised she was too tired to be thinking clearly. 'I'm sorry I snapped, Janet,' she said. 'I didn't get much sleep last night—and, no, it's not what you're thinking, you wretch.'

She explained about the dog.

But the marital status questions stayed with her as she went through to her kitchen and made a sandwich, then gathered a few scraps of meat she had in the refrigerator to take over to the dog. She'd wrap her sandwich and take it over there—they would eat together, her and the dog…

Getting back to Cam… He *was* married, and she had to remember that. People who left to 'find themselves' could easily come back. And his wife had been a good mother—Cam had told her that.

Although Lauren felt she'd managed perfectly well without a mother, she did remember times, particularly in her teens, when she'd have loved to have had a mother to talk to, to tell her things… To comfort her when things—boys, more often than not—were disturbing or upsetting her teenage self.

Her consideration of this stayed with her on her walk across to his house and around to the kennels, where she keyed in the gate code and made her way carefully to the injured dog's run.

She spoke softly to him as she approached the gloom of the kennel in the dusk, and wondered if there'd be a light. Did injured dogs need night lights?

'Hello, old boy,' she said, as she came quietly into the shelter.

'Not so much of the "old", thank you,' a deep voice said, and she let out a cry of what she hoped hadn't sounded like fear.

'What on earth are you doing here?' she demanded.

'He's my patient,' Cam said.

But the lack of sleep, concern about the dog, and the muddle she was in over her feelings for this man all crashed down on her and she slumped onto the floor, head bent, as her eyes started leaking tears.

'Hey...' Cam said, standing up and moving so he could sit beside her and put his arm around her. 'I gave you a fright. I'm sorry.'

He pulled her close against his body and she felt his lips pressing kisses on her hair.

'This is stupid,' she finally managed to mutter. 'I never cry.'

He held her closer, so his body warmed her, and just for a minute or two she relaxed against him, nestled into him.

'It's lack of sleep,' she said against his chest. 'And the dog.'

Having produced two more or less sensible sentences, she knew she should ease away—ease out of those arms that held her, away from the security that was something she'd never known...never felt before.

Had she been lonelier than she'd thought? Was that why Cam's arms were so comforting?

She didn't think so—had never felt that. So it must be Cam's arms in particular that were producing these wonderful sensations...

This was dangerous!

But although the word was like a red light, flashing

in her brain, she let him hold her, finally lifting her head for the kiss she was sure they both wanted.

The kiss was warm and comforting, but there was more than that to it. Sensuality and desire caused a physical ache deep inside her—a yearning for something she could barely understand.

She finally eased away from him, dug a handkerchief out of her jeans and cleaned up the remnants of her silly tears.

Back in control.

Almost...

Deep breath, and then sensible conversation.

'I've a sandwich, if you'd like to share, and I brought a few scraps of ham for the dog, if that's okay and if he wants it.'

She knew she was yammering on so that she didn't have to think—or, worse, talk about what had just happened—but Cam accepted half her sandwich and agreed that the dog might like the ham.

He sounded so cool and in control. She still felt confused about her weakness, and found herself feeding bits of sandwich to the dog, so she didn't have to think about the man who'd held her in his arms and somehow managed to kiss her body back to life.

'Well, he's certainly well enough to eat,' Cam said, definitely in control. 'I'll feed him mine as well, if you don't mind?'

'Go for it,' Lauren managed, but her voice was husky and a trifle wobbly.

Cam pulled her close again. 'Come on,' he said, 'I'll walk you home. We'll have some tea and toast—if you've any bread left after the sandwiches.'

'I've always got spare bread in my freezer,' Lauren said, deciding it was time to take control of the situation.

'I was almost sure you would,' he said, and she could hear the smile in his voice.

In spite of all the reasons she could list for *not* getting involved with this man, she knew she wanted nothing more than for him to walk her home, his arm around her shoulders, his body close to hers...

They did have tea and toast—but much later.

Cam was more or less dressed—his T-shirt was on inside out—and Lauren was in her faded old dressing gown, cuddly and familiar.

'I shouldn't have let that happen,' she said, her face still flushed from their lovemaking.

'And why is that, oh, wise one?' Cam teased.

She frowned at him. 'You know very well—there are dozens of reasons.'

'Like?' he prompted.

Again that smile was in his voice, and her body trembled.

Get a grip, she told herself.

'Gossip,' she said, 'which won't bother me, but might be hard for Madge to listen to, and it could hurt Maddie too.'

'Not the dog?' he teased, but she shook her head.

'It's not a joke,' she said. 'This community might be spread out about the lake but it's small, and there's nothing a small community likes better than some fresh gossip.'

'Would it hurt *you*?' he asked, not joking now, and his blue eyes looked at her so tenderly she had to bite back tears.

Bloody hell. Hadn't she cried enough for one day?

'No,' she said. 'I've been here so long I'm just part of the furniture. Although...' She thought about it, and finally admitted, '*Because* I have been here so long, it might be even more startling—juicier.'

She wasn't going to sigh again.

No tears and no sighing.

'And then there's your age,' she said bluntly. 'Lakesiders are fairly conventional people. Cradle-snatching will come up somewhere along the line.'

'Not if we got married,' he said.

And this time she wanted to sigh and cry at the same time.

'Aren't you already married?'

She was watching him closely, wanting to read his reaction. She didn't expect the smile that came.

'I *am* trying to get unmarried,' he said. 'In fact, one of the reasons I was so delighted to move out here was because my wife is in Australia and I thought it would be easier to push her to sign divorce papers from here.'

Lauren was telling herself she shouldn't feel pleased about this when he floored her completely.

'I think I was smitten the first time I saw you—or very soon after—so it seems natural to think of marriage.'

'*Smitten?* What do you mean "smitten"? And if it's what I think it means it's a passing thing, nothing more, and certainly not a basis for marriage—which isn't possible anyway, given where we're at!'

She folded her arms as she finished this rant, and glared at him—not that her glare had the slightest effect. In fact, it seemed to encourage him, because he left his stool on the other side of the breakfast bar and came to put his arm around her, pulling her to her feet and kissing her so passionately on the lips that her bones began to melt.

Dear heaven, what was she supposed to do?

Let him carry her into the sitting room?

Let him slip off her robe?

Let him kiss his way down from her mouth to her neck, to her breast?

Yes.

So she let him tease and tantalise her, until she joined in the teasing, the kissing, the movement of their bodies as they came together...

He tipped her so she was on top of him, sliding into her, his hands on her breasts making her moan as he moved and cry out as she climaxed, his matching groan of satisfaction sweet in her ears.

CHAPTER SEVEN

For the second morning in a row she was woken by Janet arriving for work, and as she flung herself out of bed she called down to her, asking her to please put on toast, and the kettle. She walked into the bathroom. She could feel him still...his skin against hers, the scent of him in the air around her.

Her body flushed with heat just thinking about it and she dived into the shower, hoping that common sense would soon return, and that she'd at least outwardly look normal and composed.

Fortunately, the morning passed smoothly enough, the only surprise arrival being Madge, towing a reluctant Maddie along behind her.

'She's starting school next week and I'm told she needs some final vaccination, before she goes. I've got her record book from London, so you can see what she's had.'

She passed a small booklet to Lauren, who checked through the vaccinations Maddie had already received.

'There's not one for meningococcal here,' she said to Madge. 'They're usually given to under-twos and fifteen-to-nineteen-year-olds, because those are the most susceptible age groups, but it wouldn't hurt for her to have one.'

She looked across at Maddie, who was looking openly mutinous.

'I hate needles,' she said, in case Lauren hadn't got the message.

'So do I,' Lauren assured her. 'I hate getting injections and giving them, but I have to give them to keep you safe.' She turned back to Madge. 'You'll talk to Cam about the meningococcal?'

Madge nodded, then added, 'You might talk to him yourself as well, in case I don't remember.'

'Madge always forgets things,' Maddie said.

Lauren felt a twinge of alarm—older people forgetting things was something she was only too familiar with—but Madge was already speaking.

'Rubbish,' she said to the young critic. 'Although I might—just sometimes—forget to keep an eye on you when I'm fishing...'

'And one day you went home without me!' Maddie reminded her.

Poor Madge flushed. 'Not all the way home—and that's enough, young lady. You're only talking because you think we might forget about the injection.'

Time to intercede.

'Okay, Maddie, come with me into the treatment room and we'll see just how brave you are.'

'Will I get a sweetie?' the child asked, eyeing the jar of jelly beans on Lauren's desk.

'Good children sometimes get two,' Lauren told her, with a slight emphasis on the 'good'.

In the colourful treatment room, she lifted Maddie onto an examination table and cranked it up. She was convinced, for no particular reason, that needles hurt less if you could put them straight into the muscle rather than at an angle.

Maddie was still counting some of the animals in a

chart on the wall when Lauren stuck a small round plaster on the tiny hole and lowered the table.

'It's finished?' Maddie demanded. 'I didn't even feel it!'

'That's good,' Lauren told her as she lifted her to the floor.

'But will I only get one sweetie?'

Lauren smiled. 'No,' she said, 'you were especially good and can have two.'

Back in the consulting room, she opened the jar and let Maddie choose—one red and one black.

With those two clutched in her hand, she eyed the jar. 'I do like green ones too,' she said, and Lauren had to laugh.

'Nice try, kid,' she said, ruffling Maddie's hair as she propelled them out the door.

'Meningococcal—is that right?' Madge asked, and Lauren nodded.

'Just phone for an appointment any time,' she said. 'Janet will fix you up.'

But even as she ushered her next patient through the door her thoughts remained with the pair who'd just departed.

Madge and Maddie.

She *had* to think of them. Had to think of the effect any gossip might have on them—and there *would* be gossip, no matter how careful she and Cam were.

The memory of a local teenager who'd committed suicide some years earlier, unable to handle gossip about him being gay—which, as it happened, he hadn't been— was still strong in her mind. Guilt that she hadn't been able to help him still sneaked into her head when she least expected it.

Her thoughts depressed her. This whole silly thing

with Cam: dinner, a few kisses, sex—very good sex—had brought light and laughter, not to mention physical pleasure, into her life, and she really didn't want to lose that.

Not just yet.

Not when simply thinking about losing it caused her pain, while thinking of *him* brought warmth flooding through her body and a bright lightness of spirit she hadn't felt for a long time.

But the idea of potentially hurtful gossip remained. Maddie was starting school soon, and Madge would begin to find interests in the area that would bring her into contact with the locals.

'So, do you think I should make an appointment to see a specialist up in Riverview?' her patient asked, and Lauren had to collect her scrambled wits and try to remember what they'd been discussing.

Stomach pain—that was it.

'A specialist would probably recommend an endoscopy—poking a tube down your throat to have a look at your stomach. But if you're only getting the pains after eating oranges, you'd be better off not eating them for a while, to see if that stops the pain completely.'

Mr March frowned at her, then lifted himself out of the chair and folded his arms across his chest. The frown turned into a full glare. 'But my tree is full of fruit,' he said. 'They're *my* oranges!'

Lauren flipped quickly through his notes—still on cards, as all the older patients' notes had yet to be computerised. And there it was. Same time every year, Mr March presented with stomach pains. Her father had actually sent him to Riverview for an endoscopy at one stage, only to be told his stomach wall lining and small intestine were all clear.

She made a new note, mentioning the oranges. She'd

transfer Mr March's file to the computer this afternoon, while his visit was fresh in her mind, but in the meantime...

'Stop eating them for a few days and see how you feel,' she suggested. 'Then, if the pain disappears, try eating just one a day and see what happens.'

She made another note, and then wondered if she was overdoing the paperwork in case her mind began to slip, as her father's had—not that she'd seen the slightest sign of it in herself.

Two more patients and she was done for the morning. And, it being Thursday, she had no afternoon session. She *did* have a late volunteering shift at the sanctuary—making sure all the animals were fed and the place locked up.

Even thinking about proximity to Cam sent shivers through her body—which was stupid, given he would quite likely be out in the backblocks somewhere, tending a large animal.

She concentrated on getting a lifetime's worth of Mr March's medical history on the computer, before tidying the house. She was putting off her trip across to the sanctuary. And the decision about what to wear was definitely a little more difficult than usual...

Finally, forcing common-sense back into her head, she fixed some sandwiches for herself and the dog—he really needed a name—and headed over to the vet's place.

Henry, she decided. That would do nicely for the dog. Henry had been a fighter too—fighting for the environment, fighting against the destruction of the natural habitat—and it was far more suitable than Tramp, Scout, or any of the other names she'd considered.

'Hello, Henry,' she said to him as she entered the dim kennel.

No spoken response this time, so at least she was on her own—and, no, that *wasn't* a twinge of disappointment that ran through her body as she realised it.

She settled herself beside Henry's head, talking quietly, touching him gently, and to her surprise he responded by struggling to roll over, so he could almost sit up, one bandaged leg stuck stiffly out to the side.

'Good boy,' she said, and fed him a piece of sandwich, patting the unbandaged bits of him. 'You should be getting most of those dressings off tomorrow,' she told him, as she ate her own sandwich.

He leaned cautiously to one side, and she lifted his water bowl, certain he'd fall back down if he tried to reach it himself.

She held it to him while he drank greedily. 'So maybe, while you're up, you'd like some real food?' she said, and reached for the bowl of dried food, holding it in front of him so he could sniff at it and nuzzle a few pieces before snaffling some into his mouth with his tongue.

'Good for you!' she said, so excited she'd have given him a hug if she hadn't thought it would hurt him.

But he must have got the message, because she was sure he smiled at her—a sloppy kind of smile, but definitely recognisable.

'Oh, you darling!' she said, and gave him a little more sandwich, feeling his tongue licking at her palm.

'Haven't you heard the expression about biting the hand that feeds you?'

She turned to see Cam, stooping at the entrance to the kennel.

'He just smiled at me,' she told him, wanting to share her delight and also to cover her reaction to seeing him— equal delight!

'Oh, yes…?'

Polite disbelief, but there was a smile in his voice again, and she felt the tremor of desire fire her senses.

Damn it all! She *had* to get over this reaction to his presence—it confused her senses, stopped her thinking sensibly, and she was reasonably sure that she *had* to think sensibly about their relationship.

Cam certainly wasn't!

But the situation—gossip, her father, so many things that really should be considered... Or should have *been* considered before this went too far...

And he was married...

And the age thing...

And, on that point, wasn't she too old to be feeling such intensity of desire? Wasn't that teenage stuff? First flush of love stuff? Not that she could remember feeling tremors of desire at the mere sound of David's voice...

Deep breath. Common sense.

'When will the dressings come off, so we can see what he looks like?' she asked, determined to sound sensible and practical and not like some teenager overcome by the enormity of first love.

'I'll redo them later,' Cam said, coming to squat beside her. 'Did you come over just to have lunch with the dog?' he asked, nodding at the bundle of sandwiches she'd set on the floor.

She turned and grinned at him. 'No, I'm on duty at the sanctuary later this afternoon, so I called in to see him first. He ate a sandwich, then sat up and had water and some actual dog food. So I imagine once you unwrap him, and he has more freedom to move, he'll probably prefer that to sandwiches.'

She put her hand on the head that was now resting on her knee.

'Won't you, Henry?'

'Henry? You're going to call him Henry?'

'I think it's a great name for a noble dog like him,' she said firmly. 'I've told him our Henry was a fighter—especially for animal rights.'

Cam settled beside her, slid a hand across her shoulders and gently brushed the skin beneath her hair. Then he pressed a kiss on the back of her neck...sending shivers all over her.

She had no memory of ever reacting to a man like this, yet that single touch had relit the embers of desire that he could flame into fire so easily.

Remember Maddie and Madge and gossip! And that he's younger than you! And married!

The mantra rang in her head even as she turned towards him and let his lips meet hers.

Fat lot of good mantras did.

At least they'd both have to get back to work before anything more could happen.

The late afternoon schedule at the sanctuary was always busy, as all the animals had to be checked to see if their wounds were healing, or if some other problem might have appeared.

The wombats were the worst. Once old enough and brave enough to leave their hollow logs, they often injured their front digging paws by trying to build a burrow near a fence post that was concreted into the ground. They had to follow their instincts to dig before they could be taken back into the bush, where they'd have to dig their own protective burrows, so it was a no-win situation.

'Poor baby,' Lauren murmured to one, as she fed it the formula especially prepared for wombats.

'Poor baby nothing,' a voice growled from behind her. 'Where's my dog?'

A man—a very large man—stood outside the sanctuary fence, a shotgun dangling casually from one hand.

'I'm sorry, sir, but this is a wildlife sanctuary—we rescue wombats and koalas and such. We don't have dogs.'

She hoped she sounded a lot more confident than she felt.

'That mad woman said she brought my dog here!' the man said, moving the shotgun slightly.

'I can't let you in because the animals can pick up germs from outside, but please look around—there's only me and the animals and that store cupboard over there. You can see right into it—nothing there. I'm sorry, but if your dog's lost maybe you could put some notices up in the village?'

'I won't put up any damn notice in the village!' the man roared. 'I'll be back!'

He turned and strode away, and now Lauren saw the ute parked in the shade of a tree some distance away. Cautiously parked, so it could barely be seen.

She remained where she was, frozen in place, until he'd driven away—not around the house to where the kennels were, but back in the direction he'd come from.

Get his number plate, some still functioning brain cell told her. But the ute was already disappearing, and all she noticed was a rusty dent in the passenger-side door.

Some clue!

She breathed deeply, realised she was holding the wee wombat far too tightly, and slowly set him down on the ground.

Police.

Aware that the one constable who was seeing out his last few years before retirement in the village wouldn't be the best person to tackle an angry man with a shotgun, she phoned the larger police station, further up the lake.

And although she'd felt tentative about phoning, wondering if it was too minor a matter to be reporting, she was greeted by reassurances that she'd done the right thing and then, to her surprise, she was transferred to someone called Brendan from 'the cattle duffing squad'.

'Cattle duffing squad?' she echoed weakly, and he laughed.

'It happens more often than you think,' Brendan assured her. 'Cattle go missing all the time, and although some have just wandered through a broken fence into a neighbour's yard, many of them are stolen, moved interstate, or sold off before they cross a border.'

'And dog-fighting?' Lauren felt compelled to ask.

'Oh, that's really nasty—and although we've been aware of a gang operating somewhere near here, we've never been able to find them. You're at the sanctuary at the end of the lake?'

Lauren agreed and the man hung up—though when exactly he or anyone else would appear she had no idea.

She'd better tell Cam he was coming, and mention the man with a gun. First, though, she would phone Helen, to let her know what was going on. Who knew what Brendan might suggest they do when he appeared. Remove all the animals?

Helen refused to panic, saying simply that she'd get someone over there to spend the night just in case there was a disturbance.

Helen's calm rubbed off on Lauren, so phoning Cam was relatively easy—until he caught on to what had happened and reacted with protective anger, asking why she'd remained in the vicinity of a man with a gun.

After hanging up, he came straight through to the sanctuary and put his arm around her shoulders, softening any rebuke in his words.

Brendan and his mate—both in the khaki uniform of country police officers—arrived within half an hour, and assured her and Cam that the animals would be safe.

'No one will come near the sanctuary with our very obvious vehicle out there.' Brendan waved his hand towards the big khaki four-wheel drive parked just outside the fence. 'These fellows know we're just as serious as they are. In fact, more so.' He turned to Cam. 'You live in the house?' he asked, and Cam explained that he, Madge and Maddie did.

'Oh, and there's a dog and a pregnant cat out in the kennels,' Lauren added.

'Is there somewhere you can all stay for a few days? Just as a precaution?'

That was Brendan's next question, and when Cam looked totally blank, Lauren spoke up.

'They can all come to my house—it's just over there.' She pointed in vaguely the right direction.

But she'd barely finished offering, when Cam said, 'The others can go, but I'll stay here. I won't get in your way, but I know where the tea and coffee are kept and I can provide some assistance behind the scenes.'

Brendan considered this and eventually agreed—with the proviso that Cam stayed out of their way.

'Madge and Maddie and the animals can all come to my place,' Lauren repeated. 'You were going to redress Henry's wounds. Do you want to do that first?'

Had some strain in her voice told him how anxious she was about him remaining in the house? Was that why he put his arm around her shoulders as he walked back into the surgery to get what he needed for Henry's wounds?

'I'll be fine,' he said, when he'd manoeuvred her away from the two men. He waited until he and Lauren were back in his rooms before turning to look into her face. 'I won't do anything foolish, but this *is* my house and I'll stay with it. Brendan is right—no one is likely to come with the police vehicle outside.'

'But they can't stay here for ever,' Lauren said, hoping the words didn't sound like an anguished wail.

'I don't think they'll need to. The police want to catch these people—not just chase them further underground. They'll already have a plan, so don't worry.'

He kissed her gently on the lips, then less gently as desire rose between them and passion fired the kiss.

She drew away reluctantly, aware they had things to be doing that were definitely more important than a kiss.

'I'll go and talk to Madge while you see to the dog. He can go in the mud room at my place, and the cat into the laundry. Both have doors that will shut to keep them separated.'

Cam paused only to smile at her. 'You've got it all worked out, haven't you?' he teased.

She blushed and shook her head. 'Not nearly all!' she told him, well aware that her organising was a cover for the disturbance going on inside her—a disturbance she might never work out.

'Well, it's never dull…' That was Madge's reaction to the sudden move. 'I've got dinner going in the slow cooker, so I'll just bring it along. Cam can look after himself.'

Lauren helped Madge organise Maddie's things, making sure they had Gummie and her favourite pyjamas.

Cam met them as they came down the stairs, ready to drive them back to Lauren's place. 'Dog and pregnant cat are all packed in—now we'd better add the humans,' he said, and turned to Lauren. 'You *are* coming?' he said.

She nodded. 'There are rooms to be organised, beds to be made, and the animals to get settled.'

But I'll be back, she said to herself. She was still on duty at the sanctuary and had no intention of abandoning her post.

She climbed into Cam's four-wheel drive, next to Maddie in the back, and they set off.

Maddie was bouncing with excitement beside her. 'We're having a 'venture,' she cried to Lauren. 'Madge says there are cock—'

'Cockroaches?' Cam offered.

'Yes, them,' Maddie said. 'They're in our house and we have to sleep at your house until the spray men can get rid of them.'

'Very nasty germy things, cockroaches,' Lauren agreed, crossing her fingers surreptitiously and hoping that her guests wouldn't meet any at her house and want to move again.

It took twenty minutes to sort out bedrooms and bed-linen, bathrooms and towels. Then Maddie insisted on a quick tour of the house before finally settling herself on the floor in the laundry, talking to the cat.

'I've got to go back to see to the animals,' Lauren said quietly to Madge. 'Cam's there, and the two police officers, so I'll be quite safe. It might be a lot of fuss about nothing,' she added, 'but I feel a lot happier knowing you and Maddie are out of the house.'

'You just do what you have to do,' Madge said, patting her on the arm. 'Maddie and I will be quite fine.'

Lauren jogged back along the track as dusk was falling, arriving at Cam's house to find the police vehicle gone—although one policeman remained in the house with Cam, and Jake, another of the volunteers, was in the sanctuary.

'Helen wanted one of us here, just in case there's trouble,' he said. 'I've set up one of the sun loungers and I will probably just sleep.'

'I do hope so,' Lauren told him. 'Just remember you're here for the animals, and keep out of any trouble.'

She finished the job she'd been doing in the stock cupboard then prepared to leave—although leaving Jake there on his own didn't sit well with her.

'Go,' he said. 'I've got Cam and at least one policeman in the house, and they've set up security cameras all over the place so they can see what's happening out here. And there are back-up officers in the bush behind the place, so I'm quite safe.'

The thought of security cameras made her decision to slip out through the side gate of the sanctuary easy, but as she took off along the path Cam appeared beside her.

'I thought you'd come in and say goodnight,' he said.

'With cameras all over the place?'

He laughed. 'They're not spying on the people inside,' he told her, slinging an arm around her shoulders and drawing her close, so she could feel the warmth of his body flow into hers. 'Anyway, I've got to get back,' he said. 'I'm fixing them something to eat. I'll walk you to the end of the path through the bush, then head home.'

And the walk home was just that. Cam escorting her—coolly and efficiently—and striding along the bush track like a guard escorting a prisoner back to prison.

Not that she wanted chat, or even kisses—which just confused her more. But this was a Cam she hadn't seen before, with tension coiled within him.

'You won't do anything stupid, will you?' she said as her house came in sight.

'The police know what they're doing,' he reminded her.

But she remembered how angry he'd been about the

injuries to the dog, and knew that anger must still be burning somewhere inside him.

'We have to assume they do,' she said, and knew she sounded glum—even upset.

He smiled and bent to kiss her lips. 'I won't do anything stupid tonight,' he said, and she knew it was a promise.

But as she watched him go—striding at first, and then, when he reached the cover of the scrub, beginning to jog—she wondered if he was even capable of keeping out of trouble should it come his way...

She wanted to go back—to check on him, to stay with him in the house—but that would be stupid.

He was tired and he would want to get to bed, so he could be ready for work tomorrow, and she should do the same—after she'd settled her house guests.

Cam fed himself, and the policeman, then showed him over the place, pointing out the different exits and where doors led. After they'd cleared the kitchen table, they chose the formal dining room in the centre of the downstairs area as the best place for them to wait, as it showed no tell-tale lights to the outside.

He wasn't needed, so he left the policeman to it and returned to the kitchen, where he made sandwiches and a flask of coffee and took them through to the sanctuary. He'd met Jake earlier, and decided that the least he could do was share the man's lonely vigil.

'Food!' Jake said with delight. 'We can make tea and coffee here, but the coffee's always instant and yours smells real. And the biscuits here have all gone stale—I doubt we've tried eating them since the bushfire crisis months ago.'

'I thought I'd stay,' Cam said.

Jake smiled at him. 'I won't try to talk you out of it,' he said. 'It'll be great to have company and it means we can take shifts. I *can* make do without sleep, but I always feel it's better for my patients if I can sneak in a few hours some time during the night.'

'Doctor?'

'For my sins! I'm a paediatrician—I work up at the new children's hospital near Riverview.'

'Tough job?' Cam asked.

Jake smiled again. 'Sometimes it is, but at other times I can't think of anything more rewarding—and those are the times you have to remember, rather than dwelling on the bad ones.'

They chatted amiably for a while, eating the sandwiches and drinking the coffee. Cam opted for the first shift, and Jake settled on one of the sun loungers.

As the night wore on, with no visitors, Cam wondered if it was all for nothing—which should have made him relieved, not cranky about the whole thing.

He found another folded sun lounger and sat for a while.

Within minutes, it seemed, he was awoken by Lauren.

'Well, you two proved terrific night watchmen,' she said. 'I'd guess you had no visitors!'

Aware he must be looking sheepish, he turned to Jake, who seemed far too fresh for someone who'd slept on the uncomfortable lounger.

'Sorry, Lauren,' Jake said. 'It was probably my shift. I'll just have a quick wash and be off.'

Lauren smiled at him. 'Have a quick wash, certainly, but then come into the house. Madge tells me there's plenty of bacon and a dozen eggs in the fridge. I'll cook you both some breakfast and make coffee.'

'Will you be all right here, or do you want to use a

bathroom in the house?' Cam asked Jake, who shook his head and headed for the meagre washroom facilities behind the store room.

'You go right ahead,' he said. 'And please tell Lauren thanks, but I won't stay for breakfast. I want to see my wife and kids before I go to work.'

His words—*'I want to see my wife and kids'*—stayed with Cam as he headed inside, calling to Lauren in the kitchen before hurrying upstairs to shower and change.

He'd enjoyed being married, and had probably taken it for granted that his wife had as well. But these last two years or so, when he'd been on his own, he'd become aware that his life was incomplete in some way. Not that he'd ever given it much serious thought—he'd just got on with things. Yet what he felt now was envy, he supposed, for Jake, having a wife and kids waiting at home for him.

As he hurriedly showered and dressed the thoughts continued to chase through his head, bringing the realisation that it was Jake's emotion—his wanting to see his family—that he envied.

Because that wanting spoke of love.

'You look good for a man who spent the night on what must be the world's most uncomfortable bed,' Lauren said as Cam walked into the kitchen. 'I'm just going to slam your breakfast down on the table and hurry back— I start work in twenty minutes and I need to check my patient list.'

She set down his plate on the already set table. There was toast in the rack, the coffee pot tantalising his senses, but as she turned away he caught her hand and drew her back.

'Let's get married,' he said, pulling her down so he could kiss her lips.

She responded to the kiss, but quickly pulled away.

'*You,*' she said severely. 'For all you look okay, you're clearly suffering from a lack of proper sleep. And what is it with you and the marriage thing? A lot of men see it more as a life sentence rather than something to rush into—and yet, although you happen to already be married, you continue to suggest it to me.'

He thought for a minute, not wanting to admit that it had been Jake's words that had brought marriage back into focus in his mind.

'I liked being married,' he said. 'The being married part more so than the marriage itself, if I'm honest. To me it was always one of those things—you grow up, get married, get a job and a house, and that's how the future is mapped out. It was what I always wanted—to grow up and get married.'

'It might be a child's dream for the future,' Lauren said, although she *was* smiling as she said it, 'but so's being a princess or a superhero.'

He shrugged, because somehow he couldn't explain it better. Unless…

'Jake didn't wait for breakfast because he wanted to go home and see his wife and kids before he went to work,' he told her. 'It's that part of being married I want.'

'Or think you want,' Lauren said gently.

Cam had sounded so gloomy that Lauren was tempted to stay, but she'd already had two late starts and she didn't want to risk Janet's disapproval with another.

'I've patients to see. We'll talk later,' she said, and whisked out through the door before she weakened.

'At least you've *got* patients,' he muttered.

As she hurried home she thought about what he'd said—not the getting married part, for all that it gave her a secret longing every time he mentioned it, but about patients. Not hers, but his.

He needed to be busy and for some reason the veterinary practice *wasn't* busy.

Henry's practice had always been a busy one, and she'd assumed it would remain the same, but now she thought about it she'd seen fewer cars there lately, and she knew Cam had had fewer call-outs because he'd been around so much.

Damn.

The locum must have let it run down—or maybe been so impossible that people had simply stopped coming.

CHAPTER EIGHT

LAUREN WASN'T THE only one worrying about client numbers at the vets.

Cam finished his breakfast and walked back into his rooms to find a total stranger sitting behind his reception desk. Pretty in a *young* way—that was the only way he could describe the girl with dark curls and a bright smile.

'Hi, I'm Debbie, and I'm your new nurse—from the agency, you know? I know I wasn't supposed to start until Monday, but I wasn't doing anything today and Harry— he's my boyfriend—was coming over here on a job, so I came along to get a feel for the place.' She paused for a moment, before adding, 'That's okay, isn't it?'

He must have nodded, because she was off again.

'I've been looking through your appointment book and it's terrible, isn't it?'

He hoped it was tiredness that made him want to strangle her. It was not that someone so bright and chatty wouldn't be good for business. It was just that he couldn't handle bright and chatty this morning.

He headed straight into his surgery—hiding—but he was aware she was quite right. His appointment book did look terrible.

The return of Brendan, one of the policemen from

the day before, provided relief. 'You don't seem busy, so come and see what we've discovered,' he said.

After telling Debbie to call him if he was needed, Cam followed Brendan into the house.

'I'll just have a look around, so I'll know where things are,' Debbie said, as if she needed to justify her position.

'The man did return—with mates,' Brendan told him, leading him to one of the laptops open on the dining room table.

'So much for the two guardians of the sanctuary,' Cam muttered.

Brendan laughed. 'They came quietly this time, and they had obviously heard about the kennels because they searched there first. We had men ready to go if they approached the sanctuary, but they didn't go near it or the house—no doubt assuming we'd left men inside, even though our vehicle was gone.'

'So they got away?' Cam said, anger stirring again at the treatment of the dog.

'Not cleanly,' Brendan assured him. 'We had a drone follow them to what we're assuming is their headquarters and a possible dog-fight site near an abandoned farm out towards the mountains. As soon as we get a chance we'll send someone in to check the place out. And we're using drones to keep an eye on things there in the meantime.'

'Sounds great,' Cam agreed. He was still anxious to see the men involved caught and punished, but when he thought about it he was also pleased to have professionals in charge.

And now that he had Debbie, who would alert him should a patient arrive, he could stay on with the policemen, checking the screens that showed the different shots the drones had taken as they followed the route towards the mountains.

But the men were packing up now, telling him they'd keep in touch, and he tossed up whether to go back into his rooms and face Debbie, or make himself coffee and a sandwich and have a think about patient numbers.

The coffee won.

'Anyone home?'

Madge and Maddie had gone into the village, so Lauren had finished her shift and come across to Cam's to find out what was happening, but the place seemed deserted.

She'd tried the surgery rooms first, and seen a note from someone named Debbie saying she'd gone to lunch, and the sanctuary had yielded only Helen, so now she stood in the big entry, calling out for Cam.

'Kitchen!' Cam answered, and she headed there to find him sitting at the kitchen table, a pen in his hand and a writing pad on the table in front of him.

'I've been thinking about your lack of patients,' she said, 'and I've had some ideas.'

He looked up at her and grinned. 'Me too, but I'll need help to know what will work.'

'I was thinking the local paper first,' Lauren said. 'The *Lake News*—Madge might have brought home a copy. It's printed right here in the village, but it goes around the lake. You could do an "Ask the Vet" column once a week.'

Cam's grin made her heart flip just a little, and his fingers tangled with hers as he passed her his list.

'Third idea down,' he said. 'Now, come and sit beside me and we'll go through them. You want coffee?'

'Yes, please—and a sandwich if you can manage one. I came straight from work and I really want to hear what's happening with the police.'

'You go through the list while I fix you something,

then we can talk.' There was a slight pause before he tease, 'If that's what you *really* want to do?'

She frowned at him. 'Yes, it is. This is serious! I want to know about the dog-fights...but, far more important, you can't just let Henry's business die—'

She stopped, looking at him, searching his face, wondering...

'Unless that's what you want?' she whispered, with thoughts of him selling the house and fleeing back to England to domestic pets and no possibility of a snake in his house swirling through her mind.

He crossed to the table and put an arm around her shoulders, giving her a gentle hug. 'Don't be silly,' he said. 'Take a look at my list and then tell me if I'm thinking of abandoning Henry's gift to me.'

The arm around her shoulders was reassuring—as was the list, now she looked at it. But the gut-wrenching, heart-stopping pain she'd felt when—just for a moment— she'd imagined him gone, told her how completely she was entangled with him now...how deep her emotions ran and how very important he'd become to her.

And yet she knew she was all wrong for him.

She concentrated on his list and actually smiled, because every single thing she'd thought of was there.

'Henry had a weekly talk on local radio,' she said to Cam, who'd returned to his coffee and sandwich-making. 'Just ten minutes, and he covered things like the best way to treat midge bites as well as animal health.'

Cam put coffee and a plate of sandwiches in front of her, then pulled out a chair so they sat together, thighs touching, the heat of his body transferring to hers.

'And how *do* you treat a midge bite?'

Lauren grinned at him. 'I'm not sure I remember Henry's advice because they never worry me. I think I've grown immune to them. But when in doubt use vinegar, my father always said. For bluebottle stings in the sea in summer, midge and sand fly bites—vinegar or bi-carb soda: his panaceas for most painful bites and stings.'

'Apart from funnel web spiders?'

Lauren had to laugh. 'Definitely not spiders of any kind! Spider bites you need to treat like a snake bite. You should keep four or five elasticised bandages somewhere handy, then you can bandage over the bite, down to the extremity of the arm or leg then back up again, phoning an ambulance as you do it.'

'Really?' Cam asked.

She nodded, because even a sensible conversation about health matters hadn't quelled the disturbances caused by Cam's proximity, and she was reasonably sure there'd be a tremor in her voice if she tried to speak.

She moved her chair, just a little, and pulled the notepad towards her, and together they went through their ideas to give his animal patient numbers a boost.

'I really should be going,' she said suddenly.

'You've only just arrived,' he said, taking her hand in his, folding her fingers so it fitted inside his palm.

It was hand-holding, nothing more—yet for some reason it was so erotic she squirmed in her seat.

She removed her hand from his clasp and shifted her chair a little further away.

'We're going to drink coffee, eat our lunch and talk about your list,' she said firmly.

'Even though we're all alone in this great big house?' he murmured, and the rasp of his voice scratched at her skin.

'I'm back!'

The call came just in time, and while Cam went to welcome his new employee properly Lauren hastily ate a sandwich and drained her coffee, then departed, yelling goodbye through the surgery door.

Madge and Maddie would be back from the village and wanting to get in, she told herself as she hurried away.

But she knew she was hurrying *from*—not hurrying *to*.

She forced herself to slow down, finding an even pace that would allow her to think.

But how to think about Cam?

About the way he made her feel?

About the physical reactions he could cause in her body with nothing more than a glance?

And why him?

She *had* met other men over the years since David, but none had turned both her mind and her body into such a state of turmoil.

She paused, forcing herself to think, telling herself she was a mature middle-aged woman and she should be able to rationalise this...whatever it was...

But standing still didn't help—and it didn't stop her hearing Cam's teasing voice in her ears, or feeling his touch on her skin...

'You've been called out to the alpaca farm.'

Cam was startled by the voice as he made his way back into the surgery. Once again, he'd forgotten he had a new nurse. He really would have to sit down and have a talk with her—find out about her qualifications, things like that—but for now just having someone to answer the phone was a bonus.

'Thank you,' he said. 'I hope it won't take long and we can have a chat when I get back. In the meantime...'

He pulled his list out of his pocket and found Lauren

had put ticks against some of his ideas—two or three ticks in some cases.

'Do you think putting leaflets into letterboxes around the lake, telling people I'm here, is a good idea?' he asked Debbie.

'An excellent one,' she said. 'I was doodling something on the computer that might do.'

She swung the screen to show a page with cats, dogs, birds and, yes, alpacas, depicted around the edge, with his name, address and phone number clearly printed in the middle. Then he noticed the heading:

Under new management!
Henry's nephew has arrived!

'That looks great,' he said, 'but is it okay to put the bit about Henry?'

She smiled at him. 'Everyone loved Henry,' she said, as if that automatically meant they'd all love Cam too.

But he knew full well he'd have to prove himself— and it appeared he'd have a lot to live up to.

Debbie was speaking again. 'You'd better get out to the alpacas—something about pregnancy testing? That Celia out there does run on and on.'

Pots and kettles, Cam thought, leaving Debbie to her work and getting the portable ultrasound out of the equipment cupboard.

Debbie was printing off the leaflets when he came back through the reception area.

'I'll stay on and answer the phone and print out more leaflets—do some larger ones for shop windows,' she said. 'Your mother phoned to say she'll be back soon, so I won't leave to put up the posters until after she comes. Is that okay?'

Still befuddled by the force that was Debbie, Cam nodded, locked the treatment room door, and departed.

Lauren, taking advantage of finishing early, had decided to walk Maddie and Madge back to their home. The dog and the cat would stay at her place, and she'd bring their gear over later.

'There's Daddy going out!' cried Maddie, who was running on ahead, and they saw the four-wheel drive reversing out of the garage.

'Stop where you are,' Madge called to Maddie, who obeyed immediately, although she was bouncing up and down with excitement at seeing her father.

Cam stopped and climbed out, swinging his daughter into the air and settling her on his hip, giving Lauren a twinge of something she couldn't understand. Not jealousy, certainly, but perhaps a kind of envy at the picture they made.

The *family* they made.

'Are you done for the morning?' Cam asked.

Lauren nodded. 'We have a very healthy population around here.'

'Same with animals,' he said. 'But if you're free, I could do with a hand.'

'Can I come too, Daddy?' Maddie asked.

Cam shook his head. 'Not today, sweetie—but go on in and say hello to my new vet nurse, Debbie.'

Maddie skipped away to catch up with Madge.

'Debbie?' Lauren asked as she climbed in the car, her pleasure at seeing Cam only slightly marred by the warnings of that stupid voice in her head—that useless mantra...

'Believe me, you can't possibly be as surprised as I was when she turned up and—'

'And started talking—if she's Debbie Bradley from further up the lake?'

'That's the one,' Cam said.

Lauren laughed. 'She's actually very good, and people trust her. I'm sure she'll give the practice the boost it needs.'

'It's almost as if she's read my list...'

He turned to look at Lauren, sharing his rueful despair, and she saw the gleam of amusement in his blue eyes and felt her heart contract.

She loved him.

It wasn't so much a question as a certainty that had suddenly struck right at her heart.

Just like that, out of nowhere, the realisation had come—and she had no idea what to do with it or about it.

She was too old for him—she knew that...knew he needed a younger woman. Someone who'd get him involved in the social life of the area—such as it was—who would have parties and go to music festivals...all the things young people in their twenties did.

She also knew she couldn't condemn him to what might lie ahead.

The shadow of her father's illness sat like a black cloud above her head whenever Cam's silly idea of marriage was mentioned. Dementia wasn't necessarily a genetic disease, but it did have genetic links in some families. Her father had often spoken of his 'mad grandmother', who, Lauren suspected, had probably had it too.

And, knowing the soul-destroying task that caring for a loved one with dementia could be, how could she risk handing that on to Cam—ten years younger than she was, who would probably still be a very active man at fifty-five if she, like her father, had her first symptoms at sixty-five?

'Anything that can help build the practice,' she said, realising it was her turn to speak in their conversation, and thankfully remembering where it had stopped.

But her mind wasn't on it. It was far too busy coping with what was in her heart.

Damn it all—why couldn't life be easy?

Hadn't she been happy enough before this man had erupted into her life?

Satisfied with her lot?

Enjoying her life?

She was happy to have an affair with him—delighted, in fact—but marriage…?

'So I think Celia will run them through the chute she has out there, and isolate one animal at a time, so all we'll have to do is the ultrasound. I'm reasonably sure she can read the screen as well as I can, but having you there to hold it will be a blessing.'

And Lauren was a blessing in other ways, Cam thought, remembering Jake's eagerness to see his wife and kids, and feeling aware of how good it was simply to have her by his side.

And a lot later in that day he'd be aware that he'd never have managed without her…

As they drove up—not towards the house, but to the paddock near the chute, where they could see Celia waiting—the woman suddenly fell to the grass.

Cam pulled up as close as he safely could, and he and Lauren both shot out and raced towards the fallen woman.

'Celia? Celia, can you hear me?' Lauren shouted as she ran, then she dropped to her knees and gave the woman a little shake, feeling at the same time for a pulse beneath her neck.

Cam reached Celia's side just as Lauren checked her mouth, then gave her two full breaths of air.

'Ring triple zero,' she said to Cam as she began compressions, counting aloud as she went.

He made the call, then dropped to his knees. 'I'll take over here—you do the breaths,' he said.

Lauren reached thirty and sank back, again feeling for a pulse.

'Nothing?' Cam asked, and Lauren shook her head.

'There might be,' she said, 'but if there is it's very weak. Often it's hard to tell, so we'll just keep going.'

He had kept the compressions going, and again Lauren breathed air into Celia's unconscious body. But this time, as Cam continued compressions, she ran her hands over Celia's head, feeling for any contusions.

There were no trees with branches she could have hit—in fact there was nothing at all anywhere near her that could have knocked her out.

'I'll do these breaths, then we'll swap,' she said to Cam, aware how tiring compressions could be, even on practice dummies.

'I'm fine.'

It was the response she'd expected. 'Yes, for now you are. But if we have to wait thirty minutes for an ambulance, you won't be.'

The look of disbelief he gave her was priceless, but he didn't argue when she took over once he'd reached thirty. Lauren counted while she watched him administer air, then looked around in frustration. She imagined the city streets where he'd lived regularly rang with the sirens of approaching fire engines or ambulances.

'It won't be too much longer,' she said, and as if conjured up by her voice an ambulance appeared, the big four-wheel drive vehicle coming smoothly across the paddock towards them.

Cam explained that they'd actually seen Celia fall and phoned immediately, while the paramedic fitted an oxygen mask to Celia's mouth and nose, then attached a valve bag to it to deliver continuous positive pressure air.

'Can you hold your thumbs to the mask either side of her mouth to seal it?' the paramedic asked Cam.

Lauren got out of the way as the second paramedic knelt by Celia's side with a resuscitator, fixing pads to her skin, checking lines and preparing to shock her heart.

The 'Clear!' signal rang out and they all moved slightly back.

The paramedic closest to Cam felt for a pulse once she'd been shocked. He shook his head, then held up a hand. 'Maybe...' he said. 'It's faint and thready, but it's there, I'm sure.'

They shocked her heart a second time, with a steadier result.

'Okay, we'll take it from here,' one of the paramedics said, and in what seemed like a remarkably short time they had her loaded into the ambulance and were driving away.

'Poor Celia,' Cam said.

'Poor you,' Lauren replied with a grin.

'Me? What? Why me?'

Lauren's smile broadened. 'Well, as well as having to preg-test the alpacas without her help, you're now going to have to work out how to look after them while Celia's off in hospital.'

'Me?'

'You're the vet,' she reminded him. 'Now, let's get on with what we came to do, and later we'll think about the animals.'

* * *

Cam, still shaken by seeing Celia so stricken, decided that was a very good suggestion—although it was slowly dawning on him that he couldn't just abandon the animals. There was plenty of grass in the paddock, but they would need some supplementary feeding, water, and definite overseeing.

Should he forget the pregnancy testing and just seek out someone to keep an eye on them? Then visit Celia in hospital and tell her he'd not done the job?

He didn't think so.

'Okay, let's go,' he said, retrieving his gear from the car, passing the laptop to Lauren and grabbing the bag with the ultrasound machine, thrusting away the thought that perhaps they could have used it on Celia, to see if her heart had been beating.

Stupid! It would have wasted precious time.

Alpacas—that was where his head had to be.

The animals had already been herded into a small paddock close to the chute, but the beasts weren't the silly, friendly creatures they'd appeared to be on first acquaintance. They circled towards the chute and then ducked off at the last minute, with Lauren herding them, while he stood ready to push the sliding gate across to secure them one at a time for the test.

'They must be friends,' Lauren said—totally unhelpfully—as two of the alpacas tried to cram into the chute together. 'Where one goes, the other goes.'

She was trying to use a garden rake she'd picked up to hold one of them back, but didn't have a hope.

Cam tried pushing the other one backwards, but got nowhere.

'Can you possibly do them both while they're crammed in like that?' Lauren asked. 'Maybe you do the one on your side, then we'll swap gear and I'll do the one on this side.'

Cam shook his head at just how much his professional life had changed, but as they successfully tested both animals with just a little extra effort—clambering up onto the lowest rung of the chute to swap implements—he found himself enjoying it all.

'Did you put the ear tag number of the one you tested onto the computer?' Lauren asked.

He looked blankly at her. 'Damn and blast!' he said. 'I didn't give it a thought—didn't even think about recording things at all…just the actual testing. But of course it has to be recorded.'

'No worries. We've got all the numbers, and if those two stay together we'll find her later.'

'It *might* be possible,' Cam answered through gritted teeth, as the next so-called pet bit his shoulder.

Somehow they got through all the animals, finding only three not pregnant. They also discovered that Celia had adjusted the gates so the animals left the chute and went into a fresh, grassy paddock with a feeding trough along one side. All the animals had headed towards it, which made it easier for them to find the pair that had refused to be separated.

Their ear tags, when checked, were forty-one and forty-two, suggesting they might be twins.

Finally, the paperwork was complete.

'And now all we have to do is find someone to keep an eye on them,' Cam said.

But Lauren was already heading for the house.

'Celia has a married daughter who lives in the area,' she said as he caught up with her. 'We'll find a phone number somewhere. And we'll have to lock up the house. We don't get much theft around here, but there are always opportunistic people who might hear she's been hospitalised and come for a look around.'

She was right, he realised, and relief that she'd agreed to come with him flooded through him. As things had turned out, he certainly couldn't have managed without her. But her presence, he thought as he followed her towards the house, was unsettling him rather than bringing the usual joy.

It was Jake's fault, of course—though he wasn't to know that a casual remark about wanting to see his wife and kids would ruin Cam's day.

Ruin his day?

What on earth was he thinking?

'Self-pity never gets you anywhere,' he could hear his mother's voice telling him.

But, hell...

He was a grown man with a daughter—what he was feeling surely couldn't be self-pity.

It was nothing more than irritation with the bloody alpacas, for whom he had yet to develop any fondness.

Shaking off his wayward thoughts, because there was work still to be done, he followed Lauren into the house, catching her in the kitchen and giving her a hug.

She turned to face him, a *What was that for?* question in her eyes, but somehow their lips met and the hug became a kiss.

And, given the way he'd been feeling all morning, it was only with the strongest of will power that he refrained from mentioning the marriage thing again.

Refrained from just asking on the off-chance...

Because he couldn't get it out of his head...

'Enough!' Lauren said, breaking away and pointing him towards the list held by a magnet to the door of the refrig-

erator. 'Ellen—that's her daughter,' she said, her finger
on a name. 'I'll phone her, because she knows me, and
she'll be able to tell us who to call to keep an eye on the
animals. Would you mind going through the house and
closing the windows, locking the outside doors, and—'

'Checking there are no appliances left on?' he finished for her.

She grinned at him. 'Okay, I know you know as well
as I do how to check things out. It's just me being—'

'Bossy?'

'Go!' she ordered. 'I've got a difficult call to make.'

It took another half-hour to make sure the family knew
what had happened, to check on Celia's status at the
hospital—she was in Intensive Care—and to organise
a neighbour to take care of the alpacas.

They were fairly quiet on the drive back. Lauren was
still testing the revelation that had struck her earlier about
her feelings for this man. She found herself sneaking
quick glances at him, as if seeing him in profile, or talking, or frowning over something, might help her work out
why she was feeling as she did—why she'd been stupid
enough to actually fall in love with him.

He was just a man, after all.

A nice man—well, mostly. He was crabby when he
was in pain, but who wasn't?

And it wasn't as if she hadn't met other nice men over
the years—even gone out with several of them while
Henry sat with her father. But the truly weird, heart-
clenching realisation of love had never featured in any
of those brief relationships.

Maybe it wasn't love she felt for Cam. Maybe it was
just some kind of heart arrhythmia and he'd just happened to be there when it happened...

Several times.

Almost constantly, actually.

She sighed, even though she'd thought she'd given up sighing.

'You okay?' he asked.

She nodded. Then, because his eyes were on the road, she added, 'Fine.'

Time to take control, she decided. *Forget this heart-love business!*

'Have you heard anything from Brendan?' she asked, but he shook his head.

'He doubted anything would happen before the weekend, and he's got the place he thinks is their headquarters covered by drones.'

Back at the surgery, they found a note from Debbie explaining that she and a friend were dropping notices in letterboxes and there'd been no phone calls.

But the note didn't finish there.

We've taken Maddie with us, so we won't go far.
    Madge said it would be okay, but here's my mobile number if you want to check.

Debbie had then listed her number, and her boyfriend Harry's number for any emergency, and signed off with a flourish, a little heart dotting the 'i' in her name.

'Even in a note she talks a lot,' Cam said gloomily.

Lauren laughed at him. 'Go on with you,' she said. 'Debbie is just what you need to brighten this place up.' She looked around and added, 'Well, a coat of paint wouldn't go amiss either!'

But their conversation, although relieving Lauren's fears about the dog-fighting man returning, had done little to dispel the aftershocks of the discovery she'd had made on the drive to the alpaca farm. The certainty of this love thing had left her mind and her body churning helplessly.

It could go nowhere—she knew that—even if the wretched man mentioned marriage at least once a day.

It just felt wrong. And the age difference, her fear of potentially facing dementia herself one day, and the suddenness made it all the more overwhelming.

CHAPTER NINE

SHE'D BARELY OPENED her afternoon session when Cam arrived, with a drowsy, unresponsive Maddie in his arms.

'Call an ambulance,' she said to Janet, as soon as she saw the child.

She ushered Cam inside her office.

'What happened?' she asked as she checked Maddie's temperature—thirty-nine degrees—something the flushed face and body had already suggested.

'She went to her bedroom to have a rest and then we couldn't wake her,' Cam said, his voice coarse with panic and concern.

She injected paracetamol into the child's limp arm and brought damp cloths to bathe the burning skin.

Meningococcal had been Lauren's first thought, and shame that she'd let events at the sanctuary take precedence over talking to Cam about the vaccination gnawed at her stomach. But as she checked Maddie's body she saw there were no tell-tale signs of the disease. She was flushed all over, but with no darker spots or splotches.

'She'll be safe in the ambulance and you can travel with her,' she said to Cam, hoping her voice would be enough to calm him down a little. 'I'll come up later, bring Madge and clothes. There's a new children's hospital just south of Riverview—it's about three-quarters of an hour's drive. There's accommodation attached to it where you and Madge can stay. I'll arrange all that when I get there.'

She wasn't sure he'd heard any of it. His whole being was focussed on willing his child to keep breathing.

The ambulance arrived, and with the paramedics' usual seamless efficiency sped away within minutes.

Lauren saw them off, then phoned Madge.

Of course Madge wanted to go, so Lauren explained that she'd collect her at six and reminded her to pack a few things for Cam, as well as for herself and Maddie.

'And some story books and a toy or two,' she added, then hung up to get back to her patients.

By the time Lauren and Madge arrived at the hospital that evening Maddie had been admitted to the ICU.

Cam kissed them both, but looked so utterly weary that Lauren handed him a bag of clothes and toiletries and sent him across to the accommodation block to have a shower and a rest.

'You're booked in there. Madge and I will both stay with Maddie while you take a break,' Lauren told him.

'Jake's here—from the sanctuary. He said he'd look after her. He did a lumbar puncture,' Cam said, in a helpless voice that made her want to hug him. 'But I don't think the results are back yet. He's thinking meningitis.'

'They'll all look after her—and we'll be with her. You go and rest.'

He kissed her again, and left reluctantly.

'Isn't that what we were talking about when I brought her in to see you?' Madge asked.

Lauren shook her head. 'Meningococcal is slightly different,' she told her. 'If this is a viral infection, rather than a bacterial one, I doubt a vaccination would have made a difference. A viral infection is most likely to have come from a virus Maddie's picked up somewhere. It could have been something as small as someone sneezing in a shop.'

'We were in town the other day and every second person seemed to have a cold,' Madge said. 'And she's been playing in that old shed a lot lately.'

Lauren shook her head. She knew you could eat off the floor of Henry's shed. Even as he'd grown older, his longtime cleaning woman would come and clean it weekly.

'She *has* been a bit sniffly lately,' Madge said, the vague tone suggesting that she was running back through Maddie's life over the last few weeks.

'Stop fretting about it,' Lauren said firmly. 'Whatever has happened has happened, and now Maddie needs us. Which is her favourite book? I'll read it to her.'

To Lauren's surprise, Madge handed her a very old copy of *Winnie the Pooh*, which Lauren recognised as one that had belonged to Henry as a child. She'd borrowed it to read herself, many times.

She smoothed her hand over the rather tired blue cover, then opened it and began to read.

Maddie's condition barely changed over the next two days—the little girl remained either asleep or too drowsy to do anything other than smile weakly at whoever had appeared at her bedside.

So when Lauren came to relieve Cam at midnight three days later, sitting next to him and holding his hand, she broached a subject she wasn't at all sure he'd want mentioned.

'Do you think her mother should be told?' she asked. 'You said she was in Australia at the moment.'

He frowned at her, shook his head, then nodded.

'I have let her know,' he said. 'I phoned her the night Maddie was admitted. She *is* in Australia—up north somewhere in the rainforest. She sends a card to Maddie from time to time. Usually with a lizard on it—Aboriginal paintings of lizards. Snakes too.'

'And...?' Lauren prompted.

Cam shook his head as if trying to focus. 'I think she said she'd come, but that she had things to arrange. She has my number, so I suppose she'll let me know.'

It all seemed very vague and totally unsatisfactory to Lauren, but she knew it was none of her business, and she didn't want to push Cam in the state he was already in.

But Maddie's mother—Kate—*did* arrive. On Sunday afternoon she swept into the hospital in a blaze, scattering 'darlings' at all the staff, crying by her daughter's bedside, then pronouncing herself utterly spent and asking to be shown to her room.

She took the room Lauren had been using. Lauren had packed and left that morning, explaining to Madge that she'd be more use back at the lake, organising Cam's practice and getting back to her own work.

Kate was still Cam's wife and the mother of Maddie. A *good* mother, she remembered Cam saying. Lauren knew she was best off out of the way.

But if Lauren's departure from the scene was low key, Kate's arrival had been anything but. The local newspaper, always eager for a bit of glamour to lift its otherwise provincial status, had caught a shot of her arrival at the airport. And the front page that greeted Lauren when she picked up the paper from her doorstep on Monday morning was highlighted by a photograph of a beautiful, petite blonde woman, a filmy handkerchief clutched in one hand.

Above it, in what seemed to Lauren to be an unnecessarily large font, were the words *UK Actress Arrives to Sit by Ill Daughter!*

Actress?

How come that had never been mentioned? she thought.

Or maybe it had...

A beautiful blonde actress...

It was even worse than Lauren had thought.

They'd married while at university, Madge had said—in rather disapproving tones. But maybe only Cam had been at university—unless Kate had been doing a drama degree of some kind?

And Cam had enjoyed being married.

That he *had* told Lauren.

Cam had phoned Maddie's mother, assuming she'd be too busy, or too involved with whatever she was involved in, to want to come.

So her, 'I'll be there as soon as I can,' had come as something of a surprise.

Until he picked up a paper in one of the hospital waiting rooms and saw the photo and the headline. As far as he knew, journalists didn't stalk the small, regional airport in anticipation of celebrities arriving—and even if they did, they'd have seen a pretty woman but would not have had any idea of her name.

Unless she'd organised the reception committee herself. Which meant, he decided, after tossing around several alternatives, that she was probably looking for work in Australia and needed a bit of free publicity.

The thought made his heart sink.

Madge had lived with them since Maddie's birth—Kate having assured him that children who grew up in multi-generation households were more stable—and even though she'd only come to help out with the new baby, she had soon become the main caregiver—and indispensable in that role, given that Kate was rarely home.

It had been Madge that Maddie had always turned to—either in excitement or concern—and Kate's departure had barely caused a blip in Maddie's existence.

But maybe he was wrong to be cynical about Kate's arrival now. She might have found some deeply buried maternal instinct and need to be with her child.

He wasn't entirely taken in by the tears she'd shed at Maddie's bedside. And yet she had sat there for nearly an hour, reading a book she'd brought about animals in the rainforest and generally becoming the centre of attention in the ward—far more than the usual number of doctors and nurses had just 'popped in' to see how Maddie was doing.

'Like hell!' Cam muttered through gritted teeth, as he thought of Kate playing the doting mother to his sleeping child.

Where was Lauren when he needed her? He needed her common-sense and calm, supportive comfort. Needed her presence by his side and, yes, her body in his bed, so he could lose his fear and dread, even for a brief time, as he lost himself inside her.

Had he conjured her up? Because she appeared early that evening, offering to sit with Maddie so he could spend some time with his wife.

She was as lovely as ever, and her smile warmed his blood, but Kate was dragging him away, informing him that he should take her somewhere special for dinner as she'd come all this way to see them both.

And when Lauren raised her eyebrows in a quizzical manner at this statement, he hoped Kate didn't notice...

* * *

She *was* gorgeous, Cam's wife, Lauren conceded to herself as the pair departed. Big blue eyes, a neat nose and full red lips—all set in pale, creamy skin, the lot framed by short, almost white-blonde pixie-cut hair.

It would be good for Maddie if they got back together—wouldn't it?

Two parents were better than one, weren't they?

She really didn't know. She'd grown up with just a father and she was okay.

Wasn't she?

Forget it.

She set aside a book about animals in a jungle—or was it a rainforest?—which looked far too complex for a four-year-old, and returned to reading about Pooh and his friends, getting a slight response when Maddie opened her eyes and said, 'Lauren…?'

'I'm here, sweetheart,' Lauren told her, gently squeezing the fingers of one small hand. 'And I'll stay right here with you until Daddy gets back, okay?'

'And Puss?'

The words were slurred, but Lauren knew what she was asking. 'No kittens yet, but it can't be long. I'll tell you as soon as something happens.'

As Maddie sighed, then slipped back into a deep sleep, Lauren wiped silly tears from her face and began to read again. She'd brought along her own copy of *The House at Pooh Corner* for after she'd finished this one, and was actually loving reading about Pooh's life again…

She was singing nursery songs from her childhood, very softly, when Cam returned—without his beautiful wife—close to eleven that evening.

'Are you going to drive back home when you leave here?' he demanded.

She smiled, and took his hand, pulled him down into the chair beside her. 'Sit, relax,' she ordered, then put her arm around his shoulders and drew him closer in an awkward hug.

As she released him, she took both his hands in hers, and looked deep into his haunted eyes.

'She's going to be okay,' she said firmly. 'She roused earlier and spoke to me—knew me—and she asked about the cat. It's a great sign, Cam. She just needs time and plenty of rest.'

And because his smile was so pathetic, and she sensed that he, too, was fighting tears, she kept talking.

'Anyway, I wanted to tell you about what's happening back in the other world. That Debbie certainly is a whirlwind. She got on to a vet she used to work for— he's retired now, and lives on the lake—and she has him coming in to cover for you. And she's put leaflets in letterboxes and posters in shop windows, and she says if she stays as busy as she is now you'll need a receptionist as well as her on your staff.'

Cam shook his head. 'I hardly know the girl—woman, I suppose—and she's doing all this for me.'

Lauren laughed. 'People are basically good, you know. By now everyone will have heard that Maddie's sick, and one thing the Lakes community does well is rally around. There are probably enough casseroles in your freezer to keep you all fed for a month!'

He smiled, and Lauren knew he'd finally relaxed.

'Go and get some sleep. I'm happy to stay tonight and doze here—it's an ability doctors have, to be able to sleep anywhere at any time. I'll go home in time for work in the morning and I can sleep in my afternoon break.'

He shook his head. 'I can't have you doing that,' he said.

She smiled at him. 'I know—but I also know that if you don't get a proper night's sleep you'll be no good to anyone tomorrow, and by tomorrow Maddie might be well enough to talk to you, or at least smile.' She paused, and when he said nothing, she added, 'Go!' in her most authoritative voice and pointed to the door.

He leant across the space between them and kissed her on the lips. Then he stood up, kissed Maddie on the forehead, and left the room.

He did sleep, deeply and dreamlessly, waking with a start at four in the morning.

Refreshed, he showered and shaved, then dressed in his last set of clean clothes—he'd have to find a laundromat somewhere or make a trip home today. He made himself a coffee, and ate a day-old sandwich out of the refrigerator, then headed across to the hospital.

He stopped at the ICU desk, to hear the latest on his daughter's progress, and was told she'd actually asked for water during the night and let Lauren give it to her from a glass. So his step was lighter as he made his way to Maddie's room—and probably lightened more by the thought of seeing Lauren.

He found her where he'd left her, sitting in the same chair, reading quietly to his sleeping daughter.

He looked at the pair of them and knew that this was what he really wanted in his life—these two, dear, precious people.

'Did you sleep?' the one who was awake asked him, and he nodded, his throat so tight with emotion he couldn't express it in words.

Instead, he crossed the room and kissed her, then drew

her to her feet and held her, snug in his arms, while he looked at Maddie and smiled.

'I've got to go,' the precious woman in his arms was saying, edging away from him. 'Did the nurse tell you she woke again and drank some water from a glass?'

She was far enough away from him now to look into his face.

'That is really good news, Cam,' she added. '*Really* good!'

CHAPTER TEN

THREE DAYS LATER, Maddie was well enough to be transferred to a room on the children's ward. She was kept isolated as her specialists wanted to ensure she stayed quiet, and she remained in bed for most of the day, still sleeping a lot.

A CT scan had revealed that the swelling in her brain had reduced to near normal, but the damaged area needed time—probably weeks—to heal completely.

'We should be able to take her home in a couple of days,' Cam told Lauren, when she arrived to do a late-afternoon shift with the little girl.

'That's great,' Lauren said, wondering just who 'we' was. She hadn't seen Cam since the night she'd stayed with Maddie, and had no idea whether or not the actress was still around.

But the kiss Cam gave her before he left told her she shouldn't be worried. Which she wasn't, really—because he *was* too young for her, and he *would* surely be better off getting back with his wife.

And if that thought made her heart hurt—well, that was just bad luck.

Madge came at midnight and insisted on staying the night.

'I've been sleeping better in that comfortable recliner

than in the hotel bed,' she said. 'I'd have been in earlier, but Cam and I went out to dinner—he wanted to talk about Kate. Why he didn't divorce her when she first left him, I'll never know. Now she's found out about the wildlife sanctuary and wants to come back to him.'

Madge paused, and Lauren held her breath.

'Apparently, saving the planet is her new thing, and she can see herself as the actress who gave it all up to save Australia's native animals. Cam's told her the sanctuary has nothing to do with him, it's just on his land, but it seems that's good enough for her.'

Madge looked at Lauren in a helpless way.

'Some people make a mess of their lives, don't they?' she said, so plaintively that Lauren had to give her a hug.

'It'll all work out,' she said. 'And won't Maddie like having her mother around?'

'Hmph!' said Madge. 'As if that woman's ever been a mother—not in the real sense of the word. She got pregnant so she could marry Cam, and as soon as Maddie arrived she virtually handed her over to me to raise—well, me and Cam. She'd found religion at that stage and was working with church youth groups, putting on strange so-called religious plays. "Street theatre", they called it. Load of old rubbish! Cam was working in a bar at night and trying to get to lectures and study by day, as well as help me with Maddie. The house was full of placards that said *All for God*—which I didn't disagree with at all. But I did think God would probably have preferred her to be a mother—for a little while at least.'

Lauren had to smile. She could imagine how much work a new baby could be, and she wondered just what Madge had had to give up to help Cam raise his daughter.

'What had you been doing before?' she asked.

Madge smiled. 'Running a very successful legal aid

business. Most of my clients were single mothers…many trying to get away from abusive husbands.' She looked ruefully at Lauren, then added, 'For a while I thought I could do it all—mind Maddie and work from home, all that stuff—but the reality was very different, and I soon knew I wasn't doing either job particularly well.'

'Oh, Madge, what a loss for you—a career like that!'

Madge smiled again. 'Not such a loss when the reward was a beautiful granddaughter who needed me and a son who needed back-up so he could get his life back together again.'

They sat in silence for a while.

Then Madge said, 'Get off home with you and get some sleep. You have to look after yourself as well as all of us, you know.'

Lauren grinned at her. 'My presence is purely selfish—it's years since I read the Pooh books.'

'Out!' Madge said, but she smiled.

Although something in that smile told Lauren she was worried, and now that Maddie was getting better, there was only Cam left for Madge to worry about. Was she concerned that Kate, if she came back into their lives, would hurt him again?

The thought brought silly tears to Lauren's eyes and an aching tightness to her throat. Knowing he was too young for her didn't stop her loving him, and she couldn't bear the thought of him being hurt.

It was a couple of days before Lauren was free to get up to the hospital to see Maddie again, because the cat had had kittens and the dog had turned cat-protector, not allowing anyone near them—which meant that when her long-suffering cleaner needed to clean the back of the house Lauren had to take Henry for a long walk.

As he knew she was the source of food for himself *and* the cat, Henry had allowed her close enough to check each tiny animal, and today, with the kittens' eyes now open, and their adventures taking them further from their mother, she couldn't resist picking up the little pure black male and tucking him inside her jacket while she and Henry walked.

When she took the kitten back, it was accepted by the others as if it had never been away. Which was why, when the day came for her to go to the hospital—possibly for the last time, she once again kidnapped—or cat-napped—the little black one and took it with her.

Cam was there, and her heart flipped at the sight of him, but the smile he offered her in greeting was wan, and something about the way he stood by the bed told her to stay clear.

Kate?

Was he back with her?

It's for the best, her head muttered at her, but her heart would have none of it. All she wanted to do was hold him—try to ease away the strain she could see in every sinew of his body.

Her body tensed…until she realised she might squash the kitten! And that thought turned her attention to Maddie, who was overjoyed as the tiny creature tumbled over her in the hospital bed, and snuggled up in her small hands.

'I *have* to go home, Daddy, so I can see them all,' she announced—which was when Kate walked in.

'You've brought an *animal* in here?' she said to Lauren, anger burning in her eyes. 'Into a *hospital*?

Lauren was taken aback by this virtual stranger being so upset. Was it because she was Maddie's mother?

'I thought it might cheer Maddie up—she's been waiting and waiting for the kittens to be born.'

'And she probably got the virus from the cat!' Kate stormed, lifting the kitten off the bed and pushing it none-too-gently into Lauren's hands.

'There are eight,' Lauren said, ignoring the other woman and turning to Maddie, 'and you can come and see them all when you get home.'

'Only when she's well enough to be up and about,' Kate said.

Lauren's stomach tightened. So Madge's fears that Kate wanted to come back into their lives had been right. The woman was obviously taking over from Madge as Maddie's carer as carelessly and thoughtlessly as she'd left her child in the first place.

Lauren walked away from them. It was more than she could bear to think about Kate upsetting Maddie and Madge with her behaviour. Moving into the house—into Cam's bed?—and then, as the limited social life at the Lakes struck her, walking away again. Hurting all of them—hurting Cam.

No wonder he looked so strained.

Although maybe Kate would find Cam and Maddie were all she needed for her to decide to stay on.

Maybe that would be best for all of them.

Because surely then her own feelings for Cam, and the anxiety they caused her, would simply fade away.

Maddie came home the following day, having been prescribed bed rest, with occasional short walks or playing with her toys as exercise.

And that afternoon Maddie's idea of a short walk constituted a visit to Lauren—although Lauren knew full well it was really a visit to the kittens.

Maddie sat quietly on the floor, Henry beside her, and played with all of them. But her hands kept going back to the little black fellow, and Lauren knew, when the time came for the litter to leave its mother, that that particular kitten would become Maddie's.

But Lauren could see the little girl was tiring.

'Come on,' she said. 'I'll drive you home.'

'I don't want to drive. I want to go through the bush. I need to smell the trees again,' Maddie said, with the querulous tones of a child still weak and unwell.

'Then I'll piggyback you home,' Lauren countered, and Maddie agreed with delight.

From the top of the front steps, she clambered onto Lauren's back. 'Daddy says I'm too big for piggybacks now,' Maddie said, her lips close to Lauren's ear.

'Daddy's right,' Lauren told her as she took up the solid weight and began to trudge towards what she still thought of as Henry's house.

They must have just passed the halfway mark, and Lauren was flagging, when Cam appeared.

'She's far too heavy for you to be carrying her like that,' Cam said, the crossness in his voice betraying the anxiety he had to have been feeling when he'd been told Maddie had wandered off to Lauren's.

'She's all yours,' Lauren said, letting Maddie slide to the ground. 'I did want to drive her, but she wanted to smell the trees.'

'Of course she did,' Cam said, his voice scratchy as he gathered his daughter in his arms. 'I think we all do, don't we, Mads?'

Maddie put her arms around his neck in a hug and smiled at him. 'I saw all the kittens, but the black one is my favourite.'

'Better that than wanting all of them,' Cam murmured

to Lauren, his face close enough for her to see the lines of strain on it, and to read a kind of despair in his eyes.

The air between them seemed charged with some kind of force, prickling her skin with heat, yet sliding icy fingers down her spine. She wanted to hold him, tell him she loved him, but knew that would make things worse.

She touched his cheek, unable not to, and said, 'You'll be all right…' as casually as she could. Because right now he looked as if nothing would ever be right for him again.

Lauren hurried home, trying not to think about what was happening at his place—refusing to think about where Kate might be sleeping.

Plenty of bedrooms, she told herself, *not that it's any of your business.*

None at all.

Apart from Maddie coming to visit and play with the kittens, and Kate cooing over the animals when Lauren was on shift at the sanctuary, Lauren had seen little of her neighbours.

After that first visit, Madge always drove Maddie over to play, and usually went on into the village to get a few groceries before returning to collect her granddaughter. One day her return coincided with the end of Lauren's morning session.

'Let her play a little longer and come and have a cup of tea with me,' she said to Madge, who accepted with alacrity.

'Anything to keep me away from that woman,' Lauren heard her mutter as they walked through to the big kitchen.

'Madge is staying for a cuppa,' Lauren called through to the laundry.

'So I can stay longer?' Maddie replied, with utter delight in her voice.

But as they sat at the huge old kitchen table Lauren could see from Madge's face that all was not well.

'Maddie's fine,' she told her, pouring Madge a cup of tea and pushing a plate of warm scones towards her.

'It's not Maddie I'm worried about,' Madge said, then bit her lip. 'I promised myself I wouldn't talk about it,' she added, looking so upset that Lauren wanted to hug her.

'Then don't,' she said. 'Just sit and relax, have your tea, and there's jam and cream for the scones. There's something I want to ask you about anyway. Last night at the Regional Fire Service meeting they were talking about getting someone in to do the books and fill in all the government paperwork. I wondered if you might be interested.'

She paused, looking at Madge.

'The RFS is a volunteer organisation,' she added, 'and we get plenty of younger men and women—and quite a few older ones too—who are keen. They practise hard, give lectures, et cetera. But book work! They seem to have a complete horror of it. But it has to be done and Nellie, whose been doing it for thirty years, really wants out. She's seventy-nine, and she feels she's done enough.'

'Well, I think that would be far more interesting than joining a quilting group or even the bridge club,' Madge said, perking up considerably.

'You could probably do both. Well, the bridge club *and* the RFS—Nellie's a bridge player. Would you like me to take you down to the service base, show you around, and maybe meet up with Nellie so she can explain the job? It's not full-time, and really there are no set hours—although it's always good to go to the meetings so you know what's going on. What do you think?'

'Lead me to it,' Madge said, a huge grin on her face. 'It's just exactly what I need, and now Maddie's spending most of her time over here, until she goes to school, I've plenty of free time to work out what the job entails.'

She called to Maddie, who left the laundry and came in carrying the black kitten.

'He's not quite old enough to leave his mum,' Lauren said gently. 'But another week and he'll be all yours.'

'But then I'll be at school and he'll have no one to play with,' she said, in such tragic tones that Lauren had to hide a smile.

'Not really,' Lauren said. 'Because the mother cat is really yours too, and she can go home with you when he goes. Debbie is busy finding homes for all the other kittens, so everything will be fine.'

Maddie beamed and flung her arms around Lauren's neck. 'I do love you, Lauren,' she said—just as Cam appeared through the laundry door, a kitten in one hand and a watchful Henry by his side.

Lauren hoped her delight in seeing him wasn't making her glow—that the warmth she felt inside wasn't visible on her face.

'Now the whole family's here,' she said, hoping her voice was light and casual. Although to her it sounded kind of squeaky—a dead give-away of her excitement.

'Not really,' Madge muttered, glaring at her son. 'Maddie, it's time to go. You need some lunch before you have your rest. Put the kitten back with his mother and meet me at the car.'

She whisked away, tea half-drunk, a jammy, creamy half-scone abandoned on her plate.

Was she upset about Kate taking over what had been her place in their lives since Maddie's birth? Or with Cam for allowing it?

Cam was looking equally bemused by his mother's abrupt departure, but rather then get involved with the family dynamic, Lauren told him about their conversation.

'I've been talking to Madge about doing some voluntary bookwork for the Regional Fire Service,' she said, as casually as she could to the man still standing in her kitchen with a kitten in one hand.

It was so good to see him, right there in front of her, and every atom in her being wanted to get up and walk over to him and hold him in her arms—kitten and all.

But the ghost of Kate hovered between them.

And, as if she'd conjured the woman up, Cam spoke her name.

'I've asked Kate—again—to sign the divorce papers,' he said, forcing his hands not to clench because of the kitten in one of them. 'I sent her the papers over a year ago, and gave her another set when she came here. Now I've told her I want them signed before she goes.'

He watched Lauren study him for a moment.

'Goes? Don't you feel you should give it some time?' she asked quietly, absentmindedly pushing half a scone around her plate—not looking at him. 'I mean, with Maddie being so sick, and things only just getting back to normal, shouldn't you at least try to see if it could work—for all your sakes?'

'Not for mine,' he said savagely. 'Nor Maddie's. Kate's barely spent ten minutes with her since she's been here, but she's seen the house, and the sanctuary, and now she pictures herself as Lady Bountiful, lording it over the locals, having fundraising parties with any celebrities she can find and generally settling in.' He paused, before adding, 'She acts all the time—seeing herself in different scenarios and playing out different parts with no thought for anyone else.'

'So what are you going to do?' Lauren asked,

And Cam realised that was really what he'd come to her to ask, and he felt ashamed. Lauren was more to him than someone he went to for help, someone he'd trusted to sit with Maddie while he slept.

Lauren was his life, his future, but what could he offer her? Not even marriage, the way things were.

He turned around, gave the kitten back to its mother, scratched Henry's ears and then slipped out through the back door, his arms aching with the longing to hold Lauren to him, his body aching to have her body pressed to his.

He'd walked over to give himself some breathing space—to smell the trees, as Maddie had said—but really to clear his mind of Kate's incessant chatter about how 'we' could do this, and 'we' could do that—all the time talking about the house and using the plural 'we', as though their marriage was already mended, in spite of their sleeping in different rooms, and his pleas that she sign the divorce papers.

'You're only just back in time,' Debbie chided him when he returned. 'Local radio wants a chat with you—they're phoning in a few minutes.'

'What do they want to chat about?' Cam demanded, not really in the mood for putting on a performance—although he had to admit Debbie's efforts on his behalf had increased the number of people seeking his help with their various animals. Business was beginning to look good.

'It's not an "on air" chat. It's what Lauren was talking to you about—you doing a regular question-and-answer thing. They can set it up so you can do it from home...

or really wherever you are. Think how thrilled people would be if you stopped preg-testing a sheep, or something, to chat about their budgie!'

Debbie picked up the receiver on the ringing phone.

'It's them,' she said. 'Go through to your office and I'll put it through there.'

Helplessly resigning himself to the force that was Debbie, he went through to his office.

Lauren had an afternoon shift at the sanctuary and, well aware she'd be as welcome as smallpox if she ran into Kate, she slipped in through the side gate. Helen was there, drawing up the roster for the next few weeks, frowning over the usually simple procedure.

'Trouble?' Lauren asked.

Helen uttered a few pithy swear words.

'It's that woman,' she said in arctic tones when she looked up from her work. 'Fair enough, Beth's left—she was always going to stop about this time—but that woman has her absolutely terrified about childbirth, undoing all the good work in the antenatal classes Beth's been going to. Claims she was hospitalised for months after Maddie's birth, but Madge tells me she was offered a job in a play and took it—three days after she brought Maddie home.'

'This is Kate you're talking about.'

'Who else?' Helen demanded. 'And even though Beth's fairly level-headed she can't help thinking about the things Kate told her. And then there's this idea she's got that we should be on the tourist map, with people coming in to cuddle the animals. Ever tried explaining the word "sanctuary" to an airhead? Because that's what she is—a dangerous airhead. How someone as kind and understanding as Cam ever came to marry her beats me.'

'Well, if you can fit them between my working hours, I'd be happy to do extra shifts, and I can easily come over in the evening to do night feeds and lock up.'

Helen sighed. 'I know you would—I'm happy to do more myself—but we started this, your father and Henry and me, as a community project that everyone could be part of, and *she's* disrupting it—popping in to grab an animal that doesn't know her for a photo shoot. Wanting signs put up for tourists. That kind of thing… People won't have it,' Helen said, and Lauren understood.

The locals were proud of their sanctuary, and did whatever they could to help. But to turn it into a commercial venture—of course they'd buck at that.

'Can you talk to Cam?' Helen asked.

Lauren shrugged. From what she'd seen, Kate took little notice of anyone else's ideas or opinions—probably least of all Cam's.

The man himself appeared at that moment.

'Debbie's talked the local radio station into giving me a talk-back session once a week,' he said, in such morose tones that both women laughed.

'It will be good for business,' Helen told him, 'and Henry did it—how hard can it be?'

'I'm more worried about sounding pathetic than having any difficulty with it.'

'You could never sound pathetic,' Helen assured him. 'Did you want something?'

'Sane company?' he said hopefully, and they laughed again. 'Actually, I saw Lauren sneaking into the sanctuary and I wanted her to look at some drone pictures I've been taking. I'm not certain I've got the knack yet. Can you spare her?'

Helen smiled at him. 'I can if you put in a plug for

some volunteers for the sanctuary on your first broad-cast,' she said, and Lauren was glad she didn't blame him for his wife chasing so many away.

CHAPTER ELEVEN

CAM LED THE WAY—not back into his rooms, but out to the shed, where he proudly displayed a drone, sitting on a table by a computer monitor.

'I found Henry's drone and fixed it up, and I've been practising with it. I've flown it over the burnt-out bush, checking for any wildlife, but apart from a couple of wallabies in the regrowth beneath the trees there's not much.'

'You've done well to get the pictures as clear as they are.'

'I've had plenty of spare time,' he said, and the hoarseness in his voice told her more than the words.

She leaned closer as she flicked through the images, stopping at one that was less clear. He caught her hand and helped direct it to another shot in the corner of the screen. His fingers tightened on hers, spirals of desire swirling through her at his touch.

Then they were gone, as he released her hand and tapped the picture in the corner, enlarging it to show the distinctive diamond shapes on the skin of a large snake. She knew it was a python of some kind.

Cam straightened up and stepped aside so she could study what he'd found. He moved a little distance from her, facing the front of the shed.

'It's killing me...this,' he said. 'Not being able to see you properly, to sit and talk with you—'

'Of course you can—we're friends, remember? And that's what friends do. Not too much, though, while you're trying to make a go of your marriage.'

'Marriage!' he snorted. 'It's hardly that.' He paused, before adding in a voice that had a hint of a tremor in it, 'It's Maddie, you see. I just can't let Kate take the divorce to court when there's even the slightest chance of her getting custody. You've seen enough of Kate to know what Maddie's life would be like.'

'Oh, Cam...' Lauren sighed as she spoke, then stood up and slipped her arms around him from behind, clasping her hands around his waist, pressing her body against his in a friendly *there-there* kind of hug.

They both turned towards the door now, and Lauren peered over Cam's shoulder, aware that he'd been looking out for Kate all along. And totally aware of the loss he dreaded.

The big black saloon that drove up caught both of them by surprise.

A smallish, very well-dressed man got out and strode towards the house.

'Is he from the radio station, do you know?' Cam asked.

Lauren, after a final hug, let go of him and came to stand beside him. 'He's not a local, I'm sure. Unless he's a fairly new arrival,' she said.

Cam shook his head. 'He doesn't look like a lakesider to me. Anyway, Debbie knows I'm here if I'm needed. Let's get back to the snake—do you know what it is?'

He sat down in front of the computer and Lauren stood behind him, not touching him, although she was aware of every line of his body, every breath he took...

They heard the visitor coming before he reached the shed, and his, 'Good afternoon,' came to them from the door.

'What is it you're looking at?' he asked, crossing to where they were, peering at the screen. 'Python of some kind from the look of it,' the man said. 'Harmless, of course, but nice to see one in the burnt-out area. Shows good regeneration.'

He straightened up.

'I'm Russell Blair, by the way,' he said, looking at Cam, 'and I've got your divorce papers here. Kate's signed them and I've witnessed them, along with that lass from your office.'

He handed the papers to Cam, who looked from the papers to the man in disbelief.

'She's packing now—Kate. I'm sorry I wasn't in the country when your little girl got sick. I'd have come down with Kate and fixed up the paperwork then. I'm going to marry her, you see. It's just that she likes the drama—stringing me along, dashing off on the slightest excuse, trying out different roles she might fancy living... But you probably know that! Anyway, it's all settled now.'

He turned from Cam, glanced at Lauren, then looked back at Cam.

'I guess you'll be glad to have it done with.'

Lauren could feel the heat climbing into her cheeks, so she fiddled with the picture on the computer, not sure that she could identify one python from another.

Cam followed Russell Blair back to his car, where Kate, with Debbie's help, was installing what seemed like masses of luggage into the boot.

'Never one to travel light,' Russell remarked, but he made no move to help.

Cam walked around the vehicle to where his wife stood at the open front door. 'Did you tell Maddie you were going?' he asked.

Kate shook her head. 'She won't care,' she said. 'She doesn't know me at all. No one really does—except for Russell.'

Well, good luck to him, Cam thought. *I've never had a clue.* And not to say goodbye to Maddie showed how little she cared about the child she'd brought into the world.

Lauren had remained in the shed, although she came to the door as the car drove off.

Cam turned towards her, face alight with joy. '*Now* we can get married!' he said, excitement filling his body.

But the woman in the doorway shook her head.

'It was never Kate or your marriage stopping us, Cam,' she said softly—and, he thought, sadly. 'Although while you were still married it was impossible…which made it easier to pretend for a bit. But the real problem remains—and that's your age. I'm too old for you. You need someone young and vibrant—someone who can give you sisters or brothers for Maddie—someone to make a family with. You need to get out and meet people, go to the pub…whatever. Get a life outside your work— for Maddie's sake as well as your own.'

She reached out, took his hand, and looked into his eyes.

'Don't make it hard for me, Cam,' she said.

And then he saw the pain she'd hidden in her practical words, only too evident in her eyes.

She slipped away through the scrub that stood between their houses, somehow making a wall of it—a no-man's-land—and cutting herself off from him.

He'd give her time to get home and then phone her, he thought, certain she wasn't really at all convinced

that whatever it was between them couldn't…wouldn't…
shouldn't continue.

But Lauren wasn't available.

She was working hard, Janet told him when he tried
to phone her. She had a lot of lost time to make up with
her paperwork and accounting. And a big meeting for
the Regional Fire Service was approaching, and she was
secretary of that. Such a lot to do…

Janet made it all sound utterly reasonable—even
mostly true—so he could hardly go crashing over there.

Except…

Wasn't Madge talking about joining the RFS—hadn't
there been talk of her doing the book work?

He'd get Debbie to babysit Maddie and take Madge to
the meeting himself.

He sat down at the computer to check when and where
the meeting was to be held. He wasn't giving up just yet.

Lauren hadn't been lying when she'd said she had a lot
to do. The end of the financial year *was* coming up, and
all her income and expenditure had to be made ready
for her accountant.

Plus, there was the RFS stuff. And the work *that*
would involve this year was going to be mammoth, as
all the donations they'd received in the aftermath of the
bush fires had to be listed, and then another list made of
what these generous gifts—even the smallest ones—had
been put towards.

And on top of that the members had to discuss a new
way forward—start thinking of a plan to be better prepared than they had been. She knew one of the main proj-
ects had to be finding a way to improve communication.
Not just between the different fire services, but between
them and the people on outlying properties, who relied

solely on the radio or their telephones—on power being connected, when often it was the first service lost.

All this busy thinking had brought her home, the scents of the scrub passing unnoticed. But she knew all her thoughts had, in part, been a way of avoiding thinking of Cam completely—just for a little while…or perhaps a bit longer than a little while…hoping avoidance would help her accept that this was how it should be.

And if even contemplating a future of seeing less of Cam caused a deep, physical ache, then she'd just have to learn to live with it.

You have to think ahead, in situations like this, she told herself as she headed upstairs to shower and change for her evening clinic.

Her at sixty when he'd be in the prime of life at fifty. Not that sixty was old…but the age difference would be more marked—especially if she did develop dementia…

Standing in the shower, warm water cascading over her, she let her thoughts continue to run riot.

All Cam-based.

It had been not just lust—she hoped—but probably also a need for closeness with a woman that had made her appealing to him. After all, she'd been there, and available, hadn't she?

But rationalising all this—and what had happened between them—didn't make her heart any less sore, or the pain of love any less overwhelming.

Not that he'd ever know.

No word of love had ever passed between them.

She was keeping the sudden revelation of her feelings to herself, while as for Cam—from their first meeting he'd been obsessed with marriage, which was probably what he needed from a practical point of view. He could hardly expect his mother to go on taking care of his household for ever.

Enough! Get dry, get dressed, concentrate on her patients, then get on with work for the RFS.

She had to find out if they could use some of the donations they'd received to put overhead powerlines underground. At the height of the fires they'd had thousands of people without power for weeks, and it hadn't been good enough.

Her session was busy, and she was late making her way back to the sanctuary, where she was on the late shift.

She snuck in through the outside gate—she could do this. Carry on as usual, get back into her old routines—her old life.

And if her heart ached with the pain of something that could never be... Well, that was for her to know—not others—and definitely not Cam.

Cam had watched her go, had heard the note of finality in her words, and thought maybe she was right—although he did wonder if she just plain didn't love him, but hadn't wanted to hurt him by saying so.

He decided it was useless to keep thinking about it and went off to see what the tireless Debbie had thought up for him now.

'We could sell products,' she announced as he went in. 'Special dog and cat food, and seeds that attract native birds. Just as an extra...you know. And I've had an email from a young man whose budgie isn't very well. It's on a self-feeder and he thinks it might be eating too much. That would be a good first question for your column.'

'My column?' he said feebly as he watched her packing up, ready to leave as soon as her ever-reliable Harry turned up.

'For the paper,' she said. 'They want it Monday. There's a note on your desk about who to email it to and the number of words, et cetera. The paper comes out on Thursday, you see.'

He thanked her and went into his office-cum-consulting room. There must be six little memos there—including the details of his 'column'. But being busy would be good.

He could hear Maddie and Madge, talking in the kitchen. He'd go and join them, maybe have a beer, and look into what kind of things could go wrong with budgerigars later.

Maddie was parading in her school uniform—having been pronounced ready to return to school on Monday by her doctors. She and Madge had gone into the village to get it earlier and had obviously made a day of it, as new shoes and a sensible wide-brimmed hat were included in their purchases.

'We can't go into the playground without a hat,' Maddie told him. 'It's a rule!'

'And a good one,' he agreed.

But when she suggested she go over to Lauren's, to show her the new uniform, Cam said it was a bit late and maybe Helen and the wombats would like to see it instead.

She skipped happily off, and he poured a glass of wine for his mother and sat down at the kitchen table.

'Were you here when Kate left?' he asked, and she shook her head.

'Although we did run into them in the village,' Madge explained. 'I really do not understand that woman—never have,' she continued. 'She was far more interested in introducing me to her fancy man in his fancy car than in saying goodbye to her daughter. Although I must admit Maddie showed little interest in either of them, just standing in front of the shop window trying her new hat at different angles.'

'Do you think Maddie realises Kate's gone for good this time?' Cam asked.

Madge sighed. 'Really, Cam, I don't think she's ever felt any connection. I doubt she has ever seen Kate as her mother—more as some exotic being who drifted into her life when she was still in the haze of her illness. She certainly hasn't any childhood memories of her. She was barely two when Kate left.'

'Well, I hope that's the end of it,' Cam said, suddenly realising he was right back where he'd started when he'd arrived in Australia—in a big old house with his mother and daughter.

Well, there was the sanctuary. And Debbie. But Lauren had been right. He had to get involved with the local community, if only to distract his thoughts from Lauren herself...

But why? He didn't *want* to distract himself from thoughts of Lauren—not a bit of it. She was the best thing that had happened to him in his entire life—including being given his own vet practice and building his own ultralight.

And he loved her.

Had he told her that?

He'd certainly told her he was smitten—but that might not have been taken as love...

And he'd certainly mentioned marriage—but had he officially proposed?

Of course not. He hadn't been able to until today, when the divorce papers had been signed.

He'd do it now—go and ask her. She was in the sanctuary. He'd seen her walk around the side of the house.

And then somehow Madge and Maddie and Debbie were all there too—going into the sanctuary.

School uniform showing off time?

He pushed ahead of them.

CHAPTER TWELVE

LAUREN WAS HELPING Helen check the stock in the sanctuary when Madge, Maddie and Cam came in through the house door, Debbie trailing behind them.

Her heart, for all she knew it shouldn't, flipped at the sight of the man she loved—loved to distraction, really.

Although how she—an intelligent, rational, not-so-young woman—had allowed herself to fall in love with a younger man, she didn't know.

Nor did she really know where things would go from here.

Or why there were suddenly all these people here...

Cam stepped away from his entourage, and would have taken her hand if she hadn't backed away.

But, seemingly unperturbed, he took his stance in front of her and spoke with calm authority. 'Lauren, I love you. Will you do me the honour of marrying me?' he asked.

You are not going to faint, Lauren said sternly to herself, clutching the desk in the sanctuary while her knees turned to jelly. *You don't do fainting*.

'Please say yes, Lauren!' Maddie said, squeezing forward to stand close to her friend and frowning. 'You look sick, like I did when I was in hospital, and not at all happy.'

'She's happy inside,' Cam said, looking serenely composed but probably inwardly laughing at the position he'd put her in—the wretch. 'Not right away, of course,' he continued, bland as milk. 'But in a few months—once we've had a chance to work things out...like which house we want to live in—'

'Lauren's!' Maddie said, clapping with delight. 'Because Henry and Puss the cat live there, and there's a little room that looks out over the lake that Lauren said I could sleep in whenever I came to stay. She used to sleep in it when she was little.'

Lauren continued to grip the desk and closed her eyes. She had a four-year-old—no, a four-and-a-half-year-old—organising her future.

'Lauren?' Madge said, her voice soft...anxious.

Lauren opened her eyes and smiled weakly at Madge. 'I'm fine,' she managed, and at the words her fighting spirit returned. 'Although whether your son will be when I finish with him over this nonsense, I can't say.'

'But *is* it nonsense?' Madge asked.

Lauren shook her head.

'Daddy just didn't do it right,' Maddie explained to her grandmother. 'He should have got down on one knee and given her a ring.'

Lauren shook her head again. This family had her beat!

'Daddy will do all that part when he's somewhere private,' Cam told his small relationship advisor.

'Can I watch?' Maddie asked.

But Cam's words had been weak, and Lauren realised just what a strain this must be for him.

'We'll talk about it later,' she promised Maddie, as Madge began herding the child and Debbie towards the door.

Lauren walked with them, thinking to escape but knowing she needed to talk to Cam.

Talk?

More like yell and shout and throw a tantrum, if she could remember how to do it from her two-year-old days.

Madge stopping her with a soft hand on her arm.

'He shouldn't have put you on the spot like that, but it would make me very happy if you did decide to marry him,' she said. 'Me *and* Maddie. And not just for dogs or cats or rooms, but because you make him happy.'

She gave Lauren a peck on the cheek and left, with Maddie talking excitedly about her new room.

'I'm off too,' Helen said, her arms raised in the air, as if well aware that a lot more had to be said.

Lauren turned to look at the man who remained, smiling genially—if a little anxiously.

'What have you done?' she muttered.

He held out his hand. She put hers into it and he clasped it tightly, pulling her closer until he could put his lips to hers in a kiss that said far more than words.

Oh, if it could only be, she thought as she leant into him, feeling the solidity of his support and her overwhelming sense of love.

He eased her a little away, so he could look into her eyes, but kept her hands captive in his.

'I know all your arguments about the difference in our ages and they're rubbish. Older men marry younger women all the time. And as for family—if you'd like children...well, you're still young enough. Lots of women in their forties are having children these days.'

Stunned by all that had happened, she could only stare at him.

'And as for your biggest fear, my darling...' He looked deep into her eyes. 'I know we've never spoken of it, but

it's your father's illness, isn't it? Your over-active imagination has you declining into some form of dementia
and me having to look after you. You've been there and
done that, and you know how hard it was, but the doctor
in you must know it's not hereditary, even though some
things that could lead to it are genetic.'

'It's a lottery,' she mumbled, and he drew her close
again.

'So shall I tell you something?' he whispered in her
ear. 'The love we share will give us many happy years,
and I would willingly care for you. You didn't stop loving your father, and I have no intention of ever—*ever*—
stopping loving you. You are my friend—my mate, in
Aussie terms—my lover and hopefully my wife, and I
will love you for ever and a day.'

He drew her close again, and his kiss told her all the
things he'd said and many, many more.

The cloud of fear disappeared, and she knew the love
she felt for him must be shining in her eyes.

'Do I need to officially say yes?' she asked, aware
that her answer was already given as she pressed her
lips to his.

'You just have to say, *I love you, Cam*,' he said. 'Because you do, don't you?'

She stepped back, her hands holding his, and looked
into those blue eyes she'd first seen in a dry gully not so
very long ago.

'I love you, Cam, more than you could ever imagine.'

And she let him pull her close again and hold her as
she knew he would—now and for ever!

They were married by the lake, their friends around
them—Maddie clutching the black kitten and the cat,

Henry the dog, who'd refused to go and live with anyone else, staunch by Lauren's side.

'It's a wonder someone didn't bring out the wombats and a koala,' Cam said, as he held his wife in his arms and they looked out over the magic of the lake that had led them to love.

'No, but there *is* a drone,' Lauren told him.

And they both looked up so the little drone from the local paper could record this special event.

And smiled.

* * * * *

REUNITED
WITH HER
DAREDEVIL DOC

SUSAN CARLISLE

MILLS & BOON

For Mary Beth Norwood, nurse extraordinaire.
Thanks for the love you've shown Nick and our family.

CHAPTER ONE

DANA WARREN SWUNG the single glass door of the US Forest Service open with a spring in her step and anticipation rushing through her veins. This would be her time. What she'd been working toward for years. Her boss had called her in. There was a fire burning in the Deschutes National Forest southwest of Bend, Oregon. New, smaller fires needed extinguishing before they joined the larger one. Her crew was next in line to jump with her as their trail leader.

She'd trained for this moment and was ready for the task. Adrenaline coursed through her at the thought of jumping. It was what she lived for and loved. There weren't many women in the smokejumper service, less than 2 percent out of four hundred, but she'd held her own beside the men, earning their respect. Because of that she'd been proud of how she'd moved up the ranks.

Heading straight for the desk of the fire manager, she leaned over his shoulder and studied the computer screen. "Whatta we have, Gus?"

"Nothing for you right yet, but I'm sure it won't be long."

Dana pursed her lips and nodded. Gus wasn't wrong often. His job was to determine the fuel of the fire, the direction, the wind velocity and make the call for the number of jumpers needed to fight it. He was good at his job.

Before either she or Gus could say more, Leo Thomas, the manager of the smokejumpers at Redmond Air Center, in Redmond, Oregon, called, "Dana. Good. You're here. Come in my office."

She dropped her pack on an empty chair outside the door and followed Leo. "Hey, my team's ready when you say—" She pulled up short. Her heart thumped hard against her rib cage. The last word stuck in her throat.

Travis.

He rose to his feet from where he'd been sitting in a metal chair against the wall. "Dana. I, uh hadn't expected to see you."

Travis took the words right out of her mouth. Not planning to see him would be an understatement. The idea of turning heel and running flashed through her mind but she'd already done that once. She swallowed hard. Grown now, she was determined to act it. Still words hung in her mouth. The last time she'd seen Travis she'd been foolish enough to try to kiss him. To make matters worse, now she couldn't seem to do anything more than stand there and stare at him.

"You two know each other?" Leo directed a hand back and forth between them.

She looked at Travis. He watched her. Her attention remained on him as she answered Leo. "Yes, we know each other."

Travis straightened as if gathering himself. "Dana and I worked together one summer a long time ago."

Leo nodded and spoke to Travis. "That's where you got your experience."

"I fought fires during my college years breaks and for the year between college and starting medical school."

Leo nodded, stepping behind the desk. "I see. I bet the medical board found that interesting during your interview."

"They did, and they especially appreciated the wilderness emergency training I have."

Leo nodded before looking at her. "Dana, I need you for a special assignment. I want you to take Dr. Russell to a spot just south of Mount Bachelor. He has a medically fragile patient who has refused to leave his cabin. The doctor fears the man has taken a turn for the worse. To make matters more difficult the bridge on the road into his place has burned and the fire is headed his direction."

Dana glanced at Travis. His blue-eyed look remained on her. She spoke to Leo, "May I speak to you alone?"

Leo sighed, turning his attention to Travis. "Please wait outside for a minute."

Travis started toward the door in one smooth motion. Still as tall and athletic as she remembered, he'd filled out. His jeans fit tightly over thick thigh muscles. He looked trim and fit. Apparently he worked out. Where he had a lanky physique of youth before now his shoulders had the wideness and broadness of a mature man. With his black hair and piercing sky eyes, he could stop her breath. Based on his appearance, Travis looked as if he could handle the grueling physical requirements this trip would require. Something that made up a major part of a smokejumper's life. What she found most disconcerting was he still had the ability to rattle her nerves.

He quietly closed the door behind him. She rounded on Leo, placing both her hands on his desk. If she went on the mercy mission then her team would go up without her. "It's my crew's turn next. This sounds like something for Rescue to handle."

"Your team hasn't been called yet. If they are, Ricky

can take the lead. Dr. Russell can't call in Rescue when he doesn't know the medical situation yet. Winds are picking up and this old man's cabin is in the thick of the forest, hard to access. With the size of the fire burning, all the available rescue helicopters are in high demand. He has to assess the situation before he can ask for one. The hope is that you two can get the man out without the use of Rescue. While you're there I'll also want you to form a fire line around the cabin." Leo nodded toward where Travis had exited. "Dr. Russell can assist."

Dana stood straight. She didn't want someone else handling her crew. She wanted to do her job. She cared nothing about babysitting a man she'd made an idiot of herself over. That had been embarrassing enough but being forced to spend time with him again only added misery to pain. "Come on, Leo. You know I've been waiting for my chance with a crew. Can't someone else take Travis, uh Dr. Russell out? My team and I know how to work together."

Leo's eyes narrowed. "There's a man up there on the mountain," he pointed the direction on Mount Bachelor. "He may be old and cantankerous by refusing not to leave when he could have, but that doesn't mean we shouldn't do what we can to save him. The man may need dialysis. You've advanced EMT training. You know the area. You're perfect for the assignment."

"Over half of these guys…" she directed a hand toward the outside office "…can be called woofers because they have the same Wilderness First Responder training as I do. One of them could go."

Leo nodded. "But I'm assigning you to see Dr. Russell gets to his patient safely and that both get back safely. I know this isn't the norm, but it's necessary. You're the best person for the job. You know that area better than any of the others around here since you worked out of the Bend district before you came back here. Dr. Russell assures me this man needs help now or he might not survive. I've given you more explanation than anyone about an assignment. You know what you have to do, do it. Now, open the door and ask Dr. Russell back in."

"Do you even know if he can still jump? I don't need two people to see about if he gets hurt." She didn't hold back her disgust.

"Why don't you ask him?" Leo suggested.

She flung open the door, stopping it just before it hit the wall. As Travis entered, she saw a shadow of concern in his eyes. Did he fear she'd changed Leo's mind? Or that she hadn't changed his mind and Travis would be stuck with her. She glared at him. "When's the last time you jumped?"

"Three months ago. I jump a few times a year. I can assure you that I'm able to manage a jump."

She fired at him, "We've moved to a new system in the last year. We're using BLM now."

"The square parachute. Yeah, I've used it. I don't have a lot of experience with it but I've jumped a time or two with one."

"Good to hear," Leo said.

Dana inwardly sighed. Travis had an answer for everything. Leo fed Travis's confidence.

"Then be here in two hours ready to go. The wind is supposed to pick up this afternoon and a front is moving in."

"I'll be ready." Travis's voice remained firm.

Leo looked at her.

Seeing no way out, Dana nodded and started for the door. She said over her shoulder to Travis, "Be on time." She retrieved her backpack from the chair on her way by, heading for the outside door with hands shaking and jaw clinched.

Exiting the building and reaching her truck, her hand rested on the door handle when fingers lightly touched the top of her shoulder. A shot of electricity flew through her. She jerked around.

"Dana."

Embarrassment heated her cheeks. She looked anywhere but at Travis.

"It's nice to see you again. I'd no idea you were working here. I'm impressed you've stayed with smokejumping. You've moved up the ladder, as well. But that doesn't surprise me. You've always had the brains and brawn for it."

"Brawn, huh? Sounds real…"

"Nice. I always thought it looked good on you." His ice-blue eyes met hers. "Your smarts and instincts have served you well."

His words made her quake. Why, oh, why did Travis still have that power over her? She should've grown up and out of the crush she had on him. Maybe it wasn't that but just embarrassment. What must he think of her? It could only be she was acting like the naive girl she'd been the last time he'd seen her.

She needed to get away. Find a few minutes to regroup before she had to spend the next twenty-four hours with him. "Yeah. I'm still fighting fires. I been working out of this base for three years. I really should go if I'm going to be back in two hours."

Travis backed away. "Yeah. See you then."

As she drove away she looked out the rearview mirror to find Travis watching her.

Travis had been struck dumb to see Dana. The last time he'd seen her he'd unintentionally hurt her feelings. He'd felt bad about it then, still did. She'd been humiliated and he hadn't known how to make it better. Dana had wanted something he couldn't give. He hadn't been happy about what had happened between them but it had been necessary at the time. He'd wounded a woman's heart he'd called a friend. That was the last thing he'd wanted to do.

In truth, he hadn't kept up with her over the years. But that didn't mean he hadn't thought about her. All the usual stuff had gone through his mind. What if he hadn't had a girlfriend at the time, what if he hadn't been entering medical school, what if they had really kissed, what if…

There had always been something special about Dana. She'd been a great friend and team member that summer. Hard work had been in the center of their time together, but there had been laughter and a comradery he'd not known since. It had been the best time in his life. One he remembered with a great deal of fondness.

Dana had changed, but then, she hadn't. She still acted headstrong and determined, willing to speak her mind. Like before, she had a body to rival any athlete. The physical demands of her job and her growth from a coltish woman he'd known before to the full-grown woman she was now enhanced her appeal. Her warm brown eyes clearly expressed her feelings.

Her thoughts had been clear through those eyes when she'd seen him in Leo's office. Total shock. Travis had recognized that feeling. He'd felt gut punched, as well. They'd have to work past that. Despite their history, he had to trust her to help him get old man Gunter to the care he needed.

A couple of hours later Travis again pulled into the parking lot in front of the large white aluminum-sided building with the long narrow windows, a tall center section and the words US Forest printed on the side. He lifted his medical pack from the passenger seat and climbed out.

He looked around the area at the other buildings comprising the firefighting center. No Dana. He'd parked beside her truck so she must be there somewhere. Starting up the steps to the smokejumpers' building, he stopped when the door opened and Dana exited.

"We need to get moving." She pushed past him. "Let's get over to Cache and get our supplies. The wind is picking up." Stopping at the bottom of the steps, she gave him a pointed look. "Remember, on this trip you take orders from me."

"Yes, ma'am."

They headed toward the building adjacent to the main office. There all the supplies and equipment were stored.

Inside Dana went to a storage locker and started removing equipment. She nodded toward a staff member behind a high wooden counter. "Art can help you with the basics." She looked at Travis from top to bottom. "Tell him not to forget to give you a Nomex shirt and pants. You need to be in something fire resistant."

"Got it." He turned to walk away.

"Wait up. Let me see your boots." Dana stopped what she'd been doing and looked at his feet.

"What's wrong with them?" He picked up one and then the other looking at the soles.

"I wanted to see the heel. You need to be wearing ones with a low heel. None of those fancy hiking boots. Steel-toed?"

He nodded.

"Those will do." Her attention returned to her locker.

By the time Dana joined him he had a bright yellow

shirt, dark green cargo pants, a black supply bag and jumpsuit lying out on the counter.

She handed him a small radio.

"I get one of these?" He turned the radio over, looking at it.

"Yes. The protocol changed a few years ago. Everybody has a radio now."

He nodded. "Sounds like a good change to me. It should've been done sooner."

Travis grabbed the shirt and pants. "I'll have these on ASAP." He stepped out of sight.

He returned to find that Art had placed two sleeping bags, fire blankets, cook can, batteries, strapping, first-aid kit, and a collapsible bag for water on the counter along with flares and a helmet.

Dana had already gathered them packaged food or MREs. "I don't need to give you instructions on packing your bag, do I?"

She wasn't cutting him any slack. He gave her a smirk. "No, I got it."

Ten minutes later they were picking up their parachute pack. They each stepped into and zipped up their jump pants. Travis pulled his suspenders over one shoulder and then the other as Dana tugged the heavy matching tan jacket on. She took time to make sure the cone-shaped neck collar stood high. Travis followed her lead.

She gathered her parachute. He took it from her. To his surprise she gave him no argument as he held it for her to slip her arms though the shoulder straps. She did the same for him. They then secured their own leg straps and closed the chest clip.

"Your chest strap is too loose." Dana stepped close.

Near enough the warm fresh scent of female filled his nose. He remembered Dana's smell. If he'd been asked if he did he would've said no, but he recognized it right away as something special to her.

All business, Dana pulled on the strap end until it fit secure across his chest and quickly moved away.

"I do know how to do this."

"Maybe so, but you're my responsibility on this trip and I intend to return you in the same condition as I took you."

He grinned. "So I'll have a guardian angel."

Her eyes rose to meet his. "No. I'm just being a safe smokejumper."

Travis adjusted all the equipment hanging on him. "I forgot how daunting and cumbersome all this equipment is."

"Yeah, but you'll be glad to have it when we're on the ground."

"Never doubted it." Maybe with a little levity she wouldn't be so uptight. Tension swirled around them. Surely they could coexist for a day.

Travis closed the Velcro of the jumpsuit at his ankles and wrists then clipped on his personal pack to his waist. Picking up his jump helmet, he then followed Dana out the door. They lumbered toward the already running prop airplane waiting on the runway.

"We're going in a Cessna instead of a Sherpa?"

"Yeah. Since it's just the two of us we don't need the larger plane." She stepped aboard.

The spotter nodded and took the large supply bag from Travis before he took a seat on the bench across from Dana.

They strapped in and were on their way down the runway minutes later.

Dana laid her head back and closed her eyes, effectively shutting him out. Travis studied her a moment.

She'd let her straight brown hair grow. It hung around her face and bounced around her shoulders. There were lines around her eyes. Had he been a part of making those appear?

In Leo's office, he'd appreciated her simple T-shirt, cargo pants and sturdy boots that might've looked unflattering on another woman but suited Dana. Her clothes had showed curves that had been girlish years ago but had a developed femininity to them now, especially the black shirt that pulled tight across full breasts. He couldn't help but notice.

Did she have a significant other? Had she found the happiness that he hadn't?

The look of devastation in her eyes that day when he'd rejected her had haunted him for a long time. It seemed to have gone deeper than it should have. When he'd told her he had to stop, the life had gone out of her eyes. Sadly a friendship had died, as well.

He'd been so focused on himself back then he'd not recognized Dana's interest. The excitement of starting medical school and his plan to ask his longtime college sweetheart to marry him had filled his head. He and Dana were good friends, partners in a grueling, demanding and dirty profession who'd gotten carried away in the heat of the moment. It was but a second in time, yet it carried lasting power.

It was the last jump of the season for them and they'd just helped put out a particularly difficult fire. They were celebrating when he pulled her into his arms and she wrapped hers around his neck. The next thing he knew their lips were only inches apart. Dana moved and he'd turned his head before their lips met.

Travis had released her and taken a step back. *Dana, I can't.*

Dana's stricken look ended further words. *Oh. I'm sorry. So sorry.*

Pain hung around them like mist on the mountains in the morning seconds before she ran. Before he could say more. The next morning he hadn't been surprised when he couldn't find her to say goodbye, but he was filled with disappointment she couldn't face him.

Maybe he should've handled it differently. Done a better job of not hurting her feelings. Dana was younger than him. He had college behind him she only had two years under her belt. At the time he thought it was just as well. If she was mad at him she'd get over him faster. In fact, he never thought he'd see her again. Yet he'd thought of her. More than once. She'd been an important part of a summer he'd remember in detail.

His focus shifted to her lips. When she'd attempted to kiss him, he'd initially been surprised but soon felt flattered followed by disappointed it hadn't happened. Although along with that came the guilt of knowing he shouldn't have feelings for Dana when he loved and planned to marry another woman.

As close as they once had been, there was more than an aisle in a plane between them now.

Dana's eyes opened. She looked directly at him. "Why're you staring at me?"

He grinned. There was that straightforward attitude he remembered well. There was something about it that brought back those secure feelings of so long ago. He shouted over the roar of the wind and the shaking of the plane. "I'd think you'd be used to men staring at you."

She blinked and her mouth drew into a line. "Men who I work with don't stare at me."

Travis shrugged. "I don't work with you."

"You do for the next day or so. So stop it."

The spotter stood and showed all five of his fingers. He mouthed. "Five minutes."

Travis looked out the small window over his left shoulder. In the distance smoke flumed into the sky. Thankfully the wind blew it away from them. He wanted to get in, get Mr. Gunter out and be gone. The worst-case scenario would be a shift in the wind with nothing but the dry undergrowth and trees as fuel between it and them.

Dana stood and started toward the door the spotter had just opened. Travis followed her. Hooking her parachute line, she rested her feet on the step. He hooked his as well but waited inside the plane. The spotter tapped Dana on the shoulder. She jumped. Travis soon joined her.

He found parachuting exhilarating. More than once he'd wondered if it was better than sex. It began with the chaos of a wildly beating heart, then the furious swish of the wind in his ears as his adrenaline pumped. Then it quickly turned into the sound of silence, the gentle tug of the airstream allowing him to enjoy the freedom and beauty of seeing the earth from above.

He looked down at Dana. Her light-blue-and-white canopy not far from him.

With his weight it didn't take him long to catch up with her. It'd be his guess she barely met the size limit of one hundred and twenty pounds. Which meant she would carry almost her bulk in equipment when they hiked. She was something else. He had recognized her fortitude years ago but now he'd aged enough to admire it.

He discerned the moment the wind current caught her, pulling her away from him and toward a cluster of trees. Despite the Ram parachute system giving her better control in the burst, the last he saw before he needed to prepare for his own landing was her canopy being grabbed by a limb.

Bringing his knees up so his feet faced the ground, Travis landed on his calves and rolled to his side before coming to his feet. He quickly pulled his parachute down, gathering it in his arms as he went. Moving with knowledge and efficiently, he took off his helmet and unclipped the parachute harness. He dropped that to the ground and loped toward Dana.

She hung about seven feet from the ground. Using her body weight, she swung back and forth trying to grab the tree trunk.

He reached up and could just touch her ankles. "Unclip and drop down. I've got you."

"Let go. I can handle this." She ground out as she glared at him.

He met her unwavering look with one of his own. "We don't have time for you to be stubborn. I've got you. Would you accept help from one of your crew?"

With a huff she gathered a length of a parachute line and clipped it to her jump jacket. "Okay."

Travis went into a stance with one foot ahead of the other. He raised his arms. She stiffened, going as straight as possible before she released the clasp. His hands grasped her waist as she slid through his arms slowing her decent. Dana's hands quickly rested on his shoulders. He rocked back as he held her weight but steadied.

As soon as her feet hit the ground he stepped back and let her go.

She pulled on the parachute. "I've got to get this canopy out of the tree."

"Can't we just leave it?"

She gave him a pointed looked that included gathered brows. "You should know better than that. Nothing has changed since we trained. We have to haul out anything we bring into a national forest. Set an example to the visitors. Also no added fuel for a fire. Plus I'll need it for my next jump after I sew up the tears." She unclipped the line and started pulling.

He joined in the effort as much as Dana would allow. A couple of times his extra muscle helped pull it free when it was stuck. Finally they had it down. Dana rolled it up.

It wasn't until then he saw the gash on her cheek. "You're hurt."

"I'm fine." She pulled off her helmet. "We need to get the kicks boxes open and stow away these jumpsuits."

He'd not even noticed their larger supply bags lying in the middle of the meadow near where he'd landed. The spotter had pushed them out of the plane. Travis caught up with her as she stalked toward them. "No, you're not. Let me have a look at you."

When Dana didn't slow he grabbed her arm. "Let me see."

She jerked her arm away from him. "Please don't touch me." Her eyes grew wide as if upset she'd shown that much emotion. Her voice took an even tone as she said, "We need to get going."

"Quit fussing and let me clean you up." He lifted her chin so he could see more clearly. "How did this happen?"

"A stick broke as I was pulling on the canopy and I turned back and it came through the face guard of my helmet. Stupid mistake."

"It just missed your eye. I'm getting my bag." He went to his supply bag and found his medical backpack. He returned to where Dana removed equipment from her kick bag. After going into his pack he pulled out a packet of four-by-four gauze pads and sterile water. "I'm going to clean you up and see what we've got."

To his amazement, she stilled and presented her face to him. Stepping closer, he went to work removing the dried blood around the puncture wound. He dug into his bag again for a tube of antiseptic cream and a butterfly bandage. "If we weren't out here I'd say you need a small stitch or two not to have a scar."

"That's no big deal." Dana shrugged the idea off.

It should be. She was too pretty to be marred. "I'll try to make the butterfly as tight as possible. Maybe it'll do the trick."

"You done yet?" Her voice held a gruff note as she looked away from him.

"Almost." He secured the tape to her face.

"Good. We should get going."

CHAPTER TWO

DANA GLANCED BACK at Travis as she wiped the sweat from her brow. The hot, dry August weather wasn't her favorite. Yet this was right in the middle of fire season and she did love her job. The one she should be doing if it wasn't for playing tour guide to Travis. He wore a stoic look on his face as they trudged across the meadow toward a stand of trees.

Her stomach squeezed. It was just the two of them. Six thousand feet above sea level in a wilderness. Her life sure had taken a drastic turn. In two days she'd right it. It was only temporary. She'd get Travis back home. After that they might see each other at the grocery store once a year and pass niceties.

She shifted the chain saw sitting across her shoulder. Travis had looked surprised when she'd pulled it out of the bag before stuffing her jumpsuit and parachute into it.

"I was just thinking it was nice not to have to carry a chain saw and then out you come with one. Are we really going to need that?"

"You never know. I believe in being prepared. I also had Art add some firefighting chemicals." She grinned to herself.

He must've seen her look because he said, "I'd forgotten what it was like to carry all this equipment plus water."

"No complaining, Doctor. You're the one who asked to come."

"I did. I'm just making conversation."

"Conversation isn't necessary." Talking meant she might discuss a subject she didn't want to. She continued walking.

"Why do you mind taking me to Gunter's place so much? I don't understand why I'm such an inconvenience to you."

"I can see why you wouldn't." She wasn't being fair to him and she knew it but couldn't stop herself. She'd been working to lead her own trail crew and instead of that she had this babysitting job, no matter how noble the reason. To make matters worse, she'd been blindsided by Travis returning to her life. Her nerves were on edge and her mind not thinking right. It was too much in one day. "My crew, *my* crew, is going up for the first time and I'm not getting to lead them."

"Hey, I'm sorry. I know you must be disappointed. I remember how ambitious you were. I'm sorry to mess things up."

It wasn't the first time. He jumbled her up all those years ago, as well. She'd wanted to find a hole and bury herself in it when she tried to kiss him. In her excitement she found herself in his arms, a place she'd dreamed of being in more than once. In that weak second she'd forgotten about his life's plans and gotten caught up in the heat of the moment. With the addition of her traitor's heart, she'd made a mistake. Adding his rejection to that of her parents and she'd closed herself off further from others. Just a few years ago she opened enough to let Ryan in and that had got her a kick in the teeth, as well. Not again. She'd learned to let her job be her love. It wouldn't disappoint her. Leave her wanting. "It is what it is."

"I had no idea you were still working out of the Black Butte base."

"I left for three years and worked in Bend to get some experience elsewhere then came back."

There was a long pause. Apparently he'd been waiting on her to say more. When she didn't he asked, "Do you still live with your grandfather?"

"He passed away two years ago."

"Sorry to hear that. I know you were close."

Her grandfather had raised her but she wouldn't have said they were close. He'd done what he had to after her parents had left her with him. They went off to follow their dreams of being musicians. That ended when they died in a bus crash.

Dana walked faster, putting some distance between her and Travis. She had no interest in rehashing her life's story. Her job was to get him to Gunter's place, not to re-kindle their friendship. Those days were gone. He'd hurt her; as unintentional as it might have been, it had been another rejection. She refused to get to know him well enough to chance it happening again.

Heading up a rise, she turned to check on Travis. He wasn't far behind. She had to give him credit for that after the pace she'd been setting.

She'd radioed base letting them know their position before they had started walking and gave them the direction she intended to go. Along with that she reported the conditions and asked for a weather report. A front was rolling in quicker than expected. She and Travis needed to keep moving if they didn't want to sleep in the rain or a lightning storm.

"We've a couple of hours walk to Gunther's land with

another hour to the house, I estimate. We should reach him by this evening. If we continue to push on."

"Good, that means if we need to get him out we'll know by tomorrow morning when the weather will be to our favor."

After locating the hiking trail they started north along it.

Travis asked, "Do I smell smoke?"

"Yeah, but it's coming from miles away," she said over her shoulder.

"I like that idea. By the way, where are we?"

She heard him shift his pack. "Fuzztail Butte Trail."

"When we stop I'll have a look on my map."

"Is that a hint you need to rest?" Dana stepped around a boulder and he followed. They were climbing higher.

"I'll be ready to stop when you are."

She said nothing more and kept going. So did he need to rest?

"Dana, tell me how you've been."

Was Travis really interested? They had been such good friends for such a short time and then she'd messed that up. "I've been fine."

"I can see that. I want to know how you've been the last eight years."

Since she'd tried to kiss him. Or since he rejected her and she'd run off? "Why don't we start with you? Are you married with two-point-five kids and a dog?"

"Okay, I'll start but only if you promise to tell me something about yourself."

She gave him a noncommittal unladylike grunt. Why did he keep pushing her about her past?

Travis went on as if she hadn't responded. "Brittney and I did get married. It lasted almost three years. Six months if you really want the truth. Of that I'm not proud.

I have no children but still hope for some one day. Now your turn."

She heard the bitterness intertwined in his words. His marriage had failed. Despite her best effort, her heart went out to him. That had to have been difficult for him. Travis had been looking forward to this big, bright future he had planned. She started down a steep grade toward the sound of rushing water. Speaking loud enough she'd be heard, she said, "I finished forestry school. Worked summers as a firefighter while in college then was hired on full time."

"So you finished your Natural Resources Management degree?"

"Yes." Pride washed through her. First one in her family to go to college, much less finish. She'd paid her way through. Her grandfather hadn't the money to help her.

Travis's voice held a note of delight. "See, we're having fun now. I moved back to Redmond six months ago."

"I had no idea." If Dana had she would've been looking over her shoulder whenever she went out. When they returned she'd be doing just that.

"Yeah, I could see that by the look on your face this morning." Travis chuckled. "Small world."

"Yeah, or bad karma," she muttered.

"I finished medical school at the University of Southern California."

The air cooled as they moved closer to the water. "Fancy. I garden when I have time."

"No husband or children?"

"No." Her chest tightened. She hadn't found anyone who lived up to him. Or would stay around long enough to make that commitment.

He quickly came back with, "I live in a condo complex that I hate."

"You never did like being closed in."

"Nope. That hasn't changed." The words came from close behind her.

"What has changed about you?" She really wanted to know.

"I don't see life through rose-colored glasses any-more."

Travis should have expected this. How like Dana to ask a challenging question. He looked ahead at the woman moving like a warrior along the narrow, packed footpath. She was as sure-footed as he remembered. She moved in and around rocks without any appearance of effort.

And kept him from fixating on the pack on his back weighing him down that held life-sustaining necessities and the Pulaski tool he'd use to stop a fire. He shifted the backpack with his medical supplies hugging his chest. The water bottle that hung off his tool belt drew his attention as it slapped against his thigh. He considered himself in good shape but he'd forgotten the stamina it took to just walk in the wilderness. Even more aggravating was that Dana looked fresh as a spring morning while he suffered.

Even with the misery he moved in, he refused to ask Dana to stop. He wouldn't show weakness. As he followed her lead across the thin, high grass of a meadow, Travis could see how easily it could burn as the dry stalks bushed his legs.

"We'll stop down by the creek for a drink and rest," Dana announced halfway down the slope.

Travis tried not to appear overly grateful. When they reached the creek, Dana set the chain saw down, removed her pack and took a seat on a rock. She reached for her water bottle and took a long draw.

He watched with fascination as a rivet of water went down her neck. His already dry mouth went dusty. They were both hot, sweaty and dirty and all he could think about was watching that rivulet disappear beneath her T-shirt. He shook his head and turned his focus to a bug moving around a pebble.

There'd been something between them all those years ago and he still felt it. Sadly, her personality seemed prickly now. Was that in general or in particular to him? I didn't matter anyway. Dana was the type of woman who would want a relationship that involved security and longevity, something he couldn't, wouldn't offer. His short, disappointing marriage had cured him of that idea.

He found a boulder across from her and removed his equipment. After going to the creek, he went down on his knees and cupped water to splash his face. The frigid liquid felt refreshing on his heated skin. From the physical exertion and the mental activity, as well.

Returning to his rock, he pulled out his water and took a long drink. Sitting, he looked at Dana. She lay back in a stream of sunshine with her eyes closed. Since they'd met again it was the first time she looked peaceful. Was she always wound so tight? He lived like that with Brittney too much of the time. Easy, comfortable was what he was looking for in his life. "How much longer to Gunter's?"

Dana didn't open her eyes. "At the top of the rise should be his property line. From there it'll take us an hour. The walking will be harder because there's no trail."

"Great, that'll give me something to look forward to." He hadn't tried to keep the sarcasm out of his voice.

"We've been making good time. I want to be sure we're there before dark." She opened her eyes a slit. "So tell me why the US Forest Service is making this special trip in?"

"Because I convinced them they'd be saving a man's life."

"Who is this Mr. Gunter?"

"He's just one of those belligerent men who refuses to listen to reason. Who can't accept he's in the path of a wildfire and is deathly ill. I inherited him as a patient when I took over the practice. I speak to him weekly over the phone. He missed last week's call. He has kidney disease. He's getting close to needing dialysis and I'm worried he has already reached that point."

"When the fire grew it left him stranded," she finished for him.

"Yep." He pulled his map out of his pack and moved to sit beside her.

Her eyes widened. A breeze blew a length of hair across her face. She gave it an impatient push away.

"Would you mind showing me where we are? As the saying goes, if you aren't the lead dog you don't see the way."

"Are you calling me a dog?" She glared at him but her mouth twitched at one corner.

Travis sat straighter. It was nice to see Dana's humor return. "I am not. I've been happy to follow but I'd still appreciate you giving me some idea of where we are and where we're headed."

She took the map from him, spreading it out over the rock. Taking a minute, she located a spot and put her finger on it. "We're here. We're going here."

"Thanks." Travis studied the map, memorizing the area. "Why do you know so much about this range?"

"Because I fought a few fires in this area when I was

working out of the Bend station and also because I like to hike here when I can."

"Makes sense. Do you know Mr. Gunter?"

"Naw. Just heard of him."

"I know you didn't have a choice about coming, but I do appreciate it."

Dana stood. "It's part of the job. Get your equipment. We need to get moving."

He folded his map, stuffing it into his front breast pocket. "I'll carry the saw the rest of the way."

"I can handle it." There was a bite to her words.

"I didn't say you couldn't but I'd like to do my share."

She looked at him a moment then nodded. "Okay. If you insist."

They worked their way up the slope and out of the trees into another small meadow. The dry grass crunched under his feet.

"There's a chance we're going to get wet," Dana called over her shoulder.

Seconds later lightning flashed.

"We need to get out of this open area." Dana picked up her pace.

Travis joined her. The saw bounced on his shoulder. He was glad he'd decided to carry it instead of letting Dana.

They were almost to the trees when a clap of thunder rolled and lightning cracked not far ahead. An instant later the smell of sulfur filled the air.

Dana jerked to a stop. Her head popped up, nose going high. She reminded him of an animal sensing danger. He started past her. She grabbed his arm. "Wait. We don't need to go in the trees. It could be moving through the canopy."

"Fire?"

"Yes. That hit something."

She spoke into the radio on her shoulder. "Base. Over. This is Dana." She gave their location. "Lightning strike in my area. Can a lookout see smoke or is there an indication on the monitors of a hit? Over."

Now Travis smelled smoke. It had been years since he'd fought a fire and he wasn't looking forward to doing the job again, but it didn't look like he'd have a choice. He might be out of practice, yet once he'd been a good firefighter.

"Come back, Dana," the radio squawked. "We've a small line of smoke about half a mile from you to the northeast."

"I'm on it. Over."

Dana took the chain saw from him and started moving. "I hope you haven't forgotten your firefighting skills."

She didn't wait for him to rely. Ducking her head, she entered the trees. Travis had no choice but to follow. They weaved in and out of the trees at a speed he would've said was impossible. As they moved, the smell grew stronger. Smoke hung in the air above them.

All of a sudden flames shot up in a tree ahead of them. The tops of two trees blazed.

Dana set the saw down. "I'll get these down. They'll go that away." She pointed ahead of her. "You start creating a fire line behind me."

Travis removed the pack off his back, unstrapped the Pulaski before looking in the bag for his hard hat and eye protection. Those found, he pulled his leather gloves out of his back pocket. Dana adjusted her white helmet and pulled a lime-colored bandanna she wore around her neck up over her nose and mouth. Finding the navy one he'd brought in a side pocket, Travis followed suit.

He hurried to the spot Dana had indicated and started

pulling the debris on the ground back until he'd created a three footwide dirt area. The fire wouldn't have fuel to burn when it reached it and would go out. He worked as fast and efficiently as he could. The skill from years ago returned. Sweat ran down the center of his back and across his face but he kept going.

The saw roared to life and soon Dana had it grinding into a burning tree. Minutes later he heard the crack of the tree as it fell away from them. He looked up long enough to see her stepping to the other burning tree and doing the same procedure. In no time it was on the ground, as well. Travis continued digging.

"Travis," Dana called. "Let's get the tops of these put out then we can finish the line and secure the burn."

Dana started delimbing the first tree. She worked swiftly and efficiently. He remembered her being an enthusiastic firefighter but she acted as a well-seasoned one now. No wonder she'd earned the title of crew leader. He really hated she'd be missing out on her chance to lead for the first time because of him.

He stepped to a burning limb and used a flapper to beat the fire out. The wide flexible plastic on the end of a handle reminded him of a broom but was effective. He used his as well until they had smothered the fire. One spot continued to persistently blaze. Travis worked to extinguish it.

A quick snapping sound was all the notice he received before a small burning limb headed his direction. Seconds later it landed across his forearm. He jerked his arm back. A ragged hole with black edges showed in his shirt. He had no doubt he had at least a second-degree burn. Gritting his teeth, he had no time to stop and care for it. He kept moving.

Dana finished removing all the limbs from the felled

tree, then cut the tree into short lengths so that it could finish burning within a controlled area. With that done, she shut off the saw. Travis continued slapping while she joined in to help him. With the blaze out, Dana removed her gloves and went down on her hands and knees. She felt along the ground for hot spots. It was necessary to make sure the fire stayed out.

"Continue to work on the fire line," she called to him. "I'll do this and help you in a few minutes." She didn't wait on Travis to agree before her attention returned to the ground.

Sometime later she joined him as he worked the line around the area where the burned trees lay. They operated in tandem. He pulled the ground back and she made the zone wider. By the time they were through and she'd declared the fire completely out, it was twilight.

Dana stopped, took a chug from her water bottle and looked around for any smoke. She glanced at Travis who stood not far from her. "I'm impressed you've kept up your skills."

Travis took a long drink. "I don't think *kept* is the right adjective. They're more like returned out of necessity. I'd forgotten the energy required to do this job and the adrenaline rush it created."

"Thinking about changing careers?" She grinned, her eyes and teeth extra bright against her soot covered skin.

"Nope. I've found I can get the same rush from taking care of a patient. A calmer, peaceful life for me." He pushed back his helmet before wiping his forehead with his bandanna.

Dana hung her water bottle back on her belt. "If I remember correctly your mother wasn't happy about you being a smokejumper?"

"She thought it was too dangerous." He shrugged.

"But what could she do about it? I was grown and needed a job."

"I bet she brags about you being a doctor, doesn't she?" Dana took a long pull of water.

"Oh, yeah. She tells everyone who'll listen."

"And your dad?"

"Him too."

Suddenly Dana was jealous of Travis. He still had both his parents. Would her parents have been proud of her, if they had noticed she was alive? "Do your parents still live in Redmond?"

"My dad does. My mom is in California. They divorced just after I started medical school. They'd been having trouble for years. It was an ugly divorce. I guess it's the family legacy to not have good marriages."

"That sounds rather sad."

He picked up his tools. "It is. But that doesn't mean it isn't a fact. Mine certainly fell into the trap."

"What kind of trap was that?"

He didn't want to tell her. Was ashamed. Disappointed in himself for not seeing what Brittney was. "The kind that looks good on the outside but has no real substance."

"You loved her, didn't you?"

"I did for what I thought she was. Until I didn't. Maybe I didn't know what love was. Who knows? It doesn't matter now." He sighed. "You always had a way of getting me to talk about stuff I didn't want to. We haven't been together a day and I'm spilling my guts." He looked around them. "Will we be at Gunter's tonight or in the morning?"

"It'll be dark before we make it but if you're willing we'll do it." Dana picked up the chain saw and made her way toward their bags. She wished they could talk more. There was a need in her to know more about Travis. She shouldn't, it wasn't her business but despite everything she still cared about him.

He followed. "The idea of having a roof over my head and being out of the elements has an appeal. I'm anxious to check on Mr. Gunter."

"Then we move on."

"Agreed."

Fifteen minutes later they were hiking through the forest again.

"We should reach the road to Gunter's just after dark. The walking by flashlight will be easier then."

"That sounds nice." Travis shifted the chain saw on his shoulder. He'd picked it up before Dana had a chance after they gathered their bags.

She was in no mood to argue with him and glad not to carry the cumbersome piece of equipment. "By the way, you did a good job back there. I was glad you were there to help."

He grinned. "I'm glad I still remember what to do."

They were still trekking through the forest as the sun set.

Relief washed over Dana as they came to the small, rutted road leading to Gunter's cabin. Weary, she made an effort not to show it. "We only have about half a mile to go."

Travis moved forward to walk beside her as they continued west.

"Why don't you take the lead here?" Dana suggested when she saw the light from the cabin. "At least Mr. Gunter knows you. I don't want us to get shot."

"Makes sense to me." Travis moved a couple of steps ahead of her. "I hope he has something hot on the stove."

Travis wasn't the only one. The emotions and hard

work of the day had taken a toll on her. She didn't like being surprised. "Does he know you're coming?"

"I tried to call him but the service here is a little sketchy, but I'll try again." Travis fished out his cell phone and punched in a few numbers.

Dana heard the ringing but no response.

Travis dropped the phone back into a pants pocket. "I guess we're going to have to take our chances."

"On getting shot?" She was only half kidding. With recluses like Mr. Gunter, a person could never be sure what would happen.

"I'll call out when we get closer. Maybe that'll get a response."

They walked toward the cabin with Travis yelling Mr. Gunter's name but there was no reaction. They stepped under the small roof over the front door.

Travis called Mr. Gunter's name again. Still there was no answer. He knocked. Nothing. After going to a small dirty window, he looked inside. "Aw hell."

Dana rushed to the window.

Travis dropped the chain saw beside the door and opened it without announcing himself.

Dana stopped in the doorway. "Trav…" She saw a man lying on a single-size bed in a corner of the one-room cabin. He wasn't moving. Even in the dim light of a lantern she could see his skin was an ashen color.

Travis dropped his pack to the floor and went down on one knee beside the bed. He placed two fingers on the man's neck to check his pulse. "He's still alive."

Mr. Gunter's eyes fluttered open.

"Dr. Russell. What're you doing here?" the man mumbled.

"I came to get you off this burning mountain." Travis grabbed his medical backpack and pulled it to him.

"You shouldn't have come," the man murmured.

"Nonsense. That's what good doctors do for their patients. Even the stubborn ones. They take care of them." Travis's tone remained even but she could see from his quick actions his concern.

"I'd say you're going above and beyond the call of duty."

Dana would too. She'd known Travis years ago but he hadn't been a doctor then. How different was he? How much had life changed him? What she'd seen in the last eighteen hours had been impressive. Was there more to learn?

"Mr. Gunter, when did you start feeling bad?" Travis asked, the worry evident in his voice.

"Just after lunch."

Travis pulled the blanket back from the man's calf and touched it. Dana could see the wash of fluid under his skin.

"You're retaining fluid." Travis pulled a stethoscope out of the bag. He placed the bell on the man's chest and the tips in his ears. After listening, he wrapped the instrument around his neck. "Irregular heartbeat and shortness of breath. Gunter, you're in failure. This is what I was afraid of. We've got to get you out of here and on dialysis ASAP."

The man weakly tried to sit up. "I can't leave my home."

"You don't have a choice." Travis's firm tone made Dana straighten. He placed a hand to Mr. Gunter's shoulder and had him lay back. "Where's your medicine?"

The man pointed to a rough wood box hanging near the rear door. A large metal bowl sat below it on a stand.

"I'll get it." Dana hurried to it. After opening the box,

she scooped up five prescription bottles and dumped them on the bed within Travis's reach.

He searched through them. Selecting a bottle, he removed two pills. "Dana, will you see if you can find some clean drinking water?"

"There's a well outside." Mr. Gunter pointed toward the back door.

Dana nodded. She passed a small potbelly stove with a rocker beside it and a book in the seat on her way to the kitchen area in the opposite corner. Picking up a jug, she then headed out the back door leaving it open so she had enough light to see.

She found a hand-pump well ten steps outside the door. It wasn't something she had much experience with but she knew the basics. Giving the handle three pushes up and down to prime the pump, she held the wide-mouthed jug under the spigot. Soon water flowed. Returning inside, she took a glass off an open shelf and filled it. She went to the bedside.

Mr. Gunter looked at her but spoke to Travis as he helped the man sit up. "Who's the pretty girl?"

"Her name is Dana Warren. She works for the US Forest Service. She brought me up here." Travis put the two tablets in Mr. Gunter's mouth. After taking the glass from her, Travis offered it to the man.

"Not too much now," Travis told Mr. Gunter. "We need to get some of this fluid off you before you eat or drink anything."

"You shouldn't have come," Mr. Gunter said.

"I couldn't get in touch with you. Apparently I was right. In your condition you don't need to stay here. If the fire makes it here—"

"That's what they say every year. I've lived up here fifty years in the same cabin. It's never gonna happen."

Travis shook his head. "That might be the case but that still doesn't mean you don't need medical care."

Dana couldn't help but be impressed with the even tone Travis used when she wanted to shake the old man for being so stubborn. "This time it's headed your way."

"We'll see about that, missy." Mr. Gunter pierced her with a look.

"The name is Dana."

Travis gave her a warning look. "I hate to put you on food duty but would you mind seeing if you can find some soup or something light for him?"

"I don't want no federal government employee messing around in my kitchen," the old man grumbled. "Can't trust a Fed."

"Well, this one you can. And you're not strong enough to stop her anyway. I hope you don't mind us sharing your food. I'd like a hot meal instead of freeze-dried beef. I'll see that it's replaced when we get to town." Travis pulled a blood pressure cuff out of his bag. "Now lie back and rest."

The old man grunted and did as Travis said.

Picking up her radio, Dana started toward the door. "I'll see what I can come up with but I need to report in first."

"Okay. Ask base to call Rescue. We're going to need a chopper here at daylight."

"Will do." Dana stepped out on the porch to make her call. After a brief discussion she returned inside. "The weather is turning for the better. The helicopter will be here in the morning. We're to meet it in an open field about two miles southeast of here. Mr. Gunter, I hope you have some transportation."

The old man grunted. "A four-wheeler in the shed out back."

Travis picked up the man's wrist and took his pulse. "Not what I'd hoped for but we'll make it work."

Dana turned to the kitchen. As she worked to put some food together she heard Mr. Gunter say in a loud whisper. "I need to piss."

"That's good to hear." Travis rose from the chair he'd pulled beside the bed. "That's what I wanted you to do to get that fluid off your body. I'd hate for you to die after you've put me to so much trouble to get here. I even had to fight a fire. Let's go outside."

A low rumble of a chuckle came from Mr. Gunter. "Fight a fire, did ye?"

"Yep." Travis helped the man to his feet.

Dana grinned. She had to admit Travis had a nice bedside manner. She bet a lot of women had experience it firsthand. She wouldn't be one of them.

CHAPTER THREE

TRAVIS GLANCED BACK at Dana as his patient shuffled beside him. She'd been smiling, then a stricken look came over her face. What had she been thinking?

She didn't seem to fit in a slot like most women he knew. It had been his experience that women were either interested in money, position or a good time. Some in all the above. Dana had grown up and into her own person. She did a tough job with grit and expertise, and more determination than he could imagine anyone else giving such a strenuous profession.

Yet through it all, he'd caught glimpses of concern for him and Mr. Gunter. He couldn't help but be fascinated by her. He'd like to learn what made Dana tick, who she had become. She hadn't been very forthcoming on their hike. Had something happened to her or had someone hurt her?

By the time he'd returned with Mr. Gunter and settled him in the bed, Dana had something bubbling on the stove and stood looking inside a mini refrigerator. She pulled out a block of cheese. Glancing at Mr. Gunter, Travis found him sleeping. He'd let the man do so while Travis and Dana ate.

Stepping over to her, he leaned over her shoulder speaking softly, not wanting to disturb his patient. "Smells good."

Dana took a step to the side. Following his lead she kept her voice down. "It's stew. I found some cans and opened them. No big deal."

He took a step back. "It is if you're hungry. Which I am. What can I do to help?"

"Pour a couple of glasses of water. I'll put the stew in bowls. I'm going to put one to the side too cool for Mr. Gunter."

While he did as she asked, Dana sliced cheese, put it on a plate and placed it on the small but functional table under one of the two windows.

As she turned back to the kitchen, she bumped into him. A zip of awareness traveled up his arm and out through his body. This reaction to Dana wasn't something he expected. Hell, he'd not planned on Dana at all.

"Sorry. This place is tiny." She hurried on.

"Functional is the intent, I believe." He pulled the chair he'd been using up to the table and waited beside it for her to bring their food.

Dana brought their bowls and set them on the table.

He took a chair. His knees knocked hers as he pulled up. Dana quickly shifted hers to the side. She acted skittish about every contact with him. What was she afraid of? He picked up his spoon, filled it. "Mmm…good."

She followed suit. "I wasn't sure how it'd turn out. I've limited skills on a two-eye gas hot plate."

Travis lifted a spoonful to his lips. "Gourmet if you ask me."

"Now you're getting carried away. How is Mr. Gunter doing?"

"Worse than I had hoped I'd find him. I'm just glad I

didn't wait any longer to come after him. The fire's the least of his worries."

She placed her hand briefly on top of the burn on his forearm. "Don't worry—we'll get him out tomorrow."

He winced and pulled away. "I'm counting on that. He needs attention I can't give him except at a hospital."

Dana looked down at his arm. Alarm filled her voice. "You're burnt, aren't you? Why didn't you say anything?"

"Because there wasn't enough daylight to spend time on me."

She reached for his hand and brought his arm closer, unbuttoning his cuff. "Travis, you still should've said something." She rolled the material back and hissed. "Oh, Travis. This must be painful."

"I can't argue with that." His lips formed a tight line. It did hurt.

Dana pushed back from the table. "I'm cleaning and bandaging this right now."

"No, you're not. Right now, you're going to finish your food. I'll see Mr. Gunter is fed and then I'll let you patch me up."

"I'll agree, but only if I feed Mr. Gunter while you clean up. Are you in any pain?"

"Only when I think about it." *Which is pretty much all the time except when I'm wondering about you.*

Her brow wrinkled as she studied him. "Have you taken anything for it?"

"A couple of pain relievers a few minutes ago."

She nodded. "Good."

In an effort to get the discussion off him, Travis said, "I'd heard of these remote cabins but I've never been in one."

"Yeah, a number of them were built as fire lookouts

by the CCC boys during the depression." Dana continued to eat.

"CCC boys?"

"Civilian Conservation Corps. They were a voluntary
group of unemployed, unmarried males between their
late teens and early twenties. President Franklin Roo-
sevelt started the program to put young men to work."

"How do you know so much about them?"

She filled her spoon. "Forestry school. And I like history. I've read a lot about the national forests."

"You really love what you do."

She nodded. "Yeah, I really like my job."

"I like mine, as well. It's one thing I've gotten right."

Dana studied him a moment before she dipped her
head to the side toward Mr. Gunter. "I can tell you're
good at your job."

"Thanks. I like to think I am."

She looked at him. "The one thing you got right...
Surely that's not true."

Travis leaned back in his chair. This discussion had
gone deeper than pleasant dinner conversation. "Let's just
say that all the plans I'd made outside of medical school
crashed and burned. I moved back to Redmond to start
over fresh and I don't make plans anymore. I just live
and enjoy what comes my way."

"Kind of sounds sad to me."

"Maybe so, but certainly more realistic." That happy
marriage, good job, house, swimming pool and kids
hadn't worked out as he planned. He'd given up on them.
He finished his soup and pushed back from the table.

Despite the conversation turning uncomfortable he
liked talking to Dana. It was the most civil and open she
had been since they had met again. For once he hadn't
had to pry information out of her. She'd maintained a dis-

tance between them all day, keeping herself closed off where none of the simple friendship they'd shared that long-ago summer could return. Their chat had consisted of short verbal remarks. He wanted to find that easiness they'd once had.

Dana gathered the used dishes. "I'll see about these while you shower."

"Are you giving the orders now?" Travis kept his tone light as he picked up his bowl.

"I thought I made it clear I was giving them before we got on the plane."

He chuckled. "Yeah, you did. But I think I should be leader now since we're in my patient's house."

Dana stepped toward him. Her neck having to crane to look him in the eyes. Her voice went low and tight, "Maybe so, but I think I'll keep the position."

Travis took a step into her personal space. He could see the flash of hesitation go through her eyes but she didn't move. Dana was strong. She'd gained that confidence since he'd last known her. He respected it. "I tell you what, when we're in the cabin I run the show. When we're outside you do."

"Okay, but I'll agree only after you clean up and let me bandage your arm. I don't need two sick men on my hands."

"Deal." Travis offered his hand.

Dana looked at it a moment as if deciding if it would be safe to take it. Finally she slipped her hand into his. Her palm didn't have the soft, pampered skin of a woman who led the easy life. Instead there was strength and purpose in her grip. The thought he could depend on her ran through his mind. She was the type of person who'd stand beside someone she loved during hard times and good times.

"I'll feed Mr. Gunter while you shower. I noticed a handmade shower attached to the back wall. My guess is that the barrel is full of rain water. Use all you want. We can't use it as drinking water. There's a well for that."

"Sounds refreshing." His mouth pulled. She giggled. The sound rippled through him leaving him wanting more. "Nice way to say freezing cold especially since temperatures can get down pretty low at night around here even during the middle of summer."

An icy shower might clear his head where Dana was concerned. The chance to take grime off would be a pleasure. Fighting fire wasn't clean work.

She moved into the kitchen. "Please be careful around that burn."

"Yes, ma'am, boss."

She smirked. "I'm not fond of that tone."

He grinned. "My apologies but I do want to point out you're giving orders inside the cabin."

One corner of her lips lifted slightly. "I'll try to make it my last one."

As he went out the back door she called with laughter in her voice, "Don't take all the hot water."

He groaned. "I'll try not to."

The tiny three-sided enclosure, the third being the side of the cabin, was situated to the right of the back stoop. He'd bathed in questionable places before, including under a hose but nothing like this. On a platform above his head was a large drum with a showerhead valve screwed into it. The floor consisted of gravel.

After putting his flashlight down on the bench just out of the water's range, Travis stripped out of his clothes, hanging them on a nail hammered into the side of the cabin. He placed his boots nearby. He picked up the bar of soap off the bench and turned the tap then stepped under the water. With a great deal of effort he stopped himself from squealing like a girl and settled for a manly yelp. He twisted the water off then soaped up. Taking a deep breath, he released the water again to rinse off. There was something freeing about taking a shower out in nature. If it only hadn't been so blasted cold. He'd brought his extra T-shirt to use as a towel. After pulling his pants on and leaving his boots untied, he hustled inside to finish dressing beside the potbelly stove.

Dana looked at him from where she sat beside Mr. Gunter. Her eyes went wide and her mouth fell open. "Invigorating shower?"

"That would be an understatement." Travis pulled on his dirty T-shirt enjoying her shocked but interested look.

"I'm proud of that shower." Mr. Gunter sat up in bed, cushioned by pillows behind his back.

Even in the dim light from the two lamps in the room Travis could tell his color had improved. Travis worked to keep his teeth from chattering. "It's a nice shower. I just wish it had a hot water valve."

"It's warm when the sun is shining on it," Mr. Gunter assured him.

Travis turned his back to the stove. "I'll keep that in mind for next time."

"Mr. Gunter, can I get you something before I bandage Travis's arm?" Dana stood with an empty bowl in her hand.

"I need to go outside again." The old man moved to rise.

"I'll help you with that." Travis hurried to the bed.

"I'll get my bag and be waiting at the table." Dana passed him on the way to the kitchen.

Travis helped Mr. Gunter outside. When he returned,

Travis settled the old man in the bed, then took the same chair he used during their meal.

Dana had supplies spread out on the table. "Okay. It's your turn to be patient. Put your arm on the table."

"Please." Travis gave her an expectant look.

Her eyes snapped. "Please."

Travis placed his arm where she could clearly see it. She examined the burn closely but didn't touch him. Was she afraid to?

Her lips formed a grim line. "That's a solid second-degree burn, close to a third. You're lucky it's not worse."

"It would've been if I hadn't knocked the limb off." He liked having Dana concerned about him.

"You should've said something." Her words were a rebuke.

"It wouldn't have mattered. We didn't have the time to stop and see about it."

"Tender?" Her head remained down as her finger probed the skin around the burn.

"Yeah."

"The blister doesn't need to rupture. If it does you'll know real pain." She wiped the area around it with an alcohol pad.

Travis said in a teasing tone, "You do care."

Her eyes flickered up to meet his then lowered again. She pulled in her bottom lip as she worked. Fanning the area dry, she then opened a two-by-two package of gauze pads. She squeezed ointment onto them and laid them over the wound. "When this needs to be changed, you'll want the bandage to come off easily."

She picked up a small roll of gaze and began rolling it around and over the pads until the area was well covered. "I want you to keep this dry and clean."

"Are you sure you're not a doctor, as well?" Dana had no trouble taking control.

"Nope, my calling is smokejumping but I do take my skills as an EMT seriously."

He watched her face. "My guess would be that you take most things seriously."

"What does that mean?"

Travis saw the slight tightening of her lips. "I just remember you were quick with a laugh and a smile. Now, not so much." He watched her. "What happened, Dana?"

She met his gaze. "I don't know what you mean."

"I suspect you do."

Dana made no comment as she finished applying tape to the end of the gauze. With efficacy, she repacked her bag. "I'm gonna clean up. It's a treat to have a place to do so when I'm out in the field. Normally I don't get a bath for a number of days."

"Says the person who hasn't stood under the water that melted from an iceberg." Travis glanced at Mr. Gunter and moved to the stove.

She giggled.

There was that sound again. The one that gripped his middle. The one that seemed to slip out unguarded when he least expected it.

Gathering her personal gear bag and a flashlight, Dana started toward the back door.

"I left my extra T-shirt for you to use as a towel," Travis called.

A few minutes later he smiled when a squeal reached his ears.

Dana stepped into the shower stall, enjoying the full moon which meant she didn't need her flashlight. Travis's T-shirt hung on a nail. She didn't intend to use it.

Something about the idea of having Travis's undercloth-ing against her body disturbed her. The warmth of it. His smell. The fact he still got to her.

At dinner she'd forgotten her hurt and found him a charming dinner partner yet sad when he'd spoken about his disappointment in how his life had gone. He'd seemed genuinely interested in what she had told him. Today they had worked together just as they had years ago. What re-ally ate at her was she still liked him.

When he'd come into the cabin after his shower with-out a shirt on her eyes had soaked him in. Travis may not have been a smokejumper in the last few years but he had obviously kept in shape. She tried not to stare but hadn't been successful. It had taken him clearing his throat to make her blink and refocus elsewhere. He had been aware of her interest. That disturbed her the most.

Getting involved with Travis wasn't a path she needed to follow. They'd only be together until tomorrow. In less than twenty-four hours they'd be back to their own lives, just as it had been before she'd walked into Leo's office.

Stepping under the water, she couldn't help but squeal. Travis had been correct. It was freezing. With teeth chat-tering and body shivering, she soaped up. The smell of smoke lingered in her hair. One of many things her ex-boyfriend had gradually grown to hate. It took at least three hair washings for the smell to wear off. She kept her hair shoulder length or above just for that reason.

Taking a deep breath to fortify herself, she turned on the tap again and rinsed off. Unable to help herself with the need to ease the cold, she snatched Travis's shirt off the nail and toweled off. It was soft and large enough to do the job. Her hands shook as she pulled on her panties and sports bra, then her T-shirt.

"Oh," she yelped when she stubbed her little toe on the leg of the bench.

Seconds later the door to the cabin opened and Travis came around the corner of the shower. "Dana? Are you all right?"

Travis stopped short. Stood there. She stared back. Why, she had no idea. She was used to very little privacy, knew that her job and her respect depended on it. But this wasn't one of the guys she worked with. This was Travis. A quiver went through her having nothing to do with the water temperature or the cool of the night. Even in the dim light Travis's look said he saw something he liked.

"I'm sorry." He turned his back to her. "Are you okay? Did you see a bear? You yelled."

"I'm fine. I hit my toe on the bench." He wasn't moving to go inside. "You were staring again."

"Men do that when they see a half-dressed woman." She huffed. "You never noticed before."

"I noticed. I was in a relationship and we were on the same team. Time and place was wrong." There was an edge to his voice.

"I know."

"That doesn't mean I wasn't aware."

Her heart hopped into her throat. Her mind might not have wanted to hear the words but her body sure reacted to them. She'd turned hot all over. "Do you mind leaving so I can finish dressing?"

"Don't take too long or I'll get worried."

Taking a shower may not have been the best choice, especially since Travis's look had steam forming on her body. She wasn't inexperienced and knew enough to recognize when a man was attracted to her. Never had Travis given her such an intense look. She quickly pulled on her pants and slipped her feet into her boots.

When she returned inside, Travis was busy taking Mr. Gunter's vitals as the man dozed.

She quietly put her belongings away. "We need to get some rest. We'll have to be up early to meet the helicopter."

"You go ahead. I'm gonna sit up with him tonight." Travis had pulled the chair back over beside Mr. Gunter's bed.

She took her sleeping bag out of her bag. "You're going to need some sleep, as well."

"I'll say, it has been an unexpectedly busy day."

Dana couldn't remember another one like it. "Wake me at two and I'll relieve you." She rolled her sleeping bag out near the stove and crawled in. Seconds later she shimmied out of her pants and put them in a pile next to the bag. Using her arm as a pillow, she closed her eyes.

"Dana, it's been nice to see you again."

She wouldn't let herself look at Travis yet it took her longer than normal to go to sleep.

What felt like seconds later, the floor creaked beside her. Her eyelids popped open to see two sock-covered feet. Her look traveled up long legs to a gently curved butt over narrow hips to a broad back and wide shoulders. "What time is it?"

"Three a.m."

"I thought I told you I'd get up at two and relieve you." She scrambled out of the sleeping bag then pulled it back up over her hips.

"You were snoring so sweetly I hated to wake you. I got some sleep sitting in the chair."

"Turn around while I pull on my pants, would you?

I can do it inside the sleeping bag but it's quicker and easier out of it."

"Sure, I'll put some wood on the fire." He turned away and picked up one of the split logs beside the stove.

"What do I need to watch for with Mr. Gunter?" She finished buttoning her pants.

"Wake me if he develops a fever or becomes agitated."

Dana moved over to the bed as Travis turned. "Take my sleeping bag. There's no point in pulling another out."

Travis woke to the sounds of movement in the kitchen. Through the window the sky had yet to lighten. He'd slept much heavier than he intended. He pulled on his pants while still inside the bag which brought on a groan. Stiffness from yesterday's activities and sleeping on the floor, none of which he was used to, had found a home in each of his joints.

He climbed out of the bag, then stretched his shoulders back and forth. He wasn't used to that type of work he'd done over the last few hours. Apparently he'd become soft through the years.

Dana's back remained to him so he had a moment to study her. There wasn't a spare ounce of fat on her. She'd pulled her hair back at her neck leaving a small stub that stuck out. Some hung around her face that she gave an impatient push every now and then with her hand.

She worked at cutting cheese. Her movements were efficient and minimal. There was nothing fussy about her. A pot boiled on one surface of the stove. She glanced over her shoulder as if she realized he watched her.

"Mornin'," he said to her but looked at Mr. Gunter. "How did things go last night? I didn't mean to sleep so long." Travis rubbed the stubble along his jaw. It already itched. He needed to shave but that wouldn't be happening until he returned to civilization.

"Good morning. Breakfast will be ready in a few minutes. I'm warming up something for Mr. Gunter."

Travis took a second to check on his patient, grabbed his shirt then stepped out the back door. He returned with his face washed, shirt buttoned and tucked in. Sitting beside Mr. Gunter, who could hardly keep his eyes open, Travis checked his vital signs.

Dana joined him with a bowl in her hand. "Left over stew broth. He did pretty good last night. Slept through me checking on him."

"Good. I'll take care of feeding him." Travis took the bowl from her. "You eat."

For once she did as he suggested. Mr. Gunter ate hardly anything.

Dana finished her meal. "I'm going out to talk to base to confirm the rendezvous point."

"If I'm not here when you come back in, I'm out back seeing about the ATV." He could eat later.

Travis had the machine started when Dana came around the side of the house. He turned it off and checked the gas and oil. "I've been thinking if I can find a couple of boards to lay across the basket and strap them to it, then put the mattress of the bed on top of that, we could get him down the road easier. Maybe cover them with our sleeping bags because they're warmer than his blankets."

Dana came to stand across the four-wheeler from him. "Sounds like it would work."

"This isn't going to be a fun ride for him." Travis added a sarcastic lift to the corner of his mouth. He looked around for boards but seeing none, he started toward the back of the shed.

"It'll be better than walking." Dana followed him.

"Can't argue with that. Either way it has to be done. The fluid is building up in his body to a dangerous point. I doubled his meds."

Behind the shed he found a stack on rough old lumber. "These'll have to do." Picking up two boards, Travis carried them to the four-wheeler and laid them across the wide but low metal basket behind the seat. "I'm worried we can secure them tight enough."

"How about nailing cross boards and using them to hold it in place," Dana suggested.

"That would work," he looked around, "if we can come up with nails, hammer and a saw."

"Surely he has those around here somewhere. Would have to have them to survive up here by himself." Dana walked farther inside the shed.

Travis followed. By the time he came to stand beside her, Dana had found a handsaw. She pulled a rusty can toward him. "You find a hammer and I'll meet you outside."

"Okay." He found a hammer lying on the bench and headed to the four-wheeler.

Dana passed him. "I'll get another board. We need to be getting on the way. The helicopter can't wait, especially if the wind picks up."

"Is that supposed to happen?"

She called over her shoulder. "Yeah. And we need them to get all three of us on board."

A minute later she returned with a board in hand. He took it from her and measured the width against the wood they already had. He quickly cut the two boards required. Positioning the cross boards so they sat the distance of the sides of the basket. He hammered the nails into place while Dana held the boards. After flipping the platform over, they put it in the correct spot.

"Now all we need is some rope or straps," Dana announced with her hands on her hips.

"I saw rope in the shed. I'll get it." Travis headed into the shed, soon returning.

Together they wrapped the rope around the platform so it wouldn't move backward or forward.

Pleased, Travis stood back. "Looks good."

"I'll put the tools away. You get Mr. Gunter." Dana gathered the tools.

Travis headed inside the cabin. "Mr. Gunter, we need to go."

The man opened his eyes.

"I need you to sit in the rocker for a few minutes. Can you do that?"

"Sure I can. Can even walk there." The older man moved to sit up.

Travis helped him. In reality the man didn't even have the strength he thought he did. While helping Mr. Gunter, Travis heard the engine of the ATV roar as Dana moved it around to the front of the house. Travis settled Mr. Gunter, then picked up the mattress and carried it outside. Laying it over the boards, Travis returned for Mr. Gunter.

Dana gathered their bags and carried a load out ahead of him. She waited beside the four-wheeler. "I'll help you get Mr. Gunter on."

Together they half lifted, half pushed Mr. Gunter up on the mattress.

Dana had already laid out one of the sleeping bags. She returned to the cabin while Travis covered Mr. Gunter with the other sleeping bag. Dana came out with the last of their bags in hand. Dana gave him his packs, then she fixed hers across her chest.

Travis placed one large bag in front of the steering wheel. The other would ride between the driver's legs.

They tied the sheet off the bed to the back side of the basket and to the front, making Mr. Gunter as secure as possible. Done, Dana picked up the chain saw.

"Put that between Mr. Gunter's feet. You drive. Your legs are shorter and you can sit farther up. I can hold the saw with one hand." He climbed on. "This is gonna be a tight fit."

Dana pursed her lips, her eyes holding a determined look. She took her seat, her hips fitting tightly against his and her back pressed along his chest. Her hair brushed his chin, a few strands getting caught in his stubble.

"Ready?" Dana asked.

"Ready." Travis placed an arm around her waist to support himself when she took off.

On a deep exhale, she turned the key and started the four-wheeler.

Travis couldn't deny being aware of Dana pressed so close yet it wasn't something he planned to act on. He'd hurt her once and he wouldn't do it again. He wasn't that guy she'd once thought he was. Life had hardened him.

Despite the bumpy ride, Dana tried to keep the four-wheeler out of the ruts with little success. Her concentration remained on the road, hoping to lessen the difficult ride for Mr. Gunter. It made the trip slow going. She glanced at her watch. It would be daylight soon. They couldn't miss the helicopter.

They were traveling through a tunnel of large timber, tall enough to block out most of the morning light. She glanced up to see the wind blowing the tops of the trees. The motor drowned out the sounds of birds or animals making their morning movements. What she did know about was the heat of Travis's body pressed against hers.

The whole scenario of the day before, and this morning, was something she wouldn't have imagined in her wildest dreams. She tried not to think about Travis and focused on her job. She'd promised herself never to let another man get into her head like her ex-boyfriend had, or before him, Travis. She couldn't let another person hurt her. It was too scary, too difficult, too much work to function again. She'd hold her emotions close and concentrate on her job and the satisfaction she received from doing it well. So far that had worked. Travis showing up again wouldn't change anything.

They came to a spot where they needed to ford a creek. "Hold on to Mr. Gunter. There's no good way to cross the rocks."

Travis removed his hand from around her. Apparently he now had both behind him, one holding Mr. Gunter.

"How much farther?" Travis asked, his hand returning to her waist. His mouth lay close enough his lips brushed her ear.

Just a few more miles, then a ride home and Travis would be gone.

"Not too much."

Dana kept them moving at a slow, steady pace. Wind having nothing to do with the movement of the ATV buffeted them. She raised her head. The slightest hint of smoke filled her nose. Was the fire moving faster?

"Smoke."

Travis had smelled it too.

Thankfully the narrow strip of road smoothed out and she increased her speed. Soon they left the woods riding into a meadow. The space would be large enough for the rescue helicopter to lower a basket to get Mr. Gunter but not great enough to land. Being in a dense area of the forest with no other roads made rescues problematic.

Dana blinked, adjusting her sight as they came out

of the dimness of the trees into the bright sunlight. She pulled into the center of the field and turned off the engine.

The whop-whop of blades announced the helicopter flew nearby. *Good timing.*

Climbing off the four-wheeler, she made sure she didn't rub against Travis any more than necessary. She radioed the helicopter pilot, letting him know they were in place. As she did so she watched Travis remove the sheet securing Mr. Gunter.

The man's skin had gone ashen again but his eyes were open.

"They're sending a basket first," she called out to Travis.

He nodded and returned to checking his patient's vitals.

Moments later the helicopter came down to treetop level and hovered over the center of the field. A human-size metal basket was lowered. It swung wildly in the wind. Dana reached out to catch the basket just as it swayed away. Seconds later it rocketed toward her. Strong arms grabbed her and jerked her out of the way.

"Are you trying to kill yourself? I don't need two patients!" Travis's words shot like bullets as they stumbled backward. He finally brought them to a standstill well out of range of the basket.

He released her as the basket bounced against the ground. "Let's get Mr. Gunter on this thing before the weather turns worse."

Together they lifted the man off the ATV. With the support of Travis on one side and her on the other, they managed to get their patient lying in the basket. Travis placed the enclosed blanket over Mr. Gunter. Dana saw to it the straps were secured over him.

Mr. Gunter looked first at Travis and then to her. "My cabin?"

"It'll be fine," Travis assured him.

"It's all I have." The old man reached a hand out, his rheumy eyes pleading.

The radio squawked. "We need to do this. The wind's picking up."

"We're ready down here. Pull him up." Dana said into the radio. She and Travis stood back allowing plenty of room.

The basket swung once so violently she feared for Mr. Gunter. The basket had just been pulled inside when the wind lashed the helicopter pushing it to the right.

"We can't hold here any longer." The pilot voice came over the radio. "Sorry. You'll have to return to base."

Dana's chest tightened with anxiety as she watched the helicopter disappear over the top of the trees and into the horizon. She glanced a Travis. They'd be together longer than she'd anticipated or wished.

CHAPTER FOUR

TRAVIS CONTEMPLATED THE fact that his and Dana's ride out of a burning forest had just flown away. This trip had turned into more than he'd bargained for in more ways than one. He looked at Dana. She'd been completely unexpected. They'd be spending even more time together.

"Understood." Dana spoke into the radio. Her voice filled with disappointment. Her gaze met his.

She didn't look any happier about the situation than he was. He had a practice he needed to get back to. One night roughing it was one thing, two was another. Losing days of work for one patient hadn't been his idea.

She took a few steps back and said flatly into the radio, "Base, it's Dana. The wind has increased. Rescue couldn't pick up Dr. Russell and me. We're returning to Gunter's cabin. We'll secure it and walk out."

"Ten-four," came back over the radio. "Be advised the fire has turned."

"Ten-four. What's the weather report?"

Base came back. "By evening, front should have passed through. It should be a calm night."

"Ten-four. I'll check in again this evening."

"Ten-four."

Travis ran a hand through his hair. "I guess we're in for a hike."

"Yep. You up for it?"

He shrugged. "I don't think I have a choice."

"You don't. Let's get busy securing Gunter's cabin." She started toward the ATV. "Then we'll be on our way out."

"I'm driving back," Travis announced.

Dana whirled to face him. "Don't think you're going to start giving me orders."

He took a step toward her. "All I want is to do the driving."

"You can ask instead of giving an order," she snapped back.

"I didn't realize I was giving an order. You don't always have to have the final word in a situation."

For a second she looked as if he'd slapped her, then she glared at him. "It sounded like an order to me."

Travis walked back to the ATV. "Instead of standing here arguing let's get started back. If that fire picks up again I want to be hell and gone from here."

A contrite look came over Dana's face before she hung her head. "I'm sorry. You didn't deserve that pettiness. This situation has taken on a life of its own. We're both on edge."

"I have to say life is more interesting around you." To Travis's surprise there was some real truth to that. Compared to the last twenty-four hours, his world looked dull. Being out of the norm added some spice to his ordered, comfortable life.

Dana came over to him. "Let's go. Thankfully right now the fire isn't nipping at our heels and I want to keep it that way. You can drive."

"Sounds like a solid plan." Travis slung a leg over the ATV and settled on the seat.

Dana placed a hand on his shoulder and slid up behind him. He started the ATV. As they rode over rough terrain, Dana grabbed the sides of his shirt. Despite the distance, Dana never relaxed. He felt the tension in her body as if she feared any contact between them.

At one time they had been friends. Shared a companionship that he'd never had with another woman. After what had happened between them years ago he didn't expect her to let go completely of her animosity, but by now he wouldn't have thought she'd still be hanging on to it so tightly. They needed to clear the air. Ease the strain between them.

The return trip went much faster. He pulled up to Mr. Gunter's cabin. Dana climbed off the ATV as soon as he stopped.

Travis turned on the seat. "About what happened years ago—"

"That was my fault. A silly girl-crush." She started toward the back of the ATV.

He continued to watch her. "Please look at me, Dana." She finally did.

"I didn't think it was silly."

"I embarrassed myself and you. I shouldn't have tried to kiss you. I shouldn't have put you in that position. I knew you had a girlfriend."

"Hey, it was a heat of the moment thing. I was flattered." After he got over the initial surprise.

He knew what being unfaithful did to a relationship, since his father slowly killed his mother with his extramarital affairs. Travis promised himself he'd never do that to someone he loved. It caused too much damage and pain. Being faithful had been important to him. That's why it had crushed him so when his ex-wife had run around on him.

"We were friends and I ruined that." She removed the chain saw from the back of the four-wheeler.

"I should've done a better job of letting you down. I've always been your friend."

She said over her shoulder, "It's all good."

He stepped off the ATV. For some reason it really mattered to him that they returned to that friendship of old. "Is it? I'd like it if we could still be friends."

"We can try. Right now, though, we need to get started on securing this area. I can't guarantee the cabin won't burn but we can at least give it a chance. You start on a fire line. I'll cut back the brush. Less fuel we give the fire the better." She raised her head. "What we need to do is hope the wind doesn't pick up. If it does it won't matter what we do."

Dana had gone into smokejumper mode. Had closed him and their discussion off.

"You start in the shed. See if there're any gas cans or flammables. What we don't need we'll bury along with anything else inside that might survive. We'll water down what we can, the best we can. Maybe that'll stop the worst of it. I'll stay in touch with base for the latest weather changes. That should give us a day's worth of work. If all remains as is, we'll stay here tonight and start out tomorrow morning. If not, we'll have to hotfoot it ahead of it."

He stood straighter. "Yes, boss."

Dana pursed her lips, giving him a contrite look. "We agreed that when we're outside I'm the boss. Let's get started. I'll start cutting back brush." She didn't give him time to respond before she started checking the chain saw. "Bring any gas or oil you find and leave it here for me. I may need it."

Travis started around the cabin. Dana knew her job.

"Hey, Travis, take the four-wheeler with you."

"We can't ride it out?"

She shook her head. "The terrain is too rough. No

roads. Only footpaths. If we're lucky. We'll be making our own path most of the time. Put it under the shed and see if you can syphon the gas out."

"Will do."

He had some difficulty finding a hose to use to remove the gas but he finally found a piece of rubber tubing on a shelf in the back of the shed. With a gas can sitting on the running board of the ATV ready, he put one end of the tube in the gas of the ATV and the other in his mouth. He sucked.

"Travis!" Dana's high pitch scream filled the air.

Gas entered his mouth and he quickly spit it out as he ran toward the front of the cabin where he'd last heard the sound of the chain saw. He slid to a stop. A large rattlesnake sat curled in front of her with its head reared high and its tail rattling. Dana stood back against a large tree. If she moved the snake could strike her.

Her attention didn't leave the snake. "Help me, Travis."

The desperation in her voice went straight to his heart and seized it. She depended on him. This tough woman must be deadly afraid of snakes to have that begging note in her voice. "Don't move."

A limb she'd just cut lay nearby. He snatched it up and slowly dragged it over the ground, distracting the snake from Dana. "Slowly move behind the tree."

Keeping her back to the tree, Dana stepped around it and to safety.

Travis dropped the limb and took a wide path around the rattler until he reached Dana. Her eyes were wide with fear and she shook. He reached out his hand and she took it. They slowly moved away from the area.

As soon as they were out of harm's way she removed her hand from his. She stood with her eyes closed taking heaving breaths. Her eyes opened. Panic still hung there.

Without thinking, he gathered her into his arms. She trembled. To his amazement she hadn't pulled away. She'd truly been terrified.

With a shuddering breath so bottomless that he felt it all the way through him, Dana stepped back and squared her shoulders. "I'm okay now. Thanks for helping out. I hate snakes. As far as I'm concerned they're the worst part of my job."

"No problem." He glanced around the tree to the snake. "It was a big one. Mean too. We'll give it a few minutes to move on."

Dana's gaze finally met his. "I'd appreciate it if you didn't say anything about how silly I acted to anyone. I just really hate snakes."

His brow wrinkled as he looked at her with astonishment. "You're afraid someone will make fun of you?"

Dana nodded, then moved away.

She was that vulnerable? That afraid to show she had a weakness? Why did she believe she must be strong all the time? He followed her. "I remember how hard you worked to prove yourself during training. Do you remember how difficult and scary it was the first time you jumped off the tower during jumper training? We talked about it afterward."

"Yeah."

"But that first real jump had been invigorating. There has never been anything like it since. I remember the huge smile on your face when you landed just after me." Dana's face had been brilliant with excitement and exhilaration. Even now he could still picture it. He wanted to see that look again.

Her face took on a soft smile. She glanced at him and it disappeared. "We need to get back to work."

Had he hurt her so much that summer that she didn't

want to remember anything about it? That saddened him deeply. He headed toward the shed. "You do know that ignoring something doesn't mean it goes away."

She grinned. "Like you?"

Travis sighed. That was more like it. The Dana he liked so much. "Yeah. I does seem like we're stuck together for a while." He went to the shed with a grin on his face.

He finished with the ATV and securing the shed, then started on the fire line. It would require hours of back-breaking work. They took a breather around midday and returned to work again. Afterward Dana joined him on the fire line.

When they were done Dana said, "Now we need to take care of the rest of the things around the cabin. We need to get the flammables buried."

"You keep piling on the excitement." He grinned and slung the Pulaski over his shoulder. "You sure know how to show a guy a good time. I'll start digging a hole."

Dana had to give Travis credit for being a good sport. He could be making the experience more difficult. She'd sure been glad to see him when she'd been cornered by the snake. They had a way for making her brain shut down. It had felt good to have his protective arms around her. She had needed them for a few minutes.

Two hours later, when she came around the side of the cabin, she found Travis on the porch with glasses of water in his hands.

"Here, you need this." He handed her a glass and sat on the bench under one of the windows. "I have the hole you requested dug."

"Great, but before you get too comfortable we still have to water down what we can."

"You keep this up and I'm going to ask to be the outside boss."

"Sorry. We've already agreed on the boss division." She gulped down the water. "I'm going to check the perimeter to see if there's anything else we need to do. I'll also talk to base while I'm doing that." She put down the glass.

"I'll start filling the hole."

"Okay. I'll be done out here in a minute and start on the inside."

"Base, this is Dana." She called as she walked away. "Can I get a weather report? Over."

Static filled the air before a male voice came on. "It's still looking calm for the night."

"What about the fire?"

"Still headed your direction. But fifty percent under control."

"Ten-four. We're staying put tonight. Will head out tomorrow morning on Coyote Loop Trail toward Bright Light lookout cabin."

"Ten-four. Stay safe."

"Will do."

Dana found Travis standing over the hole he'd dug.

He leaned on a shovel handle. "I was waiting to see if you need to put anything else in it before I cover it."

"Nope. If you have all the flammable stuff in there then I say cover it."

"Is there anything else we need to do?" Travis filled the shovel with dirt.

"I still need to sort through Mr. Gunter's food supplies and see if there is anything light enough for us to carry. We didn't bring enough food for the extra days we're going to be out. We have at least three days of walking ahead of us." She looked off at the sky over the top of the trees. It would be dark in a couple of hours.

"Did you get that weather report?"

"Yeah." She told him what base told her.

Travis continued to dump dirt over the items in the hole. "That sounds like good news."

"It was. We'll stay here tonight after all."

"I like that idea. I'd rather sleep with a roof over my head. Just in case there is rain."

She turned toward the cabin. "We'll leave at daylight and make our way as far and fast as possible."

"I'll be ready." Travis picked up his pace with the shoveling.

Forty-five minutes later Travis joined her inside the cabin. He took a seat in one of the chairs with a groan. He rubbed his lower back.

Dana winced, then turned to look at him from where she stood in the kitchen. "You okay?"

"You better not laugh at me. I'm not used to so much manual labor."

Dana had to admit Travis had been a hard worker, sharing the load and following her lead—most of the time.

She smiled. "You don't look out of shape."

"Thank you. Have you been checking me out?"

Dana snorted. She had been, but she wouldn't let him know that. "What're we in? High School."

He harrumphed. "If we were I'd be too tired to make a pass at you."

As if he really would. "I'm going to take a shower before dinner."

His brows rose. "Is that your way of telling me to cook?"

"Not really. You're welcome to see to the food if you wish. If you don't, I will."

He pulled his feet back when she started to step across his legs. "You saw to dinner last night—it's only fair that I do it tonight."

She looked at him her eyes wide with astonishment. "Thanks for that. Some guys still don't think that way."

A spot in the center of Travis's chest warmed.

A few minutes later while busy in the kitchen he heard her yelp. She'd apparently stepped under the water. He grinned. His smile quickly disappeared when the picture of her naked in the outdoors slid into his mind. That wasn't a thought he needed to let take hold. He swallowed hard and kept applying all his attention to putting something for dinner on the table.

They weren't young adults any longer. If he kissed her now it wouldn't be so easily put behind them. He didn't want to hurt Dana. But he had nothing to give her. She deserved better than a fling because they were alone in the wilderness. But that was all he was offering these days. He'd tried for a real relationship and failed at it, miserably.

Travis looked Dana's way when she entered the cabin. All his earlier convictions disappeared like a sprinkle of rain against an uncontrolled fire. Her flushed face fresh from scrubbing and her hair hanging damp around it made her look younger than her years. Dana didn't need makeup to make her attractive. She had a sparkle of life about her that made him want some of it for himself. To absorb it. Feast on it.

Come to think of it, he'd not known that feeling since the summer they had spent together. Somehow he'd been going through the motions. Being around Dana made him want to grasp life and squeeze all he could out of it.

He stepped toward her but stopped. A cold shower

would be good right about now. He gathered his stuff. "We'll eat after I get a shower."

"Then I'm going to rebandage your arm."

He said over his shoulder without slowing down, "And I need to see to your face."

"What a pair we make. Not even together twenty-four hours and we both have injuries."

Yeah, and he had other issues, as well.

As the cold water flowed over his back, he moved his head from side to side then rolled his shoulders. What would they feel like after another two days? At least his body aches and pains helped keep his mind off the uncomfortable thoughts he had toward Dana. Those had to stop. Dana sat at the table with sandwiches and soup waiting by the time he reentered the cabin.

They ate with little discussion then cleared the table. With that done, Dana pulled out her first-aid kit. "How's your arm?"

"Sweating didn't do it any favors." It had stung all day.

Her eyes softened. "I don't imagine it does."

"I gave it a good wash. With a new bandage I think I'll be good to go. And a couple of pain relievers."

"Let me have a look before I cover it."

He held his arm up in the air with the bent elbow resting on the table. She took his hand, brought it down to her eye level. He tried not to let her touch affect him but just a simple nonsexual one had him wishing for more. Did Dana have any idea what she did to him?

Her eyes flickered up to meet his. Heat flashed in them before she let go of his hand. She straightened. In a firm voice she said, "Hold it up again."

He did as he was told, never taking his eyes off her.

She looked at him, but defiance and determination rested in her eyes now.

Disappointment filled him. He'd believed they had gotten past that since they'd returned to the cabin. Found some of their way back to what they had once had. But of course their time together now wasn't any different than what they'd shared before. It was only temporary.

With a gentle touch Dana smoothed the salve over the burned area. "This'll have to hold for as long as possible. I don't have much left."

"I have some in my pack but I'll keep my shirt sleeve down all the time. That should help protect it." He watched as she reapplied a bandage. "Tell me, are you still living on your grandfather's ranch?"

"I am. I don't plan to ever move." She carefully wrapped his arm.

He looked at the top of her head. Her hair had dried. He wanted to touch it, but wouldn't. "I remember you saying how much you loved it.

"Is there anyone special in your life?" Maybe it wasn't his business but he wanted to know and didn't have another way to find out without asking.

Her gaze flicked up to his then down again. "No. Let's just say that I have a tendency to intimidate men."

He sat back and grinned. "Now there's a surprise."

Dana's gaze, darkened now, met his. She wasn't sharing his humor. "I'm sorry. That's obviously a sore spot. Will you tell me what happened?"

"My last boyfriend started to make suggestions I should find another job. That I was gone too much. He wanted me to go to work in the office. He had a problem with jealousy. Didn't like me being out overnight with other men even though it was part of my work." She huffed. "As if we weren't worn out at the end of the day and just hoping we had a chance for eight hours of sleep."

"So why were you with this jerk anyway?" For some

reason he was far more indignant on her behalf than he should have been.

Her fingers stopped moving and she looked at a spot on the other side of the room. She shrugged. "I met him just after my grandfather died. He worked in the probate office at the courthouse. I had taken some papers in. He was nice. Asked me to dinner." Her mouth twisted into a grimace. "You don't want to hear this."

"I do, if you want to tell me."

"It was a long time ago." She went back to work with the bandage.

Like it had been between them. It shouldn't, but it sort of hurt that Dana hadn't pined for him all this time.

"At first he was fascinated by my job. He told all his friends he was dating a smokejumper. If we were out with a group he wanted me to tell stories. But slowly he started to make barbed remarks. When I didn't agree with something he accused me of being controlling."

Now he understood why she hadn't liked him accusing her of being bossy.

"By that time I was moving up the ranks and he hadn't gotten a promotion he thought he deserved."

"How long did you date this guy?"

"Almost a year." She spoke softly as if ashamed.

Travis couldn't keep the snarl from his lips.

"I know. I think I was just looking for someone, anyone. I was lonely. To make matters worse, I hung on until he dumped me, in public."

Another person had pushed her away. Travis placed his hand over hers and squeezed. "I'm sorry. You didn't deserve that."

"Maybe not, but that's the way it was."

He let her hand go before he held it longer than he should. "You haven't dated anyone since?"

She shook her head. "Nope, I've focused on my job. Much easier to deal with. I don't think I'm cut out for marriage and a family anyway. I've never really had a good example to follow."

"I don't know if I agree with that. We made a good team that summer."

She narrowed her eyes. "And look how that ended."

"It wasn't one of our finest moments. Let's leave it there and move on." As she placed the final tape on his arm, he lifted her chin with a finger. "It's your turn." He turned her head so he could better see her cheek. She'd already removed her bandage.

"Looks good. There may be a small scar." He picked up a plastic bandage from the table and opened it.

"It won't be the first I've had."

Her skin was too smooth and beautifully bronzed to be marred. He brushed the back of his hand over it. "It's too fine to be spoiled."

Her gaze met his and held. The air turned thick between them that had nothing to do with a fire coming their direction and everything to do with the electricity between them.

"Don't be so hard on yourself. I've been there and done that. I was supposed to have this perfect life and marriage. It didn't happen. We can't control what others do and think."

Dana looked at him. This time her eyes filled with curiosity. "That's a statement that begs for questions. What happened?" Just as quickly she said, "Hey, sorry, that's not my business."

Travis shrugged. "Water under the bridge. Let's just say while I was busy getting through medical school my wife was out partying at the clubs and going home with my classmates."

"I hate that that happened to you."

"Yeah. The worst is I took being loyal seriously and she treated it as the least important part in our marriage. Trust, partnership, working together and growing together were important to me."

"Are they still?"

"I don't know. I've not let anyone close enough to find out. I don't do long-term relationships anymore."

"Why did your wife run around on you?" she asked, disbelief filling her voice.

Somehow that boosted his damaged ego. "She said that it was because I wasn't available. I always had to study. Or go to class. Or to the lab. I guess she was lonely."

She looked down to where she toyed with a fingernail. "I can understand that feeling. Sometimes we do stupid stuff just not to be by ourselves."

Did he carry more blame than he thought for the breakup of his marriage? That wasn't a comfortable realization. He liked it better when he'd placed all the blame on Brittney.

Dana's gaze locked with his, stayed there. She blinked. "We uh…need to finish here and get some sleep."

As sensitive as the discussion had been for both of them, at least they had broken through that glass wall between them. Those easygoing days of summer were no more. They both lugged baggage and hurt behind them that they couldn't seem to leave on the side of the road.

Dana packed away her first-aid supplies. She felt Travis's look on her but she wouldn't meet his eyes. She couldn't believe she'd just told him all that about her ex-boyfriend. She must've been tired. He'd been back in her life for less than two days and she was spilling all her secrets. Even her trail crew, who she considered her brothers, didn't know what had happened. Since Travis had shown up again it was as if she was living in a parallel universe.

And to think his wife had run around on him. Dana hoped Travis didn't think she had been taking his ex-wife's side by what she said. She believed in commitment, as well. From what she'd read between the lines, they hadn't been ready for marriage. Travis had been focused on school and his wife had been focused on herself. Dana couldn't criticize because she'd stayed with a man who ended up humiliating her. Adding to the pile of people who'd rejected her.

Travis might've hurt her feelings at one time but even then she'd admired his devotion to honesty. She stood. As she moved past him to store her kit, Travis lightly captured her wrist with a hand. She looked at him. "Yes?"

He said softly, "I've missed you. Our talks. You always had a way of making me see things differently."

"You're welcome?" She dared a look at him unsure where this would go.

"I did wonder about you. More than once."

She couldn't stop warmth from filling her. More than once he'd entered her head. Mostly as the person she judged all other men by. "Travis, I'm not that naive girl anymore. The one who had a crush on the older guy."

His gaze found hers. "I'm aware of that. I like you, Dana."

She sighed. "You shouldn't be looking at me that way."

"How am I looking at you?"

This conversation had turned a direction she hadn't expected. She took a step back. "Like I was your favorite candy."

Travis didn't move closer but her body heated as if he had. His look captured hers again. "Candy, uh? Is there something wrong with that?"

She glanced down at herself. "Yeah. I won't be your play toy. You said yourself that you don't do relationships anymore. I don't know how to do a fling."

"How do you know?"

With nervous motions she replaced her kit where it belonged. "I don't want to talk about this anymore. I think we need to keep what's between us business. That means no more personal comments or discussions."

"You sure that's want you want?" His look bored into her.

She straightened. In her firmest tone said, "I am."

"I'll agree under one condition."

"What's that?" She desperately needed him to agree.

"That I get to satisfy my curiosity."

She knew better than ask but she couldn't help herself. "About what?"

"I want to know what it would have been like to kiss you."

Her throat went dry. She shoved her hands in her pockets. "I don't think that's a good idea."

He took a half step toward her but remained out of touching distance. "Maybe not but haven't you wondered? Wouldn't you like to find out?"

Yes! No. She watched him.

"Meet me halfway, Dana," he said so softly that the roar in her ears almost kept her from hearing him.

Could she? If she didn't she'd never know. She'd wanted to kiss him then. Wanted to now. What would it hurt for them to share one kiss? She could get it out of her system. Stop wondering what it would have been like.

As she took a step forward, Travis did, as well. When they were inches apart Travis used two fingers to tip her chin up. She hardly dared to breathe. Travis Russell wanted to kiss her.

He slowly lowered his mouth.

Heat shot though her. His lips were full and firm. His first touch was gentle, tentative. She didn't back away, didn't want to. Her body trembled. She'd dreamed of this so many times. Her hands moved to his biceps, her fingers squeezing to keep from falling. Travis's hands rested on her waist steadying her. As she made a mewing sound in the back of her throat, he slanted his mouth taking the kiss deeper.

Travis pressed her more securely against him. Brushing his tongue along the seam of her mouth, asking for an invitation to enter. Dana didn't disappoint him. She wanted more. And more. This was everything she'd dreamed of, and beyond. Her mouth parted. He accepted her welcome. Wrapping her arms around Travis's neck, she clung to him.

Dana had feared she'd missed out on something special all those years ago. She had. This was what it felt like being wanted, needed.

CHAPTER FIVE

THE SQUAWK OF the radio followed by, "Come in, Dana. Come in," jerked Dana back from Travis's stupor-inducing mouth. The man could kiss. Dazed, she forced her eyes to focus and her mind to engage. She took a step toward him. She didn't want this moment to end.

They were different people now. She was stronger. Could she have some of Travis and move on?

"Dana, come in."

She pushed away but immediately missed the sizzle Travis created in her. With shaking hands, she picked up the radio. "This is Dana."

"I have an update. Fire is no longer under control. Headed your direction. Advise you move west ASAP. Over."

She felt Travis standing close behind her. "Ten-four. Will leave at first light."

"Take care. This one has turned into a monster."

"Ten-four."

She looked at Travis. "We better get some sleep. It looks like we're going to be moving fast and hard." Not waiting on a response, she went to her pack and pulled out her sleeping bag.

To her relief Travis said nothing and stepped outside. He at least was giving her time to collect herself. She needed it. The almost childish attempt at a kiss years ago came nowhere near the toe-tingling, red-hot meeting of lips they'd just shared. Travis was a master and she'd hung on for dear life. Much more and she'd be giving herself to him body and soul. Something she couldn't do.

She'd given her heart without him asking before. The hurt from his rejection still pained her. Could she live through something like that again? The bigger problem was could she resist him and live with the disappointment of not knowing what it was to kiss Travis again?

For now she had to try to settle down enough to get some rest. She'd need all her energy to make it through the next few days.

Fifteen minutes later Travis reentered the cabin. She'd already laid her sleeping bag out next to the stove. "I don't want to start a fire in the stove tonight. I don't want to have any embers left when we leave in the morning."

"Understood. You take the bed." He'd returned the mattress.

She shook her head. "I can sleep on the floor. I'm used to it."

"For heaven's sakes please let me be chivalrous for once without an argument." His tone had a bite to it.

She looked at him then. Really looked. He glared at her. "I'm sorry. I'm not used to men being chivalrous, as you put it."

He grabbed his sleeping bag from where it sat beside his equipment. "Well, you should be."

"Okay. I'll sleep on the bed. I saw a couple of extra blankets in the cabinet over there. I'll get them for you. At least you'll have some padding."

"Thank you." The early tone eased but his voice remained tight.

She dropped her sleeping bag on the bed and went

after the blankets. She handed them to him. "Thanks for the bed."

"You're welcome. Good night, Dana." With that he turned his back to her, finished making his bed and climbed inside his sleeping bag.

Dana turned off the lantern. She thought of what would have been her amateur effort of kissing all those years ago and the expertise he demonstrated tonight. She shouldn't have let it go so far, but once his lips touched hers she'd been a goner. The need to kiss him, to have him kiss her had been too strong. She wouldn't let it happen again. Couldn't let it happen again.

Rejection would soon follow. She had learned the hard way it always did for her. Dana had enough of it. First her parents. Then she'd lost her grandfather. Travis, then a man she cared for. What made her think Travis would take her seriously a second time? The only reason he'd kissed her had been to settle his curiosity. He'd said so himself.

She wasn't his type, never would be. Her life was with the smokejumpers. He would want someone to hostess dinners and to go to cocktail parties. Never would she want to shame him and that would surely happen. She wouldn't be good enough for him.

She started to remove her pants.

"Leave your pants on and settle down, Dana," came Travis's husky voice. "Unless you wish me to join you. And it wouldn't be to sleep."

She held her breath not daring to move. What if she did move? Would he act on his threat? Running a finger over her bottom lip, she remembered each and every moment of Travis's kiss. It had been far better than her fumbled attempt. Maybe she should take off her pants.

No, it was better to keep things the way they were.

They'd both quenched their curiosity. It was over now. Her eyes closed on an active day involving hard physical work and emotional upheaval to drift into erotic dreams starring Travis.

By the time she woke, Travis was already in the kitchen. The smell of coffee filled the air. "Breakfast in ten minutes and daylight in thirty."

His bags were already packed and waiting by the door. The few last-minute food supplies she'd left on the table where gone. He must have put them in his bags.

"You're up and ready to go."

"Let's just say I miss hot baths and a comfortable bed." He continued to work in the kitchen.

Trying to make light of the situation, she said, "At least you have goals. That'll make the walking a lot easier."

He glanced over his shoulder. "I'll keep that in mind when my feet start throbbing."

She went to the wash pan near the back door and found fresh water already in the bowl. "Thank you." She cupped her hands together and scooped it up to splash her face. It was warm. Travis had heated water for her. She let out a loud sigh of pleasure.

"I like to hear you make that sound."

Dana looked at him to find his back still remained to her. "Thank you. That was a true gift."

He turned and smiled. "You're easy to please. And you're welcome." After placing two mugs on the table, he sat. "Let's eat."

He said that as if his ex-wife must have been difficult to please. How sad for him. Travis deserved better.

Fifteen minutes later they were ready to go. They headed out just as the sun broke over the trees. Dana took a moment to look back at the cabin. "We did all we can to save this place if the fire makes it this far."

"I'm sure Mr. Gunter will be glad we tried." Travis adjusted his pack.

They were no longer following a footpath. Dana blazed their way. Trees towered high over their heads. They spoke little as they walked. She already missed their newfound camaraderie.

Thoughts swirled through her head. Travis hadn't been exactly short with her while they ate but things had changed since they'd kissed. She felt off center around him. As if her world had shifted but she didn't know which direction.

Had she disappointed him? Was he upset with her? Had she done something wrong?

Travis had been following Dana for a couple of hours. All of those he'd been thinking about their kiss. The one that had kept him up most of the night when he'd needed sleep. He wanted to kiss her again and again. He couldn't remember when a woman had set him on fire like Dana had.

He'd had to go outside and take a few minutes to recover. Returning inside had been difficult. He'd wanted to pull her to that awful single bed and show her what they could be together. To make matters worse he was hyperaware of her soft breathing all night. Dawn came as a relief. He could get up and do something to keep his mind off Dana.

That had been working well for him until he heard her reaction to his gesture of warm water to wash with. That soft, sexy noise almost undid his good intentions.

She called a halt to their trek. "I need to check in with base."

"Okay. While you do that I'm going to try to get in touch with the hospital and see how Mr. Gunter is doing."

Travis walked off far enough they both could have a conversation without interrupting each other.

While still on the phone he heard a roar of a large engine. He looked up to see a low-flying tanker plane.

"Travis," Dana called with a note of urgency.

He looked to see her waving an arm for him to come. He ended his call and hurried to pick up his packs.

"We need to get out of range of these guys. The fly jockeys sometimes miss their mark. The last thing we need is to have all that fire-retardant chemical all over us."

"I couldn't agree more." Travis hustled to catch up with her.

They kept moving until they were high enough to see the sky above the trees. Dana stopped in an open area and looked back behind them. In the distance an orange-red haze hung in the air. The fire retardant floated to the ground. Farther to the north, the gray of smoke still filled the sky. The fire was still burning strong.

"What did you find out from base?" Travis asked still watching the sky.

"They're expecting a storm late afternoon and most of the night. The hope is that there's enough rain in it to help. Another electrical storm isn't what we need. It would only start more fires. How's Mr. Gunter doing?"

"Stable. He'll need a kidney transplant when they're able to move him to Seattle."

Dana briefly put her hand on his upper arm, giving him a commiserating look. "You hate not being there to see about him don't you?"

Travis's gaze met hers. Was it that transparent or did Dana understand him that well? What he did know was that his ex-wife never "got him" as Dana did. Or had he not let her? "I do. He's my patient."

"We better get going. It sounds like we're going to need to find some good shelter tonight if we don't want to get wet."

"Oh, to sleep in the rain." Travis gave one last look at the sky and turned to follow her.

"Gotten soft over the years, have you, Doc?" Her tone turned lighthearted.

"More like out of practice." Relief washed through him. At least some of the tension between them had eased. Dana hadn't met his eyes all morning. He'd convinced himself he'd been wrong to ask to kiss her. He should've known better. Somehow in a weak moment he'd thought if they did, it might clear the air some. All it had done was make it thicker. He'd had no idea it would be so explosive.

"I bet it'll come back to you." The words were thrown over her shoulder

An hour of hard walking later, they reached a peak.

"We'll rest here." Dana dropped her packs and sank to the ground, her legs crossed.

Travis joined her, leaning his back against a boulder. "Where are we?"

"To the west of Skeleton Cave Trail. We may need to turn south some. The going's harder there but we have a better chance of finding some protection from the weather."

Travis dug into his personal pack and pulled out two granola bars. He offered her one. "Sounds like a must-see."

Dana laughed and took the bar. "Some of these trails were named ages ago."

Hearing her laugh was like having the sun come up just for him.

"Goodness, if I'd realized a snack bar would be that appreciated I would've given you one earlier."

"I might not have been as happy to receive it then as I am now."

He chuckled. "Point taken." Looking up at the beauty around them, he recognized that Dana belonged here. She'd be swallowed up, and shrivel up in an office building. Her world was in nature. Had her ex-boyfriend not seen that? Or had he not cared?

Dana had a wildness to her, an untamed quality that called to him. He didn't want to master it, just taste it and be carried along with it. That sense of who she was only added to her beauty. Her draw. His need.

"You're staring at me again." She took a bite of her bar. "This is the third time."

His look didn't leave her. "I'm sorry. I tend to do that when I'm fascinated by someone."

Pink that had nothing to do with the effort of walking came to her cheeks. That only charmed him more. As tough as Dana acted, she could still blush.

"What's that supposed to mean? Fascination."

He took another bite out of his bar as he continued to watch her. "Being interested or amazed by something."

Her lips tightened as she gave him a disgusted look. "I know the definition of fascination. I'm just wondering why you'd be fascinated by me."

"Why wouldn't I be? The fact that you can outwork most people I know. You jump out of airplanes. You're so feminine yet you work in a man's world. You've the most luscious lips. And you can kiss like there's no tomorrow. Need I go on?"

There was a long pause where only the sounds of birds and the rustle of the wind could be heard.

"Why're you sweet-talking me? I'm not what you want. I told you I'm not going to be your play thing."

"I'm not trying to sweet-talk you. You asked me a question and I answered it. Honestly. Whether you believe that or not is up to you."

She looked toward the forest. "What I think is you're dumping a load of bear scat at my feet."

That hurt. He'd meant every word he'd said. Had she heard so few compliments in her life she couldn't believe one when it was given? "Why would you say that? Not everyone is as ignorant as the men you've apparently been out with. You ex-boyfriend being a prime example. Just because you haven't been out with a good guy doesn't mean they don't exist."

She shifted to hold more of her back to him. Dana wasn't comfortable with this discussion but he wasn't gonna let her off the hook. She needed to know how desirable and interesting she was. To know that her kisses could turn his insides into hot liquid.

"Is this part of that bedside manner that's required to be a doctor?" She stuffed her trash into her pocket.

"How like you to put a man in his place. I can see that sweet-talking you isn't your thing. Maybe I need to try my caveman technique."

She twisted to glare at him. "Don't you dare! I have a chain saw and know how to use it."

Travis leaned back and roared with a laughter. The birds flew out of the trees and small animals hurried to their holes. It was the first real laugh he'd had in a long time. It felt good.

"I think it's time we get moving." She stood and gathered her things including the chain saw.

To her back he said, "Just because you don't want to believe something doesn't make it not be true."

Finally the ground leveled off enough he could walk beside her. A loud screech came from the sky. He looked up to see an eagle, wings spread wide soaring overhead. "This truly is amazing country, isn't it?"

"It is." Dana's voice held a sound of awe. "But for all its beautiful, wild, breathtaking elements it can be deadly, as well."

Too soon they reentered the woods and started downhill. At one particularly steep spot they had to hold tree saplings to keep themselves upright. When Dana slid to her side Travis grabbed the chain saw before it and she went tumbling. Bracing himself against a tree in order not to go down, he helped her to right herself.

Dana worked farther along, still using the trees as support until she could stand by leaning back against a tree. She reached for the chain saw. Travis handed it down then climbed past her. They followed the leapfrog pattern until they were on flatter ground.

He stopped beside Dana. "You okay?"

She shrugged and wiped her hands on her pants. "Scraped my hands but no big deal. I should be wearing my gloves."

"Let me see." He took her hands and lifted them. Both had small red marks across them.

Before he realized what he was doing he kissed one palm then the other.

"Travis…" His name was little more than a whisper across her lips.

He picked up the chain saw and started off. "Let me lead for a while." To his astonishment she didn't argue. She must have been as shocked as he that he'd kissed her hands.

Dana watched Travis's back. What had that been about? Whatever it was, he left her heart fluttering in her chest.

She'd had such a crush on Travis once. Was it so hard to believe that she could again? Would it be so terrible if she did? The thought took a firmer hold the more she was around him. She hurried to catch him.

The roar of water rushing over rocks grew stronger. Travis stood beside a creek by the time she joined him.

"Should we cross here or is there a better spot?"

Dana looked across the rocky area. "This is as good a place as any. It's miles downstream before the stream calms."

"We cross here then." Travis picked up the saw by the handle.

"Go slow. The goal here is not only to cross but to stay dry. We can't build a fire this time of the year to dry things out."

"I'll keep that in mind." Travis took a wide step putting a foot on a rock with water washing around it. Using the saw as a counterbalance, he moved farther into the stream.

When he had made it halfway across, she followed using his path. They made slow progress but wearing wet clothes all day wouldn't be fun. She concentrated on each movement of her feet. Glancing over, she saw Travis had made it to the other side. He placed the saw and his bags on the ground.

She returned her attention to what she was doing. The next step had undoubtedly been easy for Travis but was wider than she felt comfortable making. Looking around for an alternative rock, she couldn't find one.

"Stay put." Travis called. "I'm coming after you."

Before she could stay anything, he'd already left the bank.

"Give me your hand." She did and his strong one

closed around hers. "Step over here to me. This rock is large enough to hold us both."

When she teetered, his grip tightened, holding her in place before his hands came to her waist. They stood chest to chest as water rushed around them. She didn't dare look him in the eyes for fear she'd forget they were in the center of the creek.

"The last step is wide also. I'm going to step across and swing you over. Don't move until I have firm footing." She did as he said. "On three." His words brushed her ear. He lifted her with ease and soon her feet were on dry ground.

As she moved away to give him room to join her, he stepped to the bank but lost his footing when part of the bank gave way. Dana grabbed his hand and pulled. She fell to the ground hard, her breath leaving her with an *oof.* Travis came down on top of her. They were in a tangle of arms and legs. She worked to catch her breath.

"Dana, are you all right? Did I hurt you?" Panic filled Travis's voice as he scrambled off her.

Pulling in enough air to speak, she said, "I'm okay."

"You sure?" Concern darkened his eyes.

"I'm fine."

Travis stood and reached out a hand and helped her stand. He studied her. "Are you sure you aren't hurt?"

"I'm good. Really." Her voice held a gruffness. Was it from the fall or having Travis so near? She adjusted her packs. "We need to keep moving."

He picked up his belongings. "You're sure I didn't hurt you. You took a hard fall especially with my weight crushing you."

"Travis, I said I'm fine. Now let's go." Why couldn't he leave it alone? She wasn't used to having someone show concern for her. Guilt ate at her. She should appreciate his worry. They hadn't hiked far when she turned to him. "I'm sorry I made a fuss about you making sure I was all right. I've spent years trying to be tough enough to handle my job. Showing any weakness might affect my performance. I'm sensitive about it."

"You're human. You can hurt. Can show it." Had all her life been spent proving herself worthy?

She looked away. "I know. But I don't like to show it."

"Hey." He waited until her gaze returned to him. "You can let it show with me. I promise to have your back."

"Thanks. That's nice to hear." She looked at the sky. It had filled with ominous low dark clouds. "We need to start looking for shelter. One of the guys I used to work with out of Bend told me about a small cave in this area. We're going to look for it."

"Is that with or without a bear?"

Dana grinned. "We're going to plan for without."

"Good. I've almost met my quota for an eventful day."

"I have to admit this trip gets more interesting all the time. It sure would make a nice end to the day if we could find that cave."

Travis slapped the side of his leg. "Then let's go do it."

CHAPTER SIX

Travis trailed behind Dana up and over the rocks. She didn't seem to give up and acted as if nothing was too tough for her. He'd gotten so used to being around hot-house, needy women he'd forgotten what a truly capable woman acted like. The only issue he had with that was she worked at it too hard. As if she always had to prove herself.

With sure feet, she continued up the mountain, half pulling herself along. He made every step she did while searching the area for a cave opening. The chain saw shifted on his shoulder. Though it was cumbersome but necessary, he still wished he could leave it behind. But that wouldn't happen. They might need it. He moved it to the other shoulder. Still a guy could dream…

They maneuvered through a narrow space between two rocks on their upward climb. Every once in a while Dana stopped and searched the outcroppings. They marched on as dark clouds continued to roll in and shut out the sunlight, lightning flashes within them. The air thickened. The storm now hung low over the distant tree line. It would be an angry one.

"Hey, Travis."

"Yeah."

"Tell me about your ex-wife."

That came out of the blue. "What do you want to know?"

"Whatever you'll tell me." Dana made it sound as if they were having a casual conversation to pass the time.

"She is tall, has blond hair and likes the finer things in life."

Dana asked over her shoulder, "Did your parents like her?"

He climbed over a rock. "I guess so."

"Did you love her?"

Had he? Really? "I think I thought she'd be the perfect partner for the life I had envisioned. I met her in college. She'd been raised as a princess so she knew all the social ins and outs. I thought I needed that to get ahead in my profession. She dressed like a fashion plate. Wanted the house to look just so. But none of that really has anything to do with love, does it?"

Dana stopped and looked back at him. "No."

How misguided he'd been. He'd not only done Brittney an injustice but himself, as well. He'd been so wrapped up in creating the perfect picture, he produced a nightmare. Moments later Dana's excited call had him hurrying forward.

"I think I've found it." She pointed above them. "Stay here and I'll check it out."

"Dana, let me go."

With a flashlight already out, she looked at him. "I've got this. You don't have to take care of me."

"I know that, but you could let someone do it every once in a while. I've the caring gene. Remember? I'm a doctor."

She'd already started up the side of the mountain. "I'll keep that in mind."

"Watch out for a bear," he yelled.

"Will do. I promise if one's in there you'll know it almost as soon as I do."

Fear shot through him. Travis dropped the chain saw to a nearby rock. "You don't think…"

"Calm down. I think if there's one it would've shown up by now." She kept moving. Closer to the black hole she slowed. Turning on the flashlight, she crawled nearer the opening.

When he could no longer see her Travis held his breath, his muscles tensed. If there was a bear and Dana got hurt, could he get her to help fast enough? He didn't even want to think about the possibilities.

He released the breath he'd held as she backed out of the hole. "I'm fine. It'll hold both of us, but just barely. At least it'll block the majority of the rain." All of her disappeared briefly again before she back out and called, "All clear. Home sweet home. For the night."

Travis carried all the supplies he could up and handed them to her. While she took them inside he returned for the rest.

Dana had already stored what she could at the back of the cave and had their sleeping bags spread out.

"Hurry up and settle in. The show is about to begin."

He couldn't miss the delight in her voice. "Show?"

"The light show." She pointed toward the sky.

A flash of lightning in the middle of the black cloud at eye level was nothing like he'd ever seen. He sat on his sleeping bag, hunched over because he couldn't sit straight.

Dana turned around and lay on her stomach propping her chin on her folded hands like a kid watching her favorite cartoon. He followed her example.

As he relaxed, she handed him two packages of MREs.

"If you eat all your meat and vegetables then you can have dessert."

He wished that included her but he wouldn't push. Anything further would be up to her to suggest.

Thunder rolled, clouds thickened making it more difficult to see. Lightning flashed, and a second later the next flash came. He grinned at her. "I get it now. Dinner and a show. Dana, you do know how to show a man a good time."

She opened one of her bags. "What can I say? The vantage point can't be beat."

They ate in silence. It would've been hard to talk over the noise of the storm anyway. The tempest slowly worked its way toward him. The first fat drop of rain fell in front of them and quickly turned into a deluge. The air drew damp.

They watched for almost an hour before the rain turned steady. "I think this might be one of the most amazing things I've ever seen."

"It never grows old. My grandfather used to say the gods were arguing."

"That's a nice way to think about it."

"It's an amazing show of nature but it can be rough on the people below."

Even in the dim light he could see the sadness in her eyes. "That sounds like you have some experience with that."

Dana didn't say anything for a while. "My grandfather's barn caught fire. He'd run inside to save the cow and horse. They made it out but a timber fell on him. For the rest of his life he walked with a limp and had horrible scars. I learned to respect the weather."

"The hard way I'd say."

"Why did you live with your grandfather?" He'd never

asked that summer and she'd never said. He wanted to know more about Dana. Understand her.

"My parents left me with him when I was five. Time for me to start school. See, my parents were wannabe musicians. They left me with Grandpa to go on the road. They were in a bus accident and killed when I was eight."

"I'm sorry."

"It's no big deal. I think I was an accident anyway. They didn't need a kid hanging around. I didn't see them but once or twice a year and only for a day or so. I didn't really know them."

"Hey, they're the ones who missed out." Travis placed a hand on her back, gently rubbed it. She had more than her share of loss in her life. He couldn't imagine not having his parents to help support him when times were bad. They'd certainly been there for him when he'd gotten a divorce. Even if they weren't together, they still cared about him.

"That's a nice thing to say."

Another flash of lightning let him clearly see her face. It was angelic. The talk of her parents hadn't taken away from her enjoyment of the moment. She understood the majesty of the world she worked in and her place in it. Could he say as much about himself? What a nice place to be in life. "Thanks for sharing the show with me. I'll remember it always."

She smiled. "You are welcome."

"In many ways this has been an amazing trip."

"I'm going to get some sleep on that thought. Good night." She turned around, opened her sleeping bag and slipped inside. "See you in the morning." Dana positioned her personal bag as a pillow, then removed her pants and placed them nearby. She rolled to her side putting her back to him.

Just like that she forgot about him. For some reason he didn't like the idea. Why it bothered him he didn't know. He wanted her as flustered by him being near as he was by her being so close.

Everything about Dana spoke of home, family, forever. He'd tried that and it hadn't gone well. He wasn't interested in taking a chance again. Didn't trust his judgement. His discussion with Dana about love had proved he didn't understand that feeling. Still he didn't like Dana not noticing he was alive.

Last night he'd believed she did, especially when he kissed her. She responded. Acted as if she enjoyed it. Wanted more. But he'd misread women before. He'd certainly thought his ex-wife had been something she wasn't. Could he be doing the same with Dana?

Since Dana had settled in for the night it was more difficult for him to maneuver. Trying not to disturb her, he worked himself into his bag and out of his pants. His body would stay warmer by putting on clothes in the morning.

Clasping his hands behind his head as a pillow, he listened to the rain. His mind returned to Dana who lay so close. Thankfully he was exhausted and soon drifted off to sleep.

A moan and the chatter of teeth woke him. Dana had shifted beside him and now curled into him. Still she shivered. The temperature had dropped after the storm.

He unzipped his bag and then hers, pulling her against his body. She lay on her side turned into him. Her nose snuggled into his neck. A hand came to lie across his chest and a leg wrapped one of his, her feet nestled with his. Working slowly and carefully, he managed to get her bag over them and tucked around her.

Placing an arm around her waist, he pulled her closer,

if that was possible. With a sigh and warmth circling in his chest, he fell back to sleep.

The next time he woke the palm of her hand circled his middle and a soft moan brushed his neck. His manhood instantly came to attention. Feet rubbed against his, then cool toes were stuffed beneath his calf. The hand stopped over his heart. Dana stilled. He drifted off again.

The shove of a hand on his chest and a knee in the side of his thigh brought him awake. He grunted and opened his eyes to see snapping eyes glaring down at him.

"What're you doing in my sleeping bag?" Dana demanded.

Raising a brow, he kept his tone even. "You're in mine."

She blinked, then looked down at their combined bodies as if to confirm his statement. "How?"

"You were cold. Shivering. You crawled over to me. You sure do have cold toes."

She jerked them out from under his calf. "We better get up and get moving."

"It's not light enough yet. Calm down. I'm not going to attack you. Close your eyes and enjoy listening to the world come alive."

Dana eased down but remained tense beside him.

He squeezed her waist slightly. "Stop thinking. Just be for a change."

It took a few minutes but Dana relaxed against him. Her breathing even. She'd gone to sleep. They stayed like that until he could easily see the area outside. He gave Dana a gentle shake. "It's light."

Her lips brushed his neck.

He went motionless. "Dana?"

That touch found the curve between his neck and shoulder. "Mmm..."

Her hips moved along his.

She couldn't possibly know what she was doing. "Dana. We need to get up."

"I'd rather stay here." She nestled against him.

"Sweetheart, I sure as hell want to, but we're not going to. I won't have you regretting anything that happens between us ever again. This isn't the time or the place." He reached across her and picked up Dana's pants. He laid them on top of her.

He pushed the bag off him, picked up his pants and pulled them on, trying not to think about the warm, desirable Dana so nearby. Had he lost his mind? Sexual attraction had hummed like a live electrical wire between them since her boss's office. When they came together he wanted them to have more than a hurried meeting in a tiny cave in the middle of nowhere. He needed to know Dana wanted it, as well. Give her time to think. Not take her in the heat of the moment.

He dared a glance at her. She had dressed. Together they worked to pack up their supplies. They were ready to leave when he took Dana's hand.

"What?" she said not looking at him, as she tugged on her hand.

Travis held it and led her out of the cave to where they could stand up. Brushing a strand of hair back from her face, he waited until she'd looked at him. He gave her a light kiss on the lips. "I don't know for sure what's going though that head of yours right now but I've a pretty good idea. So I want to make it perfectly clear that when I have a chance I'm going to kiss you, all over. Don't doubt for a minute that I want you."

Dana had no idea what to say so she said nothing. She couldn't believe her own actions. What had she done?

She'd been keeping Travis at arm's length for days and this morning she woke to his heat and lost her mind. She spent the entire day before thinking about kissing him again, wanting him. Snuggled against Travis, she couldn't resist acting on her desire.

This trip would be a short amount of time so why shouldn't she enjoy Travis while it lasted? Their summer together was temporary, this trip would be, as well. But with a better ending. They'd return to civilization and life would go back to normal. They'd enjoy each other for a while, then have nice memories and move on.

She watched Travis for a moment as he led the way down to the path. Her chest filled with the hope of what would come. Travis hadn't said no. Instead he was postponing. He wanted her. He hadn't rejected her. Instead he promised her soon. That's what she needed to remember.

On the path she said, "I need to check in. It'll determine which way we go."

"Okay. I'll do the same." He shrugged off his large bag and fished out his phone before he stepped away.

A couple of minutes later Travis rejoined her.

"What's the word?" He took out his water bottle and drank.

"The good news is the rain put the majority of the fire out. Bad news, we still have a long walk out. How's Mr. Gunter doing?"

"The same. They're preparing to transfer him today or tomorrow." Travis picked up his bag. "What's our plan?"

"We're headed for the tower off Bessie Butte Trail. We'll stay there tonight. If all goes well we'll hike out tomorrow and someone can pick us up."

Travis nodded. "Good deal. That sounds promising."

"The downside is we've got a ten-mile hike today." She started along the trail.

What she didn't say was she hoped they could remain on the path for as long as possible. They'd soon have to get off and create their own again which would make the going harder and slower. If weather deterred them they'd be in further trouble. Being responsible for Travis added to her concern. Yet they had to push on if they wanted to make the tower by nightfall.

"We can't stop to eat today. Sorry."

"Okay." He pulled two bags of MREs out of the lower side pocket of his pants. He handed one to her. "Enjoy."

Travis didn't complain—she'd give him that. Dana took the package. She ate as she walked. Grabbing a limb to steady herself, she descended another rocky path. Over the next hour they concentrated on climbing down the mountain. They hiked out into a wide-open meadow with a stream flowing through it. Mountains created a beautiful clearing. Birds flew up in front of them as they walked.

"I have to admit I've enjoyed seeing a part of the country I've never visited. The beauty is amazing." Travis moved up to stroll beside her. "I forgot what it was to walk for days to get home after fighting a fire."

"I always find it ironic when we jump in and fight a fire for half a day then have to walk two days to get out."

"Isn't that still a score of pride for the smokejumpers? They walk out when the hotshots ride."

"Yeah. They're *much* weaker," Dana said proudly.

"You never told me why you wanted to be a smokejumper. It's an unusual job for a woman."

"That's pretty easy. My fifth-grade class went on a field trip to the base station. I thought it was the most amazing place I'd ever been. A couple of jumpers talked to us. Let us put on equipment. We even climbed in a plane. I decided that day I wanted to be a smokejumper. When my grandfather got hurt it sealed the deal."

"And you never looked back."

"And I never looked back. I wanted to be the best of the best." Complete confidence surrounded her words. "To do something that really mattered."

"There're less dangerous ways to do that."

"Sure there are, but I found a home with the smoke-jumpers. It took some major work on my part to prove myself but I have." She'd worked out more, studied harder and done jobs no one else wanted. Had proven herself worthy. Found a place where she was valued and wouldn't be pushed out. A place where she was wanted and needed.

"From what I can tell all that paid off."

Her chin rose with pride. Travis sounded as if he admired her. "Thanks for saying that. I like to think so. High praise since this trip has been such a fiasco. I thought it would be more straightforward but that's part of the charm of the job. You never know what's going to happen. How about you? Did you feel the same about medicine?"

"I did, and do. All it took for me to know I'd found my place was the look on an older gentleman's face when I told him he would be fine and could go home to his wife of fifty-five years. I just wish all my decisions had been as clear and correct."

"We all make mistakes. It's what we learn from them and do about them that matters."

Travis made a sound of agreement. "That's a deep bit of wisdom. Have you managed to follow it?"

"I've tried but haven't always been successful. I'm still working on it."

Travis looked at Dana's profile as they continued across the wide meadow. Why did she seem to have it all together while he was still fumbling with life? "Why didn't we ever talk about this before?"

Back during their summer together had he just been in his own world? Concerned only with what he planned for his life. It was just as well he hadn't let their relationship go beyond that almost kiss. He hadn't deserved Dana. Didn't like the man he'd become since then as well. They had both changed. Her for the better. Him not so much.

"I don't know. We were focused on training and having fun during our down hours. To talk about our dreams and plans maybe had been too serious."

Back then he'd had his entire life mapped out, yet most of it hadn't turned out as expected. He'd given up on plans and hopes. Now he just lived, took what came.

"There's supposed to be a footbridge along here somewhere."

Dana's statement drew him out of his musings. He looked around. They'd arrived at a wide stream.

"Since it's the dry season the water is low. If it were spring this water would be high and rushing. We'd have no chance of crossing without getting wet." She looked up and down the creek. "If we don't find the bridge it'll add an hour to our walk."

"You do love a challenge."

She strolled ahead. "There has to be some way across. There." She pointed ahead. "It narrows." Hurrying forward she called, "And look! A log."

"You've got to be kidding. A log isn't a bridge. You really expect us to cross on that?"

She grinned back at him. "I thought you liked a challenge." Picking up a stick, Dana returned to the log. "Didn't you say you wanted to work on your tightwire act?"

"No. And if I did I'd rather not start with a log lying

across a cold creek in the middle of nowhere when I can't build a fire."

"Afraid to live dangerously, are you, Doc?" Dana placed a foot on the log to test it. Bounced it a few times. "It seemed sturdy enough. Look at it this way. If you go in it's only a couple of more miles to the tower where there's a propane heater. And if your boots get wet you only have one more day to walk in them."

He stood on the bank watching her. "That's all supposed to make me feel better?"

"I'll talk to you on the other side. You're distracting me." Dana stuck the stick into the water using it to help balance as she moved farther out on the log.

She'd been distracting him for days and she expected him to feel sorry for her. "At least that's a positive. For a while there I wasn't sure you knew I was alive."

She glanced back. "Oh, I knew you were alive. That was the problem. Now hush and let me concentrate." She shifted her foot out another step.

With the next one, Dana rocked back and almost lost her footing. He sucked in a breath. She wasn't going to make it. He dropped his packs and the chain saw. If he had to go in he didn't want anything extra hanging on him.

Dana continued moving out over the water.

A crack of sound barely reached his ears before the snap of the log breaking echoed across the prairie. Dana yelped, falling in the water backward. If the situation hadn't been dire, the look of surprise on her face would've been comical. Instead she went under. The weight of the pack on her back holding her down.

Travis didn't hesitate to jump in. By the time he managed to get to Dana she'd rolled over but still fought to get her feet under her. He grabbed her around the waist. "Stop struggling. I've got you."

Dana relaxed.

They continued to float down the river.

"We're going to slowly make our way over to the bank." They kicked and paddled in unison without Travis letting her go toward the grassy edge. There he pushed Dana with a hand to her bottom while she pulled herself upward until she lay on her stomach. With what energy he had left, he grabbed a handful of grass and tugged his way out of the water beside her. They both lay there heaving.

"Are you okay?" Travis asked fearing she'd hit her head or worse while struggling.

"Yeah. But now we're both wet." She sounded disgusted.

"Should I have just let you drown?" He sat up.

"No. I do appreciate you helping me. The pack weighted me down and falling backward made it worse."

"We still have to cross over." Travis rolled to his knees and hands, then stood. He took her by the elbows and helped her stand. "This time it won't matter if we get wet or not. This time I think I'll be the outside boss and we'll try it my way."

Dana's hands went to her hips. "Which'll be?"

"Find a shallow place to cross. Our feet are already wet. Let's go pick up my stuff and see how fast we can get to some place where we can take off these wet clothes."

They walked back up the bank. Travis picked up his supplies and they kept moving. The river remained wide for a way but he soon found a rocky area.

"This should do it." He looked at her. "We'll go across together this time. Take my hand."

She gave him an indignant look, crossing her arms over her chest. "I can handle myself."

"Why do you always have to be so independent?" He pumped his hand offering it again. "It's not a sin to accept help."

"Maybe it's because I've always had to take care of myself."

His look met hers. "Then this time let me help take care of you. Grab my hand. I promise not to let you go."

Her gaze locked with his. Her eyes flickered with surprise, questions and possibly hope. Slowly she placed her hand in his.

Something significant had happened but he wasn't sure what. He stepped into the water. "I won't let you fall."

Her gaze met his. "I know you won't."

Travis got the idea her words meant more than the obvious as if she were giving him a vote of confidence she hadn't given another man. He didn't wish to disappoint her.

Dana joined him in the water and they slowly worked their way across. When her foot slipped he held her hand tightly and placed a hand at her underarm steadying her. They looked at each other. He would've kissed her if they hadn't been standing in the middle of a river. "We need to keep moving. We're almost there."

She nodded.

At the bank, he climbed out then helped her.

Dana removed her big pack and set the saw down. "Time to empty our boots."

"Now? Can't we do that when we get to the tower?"

"I recommend you don't wait. Take them off and dump out as much water as possible. Also ring out your socks. You don't want your feet to get unhappy."

"I'll be okay."

She put her hand on his arm. "I promise you won't be if you don't do as I say."

Travis took a seat on the ground beside her. "It's hard for me to believe my feet could be any more uncomfortable than they already are."

"You get foot rot and you'll find out different." She pulled off one of her boots and turned it upside down.

He did the same and water tricked out.

"Hand me the shirt slash towel." He dug through his pack and found it. She picked up one of his feet.

"What're you doing?"

She dried his foot making sure to get between the toes.

"Hey, that tickles." He pulled back on his foot.

She hung on. "I can't take a chance you don't get them dry as possible. I'm responsible for getting you back in one piece." She put that one down and started on the other. "We'll dry everything out the best we can tonight. By the way, thanks for saving me."

"You're welcome."

"I hope you brought a change of socks." She put his foot down.

Travis patted his bag. "Right here."

"Good. It'll be important you wear them tomorrow."

He shifted so that he could dry Dana's feet, placing one on his thigh. She had such a trim ankle. "If I didn't know better I'd think this was some erotic foreplay."

Her cheeks pinked. She lowered her head. "You'd think that until the skin started peeling off."

"I've seen trench foot. It's not very attractive." Travis had never been a foot guy but he liked Dana's. They were long and narrow. To his surprise her toes were polished a bright pink. "Hot pink, uh?"

Those rosy spots on her cheek grew.

He continued to dry her foot giving each toe special attention. Finished with that one, he picked up the other. Taking more time than required, he gave it the same devotion.

Dana cleared her throat. "We should be going." She picked up one of her socks and rung it out, ready to put it on.

"Don't." Travis reached inside his pack and pulled out a plastic bag. He removed a pair of socks and handed them to her.

"I can't take your socks. You won't have any dry ones."

He dug around in his bag again and pulled out a bag. "I have another pair."

"What're you, a Boy Scout?"

He raised his chin and gave her a cheeky grin. "No. I've just learned from experience to be prepared."

"You'd think I'd know better." She accepted the socks from him.

"I know you do just fine on your own but every once in a while we all need help." He suddenly wished she did need him. But could he be that guy?

"Look who's dishing out wisdom now."

With their socks and boots back on, Travis helped Dana with her pack and picked up his bags. "Which way, oh, great leader?"

"Are you relinquishing the bossing duty to me again?" She grinned.

"I am?"

"As it should be."

He gave a loud huff.

She smiled and pointed off to the north. "See that second peak over there?"

"Yeah."

"Can you make out that tiny dot above it in the sky?"

"Yep." He stood beside her.

"That's the top of the fire tower and our destination tonight. Do you think you have it in you to make it?" Her eyes held a dare.

Travis pushed his chin out. "I'll try not to hold you back."

She smiled. "I'll let you know if you do."

Travis nudged her with an elbow. "I've no doubt you'll point it out when I do."

They started across the flat plain with the knee-high grass wrapping their legs so dry bits of shaft blew in the wind around them. An hour later they reached the tree line and started their climb.

"Talk to me, Dana. Tell me about your ranch. How big is it?"

"You really want to know about that?" she asked over her shoulder.

"I do." He wanted to know all he could about her.

Dana wasn't sure how much of her life she wanted to share with him. But if she answered his questions then she had the right to ask some of her own.

"I have almost ten acres just south of Redmond with a small house and barn." It was her heaven when she wasn't working. "It needed a lot of work when I inherited it. I've spent most of my time redoing it." She wove through the trees. Thankfully the space between the wide, tall trees made it easier to walk.

"Does the house have a porch?" Travis asked from close behind her.

Why had he asked such a specific question? "It does. A large one across the front with a swing."

"From the sound of your voice you clearly love the place."

"I do. It's my home." It belonged to her and couldn't be taken away. Wouldn't leave her.

"Sounds much nicer than my condo with the thin walls. Any animals?"

Travis really was curious. "I board a few horses for a friend. Have two barn cats."

She thought to invite him for a visit but stopped herself. What they had would end when they returned to town. She didn't expect more. She couldn't count on it being different.

They came to a dense stand of timber where the ground was covered with moss and ferns. Dana took a seat on a fallen log. "Let's rest."

"I didn't know you could." Travis sat beside her. "Down here it's hard to believe it can burn."

Dana looked up to where the dappled light came through the trees. "The tops of the trees are often not so lucky. All it takes is a lightning strike and they go up."

"Still here it looks like elves should be jumping out at us."

His words said he missed little in his observations. That no doubt made him a good doctor. What did he see in her? She chuckled. "I had no idea you had such an imagination."

"Hang out with me and you might learn a lot more things. How're your feet doing?" Travis stretched out his legs.

"Pretty good. What about yours?"

Concern filled his eyes as he looked down at her. "They've been better. But I have to admit dry socks were nice. For a while."

"We should get going. We're losing daylight. I'd rather not climb the staircase of the fire tower in the dark."

Travis stood and offered her his hand. She placed

hers in it. So strong and warm. Secure. Her problem when they returned to their own world wouldn't be having taken his help but with letting it go. Yet she had to. They weren't meant to be. The only reason he was still here was because he had no choice. Otherwise he'd have been long gone.

They walked for another thirty minutes before they came to an opening where they could see the valley and the river they'd just crossed.

Travis took her hand. "This has to be the most spectacular view. Just gorgeous. This extra hike might not have been our choice but I'm glad I get to share this with you."

She looked at him instead of the view. A honeyed feeling filled her middle making it flutter. Heaven help her, Travis had started to get to her. She wanted a little of what might have been.

CHAPTER SEVEN

TRAVIS FOLLOWED DANA'S lead and kept the pace. They had started downhill again. Thankfully it was more of a meandering walk then before. Soon they were starting back up again.

"When we reach the top we only have a little ways to go before we get to the fire tower."

Sweat ran down the center of his back. His overgrown facial hair itched. Every once in a while he tugged on his damp pants, pulling them away from where they stuck to his legs. His pack grew heavier with each step. He could imagine Dana felt much the same discomfort. Since her bags were wet they must weigh more yet she didn't slow or let him carry them.

Finally they reached a rise and he could see the fire tower clearly. Without breaking her pace, Dana continued along the winding path to the top of the mountain.

The sun lowered. Light had become limited. What started out as a medical mission to help a deathly ill patient had turned into brutal days of hiking. Dana hadn't uttered a single complaint and he didn't intend to either. Despite the fact that his feet were killing him and he'd worked up a blister that hurt like the devil.

"How much farther?"

"Hour. Maybe a little more."

He took another step forward.

Dana looked up. "We're either going to have to push through or make camp."

"This close I say we push through." He wanted comfort and shelter. He had no interest in staying out in weather like last night's.

"Agreed."

Was Dana as determined in every area of her life? He suspected she was. He looked forward to getting caught up in that determination when he had her in his arms. And he'd have her there soon, especially after what happened this morning. He had been shocked at her clear want of him, but he would willingly accept it. Desperately wanted her. He would make the most of the time they had together. Even if he could only offer her now and no more. His heart would remain firmly behind a closed door.

Sooner than he'd expected, they reached a small building constructed on a metal frame that stood six stories high.

Travis had never been so glad to see something in his life. He'd seen pictures of fire towers but had never been up in one. Dark was almost on them. He was tired, hungry and damp and had had enough walking. They crossed the middle of the field.

He put his foot on the first iron rung of the stairs. It consisted of six steps then a platform and six more steps until it reached the top. Looking up, he considered the climb. "Do we stop for a rest or do we keep moving?"

"I'm afraid if I stop I won't get started again. The only downside to that idea is the outhouse is all the way down here." Dana glanced at the small building sitting thirty feet away.

"Both are good points."

"Outhouse later. Wet clothes first." He pulled himself up the first step. "I had no idea these were still being used."

"Mostly they're not for their original purpose. Many are not tall enough to see as large an area as necessary. And technology has gotten so much better they have become obsolete. We have so many better ways of detection now. Mostly they're used by hikers or tourists as a place to stay."

"A rustic hotel room." He'd take any place with a roof and some semblance of relief.

"Yeah, something like that. I'm glad to see no one's rented this one tonight." Dana's booted steps sounded behind him.

"They would've had to share." Travis looked up to find they were only halfway to the top. "We'd have asked nicely."

"Whatever way we did it, we at least have shelter for tonight and a chance to have some heat."

He looked at her. "There's never-ending fun with you."

"Thanks, I think. Don't tell me you're tired of walking in wet shoes."

"I've had enough for the day, the week and possibly the month."

Dana chuckled. "If you need any encouragement there should be a cold shower, canned food and a not-very-good bed. But it'll offer a breathtaking view."

"I'm moving on." He took another step.

"Oh, one more selling point. We won't get wet if it rains."

"All the comforts of home." Travis grinned. He liked the banter between them. It was nice they had found this in their relationship. He hoped there was more of it to come. "Based on the sky, it doesn't look like that's gonna be a problem tonight."

They were almost to the top.

Travis took the landing and started up the last six steps. Above his head was the catwalk that circled the twelve-by-twelve room, glass on all four sides. He climbed through the hole and kept moving until he stood on the catwalk waiting for Dana.

She joined him, then went to the door in the middle of the wall. Turning the knob, she grinned at him when it opened. She pushed it wide and stepped inside.

He followed. "Looks like home sweet home."

Dana chuckled low in her throat. "I think that might be an exaggeration but I'll certainly take it."

The entire building was smaller than his bedroom at the condo. In one corner was a counter, a stove with two burners, and a mini refrigerator. A table with two chairs sat nearby. In the opposite corner stood a bed of sorts made out of wood with an "iffy" mattress, but space enough for two people. In another area were two small, cushioned chairs with a shelf full of books. Simple, and everything they needed to survive.

In the middle of the room stood a round fixture, waist high on him, that had an eighteen-inch map on it.

"What's this?" he ran his hand over the top of the clear covering.

"It's an Osborne Firefinder. It is used to locate the position of a fire. The lookout would then radio in the coordinates. Each tower has one. Old-school stuff now."

"Yeah, but there was some artistry to the old-fashioned way." He continued to study the apparatus.

"Why, Dr. Russell, you continue to surprise me. You can appreciate the simpler times. I always liked the idea of the lone man waiting and watching for that puff of smoke and calling it in."

"The alone part would take a special person. I'm not sure I could be here days upon end by myself." He put his pack down. Unless he had her with him. Wow, where had that idea come from?

Dana unload her bags. "I've gotten used to being by myself so I don't think I'd mind. Enough of that. We need to get busy before it turns dark. I'll check on the propane. Why don't you check on the rain barrel?"

Travis headed out the door and around the catwalk. He located the shower that was much like Mr. Gunter's. He returned inside. "Plenty of water. My guess courtesy of the storm last night."

"Good. We've enough propane too. I found a few canned goods that were left behind. Renters are supposed to take everything with them but some leave their extras behind for people like us. We'll use it because I want to save anything we have in case we need it." Dana picked up her bags and carried them to a chair.

"Sounds like we'll have a hot meal and bath tonight. All the luxuries."

Dana smiled broadly. "Yes indeed. But before we do anything more we need to get our boots and socks off and let our feet breathe. Then pull out our supplies and clothing. Get them to drying."

She immediately went to work removing items from her backpack and supply pack. Travis followed her lead. Soon they had clothing spread out all over the place.

"The majority of my stuff is dry with the exception of my pants, socks and shoes." Travis slung his sleeping bag out across the bed.

She frowned. "And most of mine are wet."

He smiled. "That's what happens when you go swimming with them."

"Not funny. The night is warm. I'm going to hang a few of these things outside, like my sleeping bag and hope they dry some. The smaller stuff I'll put near the stove while I get together supper."

"I'll help you." He grabbed up a pile. "I saw a couple of folding chairs we could put to good use as a clothesline."

She held the door open for him as they went out into the twilight.

Travis nodded his head to the right. "The chairs are around that corner."

Dana led the way and set up the chairs. She then placed her belongings over them.

The pile was almost gone when Travis picked up a scrap of material. He held it at eye level. "Very sexy panties for fighting fires."

Dana snatched them out of his hand. "You're supposed to be helping not admiring my underwear."

He said as innocently as possible, "Hey, they just happened to pop out of the pile."

She huffed. "Okay, funny man, help me with this sleeping bag."

"What're we going to do with it?"

"I want to spread it over the rail." She picked up one end. He took the other. Together they laid it over the outside rail.

"I hope a good blow doesn't come up. They're going to find your belongings in Bend. I'd hate for another man to get to appreciate those panties."

She lightly slapped him on the arm as she went by him. "Have you thought of giving up medicine to do stand-up comedy?"

"I have not, but I just might now that you've encouraged me." He grinned.

"I am not encouraging you." She leaned toward him and glared up at him but a smile formed on her lips.

"That's what it sounded like to me."

Dana returned to straightening her sleeping bag. "Need to get your hearing checked too."

His voice dipped. "Oh, I hear just fine."

She headed toward the door, saying over her shoulder as she went, "Then hear this—I'm fixing dinner and if you want to eat something hot you better be nice to the cook."

He chuckled. "And here I was thinking I had been when I was admiring her panties."

She walked away muttering, "And we've circled back to that."

Dana liked that she and Travis had slipped back into what they'd had so long ago. He used to tease her unmercifully like she was his kid sister. Had that been how he saw her? Maybe she'd imagined there was more between them. He must've been shocked when she tried to kiss him. She'd been humiliated but he had to have been embarrassed, as well. She had never thought of it that way. Being unwanted one more time had been the only thing she could see. She'd been so naive.

It was nice to have her friend back. She hoped they remained that way. Travis kept her on her toes. His wit encouraged her to think, and even his questioning of her decisions made her listen to his views. She worked so hard in the smokejumping program to prove herself, she didn't dare show weakness. Maybe as he said, it wasn't always a sign of weakness to accept help.

Before getting started on their meal she pulled off

her wet long-sleeve shirt leaving on her T-shirt. She laid her outer clothing across one of the chairs and turned on the propane heater. Everything she had was at best damp. She dreaded putting on clammy clothes after her shower, but it was that or walk around naked. The idea of her and Travis acting like Adam and Eve both shocked and intrigued her.

A few minutes later Travis looked over her shoulder. "It smells interesting."

She jumped at him being so near after such an erotic thought. If Travis had any idea what she'd been thinking... Gathering her thoughts she continued to stir the pot. "Is that a compliment?"

"It is. What can I do to help?"

"Grab one of the bags of fruit." She pointed to their supplies.

"I do love good dried fruit." He reached for a packet.

Dana grinned. "Why do I hear no sincerity in those words?"

"Maybe because there wasn't any."

She looked at him. "We'll be home soon. I promise."

"Hey, that wasn't really a complaint. I'll admit I like finer living then we've had for the last few days but I've liked getting to know you again."

"And I've liked getting to know you too." She turned back to the pot. "After dinner I need to check your arm, especially since it got wet."

"And you need another bandage. Yours went down the river." He touched her cheek.

A tingle ran through her. She chuckled and wobbled. "We're a needy pair."

"I know I am."

An odd note had entered Travis's voice making her look at him. He watched her, his eyes dark and wanting.

Dana shivered, yet her blood ran hot. She wasn't so inexperienced that she didn't recognize when a man desired her. That morning, half asleep and toasty warm, she'd wanted him too but now...here...

"I think I'll get a quick shower before dinner." With that he went out the door.

"But dinner's ready," she murmured to the empty air.

Fifteen minutes later at the sound of the door opening and closing she said, "Sit down. This is ready." She spooned the food onto the plates. Heading to the table, she jerked to a stop. Reality had come too close to her fancy. Travis sat at the table with no shirt on. She had a full view of a broad chest with a dusting of hair in the middle. His muscles flexed and relaxed as he picked up his water bottle, taking a swallow. The ripple of his throat fascinated her. She'd seen beautiful sunsets he outdid.

"Sorry about the no shirt and boxers at the table. My mother would have a fit but I couldn't bring myself to put those damp clothes on again."

Dana didn't move.

"Dana?"

Blinking to adjust the train of her thoughts, she placed the food on the table. Despite her hunger she didn't immediately eat. How was she expected to with a half-dressed Travis feet from her? He obviously wasn't having the same problem. He forked the food in as if it was the finest of meals.

"I'd like to enjoy the last of the sunset but I'm too hungry to take the time." He glanced up. "I don't know about you but this wouldn't be my normal fare but it sure does taste good. Nice and hot. Thank you."

"My pleasure." And she meant that. She didn't usually cook for a man, but somehow she liked doing the domestic things for Travis. "What would you be eating if you weren't here having this delicious meal?"

"I really like roast beef, mashed potatoes and gravy, creamed corn and lima beans and homemade rolls."

"Goodness. That's some list." She glanced at her plate. "This doesn't come close to that. Do you cook for yourself?"

"Not very much. I'm pretty good at breakfast. Eggs and bacon. I can make a mean macaroni and cheese out of the box."

She laughed. "I don't think that counts in the culinary world as cooking."

"Mostly I eat at the hospital or out. That was one of my and my ex's biggest disagreements. I wanted us to eat together. She liked to cook but there was never a meal when I got home. Don't get me wrong—I didn't think she should be a slave in the kitchen every night but it would've been nice to have a home-cooked meal waiting a few nights a week."

"I'd think you'd have women falling all over you to cook for you."

He turned his head to the side, lowered his chin and narrowed his eyes. "Actually, I don't. I don't want just anyone to do so. It was my mother's way of showing love. I guess I see it as a declaration of love."

"Oh." Dana looked at the plate again. She couldn't do that. What if he decided he didn't want her after all? She'd never recover from the pain, and she knew that type of pain too well.

Travis finished eating and sat back with a satisfied sigh. "I'll see to cleaning up while you get a shower."

"Thanks." Just before she left, Travis stopped her. "Hey, I have a dry T-shirt if you want it."

"That would be nice."

He went to his bag and pulled out a plastic bag, then removed a shirt.

She shook her head in disbelief as she took the clothing.

Travis made a proud lift to his chin. "A T-shirt can be used for a lot of things. To start a fire, as a towel, to filter water, carry berries, even be torn to make a rope."

"You continue to surprise me."

He watched her with hooded eyes. "I think I like that idea."

Not daring to continue that conversation, she headed outside. She couldn't get to the shower fast enough. Travis's brand of charm had her thinking about things better left alone.

Quickly showering, she realized she had nothing to dry off with so she stood there for a few moments to ring her hair out as much as she could, then using the T-shirt she took off to dry with. The last thing she needed to do was show up looking like she'd just been in a wet T-shirt contest. Grateful it had turned dark and there was still some heat from the day, she looked out at the stars. The lone dim lantern inside didn't ruin the view.

Would it really be so bad for her and Travis to act on what simmered between them? It might. There was a real chance her heart could get involved. All those old feelings she had for Travis had already come rushing back. But did he feel the same?

That morning she would've taken him any way she could have him. But that had been in the heat of the moment, the heat of him. She had the day to think rationally. Still, to have him for even a short time could only be wonderful. Was she strong enough to accept that? To risk the pain for a few moments of pleasure.

She went inside. Thankfully Travis's T-shirt almost

reached her knees, covering her well. She went to check her drying clothes, touching them and flipping some.

"Dana, come to bed. If they dry, they dry. If not, we'll deal."

She turned to find Travis already lying on the single sleeping bag with his back to her. She'd wanted to re-bandage his arm but would wait until morning. Moving the lantern to the floor near the bed, she turned it off and joined Travis. She lay stiffly beside him.

"Relax, Dana. I'm exhausted. When I make love to you we're both going to be well rested. Now sleep."

Dana released the breath she didn't know she had been holding, and closed her eyes.

Travis rolled and pulled the warm body snuggled against him closer. Legs intertwined with his as if Dana wanted to crawl inside him. He had no issue with that. Now fully awake, he couldn't stop himself from appreciating her heat pressed against him. She positioned her thigh across his. He couldn't resist brushing his fingertips over the exposed skin.

She nuzzled her face into his neck, then made the sweetest sound of pleasure. Her hand circled his waist. Her fingers brushed the waistband of his boxers, then wandered away leaving his manhood hard with need.

He kissed the top of her head as his hand cupped her butt, pressing her closer. The tip of her tongue touched his neck. His manhood throbbed. "Dana? Are you awake?"

"Mmm."

"Do you know what you're doing?" It might kill him if the answer wasn't what he wanted to hear.

"Dreaming?" She flexed her hips into his rock-hard length.

"That and other things."

She kissed his chest. "Do you always talk this much in bed?"

"No, I like to do other things much better. But I want you to understand that I can't offer you anything more than right now." His hand found her chin, then his mouth her lips. He had been wanting this for far too long.

"That's all I'm asking for. To be wanted. Right now." Dana's arms moved around his neck and she held him close.

"Sweetheart, I can promise you're wanted." Her lips were as full and luscious as he remembered. His intent had been a tender kiss but when Dana pulled him tighter his desire grew as his mouth became more demanding. He ran his tongue across her plush bottom lip. She opened, welcomed him with her tongue. Such sweetness.

His hand returned to her butt, pressing her against his hardness. Reluctantly he broke the kiss. "I didn't bring any protection."

"I'm on the Pill." She cupped his cheeks and her mouth joined his.

Travis let her go long enough to remove his boxers before sliding over Dana and between her legs. His hand glided up her thigh. He pulled back. "No panties."

"Wet."

"If I had known…"

"Now you do." Her lips brushed his.

"Yes, I do." His mouth found hers again, then floated over her cheek to nuzzle her ear. "You want this?"

"Oh, yes." She flexed upward, her center brushing the tip of his hard length.

With one thrust, Dana's heat surrounded him, gripped him. Captured him. His mouth ground into hers. She returned his passion. As he plunged into her then pulled away, she rose to meet him. Her fingers bit into his shoulders. When he feared he couldn't hold back any longer Dana's body tensed, her hips rose. Her mouth left his as that sweet sound he liked so much rolled over her lips before she quivered and sighed her joy.

He pounded into her, once, twice and thundered off into his own release. One so deeply satisfying he'd had no idea its kind existed. Having sex with Dana, he'd quickly found was far better than skydiving. Pulling her close, he closed his eyes and slept the sleep of a man well pleasured.

CHAPTER EIGHT

DANA WOKE TO just enough light so she could see. Travis's warmth surrounded her. She would never have thought two days ago she'd be lying next to Travis. Those feelings from years ago were still alive. Every man she'd dated she measured by Travis and they had come up wanting. She'd never dreamed he'd return to her life, but now that he had she'd take all of him he'd give her.

She hated to leave his arms but she needed to go downstairs to the outhouse. Sliding from under his arm, she climbed off the bed. Finding the T-shirt and her boots, she carried them outside to put them on. When she returned, Travis stood next to the outside rail with two mugs sitting beside him.

"Good morning. I found some coffee and thought it worth the use of our drinking water."

Dana hesitated. He acted as if it was a normal day. For her the world had shifted.

His gaze met hers—a smile covered his lips. He reached out an arm. "I missed you when I woke."

She stepped to him. His arm came around her waist, pulling her against him as his lips pressed against her temple. He handed her a mug then picked up the other before taking a sip. "I've heard of being just above the clouds but have never experienced it. I've had a number of firsts with you."

Dana looked out at the clouds so thick they appeared as if they could be walked on. The ground wasn't visible. The tops of the trees of a far-off mountain were all that could be seen. It was as if no one else existed in the world. "I've only seen it a couple of times but nothing as thick as this."

They stood sipping their coffee as the sun slowly burnt off the mist.

Travis set his mug down, took hers and did the same. He came to stand behind her. His hands wrapped her waist as he pulled her back against him. The hard length of him pressing into her behind. She moved to turn. His mouth nuzzled her ear. "Hold the rail, Dana. I wish to give you the devotion you deserve but I selfishly didn't take time to give you last night."

"But I want—"

"Shh. Just feel."

His hands went to the hem of the T-shirt. Pulling it up, they traveled along her sides until they cupped her breasts. He lifted, and gently squeezed them. "So perfect." His lips muttered against her ear before they teased the hollow behind her ear.

She leaned her head to the side so he had better advantage. Heat pooled heavy at her center.

His fingers traced her nipples, teased them then tugged until they were hard nibs. His palms came to rest over them. She squirmed, her knees becoming weak.

His tongue traced the shell of her ear. Dana hummed low in her throat. She had turned as tight as a violin string and he strummed her.

She reached around him before grabbing his thighs. That only brought him nearer making her more aware of his rock-hard manhood. Still his skillful hands continued to do magical things to her breasts.

Her mouth fell open as her breaths turned to pants. She returned her hands to the rail so she wouldn't fall as pleasure rocked her.

Travis continued to leave tiny kisses along her hairline as one of his hands went to her middle, locking her against him while his fingers brushed her curls on the way to her center. Involuntarily she widened her legs, throbbing for his attention. He stopped just before slipping into her wet and waiting heat. He retreated.

Dana moaned her protest. Her center pulsed, begging for his touch. Her fingers turned white where they gripped the rail. She flexed against Travis, her body pleading for his continued devotion.

His lips moved to the curve of her neck as his hand returned to her center. All her concentration, her blood, focused on her center, the pounding need to have Travis's attention.

His fingertips caressed her swollen center. That wasn't enough. She arched chasing his touch.

"Turn around, sweetheart. I want to see you come against the sunrise."

Dana did as he asked but only with his help. She gripped his forearms.

"Lean back, sweetheart." One of his arms lay along the rail. "I've got you."

Dana did as he asked. She would have done anything he asked.

Travis pushed at the T-shirt, baring her breasts, and looked at her. "So beautiful." His mouth took one of her nipples and sucked as his finger entered her.

She bucked. It was as if a lightning strike had hit her sending its power zipping through her. She closed her eyes and felt. Travis's mouth continued to caress her breasts as his finger teased her nub. A tightness built, twisted, curled then pleaded for release. Dana threw back her head, pressed against the rail and down on Travis's masterful hand before screaming her release. She shuddered as it echoed in the morning air.

When her knees failed to hold her, Travis brought her against him. He held her tenderly. After a few minutes she stepped back still steadying herself with hands on his biceps.

He looked into her eyes. "Thank you for that gift. It was the most amazing experience of my life."

Dana's cheeks heated and she looked away.

Using a curled finger, Travis raised her chin so she had to meet his gaze. "You're an extraordinary woman, Dana Warren." He kissed her softly.

She wrapped her arms around his waist and pulled him tight, kissing him deeply. "I need you in me."

With a swift turn, he had her pinned against the glass. Seconds later his boxers were on the catwalk. Minutes later the birds flew from the trees at the roar of her name across Travis's lips.

Travis watched from the bed for a peep of Dana's naked sweet butt beneath his T-shirt as she checked the clothing to see if it was dry. Could a morning get any better than this? "You know, I really did think about you through the years."

Her gaze shot to meet his. "You did?"

"You're not that easy to forget." That brought a small smile to her face.

"I thought about you, as well. What did you wonder about me?"

He leaned up on an elbow to see her better. "At first I

wondered how bad I had hurt your feelings. Then I just wondered where you were. If you were happy." His voice took on a soft note. "You should know it's never wrong to let someone know you care about them. I really am sorry I hurt you."

"You didn't mistreat me. I had a crush." She kept messing with the clothes. "As I've already said, it was the heat of the moment."

"I was a self-centered young man who thought he had his whole world planned out. Was doing what he'd been told would get him ahead in the world." That was exactly what he had been doing. He'd not realized that until now. Not once had he thought about what he really wanted. Why did he feel he had to follow some established plan for his life? Why hadn't he thought about what made him happy?

"That's all a long time ago." She continued moving clothes around. "We need to get started."

"I don't see why we can't spend the day here. Head out tomorrow." Travis patted the bed and grinned.

She returned it. "As much as I'd like that idea, I don't think the forest service wants to pay me for spending all day in bed with you."

"Is there any reason we can't leave in an hour?" He winked. Dana started toward him. Her focus left him to look out the window behind him and she jerked to a stop.

He rolled, looking out, as well. "What's wrong?"

"Smoke." Her voice had lost it humor.

"There was no electrical storm."

"Most likely a careless camper." She jerked on her panties, then pulled off the T-shirt put on the bra and returned the shirt. Finding her pants, she stepped into them.

Dana had morphed into firefighter mode. What he'd hoped for wasn't going to happen.

"No matter how many times we say no burning, no campfires this time of the year someone inevitably ends up letting one get out of hand." She picked up the radio and headed for the door. "I'm calling base."

Travis rolled out of bed and started dressing.

Dana returned. "So far they haven't seen the smoke so it's still small. Since I'm so close I need to go see about it. Maybe it's just a campfire. You can head on out. All you have to do is follow the road. It's a walk but it reaches a main road. I can radio in and have someone pick you up."

"Not going to happen. I'm going with you." Travis started packing his bags.

"You don't have to."

His gaze met hers. "You're not going alone."

Her look of surprise took him off guard. "Is something wrong?"

Her eyes were bright. "No, I'm just not used to someone being that concerned about me."

He took her hand and pulled her gently to him. "What're friends for?" He kissed her and patted her on the butt. "Now let's get moving. We've a fire to see about."

She grinned, turned and picked up her belongings.

"Can't we leave some of these supplies here? Travel lighter. Come back for them."

"No, they have to go with us. We may not be back this way."

Fifteen minutes later they had their packs on. "Let's go. If it's any consolation there's no water to cross on this trip."

"I do love dry feet." He hadn't let on to her what bad shape his feet were in. If he had she would've insisted he stay behind. He'd patched himself up with the supplies he had and put on two pairs of socks. Had also taken two pain relievers while she was outside seeing to the stuff hanging there. "I'm ready when you are."

They headed down the stairs. At the bottom, Dana checked with base for more information and confirmed GPS coordinates of the fire. She set a steady pace as they walked across the field into the woods.

"How far away do you think it is?"

"Couple of miles. It shouldn't take long to get there."

Thoughts of their earlier activities kept him from thinking about his feet. He wanted to repeat them. Bring that look of delight to Dana's face again.

Dana hated she hadn't gotten Travis back to town before going off to another fire. He was a doctor not a firefighter. She'd tried to leave him behind, but from the determined look in his eyes he wasn't going to let that happen. Her heart had swelled at his support but she'd seen the gingerly way he walked. His feet pained him.

She'd glanced in the window when she'd been out on the catwalk and seen him caring for his feet. Taking longer than necessary, she gave him time to finish before she announced they should go. She hated Travis was hurt but she didn't have time to argue with him about going or not.

They broke into an open area of small bushes with an occasional tree. Travis came up beside her. Smoke filled the air. "Let's hope it hasn't gotten out of hand by the time we get there."

"I'll second that." To go home for a rest and hot bath sounded good right now. She glanced at Travis. Yet she'd miss him when they got back. But that had been the plan.

This morning on the catwalk had been unbelievable. Too many orgasms like that and her heart might burst. That Travis had given it to her only made it sweeter. It would be a precious memory of their time together.

Once again she smelled the fire before she saw it. Moving forward they found the scorched black burn line. "It looks as if we've caught it early. We need to get out in front of it and make a fire line. Stop it before it crawls any farther. I only have half a tank of gas left for the chain saw. We have to plan its use carefully."

"Hey!" A young man who looked in his early twenties came running toward them waving his hands above his head. "I'm glad to see you." He coughed. "Can you help us?"

"What's wrong?" Dana asked.

The man pointed behind him toward some rocks that had just been missed by the fire. "My friend broke his leg."

Travis turned to her. "I'll check on him then come help you. I want you to stay within my eyesight until I can get to you."

She nodded.

"If you don't promise to do as I say, I'm coming with you right now." Travis narrowed his eyes and watched her closely.

He'd make that kind of choice for her? No one outside her grandfather ever had and he hadn't wanted to. She'd been pretty much thrust into his lap.

"I'll do my best. But it's my job."

Travis's look bored into hers. Then he nodded. "Good enough."

As he and the guy hurried away she heard Travis say, "I'm a doctor. Tell me how your friend got hurt."

The wind picked up and the smoke grew heavier as she approached the fire. She pulled her bandanna up over her mouth and started to work on a firebreak.

Once she'd glanced back to see Travis standing up and

looking her direction as if searching the area. Apparently he saw her because he sat down again beside his patient. Half an hour later, he joined her as she worked the dirt with her Pulaski.

"The hurt guy?"

Travis joined in right beside her. "He's settled out of harm's way, leaning against a tree. I told both guys to stay put and we'd be back for them. I had the guy lay your damp sleeping bag and our clothes out in the sun."

"Really?"

"Yeah, we're going to need them to get the hurt one to help. I also figured we might have to spend another night out here."

"It's starting to look that way." She picked up the pace and he did the same.

It was the middle of the afternoon when they stopped and surveyed their progress. Travis stood with his gloved hands on the top of his Pulaski handle. She surveyed the black area around them, having already gone down on her hands and knees to test for any heat in the soil.

"It looks like we got it." Dana pulled her bandanna down and wiped her face on her sleeve.

"Yeah, it does."

She looked at Travis. He studied her. She asked, "What's wrong?"

"I was just thinking how completely inappropriate it would be to kiss you but I really want to."

She licked her lips and stepped to him. "It might be, but I'd sure like one."

Travis took her in his arms; his mouth touched hers with such gentleness she almost cried. She clung to him. His lips were a caress pressed against hers. When she would've taken the kiss deeper he kept it tender as if he was trying to express the depth of his feelings. Her arm went around his neck while another lay on his chest. His heart beat solid and sure beneath her hand.

Heaven help her, she would miss him when their time was over.

He pulled back, placing his black-from-smoke-and-dirt forehead against hers. After taking a deep breath, he let it out slowly. "As much as I wish we were going to be alone again tonight, I think we need to get back to my patient. We've got to work out some arrangement for getting him to a hospital."

"Can't we call in Rescue?" Dana picked up the chain saw sitting not far away.

"We could but it'll be dark before they could make it this far today. If the weather doesn't turn maybe they could make it in the morning. I still think we need to plan to get him out of here on our own."

"Agreed. Do you think the guys will be where you left them?"

"Yeah." Travis took her hand and held it as they went as if they were strolling in a park. She couldn't help but smile at the picture they must make. Nasty, sweaty and dusty from head to toe. "They were both too scared to move. Especially when I told them you work for the forest service. They knew they were in trouble then."

"Ah, I get to be the bad guy."

He grinned. "Someone's gotta do it."

As they walked up to the guys, the mobile one came running to them. "I was afraid you had forgotten about us."

She tried to pull her hand from Travis's but he hung on to it.

"No. It just takes time to put out a fire," Travis said not slowing down until they reached the injured fellow. "Ted," Travis indicated the man with a broken leg, "and

Jim, this is Dana Warren, a smokejumper with the US Forest Service."

"Ah, hi." Jim shrugged. "Sorry about the fire."

Ted gave her a weak smile. His eyes were glazed over in pain.

Travis choked back a chuckle as she glared at Jim.

"We just had a small campfire. We had to cook." The guy's voice climbed higher with each word. "I don't know how it got out. It became a brush fire like that." He snapped his fingers. "We tried to stop it but we couldn't. Everything we did made it worse. I got burnt then Jim fell and broke his leg."

After her initial disgust, Dana couldn't help but feel sorry for the guy despite him not following the law during fire season. She pursed her lips and shook her head. Young and stupid. She looked at Travis. She'd been that once. Was she now being older and stupid?

He looked at her and raised a brow. Was he thinking the same thing?

"Do you have any water?" Travis asked.

Jim said, "Yeah. Right here. We managed to save a few of our supplies. Our parents would kill us if we'd lost their stuff."

Dana rolled her eyes. Apparently they'd been more concerned with saving their butts instead of the forest. Jim went around the tree and returned with an armload of camping equipment including two CamelBak canteens.

Travis leaned his Pulaski against the tree and went down on his knees beside Ted and said in a calm, reassuring voice, "We're going to need to get this splinted and secured so we can get you out of here. You'll be fine."

Dana's heart filled with pride. After fighting a fire for the last six hours, kissing her like she was the most precious person in the world, Travis was now caring for his patient. He was the most amazing man. She hadn't been wrong all those years ago. He had been special then and he still was.

Travis sighed as he looked at Ted's leg. What he wouldn't give if he and Dana were on their way back to the fire tower. Even their gentle kiss had left him wanting more. He spoke to Ted. "I'm going to need to cut your pants so I can see more clearly what's going on."

"Okay." Ted's eyes were glassy with pain. The over-the-counter pain reliever wasn't doing much for him.

Travis looked at Jim. "You go find two solid limbs that I can use for splints. Make them as long as your leg."

"Dana, would you check on a helicopter then come help me?"

"Ten-four." A few minutes later she returned to stand beside him.

"So can they send one?" Travis asked over his shoulder.

"You were right. Not this late in the day. Tomorrow morning at the earliest. But they are expecting another front with high winds. They'll let us know if they can make a pickup."

Disappointment filled Travis as he looked back at his patient. "Just as I thought. Then we'll have to work as if we are going to have to carry him out of here. We need to clean up some if I'm going to work with his leg." He picked up his pack and carried it far enough away they had some privacy.

Dana followed him.

He pulled out his now well-used T-shirt and wet it before handing it to her.

She wiped her face and cleaned her hands. "Kind of makes you wish for a good river doesn't it?"

He grinned. "That it does. What I'm dreaming of is a hot shower with you." Dana rewarded him with pink coming to her cheeks even through the dirt. "You make me want to kiss you when you blush."

She handed him the T-shirt. "Clean your face, Dr. Russell, and I'll pour water over your hands." She took the bottle from him.

With Dana's help he managed to get his hands fresh enough he felt he could care for a patient.

"What do you want me to do?"

"Go through our supplies and theirs and find anything that can be cut up to be used as wrapping on the leg. I want you to help me with that when Jim returns. Do you think we can make it back to the tower before it turns dark?"

Dana looked at the sun. "I'd hate to chance it if we're carrying an injured person."

"That what I was thinking. We make camp here tonight and build something to carry Ted out with just in case we need it."

"I can get Jim started on that when he gets back. I'll cut some limbs and we'll make a travois, like the Native Americans used to move their goods with. Will that work?"

Travis smiled, and nodded. "That would be brilliant."

"We'll cut the ropes off the parachutes to strap the poles together and use them to create the bed for him to lie on. The sleeping bag on top should make it as comfortable as possible."

"Sounds like a plan. If Rescue can't get here we'll walk him out and have someone at the tower to meet us."

"Agreed."

Jim came running toward them. "I've got them." He held up a stick in each hand.

"Put them over there near Ted. We've another job for you." Travis went to his supply bag and pulled out his parachute. "Cut the ropes off of this. Make them as long as possible." He handed the material to Jim.

"Did you guys parachute in here?" His eyes went wide with disbelief.

"Yes, we did," Dana said evenly.

Travis took a deep breath. "Do you have a knife?"

"Yep." Jim showed him.

"Then get to work." Travis pointed toward the bags.

"Dana, will you come help me, please." Travis went down on his knees beside Ted. "I'm going to need you at his feet."

Dana went to the ground also.

"Ted, I'm going to remove these temporary splints. Then I'm going to have to cut your pants."

"Pretty ingenious splinting there, Doc," Dana said.

Travis gave her a thin-lipped grin. He'd used part of a thin flexible tent pole from the guys' tent. "Thanks. It's what I had in a pinch but he needs something sturdier if we plan to move him. That's why I sent Jim out for limbs."

From behind Travis Jim said, "Yeah, but my dad's going to be mad when he finds out it's broken."

"And your dad isn't going to be happy to learn you started a forest fire either." Travis was on the road to losing patience with the dense kid.

Carefully, Travis removed the splinting, then took scissors from his medical pack and cut up the inside seam of Ted's pants. When he could pull the material back enough, he examined the injured area. The break was just below the knee.

"It looks as if both the tibia and the fibula are broken. Without X-rays I couldn't be certain. We'll just have to treat it as the worst-case scenario." The area around it had turned a vivid red and blue. "The bone hasn't come through the skin. We need to see that it doesn't."

It would be tricky to do so with the rough ride Ted would have the next morning but Travis could only do his best.

"Dana, while I'm getting everything we need together would you mind taking his vitals. The last thing we need is Ted starting to run a fever."

"Jim, stop what you're doing and find another tent pole. I need it as well for splinting." Travis called over his shoulder.

Dana picked up his medical bag and went to Ted's head.

Jim grumbled but did as he was told. Travis took the pole, then cut the elastic cord that held them together, giving him two poles to work with.

"Temp is normal. Heartrate is elevated and pulse is, as well," Dana reported.

"Not a surprise since he's in pain. Come down to his feet now. I want you to put your elbows on the ground and support his calf between your forearms while I put more splints on. First, I'm going to wrap the area then reapply the splints."

Picking up one of the guys' shirts, Travis ripped a sleeve off. He wrapped it around the injured area. "I want this to support and not restrict blood flow." He spoke more to himself than to the others. He picked up another sleeve and applied it. "Now for the tent poles."

Dana straightened and rolled her shoulders before assuming her position again.

Travis placed one between Ted's legs. "I'm going to tie these off then I want to put one on the back and front of his leg." He looked at Dana. "I'll need you to help me with tying those." He picked up a strip of cloth.

"Okay, Dana. Now I need you to pull the end of the cloth through when I push it under his thigh." He did so and she pulled it up. Putting the last two poles in place, he tied them down. "Now let's do the lower part of the leg."

By the time he and Dana were through manipulating the leg Ted's lips were white and his eyes closed. That was a good thing. Travis had very little to give him as pain reliever. He had one dose of hydrocodone left that he'd brought for Mr. Gunter. He wanted to save it to give Ted in the morning. His ride out would be painful.

Travis patted Ted's shoulder. "I'm sorry I can't do anything more."

"I appreciate what you have done." Ted mumbled.

Dana brushed the hair back from the guy's face. She looked at Travis and her eyes were dark with concern. Dana had a tender heart. She picked up her supply bag and put it under Ted's good leg.

"Good thinking," Travis said. "It'll help prevent shock."

Dana picked up a nearby sleeping bag and opened it before placing it over Ted.

"Let's get the travois made before it gets dark."

"Jim," Travis called. "We're going to need your help."

The guy looked up from where he removed the lines from the parachute canopy. A pile of rope lay beside him.

"I need you to go with Dana. She'll show you what to do."

Without a word Dana picked up the chain saw and started into the woods.

The thing he liked best about Dana was that he could trust her. She didn't think about herself first. His ex-wife had always questioned how it would affect her. Dana was resilient. The last few days had been tough and she weathered them well. With her, he knew what it was like to have a true partner. Not just in name only.

Despite their earlier disagreements they had become friends. Real ones. The kind who could trust each other through thick and thin. The golden ones that were hard to come by. Lovers could come and go but someone who you could trust was rare, to be valued.

Dana was no shrinking violet nor was she somebody who had to have everyone's attention. She shone despite her efforts not to. Her confidence came from her skills and her love of life. She earned that the hard way. Life hadn't always been kind to her but she'd kept on moving forward, following her dream. Could he say the same about himself?

He rechecked Ted's vitals. The grind of the saw came from not far off. He went to work to see about their supplies and repacking the ones that were dry. Thankfully most of them were. He was glad to see Jim had left Dana's panties in her bag. Those he should be the only male allowed to touch.

Soon Dana and Jim returned. He pulled two limbs along behind him. Dana did the same with one about half the length of the others.

Dana seat the chain saw down and spoke to Jim. "Lay yours parallel to each other. Then cross one end over the other." Jim did as she said. She then laid the pole she'd carried over the poles a foot from the ends of the others. The poles made a triangle. When they were done one person would be able to pull or the three of them could carry when necessary.

Travis picked up the rope Jim had cut and joined them. "We need to get these tied off." Dana took a rope from him and started tying the crossed poles by weaving in and out and around.

Travis took one and started working it around one of the bottom intersections.

Dana said to the watching Jim, "Look through that pile and find the longest pieces."

Jim went to work.

Travis finished off the intersection he'd been working on and started on the other.

When he finished Dana said, "Jim, bring a rope and come help me." He did. "I'm going to tie it off over here, then pass it to you and I want you to wrap it around twice and pass it back to me. We're going to zigzag it all the way to the end. We'll tie the rope together as we go until we have created a bed."

Jim grinned. "This is so rad."

Travis stopped himself from rolling his eyes. Had he been this unaware when he'd been Jim's age? He looked at Dana. He feared he might have been.

"With the give of the rope we'll make Ted as comfortable as we can." Dana gave her work on the travois the same focus she did everything. Done, she went to the front, turned around, putting her hand behind her and holding the poles she pulled. It worked great.

Travis decided then she wouldn't be doing the pulling when the time came.

Dana looked at him. "What do you think?"

"I think you do good work." Once again she'd impressed him.

She smiled broadly. His heart swelled. He made a mental reminder to brag on her often.

"What're we gonna do with it?" Jim asked.

He and Dana looked at each other, then back at Jim.

Travis said with as even a tone as he could manage,

"We're gonna put Ted on it and you and I are going to take turns pulling him out of here if we have to."

"Oh."

"Dana, please pull it over beside Ted. I'd like to get him off the ground for the night if we can. Jim, come help us."

Dana put the travois down and picked up one of the guys' sleeping bags. Opening it, she laid it over the ropes leaving enough to cover Ted with.

"Jim," Travis squatted down beside Ted, "get across Ted from me. We're going to lift Ted while he's still unconscious. He'd be in real pain if we did it while he was awake. The longer he's out the better for him."

"What do I need to do?" Dana asked.

"I want you to hold his broken leg as level as possible."

"Now, Jim, slide a hand under his shoulders. I'll slide mine under his lower back and we lift on three."

Everyone moved to their positions.

"Ready? On three. One, two, three," Travis called.

Between the three of them they managed to get Ted where Travis wanted him. Ted did moan but settled quickly. He just did fit in the space they had made for him.

"You guys lift this end and let me get this pack under his feet again." Dana situated the pack on the ground beneath one end of the travois.

"Good job." Dana pulled the sleeping bag over Ted and tucked it in.

"I'm hungry," Jim announced. "What're we going to eat for supper without a campfire?"

Travis walked over to his pack and pulled out a bag of MREs. He tossed it to Jim. "Bon appétit."

"What?" Jim gave him an odd look.

Travis had had enough. He and Dana had been at it

since sunup and he was hungry and tired. "Just open it and eat." He pulled out two more bags. He looked at Dana. "What would you like? Vegetables and roast beef or vegetables and roast beef."

She gave him a tired smile. "I guess vegetables and roast beef it is."

Travis handed her two packages. Dana sat down where she was. Travis got their water and joined her.

"This is dried-up food." Jim sounded as if he was being asked to eat worms.

"Yeah, but wasn't it you who tried to start a cook fire in a 'no fire' time of year?" Travis couldn't stop himself from saying.

Jim had the good grace to look ashamed.

Dana ate without saying much. She looked exhausted and had a right to be. The bandage on her face had long ago fallen off. He'd kept her up during the night and they'd risen early that morning. They'd walked a distance through the woods to then put out a fire before caring for an injured person. She'd earned her rest.

Jim stood nearby looking awkward.

Dana patted the ground next to her. "Jim, come sit with us and tell us where you live."

The guy wiggled like a puppy as he joined them. Dana had that effect on people. If gruff old Mr. Gunter had warmed to her then anyone could. What made her special was she didn't work at it or realize it. She was genuine in her caring.

Soon the sun had gone behind the mountains.

Dana stood. "I'm going to get some sleep. I've had a long day. Tomorrow we'll either meet the helicopter or walk out of here. Either way we'll have to be up at daylight."

She stuffed her water bottle and paper wrapper in her bag.

"Daylight?" Jim echoed.

Travis pursed his lips. That was it for him. "You do realize that you started a forest fire today that burnt land that belongs to all of us. Your friend is seriously injured. He needs to be in a hospital and will need an operation. He has a painful trip ahead of him."

Dana stepped up beside Travis and placed her hand on his arm. "It's time we all got some rest."

Travis looked at her. She gave him a slight smile. Without another word he went to where he'd left their sleeping bags rolled on top of the parachute canopy. He opened one bag and laid it out. He then unzipped hers, placing it on top of his. Dana didn't ask any questions about the arrangement. She took off her boots and outside shirt, climbed under the top bag and removed her pants. He did the same. As far as he was concerned Jim could fend for himself.

Travis pulled Dana to him. She resisted for a moment but he slipped his arm under her head and kissed her temple. She soon rolled to her side, and snuggled against his chest.

"Hell of a day to start it out so sweetly," he whispered.

"Uh-huh."

"Good night, sweetheart." His arm rested around her waist. Despite the way the day had gone, he liked the ending. Having Dana in his arms seemed right. He closed his eyes to the sound of her soft easy breathing.

CHAPTER NINE

DANA CLUNG TO the warmth. Not wanting to wake.

"Dana, it's almost sunrise."

She even liked that voice.

She burrowed closer to the warmth.

"Sweetheart, you keep that up and we're going to put on a show for these guys."

Her eyes opened wide.

Travis grinned. He stood and pulled his pants on but not before she saw his manhood standing tall and proud behind his boxers. She groaned. Grabbing her pants, she pulled them on while inside the sleeping bag and stood.

Travis took her in his arms.

"We can't," she said looking around him.

He frowned. "Can't I at least get a good morning kiss?"

She smiled and put her arms around his neck. "That I'll do."

Travis's mouth met hers as if he was a dying man and she could save him. One of his hands went to her butt and pulled her tight against him. "Feel what you do to me?"

His kiss promised more when they were alone. But that wouldn't happen. They were going home today. And their own ways. He'd not said anything about seeing her again. She hadn't either. They both were adults and knew the score. With that thought she tightened her hold and kissed him deeply. With a groan, he released her, but acting as reluctant to let her go as she was to have him do so. So quickly she'd become attuned to him.

Sometime during the night he'd gotten out of bed. She'd woken missing his warmth and hard body holding hers. There had been enough moonshine she could see him checking on Ted.

"Is everything okay?" she'd asked.

Travis returned to bed pulling her close. "Shh. Everything's fine. Go back to sleep."

Just like that she had. As if Travis telling her things were fine made it so. He'd take care of her and everyone else, as well. She loved the security he provided when she'd had so little in her life.

As soon as he'd dressed, Travis left her and went to Ted, and started taking his vitals. The kid's lips were tight with pain. While Travis saw to Ted she stepped away to talk to base about the helicopter. She soon returned.

Travis looked at her. "What're the arrangements? When will the helicopter be here?"

She pursed her lips and shook her head. "No time soon. Best they can do it midmorning. There're only two copters and both are out on runs for more urgent cases. We'd come out better time wise by carrying him out."

Travis closed his eyes. "And every day brings another adventure."

Dana hurried to break camp. She noticed Travis using a syringe to give Ted an injection in his arm.

"What's that you're giving him?"

"Hydrocodone. I'd brought this with me in case I needed it for Mr. Gunter."

"I'm glad you had some left. I'm afraid Ted will need it." She smiled down at the guy.

He was so miserable he didn't even try to return it.

"My thought too." Travis took the guy's arm, prepared it for a shot and expertly inserted the needle. Afterward Travis offered Ted something to drink. "We don't need you dehydrated."

Jim grumbled when he had to get up. Only when Travis threatened to leave him did Jim start moving. "Maybe Ted and I should've gone to the beach."

Travis nodded. "Yeah, I think you guys should give that some thought next time you're planning a trip. Get your stuff together and let's get moving. Don't leave anything behind."

Travis joined her at the front of the travois. He leaned in close. "Let's get this guy," he nodded toward Jim, "out of here before he dies despite our best efforts to save him."

Dana rolled her eyes. "I know what you mean. If he wasn't so innocent I'd see that the book was thrown at them."

"I'll take first turn pulling," Travis announced. "Jim, you carry the supplies." Travis picked up the poles and they headed out.

They'd not traveled far when Dana was glad Travis had given Ted pain medicine. Bumping over the ground as he was, he could only be in agony.

They started their return trip to the fire tower because that was where someone would be waiting on them. The tower had the nearest road. It was slow and arduous journey. While they crossed open spaces, Travis pulled. When they came to the trees and the upward grade Travis had Jim take the front while she and Travis carried the back. He also made sure to handle the chain saw, as well.

The trip would've been easier if it hadn't been for the moaning and groaning of Jim but he did keep moving. Dana wasn't sure if it was from his fear of Travis or from the fact that he knew if he kept going there would eventually be an end to the misery. Ted thankfully slept.

Travis called a halt for rest a number of times, not only for themselves but for Ted. What should've been a two-hour trip turned into a four-hour one. It was with great relief she saw the fire tower across the open field. With the tower in sight, Jim managed to find new energy and pick up the pace.

She was even happier to see the light green forest service truck base had told her to expect. Dana casually knew the female ranger waiting. She'd brought fresh water which was eagerly accepted. The road into the fire tower had been determined too rough for an ambulance. They'd meet it at the ranger station out on the main road. It took some time to settle Ted in the bed of the pickup truck to Travis's satisfaction. He climbed in the back beside the young man.

"Jim, ride back here. I'll need your help to steady Ted."

Dana took the open seat in the cab. She spent much of the ride looking through the window to check on the passengers in the back. More times than not Travis and Jim were holding the travois poles up so the going would be easier for Ted.

Once she caught Travis's attention and he winked at her. Her stomach fluttered. He had a way of making her feel all woman. Like a girl crazy about a guy. One she soon wouldn't be seeing any more. They'd agreed to short-term.

Over the bumpy, often washed-out road it took them almost an hour to reach the paved street and another thirty minutes to arrive at the rangers' station. There the ambulance waited.

As they pulled in, the EMTs were ready with the

stretcher. Jim's and Ted's parents were there, as well. She and Travis quickly became busy, making it difficult for them to talk. She focused on the parents while Travis gave a report to the EMTs as he oversaw Ted being moved to the stretcher.

With what she needed to say to the parents finished, Dana moved away letting them fuss over their sons. She stood beside the ranger truck and watched the EMTs load Ted into the ambulance.

Travis walked over to her. "I've got to go with Ted."

"I figured you would. I've got to go to my office."

"Dr. Russell, are you coming?" One of the EMTs called as he held one of the back doors open.

"Be right there." Travis gave her one last look of regret and a wave as he loped off and climbed into the ambulance.

A heaviness fell over her as if she was being smothered. Tears formed but she checked them before they rolled. What they'd found together had just slipped out of her hands. Travis was gone again. They were in the real world once more. Things were different there.

But that was how it was supposed to happen. He didn't want forever. She had her safe life where she wouldn't get hurt. So why did it matter so much? It was time to get back to the life she'd built.

Dana looked at the ranger. "I'm ready to go."

"Sounds like you and the doctor had a few wild days together," the ranger said as she pulled out into the road.

"Yeah. It was interesting at times." Days that she'd like to have back.

"Also sounds like you and Dr. Russell made a pretty good team."

"We did." Especially in bed. She already missed him. But that was then and this was now. He'd said nothing about calling her. She hadn't asked. Hadn't had a chance. Or was it fear over what he might answer? She refused to have a repeat of what had happened years before. This time she would handle her feelings better.

At the station she pulled out her supply bag and Travis's, as well. After returning their equipment to Cache, she went to the locker room and took a long hot shower. As nice as it was, her thoughts were about the cold ones she'd had while with Travis. The smoke still clung to her hair as she blew it dry. As long as it stayed it would remind her of her time with Travis.

In the main office she found an open computer and wrote up her report being as detailed as possible but leaving out how close she and Travis had become. Reliving it through words only made the loss sharper.

On her way out, she stuck her head into Leo's office.

He looked up. "Hey, good to see you."

"It's nice to be back. You should have my report in your email."

His brows rose. "I understand you've had an interesting few days."

She shrugged and held the door frame tighter. "That'd be an understatement."

"Your trail crew is already in."

"That's what I heard." She had forgotten about them as her days with Travis had lengthened.

"I'm giving you and them a few days to rest up before I put you back in the rotation."

"Okay."

Leo's eyes narrowed. "No argument?"

She shook her head. "Nope."

He studied her a moment. "Is there something I need to know?"

She pursed her lips. "No."

Leo still studied her. "If that changes let me know. See you on Thursday ready to go up again."

"I'll be here." She made her way out to her truck.

Just a few days before, her ranch had been her haven. The place she went to reenergize. Now she dreaded being alone. There would be too much time to relive the hours with Travis, his kisses, those explosive moments on the catwalk, the look in his eyes when he desired her...

She'd known better than to get involved with him. He'd never once promised her anything. What had happened between them had all been the heat of the moment. Convenience. But for her...he'd gotten under her skin, again. She liked the guy outside of bed and in. They had rekindled their friendship. For that she was grateful.

Travis hadn't liked leaving Dana like he did. He would much rather have gone back to the station with her, hustled her through whatever paperwork she had to do and then followed her home into a shared hot shower, and then bed, with some sexual fun in both places. He sighed. Sadly that hadn't been how things worked out or been their agreement.

A night of passion had been the deal. He would honor that. But it would be difficult. He wanted more of Dana.

With his report about his care of Ted to the ER doctor finished, Travis waited with Ted and his parents until he had been wheeled into the OR to have his leg set. Eager to get away so he could clean up and possibly see Dana, he got a ride to the smokejumper station. To his disappointment, Dana had already gone for the night and the office was closed except for the dispatcher. He asked the woman for Dana's number but she told him she wasn't allowed to give that information out.

Maybe it was just as well. Travis rubbed his hand

across his jaw. He needed a shave. To get some good sleep. Dana needed the rest, as well. His feared when he had a soft mattress with a good hot meal in his belly he might not be able to sleep well without Dana beside him.

He had learned one thing on their big adventure. That since his divorce he'd closed himself off to life. He'd been so fearful of making plans and being disappointed that he'd quit thinking about the future. His personal life had become an endless stream of no emotional attachments. If he didn't care then he didn't get hurt. But was that a healthy way to live?

A half an hour later while standing under the water he wondered how Dana was doing. In bed, he tossed and turned. How swiftly he'd become used to having her next to him. Maybe she'd be willing to extend their agreement. She might even call him. If not, he'd give her a few days and call her. Ask her how she was doing. If she'd recovered from their trip. With his first plan that had something to do with a woman in a long time in mind, he went to bed with a smile on his face.

The next morning he called to check on Mr. Gunter's progress and to see how Ted was doing. He received good reports. Then there was a week's worth of work to tackle and patients to see.

Two days went by and he still hadn't heard from Dana. He called the station, determined to check on her. The person who answered told him she was there but couldn't come to the phone right then. He left a message for her to call him.

When he hadn't heard from her by late afternoon he phoned the station again. "This is Dr. Russell. May I speak to Dana?"

"I think she's around here somewhere. Hold on a minute."

He paced across his small office. Since when had he

been so nervous about calling a woman? Dana was already messing with his ordered life. He made another three trips across the floor before she came to the phone.

"Hi, Dana. It's Travis."

"Hey." An unsure note surrounded the word.

"I was just calling to check on you. See if you've recovered from our adventures."

"I'm fine. How about you?"

The warmth in her voice had returned. Suddenly this call had taken on more importance. "I'm great. Still sore but getting better every day." He cleared his throat. "I'd like to see you."

There was a pause. "This is fire season. I never know my schedule."

His heart sank. "I understand. Maybe another time."

"If you wouldn't mind coming to my place…"

"I'll bring supper and we can eat it on your porch." He wasn't going to give her time to change her mind.

"Does six work?"

"That's fine." Why did she sound so unsure? Their last morning together she had been warm and responsive to his kiss. He'd like to hear more enthusiasm in her voice. Was she afraid of him? He didn't like that idea.

She gave him her address.

"I'm looking forward to seeing you." His voice softened as he gripped the phone.

"Me too."

That note of anticipation he'd been looking for turned up in those two words. He said goodbye with a smile on his face. It shouldn't matter so much to him. He had been the one who had said he wouldn't be offering more.

As he drove along Dana's gravel lane three hours later, Travis couldn't remember being this excited about seeing much like permanency. That wasn't what he'd intended. Loose and easy had been the plan.

"I just think we need to stop this before it gets out of hand. Like eight years ago you wanted one thing and I needed another. It's no different now."

He pulled to a jerking stop before her front door, turned off the car and shifted so he could look at her. The porch light gave him enough illumination to see her expressions. "But we've been having a good time together. We're good together and you know it."

"Sure we are. Hiding out here together. In bed."

"That works for me."

Dana sighed. "Yeah, but we're both hiding from life. You because you're afraid to trust yourself to really care again. For anyone. You do know I'm nothing like your ex-wife, don't you?"

"Of course I do."

"But you can't get past what she did to you. Your plans for your life didn't work out, so now you don't intend to ever make plans with anyone else." Dana put her hand on his upper arm. "We've found friendship again. I want to keep that. I fear if we don't step back now that we might lose it. I don't want that to happen."

"Aren't you borrowing trouble? Looking for something to worry about."

The crackling of lightning off in the distance mirrored their discussion.

"I thought I could do easy, no attachments. But I can't. I'm sorry. I should've never let this get out of hand."

His world had started to crumble. He wasn't sure what he wanted but he didn't want this. Yet what Dana said was true. The longer they were together the more difficult it would be for them to break things off without her getting hurt. He'd hurt her once and he didn't want to do it again. He brushed her jaw with a finger. "Maybe you're right."

She leaned into his hand for a moment, then pulled away. "It has been sweet while it lasted. We had a...what's it called...? Foxhole experience. That's all it ever was."

"If that's the case what do you call the last two weeks?"

Dana hung her head. "A fling. It's time we let it go. While we can look back on it...fondly."

"I can think of other adjectives I'd use. May I call you sometime?"

Dana's lips tightened. Gloom filled her eyes. "Maybe one day. You know you shouldn't depend on anyone for your happiness. I, of all people, know that. I hope that one day you can learn to trust your judgment about people, take a chance on them. Just know they may still disappoint you. Remember when we talked about making mistakes."

Annoyance welled in him. She spoke as if he was the one with all the issues. He wasn't the only one in the car who needed to examine their life. "You might want to spend a little time on yourself, as well."

She straightened until her back pressed against the door. "What exactly does that mean?"

"It means that you've spent so much of your life being rejected that you think everyone is going to. You're harder on yourself than anyone is on you. Your house has to be perfect. You fear everyone is judging you and you'll be found lacking. That makes it impossible to measure up to your expectations."

"That's not true."

He gave her a direct look. "Are you sure about that?"

"Now you're not being fair."

"How's that? By telling you a few home truths? You

might just miss that one person who'll never leave you because you won't give him a chance to prove it."

She glared at him then said, "I think on that note I should say good-night. I'll pack your stuff. You can pick it up or I'll stop by your office and leave it with your receptionist."

"Dana," he stepped out of the car as she ran up the porch steps. He went no farther. Maybe it was best this way. A clean cut. Those always healed faster.

On the plane to a fire Dana closed her eyes and thought back to the discussion she and Leo had had the day before when he'd called her into his office.

Shut the door and have a seat.

She did as he asked and pulled a chair up in front of his desk. Leo had already sat in his chair.

He crossed his arms on the desk and fixed her with an unwavering look. *I'm the closest thing you have to a father now and I want to know what's eating you.*

Haven't I been doing my job? She didn't want to talk about Travis.

You know you have. The others have nothing but great things to say about your leadership. But something's not right with you. You haven't been the same for the last month or so. I know you don't share much about your private life but does it have something to do with Dr. Russell?

She pushed to the edge of the seat. *Why would you think that?*

Because for a few weeks after you came back after that trip you walked around with a smile on your face and then one day it was gone. Now you look like you have lost your best friend. You want to talk about it?

Not really. If she did she might break down and sob. She couldn't have that.

I can't make you. I can tell you that I'm here if you need me.

She stood. *I appreciate that.*

Dana had made it to the door when Leo stopped her. *Just so you know, I did a little checking on Dr. Russell before and after your trip. He's one of the good ones. Someone you can trust. Keeps his word.*

I know.

She did. Travis had proved that more than once. When he'd helped put out fires, seen to Mr. Gunter and Ted, not taken advantage of her in the cave and saved her life in the stream. The list could go on.

Had Travis been right? Had she broken it off with him because she feared he'd one day leave her and move on? Yet he hadn't acted like he was interested in leaving her. Had he changed his mind about what he wanted? What if they could've had something real together and she hadn't given it a chance out of fear?

Travis had shown himself to be steadfast and dependable. Even years ago he had been true to his beliefs. Wasn't that someone she was looking for in her life? She'd had that and thrown it away. Travis deserved better. Had earned her trust. A chance to prove himself. She wanted to give him that opportunity. When she got back from this jump she would call him. Ask him for another chance.

"Five minutes," the spotter called.

She'd trained for these moments. The cutting pain in her throat and nose. The burning in her eyes from the boiling smoke. Soot flying around her, into her mouth and nose despite the material covering them. The gasping a woman in his life. His hands were sweating. He wiped them against his jeans. What could he expect from Dana? She hadn't tried to contact him. Hadn't sounded excited to talk to him. Would their dinner be a friendly thing and nothing more? He'd accept friendship if that's all she'd wanted. It would be difficult, but he'd do it.

He pulled up in front of the white clapboard house and stopped. It was neat and tidy, with the shrubbery trimmed and blooming flowers planted along the short brick walkway leading to the steps to the porch. The porch floor and the stairs were painted a dark green along with the screened door. On either side of the door were two wooden rockers. At both ends of the porch were large flowerpots with trailing greenery. The house looked like a home, not just a place to sleep like his was. It made him feel calm just seeing it.

He carried a bouquet of wildflowers and a bag of food. The main door stood open so he knocked on the screen door. His heart beat faster as Dana padded on bare feet toward him. As she drew closer he held his breath. He ached to hold her but he'd control his urge. It seemed like forever since he'd seen her.

His eyes eagerly took her in. She wore a simple pink T-shirt and short cutoff blue jeans that showed those shapely legs that had wrapped around him. His mouth watered. Her hair swung freely around her face. He'd never seen anyone more desirable. What made her even more gorgeous was the smile on her lips despite the unsure look in her eyes.

Opening the screen, she said, "Hello. Come in."

"Hi." He brushed by her on his way inside.

That slight contact already had his body coming alive. His blood rushed south. He needed to go slow. Not scare her. Dana might be fearless in the woods but he was well aware she lacked it in her personal life. Part of that was his fault. He wanted to help repair that.

"These are for you." He handed her the flowers.

She smiled. "Thank you. I love flowers."

How did she manage to make something so simple give him such pleasure? "I could tell from your front walk."

"How's your burn? Did you have them look at it at the hospital?" Her focus went to his arm.

"I didn't. But I've had my nurse dress it each day."

Dana nodded. "Good. Come back to the kitchen."

She led him down a short hallway, past a stairway on one side and a living room area with floral-print sofa and cushioned chair, to a large kitchen. It ran along the back of the house that gleamed with white subway tile which had obviously been redone recently. Dana's decor showed her softer side much as her panties had.

He placed the bag of food on the table with the four nonmatching multicolored chairs.

"Thank you." She went to the sink, looked in the space under it and pulled out a vase. Filling it with water, she placed the flowers in, then took time to arrange them before she set them in the center of the table. "Thank you. I really do love flowers."

Travis studied her for a moment. "How're you really doing?"

Her gaze came up to meet his. "I've recovered. Nothing like a few good nights of sleep."

He turned her face so he could see her cheek. "I'm glad. I felt guilty getting you involved in all that. You were great. By the way, Mr. Gunter is on the waiting list for a kidney. Hopefully it won't be a long wait."

"I'm glad to hear that. You were the one who was the good sport during our adventure."

for breath. The push to stop the express train of panic coming at her. *Can't breathe.* She was going to die if she didn't get some help.

She reached for her radio, pushed the button but the words wouldn't come out of her smoke-filled throat. Waving her arms, she tried to get the attention of one of her crew. He didn't look her direction. She stepped toward him. Stars swam in her eyes. If she went down it would be over. They were in the middle of the forest. She needed to take a breath. And another.

Dana forced herself to keep moving until she could grab the sleeve of the crew member. Her fingers slowly let go as she dropped to the charred ground.

She'd never see Travis again. Never feel his touch. Never kiss his lips. Never be able to tell him she wanted him, how much she loved him. Never…

Over the last month Travis had learned he'd been wrong. Terribly wrong. Some clean wounds were difficult to heal. He'd adjusted to his divorce with less pain than he'd experienced with trying to get over Dana. She'd permeated his life.

Even when he took care of patients, thoughts of how they had worked together to see to Mr. Gunter and Ted popped in his mind. The worst was when he watched the news or heard on the radio about a fire burning in the national park. The first thing he wanted to do was call Dana and see if she was all right. It required a great deal of effort for him not to.

During one of his weekly calls to check in with his mother she asked, "Travis, what's going on?"

"What do you mean? I just told you about my week." He ran his fingers through his hair.

"I mean you haven't sounded like yourself the last few weeks. What has happened?"

Did he dare let that floodgate open? "You remember that year between college and med school?"

"Yes. You always seemed so happy when you called."

"I did?"

She chuckled. "You did. I figured there might be a young woman involved."

"There was. I saw her again a few weeks ago." He went on to tell her most of what had happened between him and Dana.

"What're you going to do?" How like his mother to cut to the heart of things. She and Dana shared that quality.

"I don't know. I afraid she'll want something I can't offer." Why must this be so hard?

"Like what? Love and companionship. Support and caring. The things we all want."

"But I messed up before, thought I had the perfect one, the perfect life planned out."

"Maybe that's the problem. No one's perfect. Life, love is about taking chances. Can be messy. This Dana sounds like she challenges you, can be a partner not a trophy. She's her own person who isn't dependent on you to make her way." His mother lapsed into silence. "By the way, I never thought Brittney was the right person for you."

"Why didn't you say so?"

"Would it have made a difference?" she asked quietly.

It wouldn't have. Back then he thought he knew what he needed.

His mother had given him much to think about. Over the next few days he rolled all she'd said over in his mind, and what Dana had said, as well. The way she saw him. In the beginning he denied it, but the more days that went by the more he thought Dana was right. He'd let Brittney, his lost dreams and his divorce color his life. His ex-wife was gone and done with, yet she still had control over him. That realization made him the sickest.

He needed to talk to Dana. Tell her how he felt. Beg her to open that big heart of hers and let him in. There his heart would be valued and protected. Let her know he trusted her like no other person in his life. She'd have his back and he would have hers. They'd learn to deal with their future and leave the past where it belonged, behind them.

The next day he was seeing a patient when his cell phone buzzed. He ignored it. When it immediately rang again he looked at his patient and said, "Excuse me a minute." He stepped out in the hall.

The number calling he didn't recognize, but he answered anyway.

"Dr. Russell."

"It's Leo Thomas with the Redmond Smokejumpers. I thought you'd want to know. Dana is being airlifted in to Redmond Hospital."

Travis leaned back against the wall, fearing his heart might stop. "I'm on my way."

Doris stood at the other end of the hall watching him. As he ended the call she met him. He explained what had happened and that he'd be leaving after he finished with this patient, with no plans to return.

The helicopter carrying Dana hadn't arrived by the time he'd gotten to the hospital. For the few minutes he spent in the ER waiting, he walked back and forth in front of the doors he'd been told she'd come through. Leo arrived soon after Travis did. He looked as tight-lipped and worried as Travis felt.

The second Dana rolled through the doors, Travis was beside her stretcher. She was unconscious. An oxygen mask covered her nose and mouth. He followed her into an examination room. Fortunately, he had made friends with the ER attending, otherwise he would've been sitting in the waiting room.

Travis made sure to stay out of the way so he wouldn't be asked to leave. In the state he was in there was no way he would've been rational enough to handle Dana's care. By the time they moved her up to a room, he was almost beyond reasoning with.

Leo pulled him aside and told him to get a grip, that it wasn't good for him and it wouldn't be for Dana either. Travis handled traumas numerous times as a doctor and held his emotions with no trouble, but this time it was Dana. He stepped out into the hall and composed himself, determined to remain cool in front of Dana when she woke, and she had to wake.

He loved her. That's what she'd been wanting to hear from him. He'd been too afraid to admit it to himself or her. If he didn't take the chance on telling her, he'd walk around half alive for the rest of his life. What he knew now was that he'd take all of her he could have for as long as he could have it. He wouldn't let his past rule his life any longer. He wanted to live large and that meant having Dana beside him. As soon as he could, he'd tell her.

Twelve hours later the greatest of his fears washed away when he saw Dana's eyes flutter, then open. She would live. Still there was a chance her lungs might be permanently damaged. Doctors wouldn't know if there was any major damage for a few more months. He'd be there for her if that was the case. If not, he'd live with her continuing to jump. They would make their life together work. What he'd never do was ask her to give up her job, just as she'd never ask him to give up medicine.

The second time she opened her eyes, Dana looked more like herself. Her eyes were brighter and more aware. He gave her hand a gentle squeeze. "I'm right here, sweetheart."

Her hand tightened on his briefly before her eyes closed.

Dana woke again in the early hours of the morning. The lights were low. She needed less oxygen now but he knew her throat had to feel like it had a raging fire in it. It'd be a while before she could talk; even then her voice might be hoarse.

A nurse brought in a small dry-erase board, telling him Dana shouldn't speak. She could use the board to write what she wanted to say. He had to promise he'd see that Dana used it.

Somewhere close to daylight he stepped out of the room to get a cup of coffee. Returning, he found Dana awake and watching him. He smiled. "Hello, sweetheart."

Her mouth made a movement like a smile but the mask made it hard to tell.

He hoped he was reading her expression correctly.

Dana took a deep breath. Air flowed easier now. But it hurt like the devil to breathe. If she stopped maybe the pain would too. The whoosh of air filled her ears as she exhaled. Something cupped her nose and mouth. She reached for her neck but her hands wouldn't move.

"Sweetheart, don't struggle," someone said near her ear. "Easy."

She knew that voice. The calm, caressing one. *Travis.*

He continued to talk to her. His voice flowed over her. "You're gonna be just fine. Take deep breaths. In, out, in, out. Slowly. I'm right here. I'm not leaving."

His fingers brushed her forehead. She recognized his touch. The one she'd missed so much.

"In and out. In and out."

She coughed leaning forward, pain assaulting her chest.

"Easy, sweetheart." Caution and fear filled Travis's voice.

She listened to his gentle voice in her ear and returned to sleep.

The next time she woke, her eyes flashed open to bright light. Where was she? She looked wildly around. The voice. She wanted Travis's voice. Where was it?

"Hey, sweetheart."

Dana instantly calmed. It still hurt to breathe. Her gaze met Travis's cool refreshing blue one.

"Don't try to talk." He stood beside her and smiled but it didn't reach his eyes. Instead anxiety filled them. His look moved over her as if he was studying her from a doctor's point of view. "I know your throat hurts. I need you to breathe deeply but slow and easy. It won't be long before you'll be able to talk so save it for right now. Okay? Please for me."

She considered him a moment. The lines were deeper around his eyes than they had been. His hair looked as if he'd run his hands through it more than once. Even his clothes looked slept in.

Dana would do anything for him. She nodded.

He kissed her forehead. "Just keep breathing for me, okay. In and out. In and out."

Slowly she returned to the blissful world of sleep. And dreams of him.

She woke to low lights the next time. She looked down to see a dark haired head resting on the side of the bed. Travis held her hand as if she were a lifeline. He softly snored. She tried to speak but no sound came out. A fresh puff of air in her lungs was welcome but it didn't decrease the pain.

As she flexed her hand slightly Travis's head jerked up. His gaze immediately meeting hers. She reached for the mask but he stopped her. He held her hand, kissing the palm.

"Sweetheart, you still can't remove the mask. You need the oxygen. I need you to stay calm and breathe deeply. You've a case of smoke inhalation." He hung his head and shook it as if what he had to say was unbearable. "I... I...uh...almost lost you."

She didn't miss the moisture making his eyes glassy.

"And I need you to stay here with me." His eyes and words pleaded. "I don't want you to talk. I want you to listen. I'll tell you what happened. Squeeze my hand to let me know you understand."

She did as he asked.

"If you have any questions afterward then maybe you can write them down, okay?"

Dana nodded slightly and he smiled.

"You were fighting a fire. A burst of wind came up and created a tornado of smoke. You were right there in it. You were already overcome but you found a crew member. You passed out and were life-flighted out. You've been here for three days. You're doing very well. But you still have a way to go. The more you follow the directions the quicker you'll get out of here."

She pointed to him.

"How did I know you were here?"

She nodded.

"Leo called me when they were bringing you in. I've never been so scared in my life." He took a deep breath, looking as if he was trying to compose himself. "Do you have any questions?"

She shook her head.

"Then close your eyes and sleep. That's the best thing for you. I'll be here when you wake. I promise."

Dana didn't doubt his words. He had been there for her before. He was here now.

The next time she woke, the sun shone through the window and an older nurse stood beside her bed. The mask had been removed and all she wore was an oxygen cannula under her nose. She looked around the room.

"Are you looking for that handsome Dr. Russell?"

Dana nodded.

"I sent him home for a bath and clean clothes. He's not going to be happy you woke and he wasn't here. He's been here almost four days and it was time he took a break. Why don't we get you cleaned up some so you'll look your best when he gets back?"

Dana gave her an eager nod.

When Travis returned, Dana sat up in the bed with her hair combed and a clean hospital gown on, eating ice chips.

"Travis." His name came out low and hoarse.

He hurried to the bedside, then set his coffee down on the table. Dana reached out her hand and he took it, kissing the top then bringing it to his cheek. "You still shouldn't talk."

"I'm going to."

"I'm sorry. If you need to say anything you need to write it on this board."

Dana shook her head, picked up the board and marker and tucked them under her pillow. "This time I'm the boss inside."

Travis grinned. "Okay."

"I have to tell you this." The words came out stronger. She looked at him with unsure eyes but smiled.

The tightness in Travis's chest eased. With the way they had left things, he had been afraid she'd tell him to get out.

"I was wrong." She coughed.

"Let's save this for later."

She shook her head. "No, now. I've lived my entire life with people leaving me. You were right. I pushed you away because I was afraid you'd one day leave me too. I don't care how long you stay but that you just let me be a part of your life. Sometime I have to stop running and take a chance. I want to take that on you. Even if it's just on friendship."

"Sweetheart, you weren't the only one who was wrong. I've let my past rule my life. I'm not going to do that anymore. It's time for me to live my best life. And I know that is with you, if you'll give me a chance."

She smiled broadly and nodded.

Travis leaned down and kissed her lightly. "By the way, I love you."

She cupped his cheek. "And I love you."

His heart flipped, then flopped, and raced like an express train. He took her hand and kissed her palm. "Will you marry me?"

"Yes."

"Maybe we can honeymoon at the fire tower. With a good air mattress, of course."

She smiled. "Sounds perfect."

* * * * *

MILLS & BOON

Coming next month

CONSEQUENCES OF THEIR NEW YORK NIGHT
Tina Beckett

Nicola's mind was wandering, and her thoughts slid in and out of places that were best left for another time. The hospital was huge and the names of people she'd been introduced to were starting to squish together inside the confines of her skull.

And as the space grew even tighter, something had to give. So squeezing between the cracks came the memory of a night five weeks ago. And the tall stranger she'd fallen into bed with.

She swallowed. She still couldn't believe she'd done that. What had she been thinking?

She hadn't been. And that had been the idea. She hadn't wanted to think, to talk...to remember. She'd just wanted to feel. And, God, had she ever. She'd...

"Kaleb, could you come over here for a moment?" Harvey Smith's voice shocked her back to reality, making her blink. "I want you to meet the newest member of our team: Nicola Bradley. Her specialty is internal medicine with an emphasis on diagnostics. She'll be helping us crack the tough cases."

As the hospital administrator continued to speak, she turned to greet the newcomer, and a wave of shock knocked her flat, setting off all kinds of sirens and alarms.

"Nicola, meet Kaleb Sabat. He's New York City Memorial's chief of reconstructive surgery."

She somehow met the man's cool blue eyes without flinching. How was this even possible? Was this some sort of cosmic joke? If so, the punch line was lost on her.

The man she'd shared a crazy, impulsive night of sex with was NYC Memorial's chief of reconstructive surgery? Oh, God. What should she do? What *could* she do?

Quit? Run down the hallway until she found the nearest exit? No. Nicola was no chicken. At least she hoped not.

She was going to pretend it never happened, that's what she'd do. And hope that he did the same. Or maybe he didn't even remember her.

Please, God...

"Nice to meet you, Dr. Sabat," she murmured, placing the slightest emphasis on his title.

The man's head tilted sideways for a second, his eyebrows coming together as a host of changes came over his face, the last of which was sardonic amusement.

Oh, no. He remembered. *Remembered!*

They'd both had a little too much to drink that night five weeks ago, and she'd hoped...

If she'd had any idea he'd worked at the hospital she was transferring to, she would have moved off that barstool quicker than anyone believed possible. But she'd been grieving and needed to forget.

Kaleb had given her a few hours of respite...and more.

Continue reading
CONSEQUENCES OF THEIR NEW YORK NIGHT
Tina Beckett

Available next month
www.millsandboon.co.uk

COMING SOON!

We really hope you enjoyed reading this book. If you're looking for more romance, be sure to head to the shops when new books are available on

Thursday 18th March

WE'RE LOOKING FOR NEW AUTHORS FOR THE MILLS & BOON MEDICAL SERIES!

Whether you're a published author or an aspiring one, our editors would love to read your story.

You can submit the synopsis and first three chapters of your novel online, and find out more about the series, at **harlequin.submittable.com/submit**

We read all submissions and you do not need to have an agent to submit.

IF YOU'RE INTERESTED, WHY NOT HAVE A GO?

Submit your story at:
harlequin.submittable.com/submit

MILLS & BOON

LET'S TALK
Romance

For exclusive extracts, competitions
and special offers, find us online:

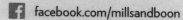 facebook.com/millsandboon

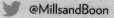 @MillsandBoon

@MillsandBoonUK

Get in touch on 01413 063232

For all the latest titles coming soon, visit
millsandboon.co.uk/nextmonth